Punished me again.

Still recovering from it. At least he didn't find the letters. Doesn't know about my scribblings. Be furious if he did. They tell too much about him, about our whole mad relationship. He'd punish me again, worse than ever.

But I can't stop writing. Only this bit of pencil and these scraps of paper allow me to retain the most tenuous grip on the last remnant of my sanity. My only link to reality, whatever that means. My reality—one continuous nightmare interspersed with all too brief periods of wakefulness. Have to keep a record of these awake times, to reassure myself they exist. That I exist! They are worth any punishment.

Oh, the punishment. He metes it out so casually these days. Simply for belittling him because he lost the blonde. Laughed at him because she escaped him. Resented my taunts, so the swine punished me.

But no matter. I survived. And in that poor nurse's death I've found hope. Proves he's not omnipotent. Not quite the Übermensch he believes himself to be—that I believed him to be.

She escaped him.

Perhaps there's still hope for me.

"Wilson
can't resist
turning
the narrative screws
another notch."

—*Booklist*

F. PAUL WILSON

TOR

A TOM DOHERTY ASSOCIATES BOOK
NEW YORK

This is a work of fiction. All the characters and events portrayed in this book are fictitious, and any resemblance to real people or events is purely coincidental.

SIBS

Copyright © 1991 by F. Paul Wilson
Illustrations copyright © 1991 by Phil Parks

Cover art by Donato

A Tor Book
Published by Tom Doherty Associates, Inc.
175 Fifth Avenue
New York, N.Y. 10010

Tor ® is a registered trademark of Tom Doherty Associates, Inc.

ISBN: 0-812-53124-8

First Tor edition: May 1994

Printed in the United States of America

0 9 8 7 6 5 4 3 2 1

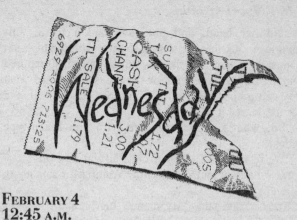

FEBRUARY 4
12:45 A.M.

IT WAS AN UNEVENTFUL EVENING UNTIL IT GOT CRAZY. Craziness had been the farthest thing from Ed Bannion's mind when he invited his younger brother into the city.

Phil came in through the Lincoln Tunnel from Tinton Falls, New Jersey, and Ed met him at a midtown parking lot. No special occasion, just keeping in touch. They went downtown and then began a steady march back up: Before-dinner drinks at The Airplane in SoHo, and off-off-Broadway play in Kips Bay, shrimp in green sauce at El Quijote in Chelsea, and finally a nitecap in the Oak Bar at the Plaza. And it was there in the Oak Bar, there in the heart of the jewel in Ivana Trump's tiara, while they were standing side by side, each with a foot on the brass rail, staring at the misty painting of the Plaza fountain behind the cash register, that the young blonde squeezed between them and ordered a double JD on the rocks.

"Hi, guys!" she said, bright and cheery with a smile that made Ed wince in its glare.

A real piece. She looked around twenty-five but she could have been thirty. Either way, she was younger than Ed. Her wavy blond hair was like a pale cloud around her head, and her face had a fresh, All-American look that contrasted sharply with the high-slit leather mini-skirt and the low-cut sweater that exposed smooth, bouncy crescents of her breasts. She had what they call a bod that wouldn't quit. Sexy as all hell, and not the least bit shy.

"So, what's happening here with you Plaza-type dudes?"

"We're not—" Ed began but Phil cut him off.

"Just hanging out," Phil said. "Waiting for something to happen."

"Yeah?" she said. "My name's Ingrid, and I'm waiting for the same thing. Isn't that something?"

"That's something, all right," Phil purred.

Ed stared at his brother who had suddenly become cool, smooth, and seductive. He hardly recognized him. Ed was a bachelor, but good lord, Phil had a wife and child back home in Jersey!

"You guys look alike. You related?"

"We're brothers," Ed said, feeling he should add his two cents. The clash of her bold and brassy attitude with her angel-soft good looks excited him. "I'm the older one—but not by much."

"Yeah?" she said with a seductive smile. "You never could tell. You guys come here often?"

"This is our headquarters whenever we're in the Apple," Phil said.

Ed struggled to keep from laughing out loud.

"Me, too," Ingrid said. "I've got an appointment with Mike Nichols this week. He's shooting his next feature right here in Manhattan, you know, and my agent's got me an audition with him. So I'm killing some time while I wait for Solly to firm up the exact time and place. What're you guys in town for?"

"We're in textiles," Phil said with this oily grin.

"Y'know . . . rugs and stuff? We sell textiles by the mile."

Ed was shocked by his brother's facile way with a lie. Phil was a Wa-Wa manager. He wouldn't know a broadloom from a flying carpet.

"Really?" Ingrid said. "That sounds boring as shit. Can you guys fuck?"

Ed saw his brother's eyes bulge as he felt his own jaw drop. That sweet face, those innocent eyes. And talking like that!

Phil glanced quickly at Ed, then back at Ingrid.

"Sure we do. What do you think we are, queer?"

"I don't know," she said. "I've been crammed in between the two of you and neither one of you has even tried to feel me up. Something's wrong here."

"My brother and I were raised to be gentlemen," Phil said.

"I kinda like that," she said, slipping a finger inside Phil's shirt, "but you can carry that polite shit too far. Want to come up to my room? It's got a great view of the park."

"I don't know about that," Phil said. "What's it gonna cost me?"

Her smile was sweet. "Cost? Nothing. My treat. But there's a condition."

Ed didn't like the sound of this.

"Phil, uh, maybe you should—"

"The both of you have to come," Ingrid said.

Ed swallowed and wet his dry lips.

"You want both of us?"

She looked at him and laughed. His expression must have reflected the excited turmoil within him.

"Yeah! Guys always run out of steam before I do. One ain't enough, know what I mean? So I like to have a back-up along. That too kinky for you fellows?"

Thoughts of herpes, syphilis, the clap, and AIDS ran

through Ed's mind. Then she ran a hand over his crotch. From the startled look on Phil's face, Ed guessed that she was doing the same to his brother.

Phil's voice was strained. "What floor?"

Before long they were twelve stories above Central Park South. Ingrid wasted no time once they were in the room. She offered them each a toot from the small vial of coke she produced, took a good snort herself, then knelt down between them and unzipped their flies.

And as the interlude progressed, it got crazier and crazier. This was one *hungry* lady.

Eventually it came to a point where Phil was sprawled back on the hotel bed, naked, moaning as Ingrid worked on him. She knelt on the carpet with her thighs spread wide as her head bobbed up and down over Phil's pelvis. And Ed . . . he knelt behind her, gripping her black garter belt like a rodeo rider hanging onto the reins of a bucking bronco, his pelvis slapping against her smooth buttocks as he slid in and out of her.

She paused and lifted her head from Phil.

"Baby, don't stop now," Phil said. His voice was thick, hoarse.

She turned her head and looked over her shoulder at Ed. In the dim light filtering across the bed from the open bathroom door, he could see her face. Her eyes glistened and her cheeks were flushed. Beautiful, and as insatiable as she was uninhibited.

"Do it faster," she said. "And harder! I want to *come*, damn it!"

Ed said nothing. He'd already come once himself, and was climbing the upslope toward number two. He picked up the pace, ramming deeper into her.

"Oh, yessss!" she said through a groan, and then went back to doing Ed.

I just don't believe this! Ed told himself for the hundredth time in the last hour.

This was the kind of thing that happened only in porno movies, in fantasies, not in real life. At least not in Ed Bannion's life. Fifteen years in this town—sixteen in August—and never anything even close to an encounter like this. When he'd got the job with Paramount he'd been a sex-starved law school grad dreaming of starlet sandwiches and orgies. Even if he was in legal and based in New York, Paramount was Paramount, right? Wrong. *Nothing!* He'd never even *seen* a starlet, let alone a star. Paramount—hah! He might as well have been working for Exxon for all the poontang he'd got through the company.

But tonight! Tonight made up for the long wait. He'd carry the memory of this to his grave. Maybe even beyond.

He felt the pressure growing within the basement of his pelvis, surging outward, building . . .

He leaned forward and reached around her, grabbing her breasts.

. . . building . . .

He buried his face in her fragrant, wavy hair, and nuzzling the nape of her neck.

. . . building . . .

Suddenly he knew he was past the point of no return. He stiffened, cried out, then bit down hard as he exploded within her.

Ingrid screamed in pain. She straightened up and twisted, pulling free of Ed as she rose to her feet. She stood there, naked but for her garter belt and black stockings, staring at Ed and his brother, her hands to her mouth, her eyes wide with what looked to Ed like shock and horror.

"What's the matter, babe?" Phil said.

"Oh, no!" she moaned. There was no passion in the sound, only revulsion and unplumbed misery. "Oh, God, *no!*"

Ed turned cold inside. Something was terribly wrong here. What—?

She turned to run and immediately slammed into the wall. She bounced off it and blindly dashed toward Ed, accelerating as she passed him.

"Christ, no! The window!" Ed said and tried to grab her leg.

But she was moving too fast. He missed her and could only watch helplessly as she rammed into the lower pane of the big double-hung window. For an instant it looked as if she might bounce off that, too, but then came a sharp crash like a shot, like an explosion, and suddenly the glass was coming apart all around her and she was still moving outward, taking a million bright dagger shards with her. And then she was gone, a keening wail trailing behind her.

Ed remained kneeling on the carpet, frozen in shock, shivering in the cold wind pouring through the shattered window, thinking this couldn't be real, this couldn't be happening, listening to the terrified wail that continued long after she was gone from view, much longer than it should have. And then he realized that the sound was coming from him.

Thursday

FEBRUARY 5
9:52 A.M.

KARA FELT THE OLD TENSION COME ALIVE AS THE CITY HOVE into view. She had been able to hold it at bay during the express ride through central New Jersey, but after pulling out of the Amtrak station in Metropark and hearing the conductor call out New York as the next stop, she'd felt it stir. Now, with the spires of the Manhattan skyline poking at the morning clouds across the river, it came writhing to life.

Ten years ago she had walked out on the city, leaving behind the two most important people in the world.

Manhattan. The City That Never Sleeps. The City of Opportunity. She and her twin sister Kelly had arrived there fresh out of their respective secretarial and nursing schools, two ingenues, a pair of Pennsylvania hicks leaving home to take their bite out of the Big Apple.

Everything went swimmingly at first. They stayed at their Aunt Ellen's place while hunting for jobs. Kelly found a nursing position almost immediately—it was the late shift, but it was a job. Kara looked over the prospects and decided she'd do better starting out as a temporary, figuring that way she'd be exposed to a variety of companies and could see how they operated.

When she found a good one that would pay enough to cover a few college courses, she'd hire on as a permanent. For Kara didn't intend to stay a secretary forever. She had plans. She wanted to write, wanted to work her way into advertising and copywriting.

So Kara started off as a Kelly Girl. She didn't like the "Girl" part but she went along. She preferred to think of herself as a secretarial gun for hire. There was no such thing as word processing then. The IBM Selectric was her weapon of choice and she wielded it with deadly efficiency. The Kelly people paid her well and kept her busy.

Who knew where she might be working now if she'd stayed on in the city? Perhaps she'd be a big name at Saatchi & Saatchi. Or maybe she'd have started her own temporary office help service. She had seen no limit to her potential in the Big Apple.

Until the Central Park incident.

That was when Kara learned that Big Apple bit back and she'd run for home.

Ten years later now, and she was on her way back to identify her sister's body. Alone. Mom was rushing back from Florida and so there was no one else to make this trip but Kara.

Kelly dead! She still couldn't believe it! And the way she had died! Naked, smashed on the sidewalk in front of the Plaza! How could someone have done that to her?

Kara's mind balked at the very question.

Since the call from New York yesterday afternoon, Kara's life had been a bad dream. Kelly, she'd learned, had been dead for more than half a day before the police had got around to calling her.

And it had been Rob of all people who'd made the call.

They hadn't spoken in ten years, yet she had recognized his voice immediately. And she had known that it was something bad, something about Kelly. Why else would Rob call from New York after all this time?

Rob Harris. She had left him high and dry. When she first met him he'd been attending the police academy. She still remembered how cute he'd looked in his hated recruit grays. When she left him he was in regular blues, and she'd been convinced the city was going to kill him.

She wondered if he'd forgiven her yet.

And now she had to see him again. At the morgue. Over poor Kelly's shattered body.

God, how was she going to do this?

▼

Kara shivered in the cold as she stood in the morning crowd outside Penn Station. The city hadn't changed much. The Penn Station-Madison Square Garden area looked older and dirtier. She noticed that the old Statler Hilton was now called the Vista. She felt the pedestrians crowd against her as they stacked up on the sidewalk, waiting for the Seventh Avenue traffic light to change. She clutched her pocketbook tightly against her. These people frightened her.

The Central Park incident came back to her in a rush.

It had been a sunny Sunday in June. She and Kelly were strolling along the Park side of Fifth Avenue on their way back from an exhibit at the Metropolitan, enjoying the day, enjoying the admiring stares from all the guys, killing time until they met the men in their lives later in the day. Kelly stopped to get a pretzel and a coke from a pushcart. While she was waiting on line, Kara wandered onto a path to listen to an old black fellow playing Delta blues on a portable electric guitar.

Without warning, she felt herself jerked off her feet,

stumbling backwards as something hard and sharp tightened across her throat, digging into the soft flesh there. She fell, and it dug deeper as she was dragged backwards. She tried to scream but her air had been cut off. She heard other screams and blurred glimpses of staring, horrified faces. Yet nobody moved to help her.

And then with a snap, the pressure was gone as suddenly as it had come.

Gasping, choking, Kara rolled over in the dirty and saw the receding back of a man as he dashed down the path, saw people darting out of his way. Her hand went to her throat. Her gold necklace, the heavy chain her father had given her a year before he died, was gone. People tried to help her to her feet but she batted their hands away. She wanted to scream at them, ask them why no one had lent a hand when she needed it most, but her voice seemed paralyzed.

"Y'shouldn't wear gold necklaces near the Park, hon," said a middle-aged woman in a housedress. "Y'should know that."

Kara wanted to strangle her, but then Kelly ran up and Kara fell into her sister's arms and began to sob with reaction.

Nowadays she didn't cry so easily.

That was when the Big Apple began to rot for Kara. It never was the same after that. She found herself constantly looking over her shoulder. She became afraid to go out alone. And she *never* went near Central Park again.

Six months after the necklace-snatching she was on the train, outbound from Manhattan, never to return.

Until now.

She looked east along Thirty-Fourth. Bellevue Hospital Center was that way, on First Avenue and Thirtieth. The morgue was in its cellar.

She shut her eyes.

Why am I here? I don't want to be here. I don't have to be here.

Which was true. Her presence here today would not speed Kelly's body back to Pennsylvania by a single minute. But she had to do this, had to make this trip. For Kelly. Kara had left her sister here, and now the least she could do was see her home.

She ignored the schools of cabs cruising the area and decided to walk. It would put off having to see Kelly.

She jumped as a hand squeezed her left buttock through her coat. She whirled and glared into the press of people around her but couldn't tell who'd done it.

God, she hated New York.

▼

Detective Third Grade Rob Harris leaned against the wall in Bellevue's lobby, smoking a cigarette and listening to the couple over by the phones. Amazing. Somebody was in the middle of pulling a variation on the old Spanish handkerchief scam in the middle of a hospital. He'd become suspicious when he saw the pencil case, so he'd sidled over to listen.

"You got da money? Da fi' thousan'? Lemme see. Good! Here. Put it in this pencil case."

"Why?" the woman said. Sheathed in a shapeless old coat, she was chunky, fiftyish, with mocha skin.

"For safekeeping. No one wants a pencil case. An' you hol' onto it. I don' wan' even touch it."

The woman shoved the bills inside the case and then clutched it between her ample breasts with both hands.

"What do we do now?"

"We wait for Chico to call and say it's okay for you to go down to da main Lotto office and collect my money."

Rob shook his head in wonder. The gullibility of

people never ceased to amaze him. This grifter was using the latest wrinkle on the Spanish handkerchief—a
phony lottery ticket. It worked like this: The grifter has
a state lottery ticket dated for, say, January 3 that has
the correct lottery numbers for that date. Except that it's
a ticket from January 31 with the "1" scraped off. The
scam artist poses as an illegal alien who can't cash the
ticket for fear of deportation. He corners some poor
sucker, usually of similar roots, and pleads for help,
promising to share the prize if the mark can prove that
he or she is "a person of substance" whom the grifter
can trust with his "winning" ticket. The mark checks
with a local Lotto stand and confirms that, yes, the
ticket does indeed have all the winning numbers. To
prove her 'substance,' this particular mark had withdrawn five thousand in cash and shown it to the grifter.
It was now in the pencil case.

Rob was sure that when "Chico" called, the scam
artist would have to go meet him immediately due to
some unexpected development. But to show his good
faith, the grifter would offer to leave his lucky lottery
ticket with the mark. He'd stick it in the pencil pouch
with the cash. That was when the switch would be
made, leaving the mark holding an identical pencil case
stuffed with dollar-sized strips of newspaper.

Rob ambled over the phone where the pair hovered
and reached for the receiver. The man knocked his hand
away.

"We're waitin' for a call, man. Use dat phone over
dere."

"Oh, okay," Rob said, smiling shyly. "Sure."

Rob moved four phones away and dropped a quarter
into the slot. The encounter seconds before had enabled
him to read the number on the other phone. He punched
it in.

Down the line to his right, the phone rang.

"Tha' mus' be Chico," the grifter said, and lifted the receiver. "*Si?* Chico?"

"Heeeyyyy, man! *Que pasa?*" Rob said in his best imitation of Cheech Marin. "Like what's happenin', man?"

"Chico?"

"Chico's dead, asshole," he said in his own voice. "And you'll wish you were too if you don't hang up the phone and walk your ass out of here pronto. And don't try to take that pencil case along because I'll be all over you like flies on shit before you reach the door. *Vamoose*, dirt bag!"

Rob had pulled his badge from his pocket and now he held it up over the sound baffle of his booth. He noticed that the grifter's face was pale as he hung up his receiver. The guy scanned the lobby and froze as his eyes fixed on the gold detective badge. He locked eyes with Rob for a second, then, without a word, hurried from the lobby.

Rob strolled over to the confused mark.

"The money still in there, ma'am?"

She looked at him in bewilderment, then unzipped the case. A sheaf of hundred dollar bills sat cozily within.

"Good. Put it back in the bank and leave it there. And next time don't be so trusting."

Rob lit another cigarette and returned to his station by the front entrance. He checked his watch. Kara was late. Normally he didn't mind waiting. He was used to it. Waiting was an integral part of the job for a NYPD detective. He'd spent entire shifts and more sitting in a cold, cramped car with his eyes trained on a single doorway. This morning he was warm and comfortable. Why should he be antsy?

She fooled him. Rob had expected her to arrive by cab, so he hadn't been paying much attention to the sidewalk. He was surprised when he spotted her half a block away, walking down from Thirty-first. He picked up the blond hair first, then the easy, long-legged gait. Kara had never learned to walk like a New Yorker.

He studied her as she neared, feeling a strange tingle spread across his chest and arms as more details of her appearance came into view. Her hair was blond as ever, longer than before, chin length now, curved slightly inward, with bangs in front. She was wearing a long, dark red cloth coat, with matching stockings, and matching shoes with a low heel; beneath the coat she appeared to be as slim as ever. She still looked painfully young. Her skin was still fair and smooth, her eyes were as clear and blue as before, her lips were still a perfect bow. As she came up the front steps, he noticed that she wore little make-up. She'd never needed much. He searched her face for wrinkles, crows feet, worry lines. Not a one. Her face was leaner, and slightly drawn, but that could be explained by grief. Otherwise, she looked trim and fit, as if she'd aged maybe five years in the ten since she'd left.

Could that be disappointment he was feeling? Had he been hoping that she'd have gone to seed since she left him? So he could tell himself it was probably for the best that they'd broken up? Or was he looking for proof that she wasn't as self-sufficient as she thought she was? That she really needed him and couldn't get along well without him?

Maybe.

From the look of things, though, Kara Wade was doing just fine.

As she reached the top of the steps, Rob stubbed out his cigarette and moved toward the glass doors. After their brief conversation last night, he'd been anticipating this reunion with both eagerness and dread. Well, the wait was over. When he determined which door she was heading for, he reached it first and pushed on the bar to open it. She glanced up at him.

"Thank—" she began, then looked at him more closely. "Rob! It's you!"

They embraced briefly. He was surprised how good it was to hold her again, even if only for a few seconds. They backed off to arm's length. His mouth was dry and his heart was thumping. After all these years?

"Yeah. It's me. I told you I'd meet you here."

"Yes, but I didn't expect you to open the door for me. Where's your uniform?"

"I made detective. Midtown North."

"Congratulations."

"It never hurts to have an old man who's an ex-cop."

"He retired?"

For an instant he was surprised she didn't know. But then, how could she?

"He had a couple of heart attacks. He gets chest pains walking across the living room, but he won't agree to a bypass."

"I'm sorry to hear that."

Sorry. Here they were talking about his father when Kelly . . .

"And I'm sorry about Kelly. It's . . . it's tragic."

Rob watched her throat work as she nodded.

"Yes." It was barely a whisper. "Which way is . . .?"

"I'll take you."

He guided her toward the elevators. He could feel the tension in her, could almost feel her body trying to run away. He'd told her yesterday that this trip was unnecessary, but she'd insisted. Same old Kara. Stubborn as ever. He looked at her grim, frightened face and decided he had to give her one more chance to back out of this. As they stepped out of the elevator into the hallway of the bottom floor, the City Morgue floor, he took her arm.

▼

"You don't have to do this."

Kara stared at Rob. He had changed considerably since she'd last seen him a decade ago. His mustache was gone, but that was minor. He was slightly heavier, and he looked older, but his face wasn't aged so much as lined. He looked *worn*. Like someone steering along the edge of burn-out. Maybe that was what a dozen years as a New York City cop did to you. At least that was what it seemed to have done to Rob.

But his brown eyes were still bright and clear, and even here in the City Morgue he still exuded the same physical presence that had attracted her way back when.

At first she'd been hesitant about his coming here, feeling it was an intrusion on her grief. But when he'd opened the lobby door for her, some of the old feelings had rushed back. It was good to see him. And it was a comfort to find a familiar face in these indifferent surroundings, especially when it belonged to someone who knew his way around and could cut through much of the red tape.

"Don't you usually have to have someone identify the body?" Kara said.

"Kelly's supervisor from St. Vincent's did that yesterday. Plus we've got a perfect print match." He glanced away. "Besides ... it's not pretty."

A burst of resentment shot through her.

"I didn't expect it to be *pretty*," she said coldly.

Rob didn't back down.

"She's a mess, Kara. And she's been posted."

"Posted?"

"Autopsied."

I know! I know! Stop reminding me!

"I. Want. To. See. Her." Kara said slowly. She was not going to back down either. "She's my sister."

She realized she'd used the present tense. She'd probably continue doing that until she'd actually seen Kelly's dead face. She didn't want to see a dead Kelly. Oh, God, she'd give anything not to have to do this. It had taken every ounce of courage she possessed just to come here. Part of her wanted to run screaming from the building, from this awful city, and take the next train back to Pennsylvania. But she knew that another larger part of her would never accept her sister's death without actually seeing her lifeless body.

Rob's mouth settled into a tight thin line.

"Okay. But I warned you."

Kara held her breath as she followed him down the fluorescent-lit hall, lined with gurneys, some empty, some not. White sheets covered the latter. She kept her eyes down and counted the drains evenly placed in the concrete floor. He led her through a set of steel double doors into a room where a gaunt young black man who couldn't have been much older than twenty sat at a small desk with a styrofoam cup full of coffee in one hand and a cigarette in the other. The sports section of the *Post* was open on the desk in front of him. Rob handed him a yellow slip of paper.

"Already been identified," the young man said after looking at the slip. "She's waiting for pick-up."

Rob's voice was flat. "She's going to be identified again."

The attendant shrugged and ran his finger down a list. He stopped near the bottom.

"Seventeen-B," he said as he rose from his chair.

He led them through another set of double doors, heavier than the first, into a larger room where the temperature was a good twenty degrees cooler. She saw a coarse concrete floor, white tiled walls, and latched drawers. The far wall was a giant mosaic of latched drawers, three high and too many in width to count. Big drawers. People-sized drawers.

Kara hung back as the attendant headed for row seventeen. He reached for the handle on the second drawer down, and pulled.

A seismic shudder ran through her.

I can't do this!

As the drawer slid out with a harsh grating noise that echoed off the bare floor and tiled walls, she forced herself forward. She *had* to do this. There was no one else.

A body bag lay on the tray within the drawer. Kara looked past it as stomach acid began to well up into her throat.

This can't be real. This isn't really happening.

She willed herself not to feel anything. She would feel later. Now she would only look.

She stared at the attendant as he pulled down the zipper and pushed back the plastic. Out of the corner of her eye she saw Rob turn away. Fists clenched, jaw tight, she forced herself to look down.

It wasn't Kelly. The caved-in cheek, the skewed nose, the swollen forehead, the misshapen skull, the bulging eye, the matted blond hair, the glass-slashed skin on her face and shoulders, the huge, crudely sutured incision running from the base of her throat down between her breasts and on downward, no, that couldn't be Kelly, it couldn't be Kelly, but it was, oh dear God it *was!*

Kara turned away, reeling as the floor began to tilt beneath her feet.

"You gonna be sick, lady?" the attendant said.

Kara waved her hand back at him. *Shut up! Just shut up!*

" 'Cause if you are," he continued, "there's a bathroom right over there."

She couldn't focus her eyes so she didn't know where "over there" was. The icy room had somehow become very hot and her skin was drenched with perspiration. She felt her knees turning to liquid, sagging.

Suddenly an arm was around her waist, lifting her.

"I've got you," Rob's voice said at her side.

He guided her through a door into a smelly little room lit by a naked 60-watt bulb and outfitted with a dirty sink, a dirtier toilet, and a mop in a bucket. He steadied her as she leaned over the bowl and lost the weak Penn Station coffee she'd had for breakfast. When the retching finally stopped, he handed her a paper towel. She wiped her face and mouth and then sagged against the wall.

Kelly is dead. My dear, dear Kelly is dead!

She felt Rob's arm go around her shoulders but she shrugged him off. She could handle this. She could have used someone to hold on to now, just for a moment, but she had to be strong, had to stand on her own. She searched for her voice and finally found it.

"Could you give me a couple of minutes, Rob?"

"Sure. I'll be right outside."

Once she was alone, the sobs began, echoing up from an empty pit that had opened inside her, quaking through her chest, making her whole body heave.

▼

11:22 A.M.

"Want another coffee?" Rob said.

"No thanks."

"Corn muffin? They're really good here."

They were seated by the front window of a tiny luncheonette on East Thirty-third. The noontime rush was still half an hour away so they had the place almost to themselves. The rich, heavy aroma of chicken soup filled the air; the peppery tang of hot pastrami wafted across their table.

"No. Thank you." A sudden thought broke through the haze that enveloped her. "They're 'good here'? You recommend them?"

"Yeah. Could use a touch more sugar, but they're almost as good as mine."

A fond memory forced its way through the gloom—Friday nights in Rob's apartment as he buzzed around the kitchen, heedless of how his amateur chef act clashed with his tough cop image, watching him follow a recipe just so far and then deciding he could improve on it, usually with disastrous results.

"You really ought to have something to eat."

"You sound like my mother."

"Fine. Listen to your mother: Eat something."

Kara allowed herself to smile. "Buzz off, Mom."

"Okay. You still smoke?"

"No. I quit years ago."

"Mind if I do?"

"Yes. I'm surprised you're still puffing those things. They're poison."

"Buzz off, Mom," he said.

Kara smiled and surrendered to the memory of how she had fallen for Rob soon after she'd arrived in the city. They met in a room full of men, in McSorley's Old Ale House, a formerly men-only tavern that had recently been forced by the courts to serve both sexes. Kara had been braver and less wise then—the Central park incident was a long way off. She'd led Kelly down to one of the toughest parts of the Bowery just so she could have a beer in that old bastion of male exclusivity. After a long wait they each were served two mugs of porter—McSorley's sold them only in pairs. Some of the men present made some rude comments, but most just stared, as if she and her sister had crawled out from under a rock. One of the starers was Rob.

Even amid all those other men, Rob stood out. He wasn't in uniform, and it had nothing to do with size, although his six-two, tightly muscled frame didn't exactly blend in with the paunches around him. It was something else. Even when there were bigger, more physically imposing men present, something about Rob subtly but undeniably announced to any room he entered that a *man* was on the premises. He maneuvered himself to their table and, despite the catcalls from his friends at the bar, sat with them.

The three of them left together, but it was Kara who fell so hard for Rob. It was Kara and Rob from then on. At least until Kara ended it.

She gazed out at the street where people hurried through the stark cold sunshine. Through the fog of condensation on the window they were motley blurs, actors on a tv with a bad tube. Kara was glad she couldn't see their everyday faces as they scurried by, going about their lives as if nothing terrible had happened. For Christ sake, Kelly was dead! Didn't they *know?* Didn't they *care?*

God, how she hated this city. And all the people in it, too.

One of them had killed her sister.

"Who did it?"

"We don't know."

"Not even a suspect?"

"Not a one."

"Great detective work!" Kara said and instantly regretted it. "Sorry. That was a cheap shot. But you must know *something.*"

Rob nodded. "We know that somewhere around one a.m. she left the Oak Bar with two men in their mid-thirties. We have descriptions of both and a good set of prints off one of the glasses in the room—you have no idea how many sets of prints you can find in a hotel room—but no ID as yet. We don't think they were registered in the Plaza. Shortly after two a.m. she came through a twelfth floor window."

Kara closed her eyes and shuddered.

"Was she conscious?"

"Witnesses say they heard her scream."

"Oh, God."

The coffee turned rancid in her mouth. Again she felt her stomach heave, but she forced it down. There was something else she had to know. She couldn't bring herself to look at Rob as she asked it.

"Was she . . . was she raped?"

There was a long pause. Finally she opened her eyes and looked at him. His face was tight.

"You're not going to like it."

"Tell me!" she said, the rage within her tearing at the surface of her control, screaming to break through and strike at someone. Anyone. *"Tell me!"*

"There was evidence of semen in both the vaginal vault and oral cavity," Rob said. His voice was robot-like, as if he had gone on autopilot and was reading from a report. "DNA analysis indicated two different men as sources. There was no sign of forced penetration. Kelly appeared to be a willing participant."

Kara's anger suddenly turned to ice. She could barely speak.

"I don't believe it. A couple of guys drag her up to their room, rape and sodomize her, then throw her out a window and you have the nerve to say that she enjoyed it? I should have known! Is this what being a cop in this city has done to you?"

Rob stared into his coffee in silence. When she was through, he spoke in a low voice.

"It was Kelly's room."

"What?"

"Kelly rented it."

"Rob, what are you saying?"

He continued to stare into his coffee.

"I'm saying that Kelly Wade, your sister, took that room herself. She signed in as 'Ingrid' Wade."

"No. There has to be a mistake."

"No mistake. She's been a regular at the Plaza for the past few months. Paid cash every time. She was known to quite a few of the staff as a good tipper, and, um, a real swinger. She'd rent a room, pick up a guy in the bar—sometimes two guys—and take them up-stairs."

"No!"

"And we found a vial of coke in her purse."

Suddenly numb, Kara slumped back in the chair.

Over Christmas she had sensed that something was bothering Kelly when she was out at the farm. She'd thought her sister was still in a funk over her break-up with that Tom creep the previous year. Kara had never dreamed it was anything like this. One night stands. Cocaine. She hadn't noticed any signs of drug abuse. But out in the heart of Amish country, who knew those signs?

An awful thought struck her. Was her habit bad enough to . . .

"She . . . she was a prostitute?"

"I don't think so. The M.E. said there was no sign of a heavy coke habit. And as far as we can tell, she didn't charge for her favors. One of the bartenders at the Plaza had spoken to a few of her, um, dates after they'd been up in her room. They said they couldn't believe they'd gotten what they'd, um, gotten for free."

Kara stared at him.

"This is true, Rob? Really true?" She fought to keep a growing sob from choking off her voice. "It can't be! You're not talking about my sister, Rob! We're twins. We spent every day of our lives together. I *knew* her! *You* knew her! This can't be Kelly you're talking about! There's got to be a mistake!"

Sadly, he shook his head.

"I wish there were. Midtown North is just a block from the Plaza. When I came in the next morning and saw the name Wade on the report, I took the case. On a whim. I never dreamed it would be Kelly. When I saw the body I . . . I thought it was you. And the more digging I did, the more bizarre it became. I mean, I haven't seen Kelly since you and I—since you left town. That's ten years, but you're right, this kind of lifestyle doesn't fit with my memory of her. Not one bit."

"She was a *nurse*, for God's sake!" Kara said. "She worked at St. Vincent's! Whenever she'd visit the farm she'd tell me horror stories about all the drug addicts and the VD and AIDS. She saw all that stuff first hand! I can't believe she'd become a . . . a swinger!" The very word left such a foul taste in her mouth that she wanted to spit. "Tell me there's a chance you're wrong, Rob."

His expression was pained.

"I wish I could, Kara, I really do. But there's too much corroboration. The Plaza people knew her. According to them, she was fast becoming a legend in the Oak Bar."

"A *legend*," she said acidly. "My sister the legend. That's just great."

Gradually, her shock and disbelief ebbed away, and Kara became aware of a growing anger at her twin. Kelly hadn't been a completely innocent victim of one of New York's myriad acts of violence. She had been an enabler. She had put herself in a situation that simply begged for trouble.

Kara was furious. It was this city, this rotten lousy city that had done it to Kelly. She hadn't come here a swinger and a coke head, but she'd ended up one.

This damn city . . . Kara had to get out of it all over again. And right now. If she had to spend much longer here, she'd start to scream.

She glanced at her watch.

"I've got to be going. Thanks for the coffee and for your help and your time."

"No trouble. Where's your car?"

"I took the train. I didn't trust myself to drive."

"Good thinking. But even so, maybe you should stay over a night."

She gave him a sidelong stare. Was he thinking . . .?

"I don't mean anything like that," he said. "I just mean you don't look so hot. You're welcome to my place."

"You still rooming with Tony?"

"No. He's married. The rent got too high so I'm over on the East Side now. But seriously, I'll sleep on the couch. No problem."

"Thanks, but I don't know when my mother's coming in and I left Jill with a neighbor so—"

"Who's Jill?"

Good God, why had she mentioned Jill? She'd never intended to. But somehow it had slipped out. *Damn.* Well, she couldn't take it back now. She had to tell him something.

"My daughter."

▼

Rob hope he didn't look as shocked as he felt.

"A daughter? You have a *child?*"

Automatically, he reached for a cigarette, then remembered she'd asked him not to smoke. He really needed one now.

"Yes. Jill Marie. A real little beauty."

Kara's mood had lightened visibly with the change in subject. Her eyes were alight with love.

Why should he be so stunned? He and Kara had had no contact in ten years. He had never married. Was that why some part of him assumed that Kara too had remained single?

"Wait a sec. You signed in at the morgue as Kara Wade. That's your maiden name."

"It's my married name, too."

"You married a guy with the same last name?"

"No, Rob," she said with exaggerated patience. "I simply kept my name when I got married. There's no law that says I've got to take my husband's name."

"Oh." He remembered how Kara had been into women's lib. Apparently that hadn't changed. "How old's your little girl?"

"Hmmm?" Kara seemed to come back from faraway. "Jill? Oh, she's eight."

Eight?

"You didn't waste much time, did you!" he blurted, then wanted to kick himself. "Sorry."

"That's okay." Kara smiled. "No, I guess I didn't. He was an old high school beau who'd been carrying the torch for me all the time I was away."

"Imagine that."

Rob remembered carrying the torch for Kara a long while himself, hoping she'd come back, or at least call. Hoping . . .

"It's true," she said. "We just sort of picked up where we left off."

Rob tried but couldn't keep the edge off his voice. "He's not a cop, I take it."

"No. He was a safe, sane, staid insurance salesman."

"Was?"

"He was killed a year after we were married. His car got caught between a granite cliff and a jack-knifing tractor trailer on a snowy night on the Penn Turnpike out near Pittsburgh."

"Jeez, I'm sorry."

She was looking at him, a hint of wonder seeping into her expression.

"You really are, aren't you?"

"Of course. I mean, that's awful. How could I be anything else?"

Her mouth worked. For a moment he thought she was going to cry, but she blinked her glistening eyes, swallowed, and seemed to get herself under control again.

She said, "That was a perfect opening for a cheap shot. And you owe me one of those."

Rob understood. One of her reasons for leaving him had been her fear of being a young widow.

"Maybe," he said, "but a dead husband and father should be off limits, don't you think?"

Kara nodded, swallowed again, and looked out the window, saying nothing.

In the silence, Rob's thoughts tripped back to the time they had spent together here in the city a decade ago. Had it been that long since he was a rookie and Kara was a Kelly Girl? After a two-year drift through CCNY, he'd finally settled on a field that really interested him. Despite all his mother's pleas to find something else, he'd decided to go into the family business—police work. And when the Wade twins came to town, he found a woman he could really care for—Kara.

Kara and Kelly, identical in appearance, but so opposite in attitude. Kelly, the free spirit, open to everything, she took to Manhattan like she'd been made for it, as if all her life she'd been waiting to be set free in The City That Never Sleeps. Kara, the thinker, the muller, did fine until her run-in with the necklace snatcher in Central Park. After that she began to see danger lurking in every corner. She started calling Rob's police career a death wish. Their last months became an endless argument, one long tug of war with a fraying rope. She wanted him to quit, go back to school, get a degree of some sort, and move out to the suburbs—Jersey, Connecticut, Upstate, anyplace but here.

He couldn't go. Rob the rookie loved the job, the excitement, the challenge, and loved the city. It was *his* city. He'd grown up here. He couldn't see what was so frightening about it.

Finally there was nowhere to go but apart. The immovable object stayed in New York. The irresistible force moved back to rural Lancaster County, Pennsylvania, saying she didn't want to be a widow at twenty-five.

Somewhere a dark god might be laughing at the irony of it all, but Rob found himself unable to squeeze out even a tiny drop of satisfaction.

Even now, after all these years, he found he still cared.

What a jerk he could be where she was concerned.

"I'll drive you to the station," he said.

▼

Rob drove her crosstown at a leisurely pace on Thirty-fourth, staying in lane instead of doing his customary bob and weave through the traffic. All around him on the street the cabs were playing their usual game of chicken with each other, while on the sidewalks the three-card monte players were set up and waiting for their daily quota of lunch-hour suckers. Rob badly wanted a cigarette.

"What are you doing with yourself these days?" he said to break the silence as they crawled past Macy's.

"Writing."

"Really? Novels?"

"Non-fiction. I do reviews, articles, criticism, that sort of thing."

"Would I have seen any of it?"

He couldn't remember seeing the Kara Wade byline anywhere.

"Not unless you're a regular reader of some of the feminist publications."

"Feminist? You write *feminist* stuff? I thought you said you wrote *non*-fiction?"

"Ooookaaaay," she said with a small, rueful smile. "I should have seen that one coming."

"So you're still into that stuff, though?"

"It's not something you're 'into' and 'out of,' Rob" she said, and he realized by her tone this was one serious subject for her. "If you really believe in something, you stay with it."

"Like being a cop?" he said.

There was something different in the way she looked at him, something new in her eyes.

'Yes. I guess so. I've never looked at being a cop as something a person could believe in, but I guess you can. But anyway, writing's what I do. I went to Franklin and Marshall when I got back home, went mostly at night, got a degree in Woman's Studies—"

Rob bit back a remark. *Woman's Studies! Christ!*

"—and began writing."

"You can make a living writing feminist articles?"

"No way. But the articles gave me enough credibility to land a contract for a book. And that's what I've been working on lately. In the meantime, I do clerical work at the local hospital—it's decent pay with an excellent benefits package, and it's mentally unchallenging enough to allow me to compose what I'll write when I get home at night. I still live on the farm. Jill and I get by just fine."

He had a feeling she was holding something back but didn't press. This wasn't the time or the place.

"And your mother . . . ?"

Rob remembered that Kara's father had died a few years before she came to New York; he had met Mrs. Wade once. A big, jovial woman who didn't look at all like her twins.

"Mom got remarried shortly after Jill was born. She and Bert live in Florida now. I'm in the process of buying the farm from her. I'm paying her off a little at a time. Mom and Bert are flying up this afternoon for the . . ."

She didn't finish the sentence. Suddenly her eyes were filling with tears. Rob didn't know what to do. He wanted to wrap his arms around her and hold her, but at the moment he was driving a car. Penn Station was dead ahead. He swung around its south side, then turned into a restricted area under its belly. He pulled the car into the curb and turned toward her. He stroked her shoulder, wondering what to say.

"I'm sorry," she said. "I'm not made for this kind of thing."

"Who is? Nobody's made for losing a sister. A twin, no less."

"I wish I could be stronger. I should be stronger."

"You're pretty damn strong," Rob told her. "It took a lot of guts to come in here and go to the morgue alone to see her. A *hell* of a lot of guts."

Suddenly her head was up and she was staring at him. Her face was blotchy, and streaked with tears, but her eyes were fierce, her teeth were clenched.

"Find those bastards, Rob!"

"I will, Kara." He had never seen her like this. "Take it easy, take it easy."

"And when you find them, I want you to call me. Because I want to see them. I want to see what kind of scum did that to my sister!"

"As soon as *I* know, *you'll* know. And we'll get them. Kelly's case won't get dropped. I've got a personal stake in this, too, you know. I promise we'll get them."

"Okay," she said. "That's good enough for me. Can I have your number so I can call?"

As he fished out a card for her, Rob didn't attempt to explain that finding the two men who'd been in the room with Kelly was a long way from convicting them of tossing her out the window, especially since the Forensics boys were saying there was no sign of a struggle. They were pushing to call it a suicide, and Kara would not want to hear that.

He said, "If I can get away, I'd like to come to the funeral."

"No! I mean, that might not be such a good idea. I'd feel better if I knew you were here working on her case."

Rob had figured she'd say something like that. Kara seemed intent on keeping him at arm's length. So what else was new?

"I'll walk you to the Amtrak platform."

"That's okay. I can make it." She started to get out of the car, then stopped. "And thank you, Rob. When they unzipped the bag at the morgue, you turned away. I appreciate that."

He was baffled.

"Why?"

"It gave me an inch more of privacy than I would have had otherwise. That was very considerate. I'm glad to see that you haven't become like everyone else in this city."

And then she closed the door and walked away toward the station doors.

Considerate, hell! he thought. He hadn't been able to look at Kelly again because she looked so much like Kara. And he hadn't been able to bring himself to watch Kara view her sister's battered corpse, couldn't watch her pain, her naked grief. So he'd turned away. That was all.

He lit a cigarette and watched the station doors for a while after she had gone inside. Kara had changed. She'd always been a strong person, with lots of drive and intensity, but the intervening years seemed to have brought everything into sharp focus for her. There was fire in her voice, and a steely determination in her eyes. Although legally she'd been an adult when they'd had their affair, she'd still been a girl inside. She was a woman now, inside and out.

And somehow he knew it would not be another ten years before he saw her again. He found himself looking forward to that.

LETTERS FROM Purgatory

Punished me again.

Still recovering from it. At least he didn't find the letters. Doesn't know about my scribblings. Be furious if he did. They tell too much about him, about our whole mad relationship. He'd punish me again, worse than ever.

But I can't stop writing. Only this bit of pencil and these scraps of paper allow me to retain the most tenuous grip on the last remnant of my sanity. My only link to reality, whatever that means. My reality—one continuous nightmare interspersed with all too brief periods of wakefulness. Have to keep a record of these awake times, to reassure myself they exist. That I exist! They are worth any punishment.

Oh, the punishment. He metes it out so casually these days. Simply for belittling him because he lost the blonde. Laughed at him because she escaped him. Resented my taunts, so the swine punished me.

But no matter. I survived. And in that poor nurse's death I've found hope. Proves he's not omnipotent. Not quite the Ubermensch he believes himself to be—that I believed him to be.

She escaped him.

Perhaps there's still hope for me.

Saturday

FEBRUARY 7
5:32 P.M.

"You coming down soon, Mom?"

Kara turned at the sound of Jill's voice. In the dim twilight leaching through the bedroom window she saw her daughter standing uncertainly in the doorway. Jill was still dressed in the dark green plaid dress and white tights she had worn to the funeral. Her dark brown hair had somehow held onto the French braid Kara had worked it into this morning.

"In a few minutes, Jill. I just want to sit here a while longer."

Jill walked over to where Kara sat by the window and put a hand on her arm.

"Are you okay, Mom?"

Kara put an arm around Jill's thin little shoulders and hugged her close. *Someday I'll be okay,* she thought, *but not yet. Not for a long time.*

"I'm fine," she told Jill. "Just sad."

It was over. Finally. Kelly had been laid to rest in a tearful ceremony late this morning. Six nurses had come all the way from Manhattan to say good-bye. Kara had been touched by that. They had accompanied the family back to the house and were downstairs now with her mother, Bert, Aunt Ellen, and a few neighbors who remembered Kelly.

Kara knew she should be downstairs playing hostess, but she couldn't manage that right now. She didn't want anybody else here in her house tonight. Except Jill. And maybe Mom.

Kara wanted them all to go home now and leave her alone with her grief. She wanted to hold onto that grief, use it to keep Kelly alive, use it to retrieve the memories of the past they had shared so intimately.

Go away! All of you!

She'd heard it was good to share your grief; that was what wakes and funerals were for—not for the dead, but for the living. To Kara, it was morbid, all of it.

"Aunt Kelly's with God, right?"

For the hundredth time, Kara reassured her little girl that her Aunt was indeed up in heaven with God.

"And she's happy, right?"

So important to Jill that her Aunt was happy. It seemed to make Kelly's death easier for Jill to accept. But it didn't work for Kara.

"Very happy. She's up in Heaven's ICU taking care of all those scorched souls they ship in from Purgatory every day. She's happy and very, very busy."

On the last word, Kara felt her voice start to crack. She hugged Jill more tightly against her.

If I start crying now, I'll never stop.

She got control and pushed Jill to arm's length, glad she hadn't turned on the lights.

"You go downstairs and play hostess with the mostess for a little while, then I'll come down and take over, okay?"

Jill brightened. She loved to be put in charge.

"Okay!"

They hugged again. Kara could never get enough hugs from Jill, or give her enough. She loved her like life itself, and strove every day to give her child two parents' worth of affection.

"Love you, bug," she said.

Jill kissed Kara on the cheek and ran downstairs.

Kara leaned back in her rocker and rocked, much as she had in this same chair, in this same room, when she'd been nursing Jill. That had given her such warm, pleasant feeling. Now she looked out at the bleak, frozen landscape and thought how well it matched her present mood.

The farm. *Her* farm. Forty acres with a house and a barn. True, the barn was falling apart and there was no livestock. Kara had no desire to be a farmer, but she was growing something: Christmas trees. That was for tax purposes, mainly. An accountant had told her that her tax rate for the property would go down if a certain percentage of the acreage was planted. Scotch pines were a perfect solution. Once she'd planted the seedlings, they needed no care beside an occasional spraying which she did herself. And someday she'd be able to sell them as Christmas trees.

She rocked and listened: Through the floor she could hear her mother moving about downstairs, clanking the pots, still so much at home in the kitchen that had been hers for thirty years but now belonged to Kara. Mom looked like she'd aged ten years since Christmas. She wasn't saying much; especially noticeable was the lack of bickering with her sister, Aunt Ellen. Hanging between Mom and Ellen no doubt was the memory that it had been Ellen who first had urged the twins to come to New York and live there as she did. Bert's voice floated up occasionally. Kara's usually jovial stepfather had been subdued this trip, muttering only an occasional phrase. He seemed to take Kelly's death as hard as a man who had lost his own flesh and blood. Kara loved him for that. And piping above it all was Jill's voice, high-pitched, incessant. Good old Jill. No such thing as a pregnant pause when she was around.

How Jill had loved Kelly, and Kelly, Jill. The two of them, separated by more than twenty years, would whisper and share secrets like two sisters, just as Kara and Kelly had when they were kids.

So many memories. What relationship, what life-sharing could be more intimate than that of identical twins? Kelly and Kara Wade had dressed alike, braided their long blond hair alike, had even played the traditional tricks of pretending to be the other.

She smiled as she remembered the time at the local county fair when they had driven one of the Little Miss Lancaster judges to distraction by taking turns showing up wherever he went. They shared the award that year.

They had grown apart during these last years of separation, of living in different states, but on the occasions they got together, it was as if they had never been apart.

Kara had always assumed she'd know instantly if something awful happened to Kelly. Wasn't there supposed to be a psychic link between identical twins? But Tuesday she had gone to bed early and had spent the night in a sound sleep. Kelly had plummeted through more than a hundred feet of cold air, screaming all the way, had had the life smashed out of her on the filthy pavement below without causing the slightest ripple in Kara's slumber.

It didn't seem right.

But then, nothing about this whole thing seemed right.

Kara picked up the list of Kelly's personal effects that were being kept for evidence. She hadn't—*couldn't*—let Mom see this. The vial with half an ounce of cocaine was the hardest to accept, but the clothing described wasn't much easier.

. . . one garter belt, black . . . two full length stockings, black . . . one pair silk panties, black, slit-crotch style . . . one bra, black, open cup style . . .

Kara forced her bunched jaw muscles to relax. This could not be her sister they were talking about here. Slit-crotch panties? Bras cut so the nipples poked through? Kelly would never wear these things. She would have fallen on the floor laughing if anyone asked her to wear this garbage.

This is not my sister!

It was Kelly they had buried today, but who had Kelly become? Who had made her this way?

Kara had to know. She knew she would not rest easy until she found out.

And who had pushed Kelly through that window?

Kara hoped that, whoever they were, they were sweating and worrying about being caught. And when Rob did catch them she hoped they got sent up for a long, long stretch during which they'd be buggered by every ferocious hood on Riker's Island.

She hoped they were spending every moment of every day in sweaty, shaky, skin-crawling, heart-pounding panic.

▼

"Phil? It's me—Ed."

"Are you crazy calling me here now? Julie and Kim will be back from church any minute!"

Ed Bannion cringed at the heat of his brother's anger. He could almost see Phil's clenched teeth, the splayed fingers of his raised hand.

"I gotta talk to someone, Phil. I'm going crazy!"

"Have you been drinking?"

"I've had a few."

"It's not even six o'clock, for Christ sake! What are you going to be like in a couple of hours?"

"Asleep, if I'm lucky."

"What the hell's that supposed to mean?"

Ed looked around his five-room Upper West Side apartment. It was empty, as usual, but never had felt so alone. He had hundreds of acquaintances, people he hung out with at night and on weekends, women he dated and occasionally slept with, men he had lunch with, played squash with. He couldn't turn to any one of them. He almost wished he'd stayed active in the Church. At least then he might be able to talk to a priest.

But there was no one for him now except Phil. And Phil didn't want to talk about it.

He sat at the kitchen table. Newspapers from Wednesday, the *Times*, *Post*, *News*, *Newsday*, *USA Today*, early and late editions, all arrayed before him. A beautiful blonde, clad only in garter belt and stockings, crashing through a window in the Plaza Hotel to end up dead on the street below—the tabloids had eaten it up, and even the *Times* had given the story considerable space. The tv news shows had reviewed the victim's life but reported that the police could come up with no answers. The victim's family refused to comment, and her tearful co-workers at St. Vincent's in Greenwich Village had nothing to say except how shocked they were.

And that was it. By Thursday she wasn't even mentioned. Twenty-four hours after her dramatic death, the papers and tv news both had forgotten about Kelly Wade.

But the police hadn't—Ed was sure of that.

And neither had Ed Bannion.

"I can't sleep, Phil. Every time I close my eyes I see her going through that window. I hear her—"

"Knock it off, will you? I never knew you were such a goddam wimp!"

Images flashed before Ed's eyes—the two of them, panicked, shaking, stumbling half-dressed out into the hallway, adjusting their clothing in the stairwell, hurrying down a random number of flights and then waiting for the elevator on another floor, taking it down to the lobby and then strolling out as casually as they could amid the uproar over the "jumper" who had landed on the pavement only moments before.

It would have been funny, a scene out of a Hollywood comedy, something to laugh about later ... if only it hadn't ended so horribly.

"Doesn't it bother you at all?"

Phil's voice softened. "Yeah, it bothers me. It was a hell of a thing. But we're not to blame, Ed. We didn't do anything to that Ingrid—"

"Kelly. The papers say her real name was Kelly Wade."

"Whatever. The fact remains that she went out that window on her own. Nothing we did in that room had anything to do with her taking that leap."

"I know, but—"

"But nothing!" The anger was back in Phil's voice. "What really bothers me is that I might get hauled in for questioning and have my marriage and career and reputation ruined because my brother can't stop whining about a whore with a snootful of coke who threw herself out a window!"

"You didn't see her face, Phil."

"Of course, I did!"

"Not right before she went out the window. It was—"

"Gotta go, Ed. Julie and Kim are back. Just hang in there and keep your shit together and don't do anything stupid, okay? *I'll* call *you* tomorrow."

"Phil—?"

The line was dead.

Ed hung up and reached for the vodka bottle. He poured some more over the ice in his glass. Absolut Citron. He'd never been more than a beer or wine drinker but he'd heard that the best way to get drunk without getting sick was with vodka. The slight lemony flavor of this one made it easier to swallow.

He sipped, grimacing as it went down.

But not *that* much easier.

He walked through the great room of his spacious condo, past the entertainment center with the stereo and giant screen tv, past the leather furniture groups. He didn't want to hear anything or watch anything, and he couldn't sit still. He stood at the picture window and looked down on Sheridan Square. How he'd reveled in owning this chic, expensive pied a terre in the Coronado, the corner of Broadway and 70th, in the heart of yuppidom. Tonight it left him cold.

"You didn't see her face, Phil," he said aloud as he watched the traffic below. "You didn't see her face."

If only he could forget how she'd looked as her head swung back and forth, staring in turn at him and his brother in those silent seconds before she ran blindly for the window; if only he could get her last expression out of his mind, maybe then he could sleep. He had only seen her face for a few seconds then, but it had differed so from the woman who had accosted them down in the bar. The face that had hovered over him for that instant had been shocked, repulsed, anguished, tortured . . . lost. But worst of all, utterly hopeless.

Why? *Why,* damn it!

The question clung to him like a whining child, following him from room to room. And it led to other questions.

Who was this woman who had called herself Ingrid

but was really named Kelly who had turned in a matter of seconds from a male fantasy sex kitten to a frightened doe? Who or what had made her that way? Why had she jumped?

And most importantly: Was Ed in any way responsible?

He wouldn't sleep until he knew.

Which was why he had spent most of the past four days trying to track down Kelly Wade, R.N. He had called in sick on Wednesday—and truly he had been sick the whole day after the incident—and had extended his illness through the rest of the week, spending his time calling the increasingly short-tempered Phil and trying to learn more about the dead woman. He had used a number of ruses, calling the personnel office at her hospital in various guises, trying to learn more about her. All he had managed to glean from them was that she had lived in the East Sixties and that the funeral was scheduled for Saturday in Lancaster, Pennsylvania. The police had been even less helpful.

He had found a *Wade K* in the Manhattan directory, listed at 335 East 63rd. He had called the number at least forty times now and there was still no answer. That had to be her place.

When he got the chance, he was going to go over there and take a look around. Nothing overt, nothing conspicuous, just get the lay of the land and see if maybe he could learn something about her.

Yes, he realized it was an absurdly stupid and risky thing to do, and he knew Phil would probably strangle him if he learned what he planned, but he had to do this. He had to learn something about this woman, something—he was almost ashamed to be thinking this—*bad*. All he wanted was for someone to let him know, just *hint*, that Kelly Wade had a long history of being a flake and a floozy and everybody had known that she was bound to come to a bad end someday.

That might not help him sleep at night. It might not make him forget that last look she had on her face, but it was a start.

And it didn't have to be all that risky. Not if he concocted a neat little story to explain his interest in Kelly Wade should anyone ask.

Ed leaned back in the chair and began inventing.

Sunday

FEBRUARY 8
10:20 A.M.

ROB HARRIS LIT A CIGARETTE AND STARED OUT AT THE Sunday morning sky. With his head propped up against the headboard he lay stretched out in his bed, thinking about where he'd been the past few years and where he might be headed—and not too crazy about either.

He looked around at the faded wallpaper which had been here since he'd moved all his second-hand furniture from his old west side digs after Tony had gone and got himself married. To the best of his knowledge, this was the first time he had looked—really *looked*—at the room.

Who lives here? he wondered.

There wasn't a picture on the walls, not a photo on the dresser. A motel room had more personality.

Where have I been?

He'd been to work and back, and that was about it. He'd put so much into the Job that he hadn't left much of a mark anywhere else. The only thing he had changed here was the kitchen, and that had been minimal, making space for some of the specialized utensils he'd picked up over the years. But the rest of the apartment? He'd seen flop houses with more character.

Marking time, that was what he seemed to be doing. Why? Waiting for what? For Kara to come back?

He flung that thought away. Ludicrous. He hadn't been saving himself for Kara. There'd been plenty of women since Kara. He glanced at the sleeping form beside him. Like Connie, for instance.

But it occurred to him that Kara had done a hell of a lot more than he with their ten years apart. She'd been married, had a child, graduated from college, and had a book in the works. Rob had had the job when she'd left, and he still had the job. Nothing more. He felt . . . jealous.

The thought of Kara brought Kelly to mind, and with her came the thought that he should have gone to the funeral yesterday. Even though Kara had let him know in no uncertain terms that he wasn't needed there in rural, Pennsylvania, and it might have been uncomfortable, he still felt he should have shown up. He'd had little or no contact with Kelly since her sister had dropped him ten years ago, but he felt he owed it to her to stand by her grave and say a prayer.

"What a jerk," he said aloud.

Next to him in the bed, Connie mumbled and turned onto her back. The movement exposed her right breast, pink and ample. Rob watched the dark nipple rise in the cool air of the bedroom. Connie squirmed, then pulled the covers up to her neck.

Rob leaned back with his hands behind his head and continued his rumination on being a jerk. Mostly it had to do with loyalty. He couldn't get past this feeling that he had some sort of obligation to be there for everyone he knew or with whom he'd ever had a potential relationship. Like Kelly Wade.

Jerk. Why was he lying here thinking about her on a Sunday morning? Did she come around to help him over the rough days and weeks and months he'd had after Kara left him? No. Oh, they'd had lunch together a couple of times and she'd tried to explain Kara's refusal to return his calls or letters, but in general she'd avoided him, going about her business without worrying too much about Rob Harris. So why did he feel he should be at her funeral ten years later?

Because you're a cop and she died in your city.

Bull. It wasn't his city. He didn't run it. And he hadn't dressed her up like a hooker and sent her trolling through the Oak Bar.

Still, Kelly had been a good kid. She had died a scarlet woman, but Rob would always remember her as the sweet young thing of ten years ago. He smiled. Kara and Kelly Wade, the two beautiful hicks looking like they'd just stepped out of a Doublemint ad. He remembered his first glimpse of her that night at McSorley's, and how the Wade twins, with their shapely, well-turned little bodies, pale blonde hair, blue eyes, scrubbed faces, and dazzling smiles had won over that all-male hangout before they'd departed.

You couldn't *not* like them. They even had a little routine: "I'm Kara, the Kelly Girl." "And I'm Kelly, Kara's sister." Corny and ridiculous from anyone else, but it had blown Rob away.

And although it was almost impossible to tell them apart except for their make up—Kelly always wore more—Rob found himself immediately drawn to Kara. Something about Kara . . .

Kara.

She'd turned out to be nothing but trouble for him. Why was he thinking about Kara when there was a shapely, passionate woman curled up against him in his bed?

Maybe because when he and Kara had been good together, it was magic. There had never been anything else quite like it for him, before or since.

But why torture himself about it? For all the passion and intimacy and ecstasy they'd shared, there had been large counterbalancing doses of anger and shouting and pain. And when she finally called it quits, she *really* called it quits—completely severing herself from him, from the city, and everyone she had known here. No calls, no letters not a word. Kelly had assured him that Kara was alive and well in Elderun but that she most definitely did not want to see him any more. He hadn't believed that. He'd traveled out through Amish country, groping through the area around a place called Bird In Hand until he'd finally found the Wade family farm and pounded on the door. Her mother had let him in but Kara had refused to come downstairs. He had stubbornly waited for hours in the warm but pitying presence of Mrs. Wade, but Kara wouldn't even show her face.

That was when it finally got through his thick Irish skull that she really and truly wanted no part of him.

That had hurt him like never before. As if the heart had been ripped out of him, leaving him with an empty hole where it had been.

Rob stretched. But that was all in the past now. Time heals all wounds. Or so they said.

Kara certainly hadn't needed much time to heal. She'd bounced back and married Mr. Right. He might be dead now, but at least she'd found him.

When's my turn? he thought. When would he find *Mrs.* Right, if there was such a person? Or had he already found her and let her slip away? Or was the job going to turn out to be Mrs. Right, like it had for so many cops he knew?

He wondered how many chances you got.

He still loved the job, but it wasn't quite the same anymore. It had been getting to him lately. The human misery he saw on a daily basis seemed to be deeper, more soul-wrenching; the scum he had to deal with seemed scummier. Was the city changing for the worse, or was it him?

That little restaurant he and Kara had dreamed of opening was looking better and better. Even though Kara wouldn't be with him, he still wanted to give it a try. He'd put in his twenty years, then use his pension as a back-up while he made the restaurant a going thing. He just had to hold out until—

He felt a hand slide up the inside of his thigh. He looked at Connie. She was awake and staring at him with her curly brown eyes. Her long dark hair flowed over her cheek and throat.

"An option on your thoughts," she said.

"Nothing. A blank."

"Come on. Your face reminded me of the first time I made you try sushi."

"Okay. I was thinking about a murder that maybe wasn't a murder and how I'm probably never going to know."

"Hey, it's Sunday. You're not suppose to be thinking about work. You're supposed to be thinking about me."

As if to emphasize that point, she ran her hand further up his thigh and began caressing him. Rob felt a faint tingle of pleasure but little more. His usual quick response wasn't there this morning.

"Not in the mood, huh?" Connie said after a couple of minutes.

"Not really."

"I hate it when you get so wrapped up in a case. You're good for nothing else when that happens."

"And I suppose you were a barrel of laughs back in October of '87?"

She laughed and punched him on the arm.

He'd met Connie during a robbery investigation when he'd been assigned to the Upper West Side. Her apartment—condo, rather—was next door to the scene; she'd heard noises and knew her neighbors were in Tortola for the week, so she called the police. Rob had questioned her and learned that she was an investment banker with Saloman Brothers. A few days later she had called him back to her apartment, saying she'd remembered a few more details. She'd greeted him at the door ... nude. They'd been seeing each other ever since.

Neither of them had any illusions that this was going anywhere. There were no problems in bed. That was fine. Connie wasn't easy to keep up with, but Rob managed. It was out of bed that they ran into problems. They moved in radically different circles. Rob had taken her once to Leo's, the watering hole where most of the Midtown North cops did their post-shift relaxing. She'd loathed the place. And Rob felt far out of his depth with her yuppie friends.

"How about going out for brunch?" she said.

"Brunch? I don't do brunch."

Connie hopped out of bed and went over to the mirror above the dresser. Rob had never met a woman so totally unselfconscious about nudity. Maybe that was because she had a great body and knew it. She pulled a brush out of her purse and began working on her hair.

"Sure you do. Every time you order breakfast when you're supposed to be having lunch, you're doing brunch."

"Oh. Okay. Let's do brunch."

She turned to him, her eyes bright.

"I got a great idea! We'll go to this place Pete McCarthy and I found up on Columbus Avenue.. It's called Julio's."

"Not another yuppie eatery!"

"No. This place is really declasse—determinedly so. It's a working man's bar left over from pre-gentrification days. It's grungy, the owner's the bartender, and the service is surly at best."

"Doesn't sound like your kind of place."

"It's not, but then again it is. Actually, it's a little like Leo's, but the hamburgers are great. Pete and I are keeping it a secret. We're only telling our closest friends, otherwise this place will be overrun."

"Just what I want to do on a Sunday—listen to your friends talk about money," he said, jabbing out his cigarette. "Almost as much fun as a tetanus shot."

"No, really." She began slipping into her bra and panties. "You'll like it."

Rob shook his head. "Sounds like too much fun for me. I think I'll pass."

It wasn't that he was into the anti-yuppie vogue. Sure, they seemed like a pretty empty-headed bunch, but he wasn't all too sure that if he had an income well into six figures that he wouldn't be just like them. It was just that he never seemed to have anything to say to her friends. They all liked to hear him talk about police work, but that was the last thing he wanted to discuss during his off hours.

"No, you won't," she said as she buttoned up her silk print blouse. "You can come back to my place while I spruce up, then we'll head for Julio's."

Rob didn't move.

"Are you coming?"

"No, Connie," he said. "Really. It sounds like a drag."

Suddenly, she was angry. Her eyes flashed.

"No! *You're* the drag, Rob! You've been moping around for a couple of days now! What's wrong with you?"

The last thing Rob wanted this morning was a fight.

"Nothing, Connie. Let's drop it, okay?"

"Drop it?" she said. "I'll drop it! But that's not all

I'm going to drop! You're no fun anymore, Rob! And you weren't so hot in bed last night either!" She turned and headed for the bedroom door. "See you in the movies, Rob!"

"Say hello to Peter McCarthy for me," he said to her retreating back.

A few seconds later, the walls of the apartment shook with the booming slam of the front door. Rob sighed.

"Women."

He lit another cigarette and stared out at the Sunday morning sky.

FEBRUARY 9
9:47 A.M.

"IT SMELLS IN HERE, MOM," JILL SAID, HER NOSE WRINKLING at the rancid odor.

Kara coughed. "That it does, Jill. That it does."

Smells like something died in here.

Which wasn't a very comforting thought, seeing as this was Kelly's apartment. Kelly had given her the key years ago, telling Kara to feel free to come visit and stay any time she was in the city.

Kara left the door open. "Wait here," she said.

She left Jill standing in the hallway by their overnight bags while she made a quick round of the rooms. Empty. Good. No one here who shouldn't be here. The odor was strongest in the kitchen. Kara opened the door under the sink and found the cause: rotten leftover Chinese take-out in the garbage sack. She tied the bag closed and brought it out to the hall. She'd throw it away later.

"All clear," she told Jill.

"What was it?"

"Week-old egg foo yung and fried rice, I think."

"Ugh!"

"You said it."

Kara helped Jill off with her coat and shrugged out of her own. She felt uneasy here, like some sort of grave-robber, or a vulture picking at the bones of the dead. But something had to be rotten here besides egg foo yung. Something had gone wrong in her sister's life. Kara wanted to know what.

She stood in the center of the main room and did a slow turn, taking in everything around her.

So ordinary.

Kara found that very ordinariness reassuring, but it didn't answer the questions that had brought her here.

The furniture was a motley assortment of new and good quality used. There were a couple of original watercolors of flower-filled fields on the walls along with a few framed posters from the Metropolitan Museum's Van Gogh in Arles show. A selection of photos of Jill and Mom and Kara herself stood on one of the end tables. The big thick *The Art of Walt Disney* sat right where it belonged—on the coffee table. Beside it was a stack of nursing journals.

This was the Kelly she knew. Not a swinger, not even a terribly exciting person, but a rock solid, steady, reliable professional who loved nursing and loved the throb and rattle of New York. Sweet and attractive. Although they were identical twins, Kara had always thought of Kelly as the better looking one. She'd had her love affairs, and she'd told Kara all about them when they got together. Once or twice she thought she'd found Mr. Right, but one had turned out to be not-so-Right, and the other, Tom, the most recent, had been keeping a little secret from her: his wife and child on Long Island.

But Kelly seemed to bounce back from those traumas like she bounced back from everything. Kara had often wished she could be as flexible, as resilient as Kelly. Which was probably why Kelly had been able to stay on in New York and Kara hadn't: Kelly could accept the city on its terms, Kara could only accept it on her own.

Which was why Kara lived in Pennsylvania and Kelly lived in New York.

And maybe why Kelly had died in New York.

So why am I in New York now? Kara asked herself.

To find a reason, some sort of hook that would help her understand what had happened. Damn it, she was going to find out why and how Kelly had changed or go half crazy trying. And she was going to tear this place apart in the process.

"When are we going to Aunt Ellen's?" Jill asked.

"Soon, honey. I've just got to look around here for a while, okay?"

Kara found something on the tv for the child to watch, then she headed for the bedroom. She'd start there.

▼

Nothing.

Kara had to admit her twin sister was boring. Not that that was bad. In this case, it was good. But puzzling.

How could a woman who liked New Amsterdam Beer, read Agatha Christie, Ed Gorman and John D. MacDonald, dressed in flannel nightgowns, and was voted Nurse of the Year at St. Vincent's twice in the last five years come to be a legend in the Oak Bar? Her major vice seemed to be Creamette pasta.

Drugs? In the night stand drawer was a prescription bottle from a Dr. Gates labeled: "Halcion 0.25 mg. One tablet at bedtime as needed for sleep." Twenty or so blue ovals rested in the bottom of the amber plastic container. It looked as if Kelly had suffered from insomnia. That might be important, but probably not. The medicine cabinet in the bathroom yielded even less. Midol was the most potent pill there, followed by Tylenol.

As she looked over the collection of lotions and creams and powders and scents lined up in the cabinet, arrayed around the sink, and clustered atop the tank lid of the toilet, Kara shook her head in wonder and dismay.

Look at this!

From Giorgio there was Red Extraordinary Perfumed Body Moisturizer; from Lancome there was Progres, Savon Fraichette, Savon Creme Exfoliante, and Effacil; Sebastian contributed Hi Contrast Gel, Sheen, and Cello-Shampoo; but Chanel had hit the jackpot: Lotion No. 1, Creme No. 1, Fluide No. 1, Creme Exfoliante, Lift Serum Correction Complex, Lotion Vivifiante, Demaquillant Fluide, Huile Pour Le Bain, Poudre Apres Bain De Luxe, Creme Pour Le Corps No. 5, and of course, the indispensable Mask Lumiere. Something called Summer's Eve Feminine Wash—"the intimate cleanser"—sat on the edge of the tub. The drawers were filled with different shades of eyeliner, eye shadow, lipstick, and make-up.

Kara never ceased to be amazed at the gullibility of her sex. It seemed to know no bounds. Even the monstrously cynical and endlessly voracious cosmetics industry, despite decades of unrelenting effort, had yet to find its limits. This collection was proof.

She had long lived with a smoldering anger toward the cosmetics industry for its alluring hype and empty promises of eternal youth and beauty. She had even sold a few articles on the subject—all to feminist magazines, of course. Magazines with no cosmetics advertisers to lose. She had wondered as she was writing them why she bothered. She was, after all, preaching to the converted. But the articles weren't totally useless: they kept her name in print, kept a little cash flowing through her checking account, and gave her credibility as a writer when she'd approached the book publishers. And her articles had been somewhat unique in that her venom hadn't been directed solely at the cosmetics industry. She'd also taken the modern woman to task for allowing herself to be so continually duped.

She was chagrined to see the extent to which her twin had bought into the Big Lie. And *bought* was the word! This junk must have cost a small fortune!

Kara guessed it was a barometer of how well skilled nurses were being paid these days.

So. There was evidence that Kelly had been moisturizing herself into Nirvana, but nowhere could Kara find a trace of illegal drugs or their paraphernalia—no joints, no unlabeled capsules, no powder-smeared mirrors, no coke spoons, no rolled-up bills, not even a razor blade.

She had ransacked the bedroom, pulled the living room furniture apart, gone through all the cereal boxes and flour canisters in the kitchen.

Nothing.

The closets were racked with Kelly's nurse's uniforms and an array of trendy outfits, some mildly sexy, but nothing blatantly provocative.

She found a couple of well-used but unlabeled videotapes under the tv. She bit her lip, wondered what was on them. Porn? Maybe even Kelly doing . . . things?

Kara glanced at Jill. She was watching *The Price is Right*. "Jill?" she said. "Can I use the TV for a couple of minutes?"

"Sure. This is boring. Besides, it exploits women."

Kara had begun raising Jill's consciousness at an early age. Occasionally she wondered if she'd started

Jill too young, or perhaps done too good a job. Sometimes Jill was *too* aware.

"*The Price is Right?*" Kara said, glancing at the screen where an overweight matron was jumping up and down and clapping her hands. "Do you really think so?"

"It makes all these ladies look dumb. Isn't that exploiting women?"

"Not really. Those ladies are making themselves look dumb. I think *The Price Is Right* exploits materialism more than anything else."

"What's materialism?"

Kara had a sudden inspiration as to how to get Jill away from the TV set for a few minutes.

"There's a dictionary over there. Why don't you look it up? Sound it out."

"Okay."

As Jill trotted over to the book shelves, Kara slipped the tape into the VCR and started it running. When the opening credits for *Desk Set* came on, she wanted to cry with relief and nostalgia. Kelly's favorite movie. The second tape was *Father of the Bride*, another of her favorites.

She swallowed the lump in her throat and called to Jill.

"Here's something better than a game show. Watch this instead."

Kara went back to the bedroom and stripped the bed, then lifted the mattress to see if something was hidden between it and the box spring.

That was when she found it.

Not under the mattress. Under the night stand. When she lifted the mattress to look beneath, it slipped off the box spring and struck the night stand, knocking it over along with the lamp atop it.

And there was the cache.

Kara had checked the night stand drawers the first time through and had found nothing but old paperback mysteries in them. But she hadn't pulled the bottom drawer all the way out. If she had she would have found this little trove.

Sleazy underwear here. More Frederick's of Hollywood type stuff—lacy open-front bras and matching slit-crotch panties in scarlet and lavender. The same under the other night stand.

Feeling slightly queasy, Kara went to the big dresser and pulled the two bottom drawers all the way out and set them on the floor. Laid out in the space under the drawers was an array of slit-sided leather skirts and low-cut blouses.

As she stared at the tawdry outfits, Kara felt a terrible sadness for her sister.

What were you looking for, Kelly? What on God's earth did you think was missing from your life that you had to go looking for it dressed up in this . . . this shit!

The sadness gave rise to anger. Why hadn't Kelly come to her if she was having a problem? Didn't she think she could rely on her own twin? Why hadn't Kelly sought her out instead of pulling away?

Or had she pulled away *because* of the problem?

Kara stood up and scanned the ransacked bedroom. Maybe she'd never know. But there had to be a reason Kelly would buy these tramp outfits and hide them—

Wait a minute.

Hide them? Why on earth would Kelly hide her trashy clothes under her dresser and night stand?

Kelly lived alone.

This didn't make any sense at all. Kara had been through all the closets, all the drawers. Everything belonged to Kelly. Nobody else was living here. Just Kelly.

From whom was Kelly hiding these clothes?

▼

It was around lunch time then, and Jill was hungry. Kara cooked up a packet of Lipton's chicken noddle soup she found in one of the kitchen cabinets and she and Jill settled down to a couple of bowls with some Ritz crackers. Kara wasn't in the mood for anything heavier.

Afterwards, she pulled Rob's card from her purse. This was as good a time as any to give him a call.

On the third ring, he answered with, "Harris."

"Rob? It's Kara Wade."

"Wh—? Kara? Hello! Good to hear from you. Everything okay down there?"

Down there. He thought she was in Pennsylvania. Good. Let him go on thinking that. If he knew she was here in the city he'd want to get together with her for dinner or the like and Kara didn't think that was such a good idea. Not with Jill along.

"As well as can be expected."

"The funeral . . .?"

"Bad. But it could have been worse. Thank you for the flowers."

"I'd have come—"

"The flowers were enough." Kara paused, almost afraid to ask the question because she already knew the answer. "Have you caught them yet?"

"No." She could hear the frustration in his sigh. "No, we haven't."

"I didn't think so."

"Don't start that again, Kara. It's not fair."

"It isn't?" She felt her own frustration ballooning within her. "If she'd been Ivana Trump you'd sure as hell have somebody in custody by now!"

"I don't know about that, Kara."

"You said you had a description of the two men and a set of fingerprints! That was five days ago!"

"Right. But the two men described were not regulars at the bar, and they haven't been back since. And the fingerprints were no help at all."

"Why not?"

"They don't match anywhere. Which is not surprising."

"Why isn't it?"

"Well, it goes along with the pick-up theory. I mean, if Kelly picked these two guys at random from the Oak Room Bar crowd, it's very possible that they don't have criminal records. And if they don't have criminal records—or haven't applied for a gun permit or a security-sensitive job—then their prints are probably not on record here or with the Feds."

"And so you won't be able to match them anywhere."

"Right."

She felt the anger rising again. She wanted to scream but kept her voice level, for Jill's sake.

"So you're no closer to finding Kelly's murderers now than you were on Thursday."

"I'm afraid that's right, Kara." Rob paused, then said, "I'm afraid we can't even say for sure it was murder."

"*What?*" Kara didn't want to believe what she was hearing.

"Just hear me out," he said quickly. "Forensics says there's no sign of a struggle in the room. And they can't say for sure whether the two guys she picked up downstairs were even *in* the room at the time she went out the window."

Kara felt as if she were turning to ice.

"Are they saying Kelly *jumped*?"

"No. Not in so many words. They're saying there's

nothing to support the idea that she was pushed. And the M.E. backs them up. He says she wasn't beaten, and that if she was thrown out the window, she didn't struggle—no broken fingernails, no skin under the nails, no bruises on her palms. And witnesses there say she screamed on the way down, so we know she was conscious."

"Kelly wouldn't kill herself," said Kara, although she knew her voice didn't exactly ring with conviction.

After what she'd found this morning, she was no longer completely sure about anything concerning her twin. However, there was most of a bottle of sleeping pills in the bedroom. If she had wanted to kill herself, why hadn't she taken them?

"We've talked to a lot of her co-workers at St. Vincent's. The ones who knew her best seem to think she was very troubled lately. Even a little depressed."

Kara thought about that. In retrospect, she could see that there had indeed been a change in Kelly over the past year. Nothing terribly obvious. She hadn't called anywhere near as often, and she had seemed a bit withdrawn on the few occasions they had seen each other. But suicidal . . .?

If there was something so terribly wrong, why didn't she come to me?

Kara was suddenly feeling pretty depressed herself.

"Does this mean Kelly's going to be written off as a crazy bimbo who threw herself through a hotel window?"

"No," he said slowly. "Not by a long shot. That doesn't sit well with me."

Her spirits rose a tiny bit.

"Why not?"

"Kelly had to hit that window with tremendous force to go through it the way she did. Jumpers just don't do it that way. They open the window, step out on the ledge, and go. They don't do what Kelly did. Besides, I used her purse keys and did a quick search of her apartment the day after her death. I didn't find a suicide note or anything like it."

Kara looked around. Maybe that explained some of the uncharacteristic disarray she'd noticed during her own search.

"So we're back to murder," she said.

"I don't know where we are, Kara," Rob said. His voice was tired. "But I promise you: I'll keep this case open as long as they let me."

"Thank you, Rob." She believed him. "Can I call you again on this?"

"Call me any time. You know that."

"Thanks."

Kara hung up and stared across the room at the pile of papers she had pulled from one of the closets. She was going to go through everything there until she found an answer.

Kelly a suicide? No way.

"Was that Aunt Ellen of the phone?" Jill said.

Kara suddenly had an insane urge to tell her the truth. *No, bug. That was your father.*

"Just a policeman."

She looked at Jill. She so resembled Rob. The idea of Jill and Rob being in the same city was almost unnerving. If they ran into each other, there was no way he could miss the resemblance. And then he would know that he had a daughter.

Rob was a good man. Seeing him again had released an almost overwhelming attack of guilt. She never should have kept her pregnancy a secret from him. She saw that now, but at the time it seemed the only thing to do. Nothing was going to deter her from having the baby, and nothing was going to convince her to raise the child in the city. And there was no way Rob was going to leave the city willingly. She could have used the pregnancy to coerce him into quitting the NYPD and moving to the suburbs, but what kind of marriage, what kind of life would that have been? He would have felt like a prisoner, or a hostage. He would have come to resent Kara, maybe even resent his child. The result would have been intolerable for the three of them.

So Kara had done the hardest thing she had ever done in her life. She left the man she loved and returned home to have her child and raise her by herself. The idea had shocked, offended, and embarrassed her mother, and even Kelly had thought she was crazy, but they'd all stood by her just the same. For awhile the farm had been a war zone ... until Jill was born. Jill brought them all together again.

It hadn't been easy raising a child on her own, but Kara had managed. She'd done it away from the city where they were safe, where she could instill in Jill the values she thought important. She was proud of the result. Jill was her own little person and Kara loved her more fiercely than she had ever believed she could love anything.

But did she need a father? That had plagued Kara for the past ten years. Soon the vague questions Jill had asked about the father she had never seen were going to become more pointed. Vague answers would no longer suffice. What was Kara going to do then?

And Rob. Kara realized she still cared very deeply for him. He had a right to know he had a daughter, just as Jill had a right to know her father.

What had seemed so simple, so clear, so cut and dried, so black and white ten years ago was now a mass of confusion. A mess. One she would have to straighten out someday.

Someday, Kara thought. Someday she'd get them together, and pray that they'd both forgive her.

▼

5:45 P.M.

"Aren't we going to Aunt Ellen's now?" Jill said. She was getting whiny, which meant she was hungry.

"After dinner."

"Where are we going to eat?"

"Anyplace close where we don't have to wait," Kara said as she stood inside Kelly's door and helped Jill into her coat. On the way in they'd passed someplace called Pancho Villa a couple of blocks down on First Avenue. "How's Mexican food sound?"

"What's that?"

"Tacos and stuff. We had tacos once, remember?"

"I think so. Are you mad, Mom?"

The question caught Kara by surprise.

"No, Jill." She smiled for her. "At least I don't think I am. Why?"

"You've got a mad face."

"Do I?" *Yes*, she thought, *I probably do.* "I'm sorry. I don't mean to. Actually, I'm not mad. Just frustrated. And it's got nothing to do with you."

"What's frustrated?"

"Let me see. Imagine you're paddling a canoe in a river and you want to get to a certain spot on shore but the current keeps pulling you away. And no matter how hard you paddle, you can't get to shore. As a matter of fact, the current keeps pulling you further and further away. How would you feel?"

"I'd feel scared."

Kara laughed and hugged her daughter. "I guess you would!"

And maybe I'm scared, too.

Scared because she couldn't get a handle on what had been happening in her twin's life. Kelly had become an enigma. Kara had more questions about her now than before. Except for the hidden clothing, everything Kara had found was so damned ordinary. She had spent much of the afternoon going through Kelly's papers. Her sister, it seemed, was a scrupulous record keeper. Kara had found a copy of her apartment lease, the warranties and instruction manuals on all her appliances, and a shoebox crammed with receipts for what looked like every single purchase she had made last year. Kelly, it appeared, was preparing to do her taxes. But nowhere was there a single receipt for the sexy clothes Kara had found.

She kept receipts for *toothpaste*, damn it! Why wasn't there one for that new leather skirt under the dresser?

Why was the sleazy part of Kelly's existence so rigidly walled off, so tightly compartmentalized from the rest of her life? Who was she hiding it from?

Kara had always thought she knew her twin. Now she wondered if she had known Kelly at all.

But there was someone who might at least know something: the Dr. Gates on the label of Kelly's sleeping pills. Kara had called the drug store on the label and the pharmacist had told her that the prescription had come from a Dr. Lawrence Gates, a psychiatrist in Chelsea. Kara hadn't been that surprised at the specialty. Maybe he was just what Kelly had needed. Getting to him was the first thing on Kara's list of things to do tomorrow.

Tomorrow. She hated the idea of staying overnight in the city, but couldn't see any alternative. Silly to waste a couple of hours each way fighting the traffic in and out every day. For years Aunt Ellen had been asking her to come and stay with her for a few nights. This time Kara would take her up on it. No rush to finish up here. She could take her time. Kelly's check book showed that her rent was paid up to the end of the month.

"Come on," she told Jill. "It's taco time."

As she led Jill out through the front door of Kelly's apartment building into the chilly twilight, she almost bumped into a man standing on the front steps.

"Very sorry," he said with the start of a smile.

Kara was about to smile in return and excuse herself when she noticed his eyes widening in shock and the color bleaching from his cold-reddened cheeks.

"My God! It's you!" he cried. "Dear sweet Jesus, it's you! You're alive!"

Startled, Kara clutched Jill against her and pressed back against the building's front door which had closed and latched behind her.

"What's he saying, Mom?" Jill cried. Kara could hear the terror in her voice. "What's he saying?"

Kara didn't answer. Her mind was racing, trying to recall the various options she had been taught in her women's self-defense courses. But she'd been poised and ready in those classes, and standing on a padded gymnasium floor. This was on a set of stone steps with a child clinging to her.

But the man didn't seem to be threatening them. More confused and frightened than anything else. And he was backing down the steps, away from them. Well dressed, like a fortyish yuppie, but that didn't mean he couldn't be a nut case. Kara decided to hurry him on his way.

"I don't know what your problem is, buster," she said in her toughest voice, "but you'd better take it somewhere else! And quick!"

At the bottom of the steps he stopped and squinted up at her. He seemed to regain some of his composure.

"I . . . I'm terribly sorry," he said. His voice was quavering. "For a moment there I thought you were someone else. But I see you're not. Your hair is straighter and . . ." His voice trailed off. "You're just not her."

A thought struck Kara.

"You knew my sister?"

The man suddenly seemed very tense, as if he were preparing to run away.

"Sister?"

"Yes. Kelly Wade."

The man glanced around, looking indecisive. Then he took a deep breath and looked directly at Kara.

"Yes. I knew her. It's just terrible about her . . . about what happened to her."

"Did you know her well?"

"No. Just a little. Hardly at all."

Kara's hopes fell. This fellow wasn't going to be any help.

"Do you live here?" she asked.

"Uh, no. I was just coming by to, uh, see if there was any family around so that I could express my condolences."

"I'm family."

"Yeah. I can tell." He managed a quick, nervous smile. "You could be her twin."

"I am."

Another quick smile, little more than a flicker. "No wonder. The resemblance is spooky."

"And this is my daughter, Kelly's niece."

"How do you do," he said to Jill, and Kara immediately liked him for speaking directly to the child. "I'm terribly sorry about what happened to your sister," he told Kara. "I . . . I wish there was something I could say."

An idea occurred to Kara. This fellow seemed like a harmless sort, and genuinely upset by Kelly's death. He was the only person Kara had met today who knew Kelly; maybe he could give her some insight into her sister's life in New York before the end.

"We were just going out for a bite to eat. Want to come along?"

As long as they stayed in a public place like a restaurant, what harm was there?

"Oh, no," he said, quickly. "I've got to be going."

"Okay," Kara said and started down the steps with Jill at her side. "Good night, then."

They were on the sidewalk and on their way to the corner when he trotted up behind them.

"Maybe just for a few minutes."

"Fine," said Kara. She held out her hand. "I'm Kara Wade, by the way."

He shook it and seemed to fumble for his own name.

"Ed," he said finally, "Ed Bannion."

▼

"I met her at St. Vincent's," Ed was saying. "She took such special care of my mother when she had complications after her gallbladder surgery. I was very impressed with her."

They were seated near the window on the second floor of Pancho Villa's. Kara licked the salt off the rim of her margarita and watched the rush hour traffic thicken in the growing darkness outside. Jill was next to her, dipping tortilla chips into the bowl of salsa and listening to the strolling guitar player singing two tables away. Ed sat across from her, sipping his own margarita.

Now that they were inside and in the light, Kara saw that he was a fairly good looking man, late thirties, with thinning brown hair. He might have been more attractive if he weren't so tired looking. There were dark circles under his eyes; he seemed tense.

"You don't work at the hospital, then?" Kara said.

"Oh, no. Why do you ask?"

"I thought you might be a doctor."

"Actually, I'm a lawyer."

"How well did you know Kelly?"

"Not well at all, unfortunately. We had lunch together a few times. I liked her a lot." He shrugged. "It might have developed into something more, but . . ."

Kara nodded. *But Kelly's time was cut short.*

Ed said, "I sensed she was a very special person, but I know hardly anything about her. What can you tell me?"

Kara told him about Kelly's passion for mystery novels and 60's folk rock, how her favorite thing was to lie on her couch munching Dorito chips while reading John D. MacDonald and listening to the Byrds or the Lovin' Spoonful. She liked middle period van Gogh paintings and old Tracy and Hepburn movies. Jill added in her own anecdotes about her best times with her Aunt Kelly.

Ed listened attentively. If anything, he appeared puzzled, as if he wasn't hearing what he expected.

Then it was their turn for the strolling guitarist. He stepped up to their table and wanted to know if they had any requests. He was dressed as a caballero and wore a huge sombrero. Kara was about to say no when Jill piped up and asked for the only Mexican song she knew.

"La Bamba!" she said.

Kara and Ed listened politely while the singer ran through the song. He offered a more traditional rendition than the Richie Valens-Los Lobos version Jill was used to, but she seemed enthralled nonetheless.

During the song, Kara realized that this encounter

was not going the way she had hoped. Ed knew less about Kelly's New York life than Kara did. The information was flowing the wrong way. But at the moment she didn't see a way out.

The three of them clapped when the guitarist finished. He added a nice accent to the restaurant's ambience, but Kara was glad to see him move on to another table.

"Can I go over and listen, Mom?" Jill said.

"Sure," Kara told her. "Just don't get in his way."

Ed smiled as he watched her go. "Looks like that singer has got himself a fan."

"Jill loves music," Kara said. "So did Kelly."

"What a shame," Ed said, shaking his head and staring down at the tablecloth. "I was so shocked when I read about her fall. So tragic."

"Fall?" Kara said. She glanced around to make sure Jill was out of ear shot. "Kelly didn't fall! She was pushed!"

Ed's head snapped up. His face was pale and his eyes were wide as he looked at her.

"No-no! She fell! It was an accident!"

Kara was surprised by his vehemence.

"Why do you say that?"

"Because," he said slowly in a calmer tone, although he still appeared upset, "I simply cannot believe that anyone would want to harm her."

"Neither can I," Kara said. It was a natural conclusion. Who would want to hurt Kelly? "But it's true. She was murdered."

"Oh, God!"

Ed ran a trembling hand across his face. He had gone another shade paler. He looked as if he was going to be sick.

It occurred to Kara that if the thought of Kelly being murdered upset him like this, he must have cared for her a lot more than he had let on. Obviously he knew nothing about Kelly's bizarre sexual behavior—and he wasn't going to learn of it from Kara.

"I'm sorry if I upset you," she said.

"No, it's all right. It's just such a shock. Do the police have any idea . . .?"

"Nothing," Kara said without trying to hide the bitterness that leapt into her voice. "They've got a description of two guys and a set of fingerprints, but no suspects."

"Are they . . . are they close?"

"Apparently not. And I'm afraid that if they don't find someone soon, they'll forget about Kelly. But I won't let them. I'm a very persistent person. I'll be on their backs. I won't let Kelly's file wind up on the bottom of their stack of unsolved murders."

"Good for you," Ed said, but his voice was flat.

He still appeared to be in a state of shock, but his color was better. He seemed to be pulling out of it.

Kara noticed that Jill was on her way back to the table.

"Let's change the subject, shall we?"

"Gladly," Ed said.

He paused, staring off into space, then seemed to come to a decision. He reached inside his coat pocket and withdrew a card.

"Here's my number."

Kara recognized the mountain logo. "You work for Paramount?"

"I'm with their legal department. I do mostly corporate law now, but I can still help you with the police. I want you to keep me informed as to what's going on with your sister's case. Because if there are any problems, of if they start giving you the runaround, they'll start hearing from me as well."

Kara was touched.

"That's very nice of you. Kelly was lucky to have a friend like you."

"It's the least I can do."

▼

I'm certifiably insane, Ed Bannion thought as he rode across town in the back of a cab. He had dropped the woman and her daughter off at the dead sister's apartment and was now eager to get back to his own place on West 70th. *Insane! That's the only explanation for what I did tonight!*

He blamed it on the uncanny resemblance between the two sisters. For a moment there he'd actually thought the dead woman had come back to haunt him. He'd been so shook up he'd given her his real name. Idiot! After that, there was no turning back. Thank God he'd had the foresight to prepare a little story ahead of time. Never could have made up one on the spot.

And her talking about her dead sister as if she were all sweetness and light, Florence Nightingale herself. The little girl backed her up, too. Hard to believe they were talking about the sex kitten he'd had in the Plaza last week.

But maybe ... maybe they weren't. Maybe they were talking about that frightened miserable woman he'd seen just before she ran for the window.

And then the sister—the live one, Kara—had dropped the bombshell: murder.

Murder!

He'd almost dropped his margarita! Even now it sent a sick shudder through him. How could they think it was murder? She went through that window entirely on her own!

Ed had sat there wanting to retch, wanting to get up and run from the restaurant. He'd seriously considered excusing himself to the men's room and not coming back. But he'd made himself stay calm while his mind raced, and had then come up with an idea. Only time would tell if it was the craftiest or stupidest act of his life.

His card.

If he could stay in touch with her, she could keep him abreast of where the police investigation was headed. He had to know. So far it sounded as if he and Phil were safe. Nothing to link either of them to the girl or to the Plaza. But they were hardly home free. And if something new turned up, he wanted to know. If the case was being downgraded to inactive, which he prayed it soon would be, he wanted to know that, too.

But then there was something else.

Ed found himself strangely attracted to this Kara Wade. She was beautiful, yes, but it was more than that. He felt oddly close to her. As if . . . as if he already had a relationship with her. Because of her sister, he felt as if he'd already made love to her.

Pretty weird.

He had a feeling that his life was never going to be the same again. Something within him had changed last Tuesday night, as if he'd passed through a flame and had come out a different person on the other side. He was going to have to take charge of things a little more instead of simply letting them happen to him. And he felt protective toward Kara Wade, as if he owed her something.

Maybe he did. Maybe he owed her a sister.

An odd thought.

Whatever happened, he fully intended to see more of Kara Wade.

▼

Kara had left Jill on the couch watching tv while she straightened up some of the mess she had made of the apartment. When she was done, she found Jill sound asleep. The thought of spending the night here in Kelly's apartment gave her a mild case of the creeps, but she didn't have the heart to wake Jill and drag her over to Ellen's. Something ghoulish about sleeping in Kelly's bed, so she curled up beside Jill on the couch. Besides, it wouldn't be so bad staying here if they were together.

Kara closed her eyes and fought off the intense loneliness that pressed in on her. Even snuggled up close to Jill, she felt so alone.

Kelly was gone. How would she ever get used to that? It had always been the two of them. When they had come to New York together they used to sing that Paul Williams song, "You and Me Against the World." She remembered how she liked the Helen Reddy version and Kelly preferred Paul Williams' because she liked the bridge that Reddy had left out. And even when Kara had returned to Pennsylvania, leaving Kelly behind, her twin had only been a phone call or less than two hours' drive away. And even if she'd been in Pago Pago, just knowing Kelly was *somewhere* she could be reached had made all the difference.

Now Kelly was out of reach forever.

Kara bit back a sob and hugged Jill tighter.

You 'n' me, kid. Just you 'n' me.

FEBRUARY 10
11:45 A.M.

KARA ARRIVED EARLY AT DR. GATES' OFFICE—ON THE THIRD floor of a brick and glass office building on Seventh Avenue in Chelsea. She was surprised at the size of his waiting room. So tiny. But then, one psychiatrist seeing one patient an hour wouldn't need much space. It was decorated like a comfortable den in someone's home—warm colors, soft furniture, subdued lighting, and a glowing tropical fish tank built into one of the walls.

Jill headed immediately for the fish tank. Kara headed for the secretary-receptionist seated at the desk in the corner, typing on a computer keyboard. Directly to the receptionist's right was a heavy wooden door marked "CONSULTATION."

It hadn't been easy to worm her way into Dr. Gates' appointment book, but through a persistent series of calls starting early this morning during which she refused to take no for an answer, Kara had managed to extract a promise of a few minutes with him on his lunch hour.

The receptionist told her that the doctor was with his last patient of the morning and would see her when he was through.

"Would it be all right if I left my daughter out here with you while I talk to Dr. Gates?" Kara said.

The receptionist's expression was sour when she looked up from her keyboard.

"We do not provide baby-sitting services here."

"I realize that," Kara said. "But I'm from out of town and have no one to leave her with. This was a last minute arrangement. My appointment's only for a few minutes. She'll be no trouble, I assure you."

"Well . . ." She glanced over to where Jill was quietly counting the fish in the tank. "Since it's only for a few minutes. But don't make a habit of this."

"Thank you. I really appreciate it."

Kara seated herself on the sofa and wondered if Kelly used to sit in this same spot before her appointments. The now-familiar wave of sadness washed over her.

Kelly, Kelly, Kelly . . . what was torturing you?

Kara hoped Dr. Gates knew.

An attractive woman in her mid-twenties came out of the consultation room. Her expression was grim. She did not look at Kara or Jill; instead she stopped at the receptionist's desk. While she arranged her next appointment, Kara called Jill to her side.

"Okay, Jill," she said, putting an arm around her waist and hugging her close, "I'm going to go into that room and talk to the doctor about your Aunt Kelly."

"When are we going to Aunt Ellen's?"

"Right after this. I'll only be a few minutes so I want you to stay here and read or look at the fish."

"Can't I come?"

"This is grown-up talk. Boring stuff. Besides, I think Dr. Gates will only want to talk to me. Maybe you can look at these magazines."

"They look boring."

"Mostly they are," Kara picked up a copy of the *New*

Yorker and flipped through the pages until she found a cartoon. "But this one has some funny drawings in it. And if you're lucky, you may even find the Addams Family."

"Really?"

She took the issue and began flipping through it page by page. Kara guessed it would take her at least half a day to go through all the issues in the waiting room.

"The doctor will see you now," the receptionist said.

Kara's stomach constricted as she rose from the chair.

"I'll be right next door, Jill," she said. "Don't budge."

"I won't, Mom."

Kara walked through the door into a much larger office. It was decorated in a comfortable fashion similar to the waiting room. A large picture window took up most of one wall; daylight filtered through the drapes. Rows of books, some so old their spines were cracked and warped, lined the walls. A couple of upholstered chairs, something that looked like a recliner, and an antique mahogany desk that had to be six feet long.

Where's the couch? she thought.

A man was sitting at the desk, writing. He glanced up at Kara and froze for an instant, then he shot to his feet.

"Eeshtenem!"

"What's wrong?"

He recovered quickly and motioned her forward.

"Come in, please," he said. There was a trace of an unidentifiable accent in his voice. "I must apologize for my reaction, but you took me by surprise. This is extraordinary, most extraordinary! The resemblance is incredible!"

Kara was impressed with Dr. Gates' appearance. He looked to be about fifty, tall, very trim, with soft blue eyes, sandy hair graying at the temples, and a neat, sandy mustache. He was expensively dressed, wearing a camel hair sports coat, dark brown slacks, a yellow shirt and brown knit tie.

"We were twins."

"Yes, I know. She mentioned you many times."

Kara was immediately curious about how Kelly had spoken of her. As if reading her mind, Dr. Gates told her.

"She had a deep affection for you."

Kara felt her throat constrict. *It was mutual.*

"Please sit down," Dr. Gates said, indicating a chair in front of his desk. "And let me express how shocked and saddened I was by Kelly's death. It was a terrible blow, and the sensationalized coverage in the press only made it worse. After nearly a year and a half of seeing her as a patient, I'd come to think of her as almost a friend. She deserved far better treatment than she received."

"Thank you, Doctor Gates. I'm sure then you can appreciate the need that has brought me to you. I need to know what you were treating Kelly for."

His smile was sardonic. "That seems to be a popular subject these days. The police are after the same information."

Good, Kara thought. *At least they haven't given up.*

"And you must believe me, Ms. Wade," he continued, "That I am sincerely sorry to say that my answer to them will be the same as to you: No comment."

"She was my sister, Doctor Gates. My twin. This is not idle curiosity on my part. I must know what it was that led Kelly to the Plaza and got her killed."

"I'm afraid I can't discuss that with you, Miss Wade. It's privileged information."

"I've never heard of such a thing!"

"Nevertheless, that is my policy."

▼

Crosstown traffic was a killer, as usual, so Rob Harris arrived at Dr. Gates' office a little later than he had intended. He introduced himself to the receptionist and was relieved to find that the doctor was still in his consultation room.

Dr. Gates had refused to cooperate over the phone. Rob knew from experience that many doctors automatically refused to divulge medical information on their patients, even when foul play was suspected; some did it as a power play, and others actually thought they were protecting a dead patient's rights. Psychiatrists were the most stubborn. But he had learned over the years that the mere physical presence of a detective flashing his badge in the office often had a tongue-loosening effect on these docs.

"Please have a seat," the receptionist said. "The doctor should be through in a few minutes."

Rob glanced at the little girl sitting in the corner flipped through a magazine at breakneck speed, then back at the receptionist.

"Kind of young for psychotherapy, isn't she?" he whispered.

The receptionist did not smile.

"Her mother is with the doctor," she said coldly. "Please be seated."

"Sure. Right."

He checked out the tropical fish in the tank. He didn't know what kind they were, but they were bright, beautiful, and graceful. He took a seat on a couch against the far wall and glanced at the little girl a few feet away. She was tearing through that magazine, stopping only to look at the cartoons. A skinny little thing dressed in Oshkosh overalls and a plaid flannel shirt, with long, dark brown hair twisted into a single braid. Cute. Rob had never been crazy about kids—usually they were pests—but this one was pretty well behaved. She seemed oblivious to him. So much the better.

For some reason, Kara popped into his mind. Rob leaned back on the sofa and sighed. In a way he was glad she was in Pennsylvania and not in the city. That made it a little easier telling her on the phone that the investigation was just spinning its wheels. But damn it, he didn't have diddlyshit to work with. Two unmatchable completes and a partial off a hotel water glass; a description of two white males that could fit one out of every four guys on the Upper West Side. And Forensics saying there was no evidence of foul play. He was glad he hadn't been sitting in front of Kara when he'd told her that.

This psychiatrist was his last lead. Rob had picked up from one of Kelly's co-workers that she'd been seeing Dr. Gates regularly for a year or more, ever since she went through a nasty break-up with some guy she'd been seeing for awhile. Rob had checked out the guy—married with children, no less—and his whereabouts last Tuesday night were accounted for. So Dr. Gates looked like the last hope for a solid lead. And not a very bright hope.

Rob picked a magazine off the top of the nearest pile. It was *Cosmopolitan*. He was about to toss it back when the vast exposed areas of smooth skin on the cover model caught his eye. Next to her left arm was a heading: "10 Ways to Keep Him Satisfied!" That sounded interesting. As he opened the issue, he heard a little voice from the corner.

"My mother says *Cosmo* exploits women."

He looked up. The little girl was still concentrating on her own magazine, rapidly paging through it. Since there was no one else around . . .

"I'm sorry. Did you say something?"

"*Cosmo* exploits women," she said without looking up.

"Really?"

"Yep. My mom says."

She still hadn't looked up.

"So you said. But what do *you* think?"

"I think so, too."

Oh, great. A feminist munchkin.

"How come?"

Finally she looked up. Her eyes were a pale, pale blue, and she was more than cute. Adorable. Rob's heart warmed instantly at the sight of her face.

"Look at that cleavage," she said, pointing to the cover.

Rob bit his lip to keep from laughing. *Cleavage?* What did this little thing know about cleavage?

"How old are you?"

"I'm nine."

"No, you're not. You're *thirty*-nine at least. Maybe forty."

She smiled, showing straight, white teeth that seemed too big for her mouth.

"I'm nine. And a half." She pointed at the *Cosmo* cover. "And *that's* cleavage."

Rob looked down at the cover.

"Oh, my!" he said. "You're so right! Look at that cleavage! It's awful."

He quickly pulled out his pen and began scribbling on the cover.

"What are you doing?" the girl said, craning her neck to see.

"Getting rid of the cleavage!"

She hopped out of her chair and plopped down next to him. Her expression was concerned as she watched him filling in the model's exposed pectoral areas with black ink. She glanced at the receptionist who was busily typing out the dictation coming through her earphones, then back to Rob.

"You can't do that!" she said in a loud whisper.

"Of course I can!" He scribbled harder. "I'll teach them to exploit women!" He opened the magazine, then slapped it closed. "Oh, no! Full of cleavage! Cleavage everywhere!"

The little girl was giggling. Rob found that he loved the sound. He didn't want her to stop. He handed her his pen and began pulling magazines at random from the pile.

"Here! We'll become cleavage police! Take these! We'll search every one of them!" She was laughing now. He pointed to the cover of another issue of *Cosmopolitan*. "*More* cleavage!" He opened a *Time* and gasped. "Oh, my Lord! This is the worst yet!"

When she saw what he was pointing to, she began to belly laugh, loud enough to cause the receptionist to look up from her dictation.

The sound of her laughter broke Rob up. He began laughing along with her.

"Quick!" he said, handing her the *Time*. "Do something about that! Cover her up!"

▼

Dr. Lawrence Gates was insufferably arrogant. And Kara thought that was a generous assessment.

Throughout her carefully reasoned plea for information, he had sat and watched her in the way one of his patients in the waiting room might watch the fish in the tank. Her words beaded up and rolled off him without marring his impenetrable surface.

Cold. Aloof. Remote. Oblivious to Kara's anguish at being in the dark about what had led her twin to her death on the sidewalk in front of the Plaza Hotel. He just sat there twirling a key ring on his index finger. Two twirls and then he'd grab it; then he'd do it again. Twirl-twirl-stop. Over and over. It was annoying the hell out of Kara, especially since she wasn't getting anywhere.

"So you see," she said, "I need to explain to myself why Kelly had slutty clothes hidden in her apartment. We had a good upbringing. We were taught to respect ourselves. Who was she hiding those clothes from? Who was she afraid of? The police will want to know too."

"I'm sorry," he said abruptly, as if a bell had rung. "I sympathize with your plight, but it changes nothing. I do not discuss my patients with anyone—not with their parents, not with their spouses, not with their siblings, not even with their identical twins. You'll have to go now."

Kara stared at him in shock. That was it: he had a timer in his head and he had been sitting there waiting for it to go off. Suddenly furious, she went on the offensive.

" 'Go now'?" she said, keeping her voice low with an effort. "Fine. I'll go. But I'll go from here to a lawyer. And I'll be back with a subpoena for your records, and maybe a summons to boot. The police are talking about the possibility that my sister committed suicide. If that turns out to be true, I'm going to want to know why her psychiatrist didn't spot the risk and do something to head it off. You may find yourself trying to explain that at a malpractice trial, Dr. Gates."

Kara saw him stiffen. She'd broken through to him. Finally.

Suddenly she heard a faint noise from the waiting room. Laughter. Jill's. She'd recognize that laugh anywhere.

"Excuse me for a moment," she said to Gates, and went to the door. She pulled it open, stuck her head through, and froze.

Rob was there. Oh, God, and he was with Jill.

Jill looked up and saw her. Her face was flushed from laughing so hard.

"Mom, look!" she said, holding up the *Time* magazine on which she'd been scribbling. "I'm drawing clothes on this naked Perdue chicken!"

Rob looked up, too. His smile vanished, replaced by frank surprise.

"Kara! What are you doing here?"

"The same as you are, I imagine," she said, masking her anxiety as she stepped out into the room.

She sensed movement behind her and saw Rob's eyes focus over her shoulder.

"Dr. Gates?" he said, reaching into his breast pocket and pulling out a leather folder. He flipped it open to reveal a gold badge. "I'm Detective Harris, NYPD homicide. I'm investigating the death of Miss Kelly Wade and I'd like—"

Gates stepped over to the receptionist's desk and fanned through a small stack of letters. He didn't bother looking up as she spoke.

"Save your breath, detective," he said in a voice that dripped with *ennui*. "As I told you or one of your underlings on the phone this morning, I do not discuss my patients with anyone. That includes twin sisters and their *gendarme* boyfriends."

"Now just a minute—!" Kara said.

"Nor will I be intimidated by threats of lawsuits or police state tactics."

"You're carrying this privilege business to a ridiculous extreme," Kara said.

Gates casually stepped over to the door to the hall

and held it open. He looked at Kara with expressionless eyes.

"You wouldn't say that if you were one of my patients. Please leave. Both of you."

Too angry and frustrated to dare try to speak, Kara took Jill by the hand and led her out. As she strode toward the elevator, she heard Rob speaking to Gates. She couldn't make out the words, but his tone was angry. She hoped the elevator was already on this floor so she could get away without talking to him, but he caught up to her while she was waiting.

"What a tightass," he muttered as he stopped at her side.

Kara glared at him. She couldn't keep the anger out of her voice.

"Your timing was flawless!"

"Me?"

"You! He thinks we're in this together, that I brought you along to twist his arm!"

He reddened. "What? That's bullsh—!" He glanced past her at Jill as she stood at Kara's other side. "That's crazy. I didn't even know you were in town. If you'd have told me—"

The elevator arrived then. It was empty. The three of them got on. Kara let Jill press the lobby button. She realized she was overreacting. Maybe it was seeing him with Jill.

As the car started down, she turned to Rob.

"I wasn't aware that I had to let you know whenever I crossed the river. Anyway, I'm getting out of this city and away from its cold, uncaring, selfish people as soon as I can. God, I hate it more than ever!"

"How about lunch?" he said.

"No, thank you."

He nudged her gently and smiled. "Even if you hate

the people, you've got to like the food. And I bet my friend Jill's as hungry as a horse."

"Yeah, Mom," she said, tugging on Kara's arm. "I'm starved."

"We'll eat at Aunt Ellen's. She's expecting us." She turned to Rob. "You remember Ellen, don't you?"

He smiled. "Of course. She liked me."

"She likes anyone who's Irish. Anyway, Jill and I are supposed to have lunch at her place today."

Rob shrugged. "Okay. Maybe next time. I'll give you a raincheck on lunch, Jill. Some place that doesn't exploit women."

Jill giggled. "Or serve chickens with cleavage!"

Kara didn't have the vaguest idea what they were talking about, but the instant rapport between the two of them alarmed her.

"Great kid you've got there, Kara. A real piece of work."

"I thought you didn't like kids."

He looked embarrassed. "Yeah, well, most of them are a pain, but your Jill is something else. You've done a great job with her. You should be proud."

"I am," she said, and she could barely hear her own voice.

Finally the elevator doors opened on the lobby. She said a quick goodbye and hurried Jill out to the street.

▼

2:06 P.M.

"I do wish you'd stay another day or so," Aunt Ellen said as she sipped her sherry.

Kara took a sip of her own. She didn't usually drink wine in the afternoon, and wasn't at all used to sherry.

But once you got past the sweetness of the first couple of sips, it wasn't half bad.

Ellen had greeted them at the door where there had been a round of embraces and a few new tears shed over Kelly. She looked great as usual. With her carefully coiffed and tinted hair, her tasteful make-up, and trim figure, she appeared a good ten years younger than her fifty-eight years.

They'd sat in the living room of her richly furnished Turtle Bay condo and talked awhile, and then Lucia, her Filipino cook and housekeeper, had served lunch. Kara thought she could never get used to a maid, but decided she could probably adjust to having a cook fairly quickly—especially one as skilled as Lucia. Her aunt seemed to take the service for granted. Her husband had been a partner in a Wall Street brokerage house. He was gone now but he had left her extremely well off.

After lunch had come the sherry. Kara had almost refused, then decided she needed it. After her encounter with Dr. Gates, and then seeing Rob and Jill together, she really needed it.

"And see how Jill loves to play with Bella," Ellen said.

Kara glanced over to the sunny window seat where Ellen's black Persian was allowing Jill to stroke her fur.

"I'd love to stay," Kara said, lying, "but I've really got to get back to the farm."

"Oh, pooh. What for? It's not a real farm. I mean, it's not as if you grow things and keep livestock."

Kara smiled at her aunt. Ellen was the only one she knew who could say "Oh, pooh" and not sound ridiculous.

"Oh, no, you don't," Kara said. "You're not going to get me into that old argument. You call Mom in Florida if you feel like mixing it up."

Kara's mother, Martha, was Ellen's sister. It seemed that Ellen had lived here in Turtle Bay in the shadow of the U.N. complex forever, while Martha had stayed on the farm. They had argued about which was the better life ever since Kara could remember. She and Kelly had called them Country Mouse and City Mouse.

Strange how generations follow similar patterns, she thought. Mom and Ellen had chosen different roads early in life, just like Kara and Kelly. But Martha and Ellen were both still alive.

"Didn't you tell me that Rob was in charge of the investigation?"

"Such as it is, yes."

"And yet you brought Jill in? Do you think that's wise? I mean, considering that he's—"

"I didn't have much choice. There's no one to leave her with back home."

"You can leave Jill with me anytime. You know that. By the way, what about Kelly's things?"

Kara took another sip. "I don't know. I'll have to come back for them."

She knew that the smart thing to do would be to spend the next few days packing up anything of Kelly's she wanted to keep and shipping it all back to the farm. But she had a blind urge to flee the city. Not tomorrow. Today. Now.

"Suit yourself, dear. I know you have to do what you think best. We all do."

Something in her voice made Kara look more closely at her aunt. She saw that her eyes were glistening, and her lips were trembling. Kara got up and went around the coffee table to sit next to her. She took Ellen's hand.

"What's wrong?"

"You blame me, don't you," she said. A tear slid down her cheek, trailing mascara in its wake. "That's why you won't stay here."

"Blame you for what?"

"For Kelly's death!"

She was crying now, and trembling all over. Kara put her arms around her.

"Don't be silly! No one blames you at all."

"Martha does! She hasn't said so, but I know she thinks that if I hadn't encouraged you two to try life here in the city, Kelly would still be alive!"

Yes, Kara thought with a pang, *she probably would be.* But she couldn't say that to Ellen.

"She thinks nothing of the sort. Kelly made her own choices. Someone is to blame for Kelly's death, Aunt Ellen, but it's not you. It's not you."

The older woman clutched her and stifled her sobs. Then she straightened up and dabbed her eyes with a napkin.

"Won't you stay the night? I've felt so terribly alone here since Kelly died. She only stopped in once in a while, but just knowing she was in the city made me feel as though I had family here. Won't you and Jill please stay? Just this once?"

"Okay, Aunt Ellen," Kara said, forcing a smile. "Just for tonight."

She hoped she wouldn't regret it.

▼

6:02 P.M.

Before dinner, Kara made a quick trip back to Kelly's apartment to pick up the clothing and personal items they had left there. She was barely in the door when the phone began to ring. Thinking it was probably Rob, she let it ring three times, then wondered it if might be someone else. A friend fo Kelly's, perhaps. She picked it up on the fourth.

"Miss Kara Wade?

It was Dr. Gates. She recognized the slightly accented voice immediately.

"Speaking."

"I'm glad I found you. I spent most of the afternoon calling this number."

"Is something wrong?"

"I'm not sure."

Kara felt a chill run over her skin.

"What do you mean?"

"Miss Wade," he said, "I've changed my mind. Please do not think that your threat of a lawsuit or the presence of your policeman friend in my office today have anything to do with this decision. It is simply that upon further reflection I've concluded that it might be in the best interests of all concerned if I break confidence and discuss your late sister's medical history with you."

"Best interest? What does that mean?"

"I'll discuss everything with you in detail tomorrow morning at ten o'clock in my office. I do not see patients on Wednesdays so there will be no time pressure. Can you be here then?"

"Yes, of course, but—"

"Ten o'clock. Good night."

And then he hung up.

Kara stood and stared at the buzzing phone. What had made him change his mind.

The chill hit her again.

She almost wished he hadn't.

LETTERS FROM Purgatory

The new one is just like the last one, the lost blond. Exactly like her. Resemblance is truly remarkable.

He wants the new one. Hasn't told me about her, but I can tell when he wants someone. Can sense whenever he's excited, and he's very excited by this new one.

Poor thing. Hasn't got a chance. Only hope is to stay away from him, never come near him again. Once he gets his hooks into her, that will be it. She'll be at his mercy.

So it's all up to her now. Stay away and stay well, or come back and be driven mad. Like me.

Me. Mad. Crazy. Insane. Meshugge.

All his fault. The swine, the dirty, filthy, stinking, parasitic scum. I'd have had a normal, productive life without him. A spouse, a child, a future without him.

But I have nothing. Not even hope.

I'd kill him if I could. If only I could! If only I had the means. But I do not. I'd kill myself if I had the nerve—ram this pencil through my eye and into my brain and end this misery. But I do not. I'm a coward. I'll have to wait and hope that someone else will do it. I can only hope.

But why bother hoping? No one knows about him, or about what he can do. Only me.

And to think that once I loved him.

FEBRUARY 11
10:09 A.M.

THEY SAT AS THEY HAD YESTERDAY: DR. GATES BEHIND HIS mahogany desk in a high-backed swivel chair, Kara in the armchair facing him. A chart lay open on the desk before him. His hands were held before his lips, palms together as if in prayer, as he stared at her with his watery blue eyes.

What little Kara had eaten of the huge breakfast Ellen's cook had served—waffles for Jill, eggs Benedict for her—weighed heavily in her stomach. She'd left Jill at Ellen's, following the cat from room to room.

Finally Dr. Gates lowered his hands. His tantalizingly accented voice took on a lecturing tone.

"I wish to emphasize, Miss Wade, that asking you here was not an easy decision for me. A psychiatrist deals with the most intimate details of his patients' lives, details they keep from their friends, their spouses, even their internists and gynecologists. Because of this intimate knowledge, a psychiatrist must be the most rigorous of all physicians in preserving the confidentiality of his patient records."

"I appreciate that," Kara said, and meant it.

"Good. But there are details of your sister's case that

are extraordinary, details I assumed that you, as her twin, would know. However, it occurred to me yesterday after our conversation—or more properly, your tirade—that you appeared completely unaware of what your sib has been through. That raised the possibility that you might share her diagnosis."

Kara shook her head in bewilderment. "I don't understand."

"You will by the time I am finished. But you may not like hearing what I have to say. It is not pleasant. It will make you angry and you will probably resist accepting it. But let me start at the beginning."

"Please do," Kara said. Her throat had gone dry.

Dr. Gates leaned back in his chair and picked up a pair of keys on a ring. As he had yesterday, he began twirling the ring on his index finger.

"Your sister first came to me sixteen months ago complaining of insomnia and poor concentration. I'm a consultant at St. Vincent's and I occasionally treat some of the nursing staff there on a courtesy basis. The precipitating event in her life appeared to be the break-up of an affair in which she felt her trust had been betrayed by her lover."

That would have been Tom, Kara thought. The lying, married bastard from Long Island.

"But as therapy progressed, I began to suspect that your sister was suffering from a disorder far more serious and complex than a simple reactive anxiety-depression syndrome. She wanted to continue therapy. As I probed deeper, I became alarmed. Finally, we tried hypnosis. It was then that I confirmed my presumptive diagnosis."

He paused, and Kara found that she was gripping the arms of her chair so hard it hurt. What was he waiting for?

"Well?"

"Your twin, Kelly Wade, suffered from multiple personality disorder."

Kara blinked and relaxed her grip on the chair arms. Multiple personality disorder. She'd heard of that.

"You mean like in *Sybil* and *Three Faces of Eve*?"

He nodded. "Precisely."

"How . . . how many did she have?"

"Two that I know of. The Kelly Wade personality you and everybody knew, and one other."

Kara leaned back, shocked. Two personalities? Weird, but it could have been worse. She could accept this. It wasn't so hard. She wasn't angry.

But *another* Kelly inside her twin? How come she had never guessed?

"Did this other personality ever come out?"

"Yes. Many times. Right here, when Kelly was under hypnosis."

This was fascinating—disturbing, but somehow fascinating too.

"What was she like?"

"Quite different from Kelly. The second person called herself Ingrid, by the way."

The name electrified Kara. She sprang from her seat.

"Ingrid? *Ingrid?* Kelly signed into the Plaza under that name! That means it was . . . was 'Ingrid'—the other Kelly—who was picking up those men!"

In a way it was an enormous relief. Kelly hadn't changed—it had been that other personality taking her over and doing those crazy awful things!

"I imagine so," Dr. Gates said, still cool and clinical. "Ingrid was, ah, rather promiscuous."

"And the clothes!" Kara said, still on a roll. "That's why they were hidden! Kelly wasn't hiding them from anyone! It was Ingrid hiding them from Kelly! Now I understand!"

Kara turned away and fought the tears that sprang

into her eyes. It was so good to understand. And poor Kelly. What she must have been going through.

She sat down again.

"God, it's so bizarre! What could cause something like that to happen?"

"It is almost always severe trauma." His eyes bored into hers. "*Childhood* trauma."

"Kelly had no childhood trauma. Neither of us did. We were 'the Wade twins.' Everyone loved us. If anything, our childhood was uneventful—blissful and uneventful."

"Ingrid has a different story."

A chill tiptoed down Kara's spine.

"What . . . what did Ingrid say?"

Dr. Gates leaned forward and stared at her.

"Do you truly have no idea what I'm talking about?"

Kara met his gaze and tried to override the growing fear that he was going to say something awful, that here was the part she couldn't accept.

"No. Not the faintest."

He leaned back and rubbed his eyes, then leaned forward again. He took a deep breath.

"Very well. I'll say it flat out: According to Ingrid, she was sexually abused on a regular basis between the ages of five and nine."

"No! That's crazy! By whom?"

"Your father."

Kara felt her body go numb. The room swung around and the lights seemed to dim for a few seconds. She fought for focus and managed a single word:

"*What?*"

"That is what Ingrid told me, and she was quite detailed."

"My *father*? Never!"

"It fits, Miss Wade. It's that type of abuse, that degree of trauma that incites the formation of a second personality."

Kara was on her feet again, shaking with revulsion.

"Listen to me, Dr. Gates! Nothing like that ever happened! So get this straight, and get it straight now: My father never committed incest! It never even crossed his mind! If it had, I'd have known about it!"

Gates leaned back again, twirling that damn key ring.

"I told you that you would resist the facts. Your sister went through a period of denial too."

Kara's revulsion was now turning to anger.

"I will not have my father defamed! He was a good man who's been dead a dozen years and can't defend himself! Besides, Kelly would have told me!"

"Kelly didn't know."

That brought Kara up short. She stared at Dr. Gates without speaking.

"Listen," he said, "and perhaps you will understand why I asked you here. The regularly repeated trauma of such magnitude can cause a child's mind to create a second personality as a defense mechanism. The second personality takes over during the times of recurrent trauma. There is no communication between the personalities. The secondary personality shields the primary personality, forming a barrier between it and an intolerable reality, thus allowing the child to go about her everyday life as if nothing happened. And in a sense, nothing does happen to the primary personality—the second personality absorbs all the trauma."

"It never happened!" Kara said.

"When the trauma stops, the second personality is no longer needed. But it doesn't dissolve, it doesn't go away, it merely becomes dormant, ready to leap to the surface should the first personality be traumatized again. I believe that the traumatic break-up of Kelly's last relationship—the lies she had believed, the betrayal she felt—awakened Ingrid. Kelly managed to handle the emotional trauma in a mature manner, but Ingrid was awake. And Ingrid wanted out. It was that tug of war going on in her subconscious, and the unexplained lapses in memory when Ingrid managed to take over, that eventually brought Kelly to me."

Kara sank back into the chair and closed her eyes.

Kelly . . . Ingrid . . . it had to be true. It explained so much. But the rest of it . . . sickening . . .

"All right," she said slowly. "I'll grant the existence of this Ingrid personality. But she's a liar. You said she was sexually promiscuous—"

"Many sexually abused children grow up to be promiscuous, a reflection of how they were taught to relate to a male during their formative years. Just as physically abused children grow to be violent adults."

"Kelly was not abused, dammit! I was there! I grew up with her! The Ingrid part of her is lying!"

"Perhaps. I have no way of knowing. Ingrid often spoke of how her twin sib was also regularly abused by their father."

Kara was out of her seat again. She wanted to hurl herself at Gates and throttle that bland, matter-of-fact expression off his face.

"Are you deaf? It. Never. Happened!"

It couldn't have happened! Not Dad. Never. She saw his weathered face, his easy smile, his gentle blue eyes. He never even raised his voice. Dad was a . . . a *prude*! She remembered how embarrassed he'd be whenever she and Kelly as teenagers would pass him in the upstairs hall in their underwear. He'd shout at them to get their robes on. He couldn't have—

"She said her twin sister was named 'Janine,' " Dr. Gates said softly.

"There! What did I tell you! This Ingrid is all screwed

up! If she can't even get my name right, how can she have any credibility about the rest of her story?"

Kara turned and headed for the door. She had tolerated as much as she could of this nonsense.

"Thank you for your time, Dr. Gates. I've heard all I want to hear."

He did not raise his voice but, as her hand reached the door knob, Kara heard him with numbing clarity.

"What if the Janine she speaks of belongs to you, Miss Wade?"

Kara froze. Her anger vanished as if it had never been, replaced by a cold, sick fear crawling through her chest. She turned and leaned against the door, facing him.

"Why are you doing this to me?"

"I am not doing anything to you. I am giving you the information you demanded yesterday, information that might be of vital importance to you."

She hung there, weak-kneed, trying to comprehend the unthinkable, but the thoughts would not take form. Her mind fought them off, drove them away.

"Please sit down," Dr. Gates said. For the first time there seemed to be real concern in his voice.

Kara shook her head. "No. Just finish this and let me go."

"All right. I'll put it all in a nutshell. Your twin sister developed a separate personality to shield her from a massive childhood trauma. I dealt with that personality. I know it existed. Therefore, since you and your twin grew up so closely together, and since you have no memory of your sister's trauma, I thought it fair and prudent to warn you that it is entirely possible that you, too, may have developed a second personality to shield you from that same trauma."

"Okay," she said slowly. "You've warned me. Maybe there was a trauma. Maybe we've both repressed it. But that doesn't mean it absolutely had to have been . . . incest."

"Judging from Ingrid's promiscuity, I'd say there's a high probability that—"

"But you can't be absolutely *sure* can you?"

Grant me that! Please grant me that!

"No," he said after a pause. "It's hard to be absolutely sure of anything in this case. Especially with Kelly gone."

Thank you.

Now. There was one more thing she had to know before she fled this place, this man, this city.

"How could I tell if I had another personality?"

"If you have black-outs, memory lapses, new items around the house that you don't remember purchasing, you might suspect, but short of a chance encounter with a friend or relative when the other personality was in charge, you couldn't actually *know*. Except perhaps . . ." His voice trailed off.

"What? Tell me!"

"Hypnotism can sometimes bring the other personalities to the surface, but it's not foolproof. And it can be risky."

Kara turned and opened the door.

"Good-bye, Dr. Gates. And thank you for your time."

She forced her feet to carry her from the office, to the elevator, and out to the street. Everything around her seemed blurred, as if she were moving through a fog.

I'm sleepwalking, she thought. *This is a nightmare, and any minute I'm going to wake up.*

She took a cab back to Kelly's apartment. She couldn't face Jill and Ellen now, not feeling as sick and . . . defiled as she did. She had to pull herself together, put things in perspective.

But how?

As soon as Kara stepped through Kelly's front door she realized she had made a mistake. She didn't want to be here. Not now. Not alone. She needed someone to talk to, she needed to bounce all this off someone. But who? Certainly not her aunt. Ellen was practically a basket case as it was.

Only one person in this lousy city was fit to hear it. She didn't want to call him, but there was no one else.

▼

1:51 P.M.

When they'd told him he had a personal call from a woman, Rob had assumed it was Connie. She'd been bugging him since Sunday, wanting to forget their falling out and get back to their old arrangement. Rob wasn't interested. So he was surprised to hear Kara's voice on the line. He had expected she might possibly call for a progress report in a few days, but not this soon, especially after the way she had all but run from him yesterday, literally dragging her cute little girl after her.

"Are you very busy today?" she said. Her voice had a strange, dull sound to it. Almost as if she'd been sedated.

"Yeah. It's a zoo. You back at the farm?"

"No. I'm still in the city. Um . . ." Her voice trailed off.

Rob waited, then said, "Kara, what is it?"

The words came out in a rush: "Rob, could you come over?"

"Come over where?"

"I'm at Kelly's."

"What's wrong? Did you find something?"

"No. But I've learned something about her you should know. I need to talk to you about it. When can you come over?"

"I won't be able to get free for at least two hours. Maybe more. How about five?"

"Okay. You know where?"

"West Sixty-third."

"Right. Don't be late, okay? And come earlier if you can."

"Sure. See you then."

Rob hung up slowly. What was going on? This did not sound like the Kara Wade he had dealt with during the past week. So tentative. As if someone had knocked the pins out from under her.

Rob did a rush job on the report he had turned in on the double homicide on West 48th, but still it was a little after five before he got over to Kelly's apartment.

Standing in the building's vestibule, Rob realized that he actually was looking forward to seeing Kara. Why? He was still attracted to her, but obviously she hadn't the slightest interest in him. In fact, she seemed to be trying to avoid him. Why should he be looking for another dose of frustration?

Well, for one thing, this time she had made the first move.

Don't get your hopes up, turkey, he told himself as he reached for the bell.

Kara buzzed the inner door open immediately. She was waiting at the apartment door when he reached the second floor.

"I'm glad you're here," she said. "Come in."

She looked awful. Drained. Small, almost frail within her oversized cable knit sweater. Her features were tight, her mouth grim, her eyes red and . . . haunted looking.

"Are you okay?" he said as he stepped inside and shucked off his coat.

"Yes. Sure. Of course. I'm fine."

Her assurances had all the depth of feeling of someone being held hostage. Instinctively, he glanced around the front room of the apartment.

"Anybody else here?"

"No. You want a drink?"

"Sure."

"Still scotch?"

"Uh-huh." Rob was disproportionately pleased she remembered.

"Good. Because that's all she's got."

"With a couple of rocks."

As Kara went to the kitchen counter, Rob stepped across the room for a quick look into the bedroom—a mess, like it had been pulled apart. How long had she been here? He followed her into the kitchen. He noticed a half-empty glass on the counter beside the Dewar's bottle.

"I see you've got a head start on me."

She poured some into a fresh glass for him and then a little more into her own.

"I've got a couple of *laps* on you," she said as she handed him his drink.

He looked at her eyes more closely.

"Yeah. I guess you do."

"But it doesn't help." She raised her glass. "Here's to the psychiatric profession."

Despite the dubious sincerity of the toast, Rob clinked his glass against hers and took a long pull on the drink. It felt good going down. Then they settled back and stood there in the kitchen under the fluorescent light, each leaning against different sections of the counter that ran at a right angles along two walls.

A vision flashed through Rob's mind—the two of

them, married, standing here like this every night dis-
cussing the events of the day while dinner cooked—
then was gone. But it left in its wake a bittersweet trace
of a warmth that could have been.

He shook it off and looked at her.

"Don't let that Dr. Gates get you down too much,
Kara. We'll get a subpoena for Kelly's records. It may
take some time, but eventually—"

"He called me last night," she said. "Said he'd
changed his mind. I went over there this morning and
he told me the whole story—Kelly's complete case history."

"That's a real turn-around."

"I almost wish he hadn't."

Rob saw the misery in her eyes and realized she
wasn't exaggerating.

"Want to talk about it?"

"No. Yes. I don't know. I just think maybe you
should know what was going on in Kelly's head—what
Dr. Gates *says* was going on in her head—in the
months before she, uh, fell."

"It couldn't hurt, and it might help."

"Yeah. I guess so. Let's go inside and sit."

They were half way to the sofa when the buzzer
sounded from downstairs.

"Who in the world—?" Kara said, and went to the
speaker.

Someone named Ed was here. She seemed to know
who he was and buzzed him up.

Rob gave Ed a quick once-over when he arrived:
about five-eleven, pushing forty, brown hair, medium
build, yuppyish. His eyes darted from Kara to Rob.

"Oh, sorry," he said. "If I've come at a bad time . . .?"

"No. Come on in," Kara said with a resigned tone.
"Ed, meet Rob Harris. Rob, this is Ed, an old friend of
Kelly's."

They shook hands and Rob noted that Ed's palm was moist.

"Nice to meet you, Ed," he said. "I didn't catch your last name."

"Uh, Bannion," he said.

Kara said, "Ed's a lawyer with Paramount. He's offered to help with any legal problems connected with Kelly." She turned to Ed. "And Rob's a detective with the New York Police. He's working on Kelly's case."

For an instant, Rob thought Ed's eyes were going to bulge out of their sockets.

"Oh," Ed said to him. "How interesting. Miss Wade, uh, Kara, told me you suspect foul play. Any, uh, suspects yet?"

"Not yet. But we're closing in on a couple of guys."

Ed's expression was tight, almost a mask.

"Really? Great! I, uh, hope you catch them soon."

"Only a matter of time. By the way, how did you know Kelly?"

"She was his mother's nurse when she was in the hospital," Kara said. She seemed impatient. "Ed, you might as well come in and hear this, too."

"You think that's wise, Kara?" Rob said.

He didn't know what Kara was going to say, but he felt he should hear it first. Plus, Kara's words were getting slurry and she looked a little unsteady on her feet. How many drinks had she had?

"I don't know if it's wise or not, but Ed thinks the world of Kelly and the way the papers treated the circumstances of her death you'd have thought she was a hooker or something. I just want to set the record straight, let him know that none of it was her doing. You want a drink, Ed?"

"Yes. Uh, no. No, maybe I'd better not."

Ed looked ready to jump out of his skin. Rob wondered why.

"All right," Kara said. "Let's sit down and I'll tell you all about it."

▼

A cop! Dear sweet Jesus an honest to God New York City detective!

Ed could feel his armpits growing steadily wetter as the perspiration poured out of him.

What am I doing here with a cop, for Christ's sake?

He really wanted that drink Kara had offered, but he didn't dare take it. He had to watch every word he said. No telling what might slip out if he started drinking. And besides, he didn't want to leave fingerprints anywhere. Kara had said the cops had fingerprints of the guys her sister had been with before she died.

Jesus! Why did I get myself involved in this?

He realized Kara was talking to him. If the round table were a clock, she would have been at noon, Ed at six, and the detective, Harris, at three.

"I spoke to my sister's psychiatrist today. I think you both ought to know what he told me."

Kara paused to take a sip of her drink and Ed realized that she was about two sheets to the wind. She appeared to be stretched to the breaking point.

"He told me that Kelly suffered from something called a multiple personality disorder."

"No kidding," Ed said. He'd read *Sybil* twice. He'd always found the subject fascinating. "I've heard that kind of thing's supposed to be very rare."

"Yeah, well, Kelly had a second personality called Ingrid. She was the one doing all the crazy things, not Kelly."

Detective Harris sipped his own drink. " 'Ingrid?' That was the name she used at the Plaza that night."

Kara nodded. "Right." She turned to Ed. "That's why

I wanted you to know. I didn't want you to think she was some sort of hypocrite playing Florence Nightingale in the daytime and Irma La Douce at night. She had a real problem and she was fighting it. I know she could have beaten it if she'd had more . . . time."

Her lips quivered and she bowed her head. Ed's heart damn near broke for her. And for the dead Kelly. Apparently she'd been a very troubled woman. Ed's stomach got queasy. He hadn't known she was mentally ill when he was . . . God, he'd been humping her, he'd even *bitten* her, some poor sick girl who didn't even know she was there.

He felt dirty.

"I understand," he said. He desperately wanted to lighten Kara's load. "But I never could think badly of your sister. No matter what."

He noticed Detective Harris staring at him. The cop nodded at Ed, as if to say, *Thanks.* Which was kind of strange. Was there something going on between these two?

He felt a compulsion to keep talking, to keep the silence at bay.

"But if I remember correctly from *Sybil*, don't most multiple personalities have abused childhoods?"

Immediately Ed knew he'd said the wrong thing. Kara slammed her glass on the table and was on her feet, glaring at him. Her face was livid.

"It never happened! Never! Don't you dare say that about my father!"

Ed was stunned.

"What? I didn't—"

"Get out! Get out of here!"

Ed stumbled to his feet and Harris rose with him.

Harris said, "Maybe you'd better . . ."

"Yeah."

Harris walked him away from the table. He turned to him at the door.

"Let me have your card," the detective said. "I may want to call you."

Ed's bladder suddenly wanted to empty.

"Why?"

"There are still a lot of unanswered questions about Kelly Wade. Maybe you can answer a few."

"Sure," Ed said, fighting the urge to run.

He fumbled out a card and shoved it into the detective's hand, hoping he wouldn't notice how his hand trembled.

Harris glanced at it then slipped it into his pocket.

"Great. We'll be in touch."

And then Ed was out in the hall, slowly fleeing for the street, wondering how he would explain to his office why the NYPD was calling him. He cursed himself every step of the way.

Shit-shit-shit! You're in deep shit, Ed! And you deserve to be in deep shit. Because you're an asshole, Ed! Only a primo five-star flaming asshole could get himself into a mess like this!

▼

"You can go, too," Kara told Rob as he closed the door behind Ed.

He turned and stared at her. She was still standing by the table, looking as if she was going to come apart. He couldn't leave her like this.

"Can I finish my drink first?"

"Sure."

He slipped into his chair again and took a small sip. He'd have to nurse this one. Finally, Kara slumped back into her own chair. She ignored her drink and stared at the wall.

"What's wrong, Kara?"

"Nothing."

"Want to talk about it?"

"No."

He rattled the ice in his glass. "You didn't ask me over here just to tell me that Kelly had a multiple personality. You could have told me that on the phone. If you want to talk, I'll listen. If you need a friend, I'm here."

Kara continued to stare at the wall, but Rob noticed tears gathering in her eyes. She spoke without looking at him, and her voice was so full of pain that he felt his own throat begin to constrict.

"He says our father molested us as children."

Rob was numb for a moment. He'd never met Kara's father. He died before she came to New York.

"Good Lord, is that . . . is that true?"

"No!" she said through her teeth. "Never!"

"Then what's the problem?"

Kara went through her conversation with Dr. Gates almost word by word. Rob listened with growing alarm, piecing together the picture, sensing what was coming and not wanting to hear it.

Finally, toward the end, Kara seemed to run out of steam. To spare her further torture, Rob finished it for her.

"So you're afraid you might have a second personality, too, this 'Janine,' hiding inside of you."

Kara shrugged. "Yes and no. I know Ingrid was lying about my father, I just know it! But *do* I know it? I don't know what I really know anymore! Am I talking complete nonsense or does any of that make sense to you?"

Rob reached out and put his hands over hers. She didn't pull it away.

"It makes sense. I just don't know how to help you. I wish I did."

She got up and walked past him. A few steps and she was in the living room. Rob turned in his chair to watch her as she sat on the sofa with her hands clamped between her knees.

"I've got to know, Rob. I can't go through the rest of my life not knowing. I'm a mother. For Jill's sake, if not my own. I've got to know if I'm okay inside. I mean, am I all one piece or is there a time bomb named 'Janine' ticking away in my head? I've got to *know*!"

She looked so miserable, so tortured. Rob went over and sat next to her.

"What about hypnotism? Didn't Gates say that's how he found this Ingrid inside of Kelly?"

She nodded. "Yes, but . . ."

Rob waited.

"Rob, I'm so scared!" she said.

Instinctively, he slipped his arms around Kara and pulled her against him. She buried her face against his shoulder. Her voice was muffled.

"I've got to know, but I want it to come out all right. I mean, what if Ingrid was telling the truth? God, what if there *is* a Janine inside of me?"

"Don't you think you'd know?"

"Kelly never knew until Gates discovered her other side. What'll I do?"

Rob thought about that. He tried to put himself in her place. What would be best for her?

"I look at it this way," he said slowly. "If you take a chance and it turns out something's there, it'll be painful, painful as all hell, but at least you'll know where you stand and you can start dealing with it. The way it is now, you're nowhere. And you'll remain nowhere until you have some facts to steer by."

"Will you come with me?" she said after a long pause.

That sounded as if she'd made up her mind.

"Of course."

"I mean, will you sit there with me while I get hypnotized?"

A shiver darted through Rob. That could be an eerie scene if there really was another personality inside Kara. But he realized that he wanted to know too.

"I guess so. If he allows it."

She lifted her head but remained leaning against him.

"Oh, he'll allow it, or I'll find someone else!"

"You don't trust him?"

"I don't know him well enough yet to let him get me alone in a room and hypnotize me and then later tell me what I said and did! Uh-uh!"

"I hear you. I'll be there."

"Thanks, Rob. Do you think you could drop me at Ellen's? Jill and I are staying there."

"Sure."

They sat in silence for a while. When Rob glanced at Kara, he saw that she was sleeping. For the first time since he had seen her last week, her face looked relaxed, free of grief and trouble. The way it should be.

He slipped his arm from around her and eased her head down onto one of the throw cushions, then he lifted her legs and stretched her out on the sofa. Her sweater slipped up in the process, revealing a band of smooth white skin above the waist of her slacks. Rob felt a surge of desire, an urge to slip his hand under that sweater and cup one of her breasts. He remembered Kara's breasts, their perfect size, the rosy nipples, how he'd fondled and kissed them and—

This was no good. He turned away and hunted up a blanket. He threw it over her and then retreated to the kitchen where he smoked a badly needed cigarette. He looked up Ellen's number in Kelly's phone list and called her to explain the situation. The older woman seemed to understand and said she'd tell Jill.

Rob decided to stay the night. He didn't want Kara to wake up alone in this place.

LETTERS FROM
Purgatory

So smug. The swine is so sickeningly smug. He's set his little trap. He sees her falling into it, see the jaws snapping closed, all in slow motion. He's enjoying this so much that he's dropped his customary insufferable impatience and is taking his time to savor the stalking.

Only a matter of time, he thinks. So supremely confident.

Makes me want to retch.

Such a terrible injustice that he should be able to continue on as he does, unchallenged, unsuspected. Someone should do something. If only someone could. The situation cries out to heaven for rectification.

You'd think God would have had enough by now, would step in and squash him for what he has done to me and to others, crush him for becoming such an abomination.

Deus ex machina!

Please!

But this isn't Greek drama. This is real life, if anyone would dare call what I have a life. Being dead would be better.

No way to stop him, but must be some way to hinder him, or at the very least, harass him.

Yes. Harass. I should try. Worry his heels, the rotten swine. He'd no right to punish me like that when I laughed at him. Wasn't fair. None of this is fair, but that went beyond his usual mean spiritedness.

Cruel. He's so cruel to me.

I wonder . . . wonder if it's possible to strike back?

Have to think on that. After all, I've got plenty of time to think. All the time in the world.

FEBRUARY 12
6:45

THE DAY STARTED OFF WITH A SHOCK.

Kara opened her eyes in the early morning light and didn't know where she was. Lying on a lumpy sofa in a strange room. With this splitting headache, starting at the temples and radiating forward and backward to her eyes and neck. The room smelled of stale cigarette smoke, and echoing through it was this deep, coarse, terrifying noise. Despite the pain it cost her, she lifted her head and looked around.

A man in sitting in a chair nearby.

Not sitting, actually—sprawled was more like it. Head lolled back, legs splayed, arms akimbo over the sides of the chair. For a moment she thought he was dead, then she realized that he was the source of the awful noise. Snoring. Rattling the windows, as the old saying went.

And then she recognized him.

"Rob?"

What was he doing here in—?

Suddenly she remembered last night. That fellow Ed had been here. She had told them both what Dr. Gates had said about Kelly. Why? Why had she done that? And why had she drunk so much?

Rob bolted upright in his chair, rubbing his face, mumbling sleepily into the dimness.

"It's okay, Kara. I'm here. I'm right here."

Kara gently eased her throbbing, spinning head back down onto the sofa cushion. She felt under the blanket. She was still dressed, her clothes still buttoned and zippered up tight. Rob hadn't touched her. But of course, he wouldn't have. The world's last knight in shining armor had sat up all night watching over her.

Kara groaned and squeezed her eyes shut. What was she going to owe him for this?

▼

"Sure you're not hungry?"

Kara nodded silently and took another tiny sip of her instant coffee.

"Really sure? There's eggs in the fridge. They still look good. I could whip up a cheese omelette before I go. Nothing to it."

Kara held up her hand for him to cease and desist. She had forgotten what a relentlessly cheery morning person Rob was. Now it was all coming back to her. Even when their relationship had been at its closest it was the one thing about him that had annoyed her the most. Apparently he hadn't changed. He'd spent all night in a chair and here he was bouncing around at the crack of dawn offering to make breakfast for her.

"No. Thanks. I'm sure. Please. Go. You'll be late."

"Okay. Let me know when you set things up with Gates. Try to make it after five."

"Okay." She looked up at him. "Thanks, Rob. You didn't have to stay last night, but I appreciate it."

"What are friends for?"

"Are we still friends? After all that's happened?"

He shrugged. "It took me a good while to accept the

fact that we just weren't meant to live happily ever after, but that doesn't mean I stopped caring about you. Why? Did you stop caring about me?"

Kara shook her head slowly. "No. That's why I wouldn't speak to you anymore back then." *Well, that's part of the reason.* "I knew we couldn't work out, but I was afraid I'd change my mind if I saw you again."

His smile was small and sad. "I was hoping you'd say something like that. Maybe we can relax a little more with each other."

I wish I could, Rob. But I can't.

"Sure. That'd be nice. And thanks again for standing guard last night. I owe you."

He grimaced and rotated a kink out of his back.

"Yeah. You do. And you can show your gratitude by letting me cook you dinner before you go."

Despite the pain in her head, she laughed. Memories of the awful concoctions he used to whip up threatened the delicate state of her stomach.

"Oh, Rob—"

"No, I'm serious. I've gotten better. I'm actually pretty good now. Please. It'll mean a lot to me, and you'll enjoy it. I promise."

She looked at him closely. It really did seem to mean a lot to him.

"Okay."

He beamed and stuck out a hand. "It's a deal?"

"Deal," she said and shook his hand.

He waved and headed for the door, pulling a cigarette pack from his pocket. And whistling, no less.

▼

4:42 P.M.

Rob sat in Doc Winters' tiny, rickety waiting room and glanced at his watch. Getting close to five. He was supposed to meet Kara soon, but first he wanted to talk to Doc Winters. He was one of the department shrinks. He treated the cops when they needed it and he was also available for consultation when they thought they had a psycho on the loose.

But right now Rob wanted to find out what Doc Winters knew about a fellow shrink named Lawrence Gates, M.D.

Rob had taken an instant disliking to Gates yesterday, and now that he knew Gates might be putting Kara under hypnosis this afternoon, he wanted the skinny on him. He'd run a check—no criminal record, no complaints lodged with the State Board of Medical Examiners, not even an outstanding parking ticket. Clean. But so what? Pre-med at NYU, graduate of Flower Fifth Medical School, psychiatric residency at Downstate Medical Center in Brooklyn. Fine. At least he was well trained. But what Rob really wanted to know he couldn't get from an AMA register or a CV. He needed someone who knew the guy.

Doc Winters said he knew him.

Rob could have asked about Gates over the phone but he wanted to be with Winters, wanted to watch him when he answered. These shrinks were like a secret society, never wanting to say anything bad about each other in public. If he could get in front of Doc Winters, Rob knew he could tell if he was hedging.

The door opened and Rob recognized Bobby Kurtzman coming out. He nodded once to Rob and hurried off. Rob shook his head. Poor Kurtzman. He'd shot a kid he'd thought was armed. Turned out he wasn't. The kid recovered and was fine now. Kurtzman would probably never be the same.

Inside, Rob found Doc Winters, a white-haired, heavy-set man of about sixty. He wore a bulging white shirt and gray suit pants. The suit jacket was nowhere to be seen. His office was cramped, and his desk was piled high with papers, journals, correspondence, patient files.

Although Rob had met him a few times before, he introduced himself anyway.

"Sure, Harris. I remember you. You called me about Larry Gates, didn't you?"

"Right."

"Is he in trouble?"

"Should he be?"

"Don't play wise with me, detective."

Rob realized that remark had not been a good choice. He'd forgotten that Doc Winters tended to be a crusty old fart.

"Sorry. I just want a personal opinion of the man. He'll be treating a friend of mine and I just want to know if he's the right man for the job."

"What's your friend's problem?"

"Don't know yet. Might be a multiple personality."

Doc Winters' eyebrows shot up. "Really! Don't come across them too often. But she couldn't be in better hands."

"How'd you know she's a she?"

"Nine out of ten multiple personalities are female. Larry's an expert on them. He was on my service as a resident for a while when I had a post at Downstate. Brilliant guy. From day one he's had a special interest in multiple personalities. He's done a few papers on them. Good stuff."

Doc Winters seemed genuinely enthusiastic about Gates. Rob was encouraged.

"Okay," Rob said, extending his hand. "I guess she's with the right man then. Thanks a lot."

"He's Hungarian, you know," the doc said as Rob turned to leave. "An immigrant. Real name is . . . let me think." He tapped a pencil against his jaw. "Ah! Gati. Lazlo Gati. Had it changed when he was in premed, I believe. Worked real hard to lose his accent. Did a damn good job, too. Said he was an American now and wanted to be accepted as one. Have to admire a man with that kind of determination."

"I guess you do," Rob said.

"Doesn't even have to practice. I understand he's rich as Creosus since his sister died in West Virginia a few years ago, but he still keeps going. A dedicated guy."

"Thanks again, doc."

Lazlo Gati, Rob thought as he hurried for his car. He'd have to see what he could learn about Lazlo Gati.

▼

Kara waited for Rob.

She stood in the cold outside the Karmer Medical Arts Building where Dr. Gates had his office and breathed the fumes from the traffic crawling downtown along Seventh Avenue. She could have waited in the lobby where it was warmer but a vague apprehension prevented her from entering the building alone.

She'd left a message for Rob in the detective squad room at the precinct house and on the answering machine at the home phone number he had given her. She didn't know if he'd received it, but she did know she was not going in to see Dr. Gates alone.

Kara had contacted Dr. Gates' office this morning

and told the receptionist that she had to speak to him. He had called back twenty minutes later and said he could see her briefly at lunch. She'd said she needed more time. He agreed to see her after today's hours, around five-fifteen.

She glanced at her watch: 5:14.

Just then a dirty, nondescript sedan pulled into the curb and parked under the red and white NO PARKING—TOW AWAY ZONE sign. Rob hopped out, wearing a sport coat, an open shirt, and no overcoat. He smiled.

"Made it!"

"Is your car going to be here when we're through?" Kara asked, pointing to the sign.

Rob in turn pointed to the vehicle identification card lying on his dashboard.

"That lets me park anywhere. Come on. Let's get inside. It's freezing out here."

Dr. Gates' receptionist appeared poised to leave, waiting only for their arrival.

"He'll see you inside," she said, pointing to the closed consultation room door, and then she was out, locking the hall door behind her.

Dr. Gates' face registered frank surprise when Kara walked in with Rob.

· "I expected you to come alone, Miss Wade," he said with that mysteriously accented voice.

"Detective Harris is along as a friend," she said.

"That is immaterial. I thought I made it clear to you that I will not discuss your sister's medical history with anyone but you. *Especially* not with the police."

Kara sensed Rob bristling beside her. She gave his arm a quick squeeze.

"I'm not here to discuss Kelly. I'm here to find out about myself. I want to know if I've got a second personality hiding within me as well."

"Very well. Arrange a regular appointment and we'll begin therapy."

Kara had expected that. But she had other ideas.

"I can't wait that long, Dr. Gates. I need to know now. Today. I'm heading back to Pennsylvania tomorrow. If you won't help my today, I'll find somebody back there who will."

"I can't possibly help you in one evening!" he said.

"I don't want therapy, Dr. Gates. At least not until I have a diagnosis. And you said you could make that diagnosis through hypnotism."

Dr. Gates was shaking his head. "No. It's much too risky."

"What's the risk? Hypnotism is used in stage acts. I thought it was pretty safe."

"In your case it might not be. If indeed you have a second personality akin to your twin's, it is most likely dormant. By attempting to reach it while you are under hypnotism, we run the risk of awakening it. You may or may not have a multiple personality, Miss Wade. If you do, it is presently a *potential* problem. I do not wish to be the one to turn it into an *active* problem."

"He's got a point there, Kara," Rob said.

Kara didn't look at him. She hadn't considered the possibility of awakening the someone else inside her. The very thought of it gave her a crawly feeling in her stomach. But she couldn't go on not knowing.

Besides, there's no one in here but me.

"It's a risk I'll have to take."

Dr. Gates shook his head. "Then it's a risk you'll take without me."

"Very well," Kara said. She turned and reached for the door knob. "But I'll find someone who will. And when I do, I'll have him drop you a line and let you know how it comes out. Come on, Rob."

This was her ace play. She hoped he went for it. She

was banking on the fact that the prospect of discovering a pair of twins, each with multiple personalities, would be too tempting for him to pass up. He wouldn't want to share the discovery with another shrink. He'd want it all for Lawrence Gates, M.D.

But when he didn't call her back as she crossed the waiting room, she thought she had lost: She was reaching for the deadbolt knob on the door to the hall when she heard his voice behind her.

"Wait. Come back. Please."

Kara turned and faced him across the combined lengths of the waiting room and office, but did not move toward him.

"I didn't think there was anything to discuss."

He got up from behind his desk and approached her.

"Are you really so set on going through with this?"

"Absolutely."

He pulled the door open wider and gestured to the chairs before his desk.

"Come in and sit down. Please. There is much to discuss before we do anything."

▼

Rob had to admit it, Kara was one cool character.

Remind me never to play poker with you, lady, he thought as he watched her sit and deal with Gates.

Rob didn't care how highly Doc Winters thought of Dr. Gates. Rob's antipathy after their brief meeting yesterday had been consolidated by today's lengthier encounter. The guy thought he had all the answers, like he talked to God every night.

But there was more to it than that. Rob didn't trust him. He had no rational basis for the feeling but some primitive instinct deep inside warned him not to turn his back on Dr. Lawrence Gates, *ne* Lazlo Gati. Over the years, Rob had learned to trust his instincts.

At least now he could explain that accent.

He was glad he was here. He wouldn't want Kara to be alone with him, especially under hypnotism.

"I hope I have made my position clear," he was saying.

"Perfectly," Kara replied. "You've explained the risks backwards and forwards. I'm going into this with my eyes open. Detective Harris is a witness: I won't hold you responsible for anything that goes wrong."

Dr. Gates looked at him with his cold, watery eyes.

"Are you a witness to that, Detective Harris?"

"Yes," he said. "But a reluctant one."

"Ah!" Gates said, turning back to Kara. "Your friend shares my reservations."

"Because I *am* her friend," Rob said.

He hated this whole idea. It sounded risky to him. Why couldn't Kara leave well enough alone?"

"I appreciate that," Kara said, glancing at him, "but neither of you have to live with the possibility of a 'Janine' hiding inside you. I do. And this is how I choose to deal with it. Enough said."

Gates shrugged. "Very well. Detective Harris, if you'll excuse us, I'll begin the—"

"I'm staying," Rob said. "I'm her witness."

Gates' eyes swept back and forth between the two of them.

"I see. There appears to be a lack of trust here."

You might say that, Rob thought, but said nothing. He was going to sit right here and watch. No way was Gates going to make "an unprecedented discovery" by fabricating a second personality or by planting any post-hypnotic suggestions. Rob was going to make sure it stayed clean and simple.

"Don't be offended, doctor," Kara said. "Would you

allow yourself to be hypnotized by a person you had never met before yesterday and never heard of until the day before?"

Rob thought that sounded pretty damn logical, but Gates' expression was grim as he thought about it. Then he smiled. The effect was startling—it was the first time he had done it all afternoon.

"*Touche*, Miss Wade. Your policeman friend can stay."

▼

The actual hypnotism procedure was nowhere near as dramatic as Rob had expected. No watch swinging back and forth on a chain, no spinning spiral to gaze into. As Kara sat there not four feet from Rob, Gates dimmed the lights and pulled out a metronome. He started it ticking, then told Kara to close her eyes and listen to the tick. He spoke to her in a soothing voice, telling her to relax different parts of he body, and that was it.

"Kara Wade," he said, "I want you to think back, back to your childhood. Do you remember when you were six years old?"

"Yes," Kara said in a dreamy voice. Her eyes were closed and she appeared totally relaxed.

"Do you remember being alone with your father at any time?"

"Yes."

"Do you remember him undressing you and touching you in places he didn't usually touch you?"

"No," she said, as if the question were the most natural thing in the world.

Rob was convinced then that Kara was in a trance. He knew how she felt about her family. If she were awake she'd be on her feet and raging after a question like that.

"Is anyone else listening?" Gates said. "Is there anyone named Janine listening? If she is, I'd like to speak to her."

Janine. Rob had heard Kara mention someone named Janine. He held his breath, half expecting to hear a voice like the one that had come out of that little girl in *The Exorcist.* But Kara kept quiet, thank God.

Gates sat there twirling a key ring. *Twirl-twirl-stop. Twirl-twirl-stop.* It was getting on Rob's nerves.

"Janine!" Gates said in a sharp tone. "Are you there? Speak to me if you can hear me! Don't play games! Speak to me now!"

Still no answer. Rob exhaled.

Gates scribbled on a memo pad and handed Rob the sheet.

I'm going to my files for more past history. Watch her.

Rob nodded and Gates slipped out through the flush door behind his desk. He watched Kara as she sat with her eyes closed, looking like she was asleep but sitting upright. If he didn't know better he'd have said she was stoned out of her gourd. He let his eyes roam about the room, taking in the antique furniture and the hundreds of books lining the walls.

Something drew his attention back to Kara.

Her eyes were open.

They blinked once, twice, then her head turned toward him, slowly, smoothly, like a gun turret rotating atop a tank. Her eyes fixed on him, vacantly at first, then they seemed to focus.

Then she smiled.

Rob nearly jumped out of his seat. He had never seen a smile like that before, at least not on Kara. It was little more than a pulling back of the lips. There was no warmth, no humor in it. In fact there was nothing in the eyes to confirm that it really was a smile at all. Maybe it was just a baring of the teeth. Whatever it was, it drove a spike of icy fear through Rob's gut.

Whatever it was, it wasn't Kara's smile.

And then, still smiling fixedly, her head rotated back the other way. When it reached its previous position, the rictus faded and Kara's eyes closed again. She made no further movement.

Gates returned a few minutes later with a folder in his hands. He took one look at Rob and stopped in his tracks.

"What's wrong? Did something happen?"

Kara answered first. "No."

Rob started at the sound of her voice and tried to gather his thoughts. His reflex was to tell Gates nothing. He went with it.

"No," he said, half choking as he waved a dismissing hand. "Everything's fine."

Rob had no intention of giving Gates any ammunition. If there was something there, let Gates find it and confirm it on his own.

But as the time dragged on, Gates' best efforts turned up nothing. He asked Kara all sorts of bizarre questions about intimacies with her father—some of them pretty foul-sounding—which she denied one after the other.

After a full hour of this garbage, Rob had had enough.

"I think it's time to call it quits, don't you?" he said.

Gates looked at him, leaned back in his chair, and nodded. He looked disappointed.

"I believe you're right." He turned to Kara. "Kara Wade, when I count to three and clap, you will awaken feeling alert, relaxed, and refreshed, with no memory of the past hour."

He counted, clapped, and Kara opened her eyes.

"Well?" she said, looking back and forth between the two of them. "Did anything happen?"

Gates shook his head. "Nothing."

She turned to Rob, smiling hesitantly, hopefully. "Really?"

Rob rose slowly to his feet, as much to stretch his cramped muscles as to give himself a second or two to listen to his racing mind. What to say? Tell her how she'd looked at him with that vulpine grin, an expression that was as much at home on her face as swastikas on a synagogue? Tell her and snuff out the relief glowing so brightly in her eyes now as she looked up at him, make her spend the rest of her life under a cloud of doubt? Or let it ride and see what happened?

Rob smiled back at her. "Really."

She leaped from the chair and embraced him, laughing.

"Oh, God! Thank God!"

And then she was crying, gripping his lapels and sobbing against his shirt. He slipped his arms around her and gently held her for a little while.

Too soon she straightened up and back away.

"I'm sorry," she said, taking a deep breath and wiping her eyes. "It's just that I've been so worried! So frightened!"

Dr. Gates said, "I do not feel we should rest too easy, Miss Wade. We have not completely ruled out the existence of a second personality."

"Maybe you haven't," she said, "but I have." She stepped forward and thrust out her hand. "Thank you, Dr. Gates. Please send me your bill."

Gates rose and shook it once. "Please be careful, Miss Wade. There remains the possibility that this experience may have awakened something. If you suffer any unusual experiences, black-outs, memory lapses, please do not hesitate to call me."

"Don't worry," she said smiling brightly. "You'll be the first to know."

And then she had her arm crooked around Rob's and was leading him from the consultation room.

"Let's celebrate!"

▼

7:20 P.M.

This was not exactly what Kara had meant by celebrate.

She had been thinking of a bar or a restaurant, someplace with lots of people and laughter, even if it was desperate laughter. Instead, Rob had called in her promise to allow him to cook her a meal. He had insisted too that Jill and Ellen join them.

Kara had said absolutely not, but he had gone ahead and called Ellen's place. Ellen had demurred, but Jill had been thrilled, leaving Kara with little choice but to agree. She had been briefly furious, but then remembered what a good friend Rob had been these past two days, and the anger evaporated. Leaving only anxiety about putting those two together for so long. But Rob hadn't noticed any resemblance between Jill and himself two days ago, so there was a good chance everything would work out tonight.

So far, so good.

She was sitting now in the tiny living room of Rob's one-bedroom apartment, sipping wine and watching him as he stood in the even tinier kitchen and showed Jill how to slice scallions. The air was redolent of garlic and oil heating in the wok; laughter from Jill and Rob mixed with the sounds of the St. John's basketball game on the TV.

Rob and Jill. It was scary the way they hit it off. Rob, who used to say he never wanted to be tied down by kids, must have been repressing his nurturing needs all these years. Jill had somehow tapped into them. Maybe it was their blood relationship. Maybe somewhere inside, on a subconscious level, they had recognized each other. Whatever the reason, they were instant buddies.

Seeing them together like this made Kara intensely uneasy. She wanted no new ties to Rob. Their break up ten years ago had been excruciating. She didn't want to go through that again — for both their sakes. And she did *not* want to try to explain why she had raised his daughter all these years without telling him she existed. Because she wasn't quite sure herself.

But the bonding between Jill and Rob didn't explain all the tension she sensed coiled within her now. After passing the hypnosis test this afternoon she had expected to feel relieved, exhilarated, free, *cleansed*. And she had, briefly. But then an ill-defined malaise had set in, a vague, pervasive sense of something not-quite-right that she hadn't noticed before.

Maybe it was the city. That had to be it. It was always the city. A good thing she and Jill were leaving tomorrow. Not a moment too soon. If she stayed much longer there was no telling what might happen. She could even imagine herself falling in love with Rob again.

She wondered if she had ever really stopping loving him.

"Jill," she said, rousing herself, "come on over here and sit with me and let Mr. Harris get the cooking done."

Jill hopped of the stool and ran over to where Kara was sitting. Rob had tied an apron around her neck. It dangled around her knees and she almost tripped over it.

"He needs my help, mom," she said in a loud whisper. "He wants me to cut the scallions real thick, and we always cut them thin."

"I think you can cut them thick when you're putting them in a wok," Kara whispered back.

"Really?" She glanced at Rob with new respect. "How come we don't ever wok?"

"We will, if you want to."

"Yeah!" Her eyes were bright with excitement. She loved to cook. "It's fun!"

"Okay. Then we'll buy one as soon as we get back to the farm."

Jill glanced furtively at Rob and lowered her voice further.

"He doesn't exploit women, does he." It was a statement.

"What do you mean?"

"I mean, *he's* doing the cooking and *you're* sitting out here. That's good, isn't it?"

"And *you're* helping him. Sharing the jobs, that's what's really important."

Jill nodded sagely. "Right." She turned and headed back toward the kitchen.

"Where're you going, bug?"

"To help him with the shrimp. He doesn't clean them as good as we do."

"Well," Kara said.

Jill rolled her eyes. "As *well* as we do." She cupped a hand around her mouth. "He leaves some of the black stuff along the back." She made a disgusted face.

Kara laughed. "Then maybe you'd *better* help him."

▼

After dinner there was coffee and Kahlua. When Jill left the table to use the bathroom, Rob turned to Kara.

"What a *great* kid she is! I love her!"

Kara kept a two handed grip on her coffee cup to keep it from shaking.

"Thank you."

"Even if she is bit of a spaz," he added with a smile.

"Give her a break, Rob. She's never even *seen* chopsticks before!"

"All right. But I'm giving her a pair to practice with. Next time you're back in town, we'll do this again and I expect her to be a pro."

There won't be a next time, Kara thought with genuine regret.

"What's on the schedule tomorrow?" he said.

"Got an appointment with my editor—to see if I can get an extension on the deadline for my book—and then it's back to the farm."

"Ever think of trying the city again? It's a great place for writers."

Kara gave him a level stare and returned the ball to his court.

"Why don't you open that restaurant you've always talked about? Lancaster can always use another good restaurant. And no matter how great New York is for writing, it's a lousy place to raise a child. Besides, I like writing at the farm."

Rob sighed resignedly. "Got a title for your book?"

Kara was grateful for the change of subject.

"It's called *Feminism and Fascism.*"

He raised his eyebrows. "Catchy. What's it about?"

"It's basically cautionary, showing how some of the movement's more radical methods and legislative drives may be turned around on us some day and do us harm instead of good. Right now I'm working on a chapter that shows why we shouldn't wail and moan about so-called 'sexual bias' in tests like the SATs. The whole purpose of the movement is to show we're just as sharp, just as smart as males, so how better to prove that than by outscoring them on any test males take? If we're equal, why should we insist on special treatment?"

"I'll buy the first copy," Rob said. "When do you think it'll be published?"

Before she could reply, Jill's high-pitched yelp came from the bathroom.

"Whoa! Does *this* ever exploit women!"

Rob's eyes widened and he leapt from his chair.

"Oh, Christ! My *Penthouse*s!"

▼

"Can we see Rob again soon?" Jill said as they stepped inside Ellen's front door.

"Oh, so it's 'Rob' now, is it?" Kara said, relieved that she had been able to get away without making any more promises to him.

"He told me to call him that."

"Well, you should still call him 'Mr. Harris.' "

"Can we have him come down and visit us on the farm?"

"Next time he's in Elderun," Kara said, "I promise we'll have him over for dinner."

"Good! 'Cause I like him a lot," she said, and ran toward her bedroom.

Kara bit her lip as she watched her daughter scamper away. Soon or later she was going to have to tell them. But *when?*

LETTERS FROM

Purgatory

So excited. Don't recall ever seeing him this excited. Thinks he has her now. Absolutely sure of it.

Too bad. Because he's rarely wrong.

Her only hope is to flee, to get as far away as she can. But she won't. They never do. He won't let them. Especially not this one. He wants her so very badly.

Wonder why.

He'd never tell me, even if I asked him, but think I know why. Because this one is the twin of the other one. So angry when he lost her. No one's ever gotten away from him before. So having this new one, this twin of the other, is just like having the lost one back again.

That must be the reason for his excitement. Like a little child, really: furious when he doesn't get his way and euphoric when he does.

I'd love to see him thwarted again. Wish I could find a way to warn the new one, but of course that's impossible as long as all my free hours are spent caged in this place.

Must be a way. I'll have to work on it. Yes. That's my project.

Of course, if the new blonde goes far enough away, I won't have to warn her. But think I'll work on the plan anyway. For I don't think she has a chance.

Friday

FEBRUARY 13
5:36 P.M.

ED BANNION HAD SPENT A LOT OF TIME IN THE NEW YORK Public Library since his visit with Kara Wade two nights ago. He'd checked out what books he could, and every spare minute of his free time during library hours had been spent pouring over psychiatric journals. He'd done an awful lot of reading on multiple personalities and had become adept at translating Psychobabble into plain English. Anyone who thought lawyers lived in doubletalk should try reading this garbage for a couple of days.

And the more he read, the more he became convinced that the medical profession didn't know squat about the human mind. Right now he was studying the section on dissociative disorders in the *DSM-III-R*. Multiple personality disorder was listed there. He'd read it so often he knew the diagnostic criteria by heart.

Diagnostic criteria for 300.14 Multiple Personality Disorder:

A. *The existence within the person of two or more distinct personalities or personality states (each with its own relatively enduring pattern of perceiving, relating to, and thinking about the environment and self).*

*B. At least two of these personalities or personality
    states recurrently take full control of the person's
    behavior.*

So why was he reading this again? Hell, why was he
even *here*? It was Happy Hour on Friday. He should
have been heading for one of his usual weekend haunts,
like Nomura's, huddling with the regular crowd around
the sushi bar, drinking Kirin and scarfing down Califor-
nia rolls. But he had no desire for that scene tonight.
What was wrong with him?

It was that woman, that Kelly Wade. Her tortured
face before she went out the window still hovered about
him.

At least now he had an explanation. The second personality, the one named Ingrid, was the one that had
picked up Phil and him. Ingrid had been the sexual ac-
robat. And then for one reason or another, Kelly had
come back. She'd been shocked and repulsed by the situation in which she suddenly found herself. Must've
figured out that her other half had got her into it. Right.
The Jekyll half had suddenly awakened in the middle of
one of Hyde's orgies and it scared the shit out of her.
So she panicked and started bouncing off the walls
looking for a way out. Unfortunately she found the window before she found the door. She probably didn't
know the window was twelve stories up.

Or did she? Had she seen that window as a way out
of more than just the hotel room?

Ed sighed and leaned back and rubbed his weary
eyes. Whatever the case, he wasn't responsible. He and
his brother had merely accompanied "Ingrid" up to her
room for a little dirty fun between three consenting
adults. What happened after that was not their fault.

So why do I feel so damn guilty?

He looked up and saw the librarians going from table
to table, shooing everybody out. Closing time. Ed left

the journals where they were and headed for the street. He hunched his shoulders against the icy wind as he pushed his way through the crowds clustering on the corner of Fifth Avenue and Forty-second Street.

Getting dark. Friday night in the Big City. The tunnel rats and bridge brats from Jersey and Long Island were already making their entrance despite the cold. He studied some of the bright, eager, excited teenage faces, watched them puff their cigarettes, trying to look cool, look tough, trying to look like real New Yorkers but giving themselves away immediately with their Hard Rock Cafe sweatshirts. Ed realized with a start that he had twenty years on them. He wondered if he'd ever looked that young, or felt that alive.

Feeling old, he hailed a cab and pondered the guilt question as he rode home. By the time he stepped into his apartment he had given up on it. What did it matter? The woman was dead.

He went immediately to the kitchen and poured himself a stiff Absolut Citron on the rocks. He was beginning to really like this stuff, actually looking forward to it, and that concerned him a little. Sipping slowly, he went over to the entertainment center that took up most of the inner wall of the living room. He browsed through his CD collection. He had a new multi-disk player and had bought a new pair of trimline speakers with fabulous bass, but could find nothing he wanted to hear. He turned on the TV. He had a built-in rear projection model with a 48-inch screen and full cable hook-up. Between MSG, ESPN and Sports Channel, there had to be *something* diverting on.

Ah. The Knicks were on. He sat down, figuring to lose himself in bitching about why they weren't a better team.

It didn't work.

Kelly Wade was there, standing next to him, naked, looking down at him like he was some sort of roach.

Ed closed his eyes. Maybe it wasn't all guilt. Maybe he wasn't feeling guilty so much as feeling *dirty*. He'd been humping a mental case and he'd *liked* it. Sure, he hadn't known then, but he knew now, and he *still* liked it. He saw her blond hair, her equally blond bush, the black garter belt against her creamy white skin, the tiny navel, the curve of her hip, her questing mouth . . .

He wanted her *again*!

But not just her, not just Ingrid. He wanted Kelly, too. He wanted them both, the good girl and the dirty girl, madonna and whore all rolled into one.

Ed shook his head.

What a pervo you're turning out to be.

Which made him feel even guiltier. This was becoming a fucking merry-go-round.

And the merry-go-round carried him toward the second twin, Kara. Wednesday night she'd looked almost as tortured as her sister. And when Ed had mentioned child abuse, she'd exploded and started talking about her father.

This was heavy shit.

He went over and poured himself another. *Child abuse.* What a world. He was glad he'd never had kids. He looked around the apartment. What *did* he have? He stared at the elegantly matched, cool-toned furnishings which so perfectly complemented the aloof, distant, abstract paintings, at the racks of electronic gadgetry that surrounded him. He was going to hit the big four-oh soon and what did he really have? A good income, yes, but from a career that had plateaued five years ago; no wife, no family, and an apartment that was more like a Sharper Image catalog than a home. Just a short while ago all of this had mattered so much. The apartment had seemed so full. Now it seemed barren, deserted.

Empty even when he was here. *Especially* when he was here.

Time for a change.

Right. Easy to say. *Could* he change?

Yes. Because he wanted to. The incident in the Plaza had changed his perspective. On everything. As if some inner clock had begun tolling childhood's end. It was time to get involved in something besides finding that latest hot bistro on Columbus Avenue. Time to grow up. Time to begin sharing his life. He was aware of a growing need, a deep yearning for someone else, not just to share his apartment, but his life.

Maybe Kara Wade was the answer. She needed somebody, he could tell. And he was drawn to her. Maybe he should concentrate on her. He could help her. Really help. Maybe she would be drawn to him as a result. That would be nice. But even if it didn't turn out that way, maybe he could do something for her. Something that mattered.

Saturday

FEBRUARY 14
5:42 A.M.

KARA AWOKE IN HER OWN BED IN HER OWN HOUSE WITH THE predawn light filtering through the frost on her own bedroom window. It was great to be back home.

She hopped out of bed and padded across the cold bare planks of the floor to look out at the farm. *Her* farm. She rubbed the rime away and watched the rows of scotch pines on the south slope taking shape in the growing light. She opened the window and thrust her head and shoulders out into the cold, still air.

The morning was hers. For these few minutes she owned it. No one was stirring except her. You couldn't do this in New York. She'd tried when she was there. She'd stayed up all night and she'd risen before the sun, but she'd never had the city to herself. Before the last of the all-night party people had gone home, the city's swarms of delivery trucks were up and out and clattering along the streets.

But here at the farm the morning was all hers. And someday, when she paid it off, the farm would be all hers as well. She hungered for that day.

She closed the window and rubbed her hands together, glad she had the weekend to whip this place into shape and get a little work done on her book. Come Monday morning Jill would go back to school and Kara back to her job at the hospital. It was time to put the ugliness of Kelly's death behind them and get their lives back on track.

She glanced over at the Apple II+ on the writing table. She had bought it second hand as a word processor for her book and it was calling to her now. And well it should. The publisher had refused to authorize an extension of her deadline. They had the book scheduled for next spring's line up and didn't want to change their plans. She had to get cracking.

But she'd been having trouble with the chapter on abortion. Intellectually, she was pro-choice. Emotionally, she was torn. She couldn't help but think that if she and Rob had ended differently—if he had beat her or otherwise mistreated her—she might have had an abortion rather than carry and deliver their child. And then Jill, wonderful Jill, would never have existed. A horrifying thought.

But that didn't explain the conceptual problems she was having with the chapter. She had been deeply disturbed by the latest statistics from India: out of every 8,000 abortions in Bombay, only one of the fetuses was male. The Indian women were having amniocentesis, and if the child was female they were aborting it.

Kara could see that as obstetrical advances filtered down to the over-the-counter level—now there were home pregnancy tests, and soon there would be oral abortifacients, and perhaps even a home amnio kit—the concept of abortion on demand became a two-edged sword. In India, daughters were expensive to marry off, so people were deciding by the thousands not to have daughters. What would a trend like that in the Western countries do to the woman's movement? And what would be the next to disappear? Freckles? Green eyes? Short stature? Mousy hair color? Where would it end?

Maybe that was the approach to take—*Where do we draw the line?*

Kara was suddenly excited. If she got to work right away, she could get a page done before Jill—

"Mom! Mom!"

Jill came racing into the room and threw her arms around Kara's waist and hugged her. She was trembling.

"Jill, honey! What's the matter?"

"Where were you last night, Mom? Where'd you go?"

"I didn't go anywhere."

"Yes, you did! I came looking for you last night and you weren't here!"

"Don't be silly, of course I was. You must have been dreaming."

Kara looked down at Jill. She was genuinely frightened. She looked as if she was about to cry.

"But I wasn't! I thought I heard a noise and I got scared, so I came in to see you and you weren't here! I called and called but you wouldn't answer me, and I looked all over for you but you weren't here! I was so scared! I thought you'd left me!"

"I was right there in bed all the time. Tell me what you did after that."

"I went back to my bed and hid under the covers. I was crying. I . . . think I fell asleep again."

"And then you woke up and now I'm here. It was a nightmare, Jill. You only *dreamt* you were looking for me." She hugged her daughter tightly against her. "I'd never go anywhere without you. You know that don't you?"

Jill nodded. "But it seemed so *real!*"

"I know." She kissed her. "The worst ones always

do. But it's over now, and I'm here, so why don't you get into your robe and we'll go make breakfast."

"Can we have scrambled eggs?"

"Sure."

"Good! I want to try my chopsticks on them!"

As Jill trotted off, Kara sat on the edge of the bed and fished around for her slippers. The mention of the chopsticks brought Rob to mind. He was another reason she was glad to be back at the farm. She'd spent most of the week holding her breath, praying he wouldn't see the resemblance between himself and Jill. How could he miss it? But he had, thank God.

Well there was no sense in worrying about what might have happened. Right now, she had breakfast to cook and a book to write.

She found her slippers and was about to slip them on when she caught a glimpse of the sole of her left foot.

It was filthy.

She checked the right and found the same. The bottoms of both of her feet were covered with dirt. Not house dirt, but outside dirt.

Yard dirt.

But she'd showered right before bed last night. Her feet had been clean, she was sure of it. This wasn't possible, unless . . .

A chill stole over her. Jill's dream. What if it hadn't been a dream? What if Jill had really come looking for her and she hadn't been here? But where had she gone? Outside? Barefoot? That was crazy!

Crazy. Dr. Gates had said to let him know if anything strange happened—blackouts and things like that. Did he mean sleepwalking, too? Kara had never done that before. At least that she knew.

What's happening to me?

Probably nothing. Probably just a reaction to the stresses of the past week. But if anything like this happened again, she was going to be on the phone to Dr. Gates immediately. As much as she disliked the man, he had a head start on any other shrink as far as this case was concerned.

As Kara put her slippers on and reached for her robe, she realized that the day had suddenly changed. The morning was no longer as bright. The buoyancy she'd felt on arising had vanished, replaced by a leaden weight of uncertainty. The Apple no longer called to her. She sensed it was going to be a very long day. And an even longer night.

▼

4:20 P.M.

"You're spending an awful lot of time on this jumper, Harris."

Rob had been expecting this. He was surprised he'd been allowed to carry it this far. But the time had come and now he was sitting across the desk from Detective Lieutenant James Mooney, chief of Midtown North's detective squad, readying an explanation. Mooney's office was a walled-off cubicle furnished with a standard issue green metal desk. He had a window, but like all the other windows in the precinct house, it was covered with steel mesh. Late afternoon sunlight strained through the mesh.

Mooney himself was a balding, jowly, overweight bulldog who usually had half a cigar stuck in the corner of his mouth. He seemed tough until he began speaking—he had a tendency to whine. But he did manage to keep the precinct's detective squad under tight control and yet remain approachable.

Rob had pulled the weekend along with Mooney. The

lieutenant liked to use his Saturdays on duty to close up all the open files that he could.

Rob said, "There's a possibility she didn't go out that window on her own. She may have had a push."

"Forensics doesn't think so."

"Forensics has been wrong before."

Mooney removed the cigar to sip from his coffee mug, the contents of which had come from the bottle in his bottom drawer. Specks of ash fell from the cigar's cold tip onto the manila folder that held the paperwork of Kelly's case.

"I read your report, Harris. You've got one very disturbed girl here, under psychiatric care, on schnozz, who jumps naked through a twelfth floor window from a room where Forensics says there's no sign of a struggle. The M.E. says her body shows no signs of a fight, except for one love bite on her shoulder. We've got people with their heads blown off waiting for their perps to be found. Don't waste your time with this one. Close it!"

That was precisely what Rob was trying to avoid.

"I think we're missing something here, lieu," he said. "I've got a gut feeling that this psychiatrist is involved somehow."

"Anything concrete?"

"No, but—"

"Then close it."

"One more week, lieu. That's all I want. I'll squeeze it in between the DiGilio and Stern cases."

Mooney's eyes narrowed as he looked at Rob.

"You got something personal in this?"

"Nah," Rob said, leaning back in his chair and hoping he was convincing. Mooney didn't like his cops getting into cases where they were personally involved. "It just interests me, you know? Ever have a case that got under your skin and made you itch?"

Mooney's eyes got even narrower. His whine became more pronounced.

"You ain't thinking of writing a book or any shit like that, are you?"

Rob laughed. "Hey, lieu, you've read my reports! What do you think?"

Mooney stuck the cigar back in his mouth and smiled.

"Yeah. You've got a point there. But Christ, every other guy in the department seems to be writing a book!"

Rob nodded. Ever since Bill Caunitz, a former detective with Mooney's rank and position, began hitting the best-seller lists and appearing on *Good Morning America*, a lot of guys were trying their hand at fiction, but not with much success.

"Give me another week, lieu. If I can't prove foul play by then I'll close it myself."

"You'd better. And don't come back next week with some sky blue theory. I want hard stuff or we close. Got it?"

"Got it."

Rob knew Mooney was hoping he'd find nothing. The lieutenant liked grounders—open and shut cases. If Kelly Wade's case remained a suicide it would be closed and forgotten. But if it became reclassified as a murder it stayed open until solved. Unsolved murders were never closed, and that could mean filing semi-annual DD5 Supplementary Complaint Reports into eternity.

Rob took the file and returned to his own desk in the squad room. It was the same color and style as Mooney's, only older and more dented. A few phone message slips on his blotter. None from Connie. He wondered why he felt relieved. Another love affair down the tubes. It was getting to be a habit.

He picked up the sheet with the notes he'd made on that lawyer yesterday and tossed it out. Ed Bannion checked out okay: a tax attorney with no record. Still ... one nervous guy. Rob uncrumpled the sheet and slipped it into the back of Kelly's file, then went over the new information he'd dug up on Dr. Gates—or rather, Lazlo Gati.

It hadn't been easy. Little Lazlo's immigration papers said he was seven years old when he arrived in the United States. He took the oath of citizenship at age 21 and had his name changed to Lawrence Gates that same year. Beyond that, Rob had come up blank. Then he'd remembered Doc Winters' passing remark about an older brother and sister who'd died in West Virginia a while back. A department contact at a Wheeling newspaper faxed him a couple of articles. The first to come through was three years old and concerned Marta Gati's death in a fire that gutted her house. The circumstances were deemed suspicious, especially since the young handyman and the maid had disappeared. Interesting, but it told Rob nothing about Dr. Gates. Then another article came through, a few years older than the first, concerning the death of the senior Gati sibling, Karl, an independent mine owner who suffered a fatal heart attack.

Rob hit paydirt in the second article. It contained an interview with Karl's sister, Marta, wherein she chronicled the family history. A fascinating story.

The Gati family had run one of Hungary's major mining concerns since the turn of the century. Somehow, through bribery and political influence, they managed to survive the Nazi occupation with all six members alive and the family fortune hidden away nearly intact. When the communists took over, however, they decided to flee. They gathered up all the gold and jewels they had squirreled away before the war and headed for the border. Mama and Papa Gati sent the kids across first. They were supposed to follow soon after but they never showed up. The children later learned that they had been captured and shot. Karl, the oldest of the three brothers at twenty, took over as head of the family. There was no opposition. Lazlo was just a boy at the time, and Marta and the other brother, Gabor, both suffered from unspecified but apparently disabling birth defects. The article mentioned that Marta was confined to a wheelchair.)

Karl turned the gold and jewels into cash and brought the family to the United States. He settled them in West Virginia where he invested their money in the familiar business of mining. He did very well, moving from comfortably well-off to extremely wealthy. Lazlo was accepted at NYU premed and moved to New York, taking the sickly Gabor with him. They all felt Gabor could get the best care in the various New York medical centers when the need arose, but apparently he died anyway. Marta was proud of her younger brother, Lazlo—she never referred to him by his American name—who was now a respected new York psychiatrist. And now that Karl was dead, Marta was all alone in the big house he had built for her, but she was not afraid. She had a loyal staff to take care of the place for her.

Rob shook his head as he folded the glossy fax sheets and slipped them back into the folder. Some loyal staff! The place burned to the ground a few years later, taking her with it.

He had one more slip of paper on the Gati family: a copy of Gabor Gati's death certificate, dated eight years ago.

Immediate cause of death: *cardiopulmonary collapse;*
secondary to: *overwhelming infection;*
secondary to: *multiple congenital defects.*

So, Dr. Lawrence Gates' older sister and both his brothers had all died suddenly a few years apart, leaving Gates as the only heir to a considerable fortune. How convenient.

This was all a sidebar, though. There might or might not be something fishy there, but it had no bearing on the Kelly Wade case, at least none that Rob could see.

He had the file cover half closed when the signature of the attending physician on the death certificate caught his eye. He looked closer, blinking. No, he was wasn't mistaken. The signature read:

Lawrence Gates, M.D.

Now that might not have been illegal, but it sure as hell was irregular to have one brother sign the other's death certificate.

Rob decided he'd better have another talk with Doc Winters about his former resident.

FEBRUARY 15
5:33 A.M.

SHE WAS AWAKE.

And as soon as she realized it, Kara threw down the quilt and top sheet and felt the soles of her feet. She couldn't see in the predawn gray, but they seemed okay. She snapped on the bedside lamp and looked.

Clean. Thank God, they were *clean*!

The sense of relief brought her close to tears.

She'd never paid much attention to washing her feet, it was just part of her shower routine. But last night she'd washed them carefully, inspecting them again before she turned out the light. They'd been clean.

Sleep had been a long time coming, kept at bay by the nightmare possibility that sleep might release another someone within her, might allow that someone to use her body. No matter how often Kara dismissed the idea, it crept back. Exhaustion finally overpowered apprehension and she drifted off.

But it was okay, now. Her feet were clean. They had been spotless last night, and they were spotless now.

She hopped out of bed. Her muscles ached from the aerobic and Nautilus work-out she'd put herself through at the gym yesterday. But it was good pain. Constructive pain.

She took a deep breath. Sunday. This was going to be a good day. She'd been too tense to do much writing yesterday. But with the early start she was getting now, she'd make up for that today.

She padded to the bathroom to brush her teeth and throw some water on her face. The medicine cabinet over the sink was open. Jill must have been up during the night and not pushed it closed firmly enough. She grabbed the toothpaste tube and slammed the door shut.

And stared.

Someone had written in lipstick on the door's mirrored surface.

Kara please
dont hate me
I want to
come back

Kara felt the toothpaste slip from her fingers as she stood there and trembled. It took all her strength of will to keep from screaming. She leaned on the sink and steadied herself. She had to be calm. She had to control this situation. Most of all she had to protect Jill from it. She couldn't let Jill see the writing, and she couldn't let Jill see her mother like this.

Forcing her hands to be steady, Kara took a handful of tissues and began to rub at the letters. First they smeared and merged, and then with increased effort they began to fade. When they were gone and only her own ashen, frightened face showed in the glass, she carried the wad downstairs to the kitchen garbage.

As she stood in the kitchen, she felt off-balance, physically as well as mentally, as if she were tottering on the brink of some sort of breakdown. It would be so easy to give in to the impulse to run screaming from the house, to lose herself in panic, to exhaust herself in blind flight. But there was Jill to think of. And there was the overriding realization that she could not run from this.

She went through her purse and found Dr. Gates's card. It was early and it was Sunday, but she had to call him *now*. She had to do something, make an attempt to speak to someone who knew about these things, even if it was only to leave a message on his answering machine, tell him that she was falling apart and ask him what she could do about it.

"Dr. Gates' service," said a woman's voice after three rings.

A real person! An answering service! They'll know where he is!

"Hello, my name is Kara Wade, I'm a patient of Dr. Gates' and I need to reach him immediately. Can you connect me?"

"I'm sorry. Dr. Gates is not available for the weekend. He'll be picking up his messages tomorrow morning. Dr. Fleischer is covering any emergencies. Can I have him call you back?"

No, that wouldn't do. Only Dr. Gates would understand the situation and know she wasn't hallucinating. She thanked the operator and hung up. She'd have to wait until tomorrow.

Delusions . . . hallucinations . . . she walked over to the kitchen garbage pail and stared at the clump of red smeared tissues. Still there. She touched it. Still very real.

She glanced up at the clock over the sink. Ten to six. It was a long, long time until tomorrow morning. But she could do it. She could make it. She could handle this until then.

▼

11:35 P.M.

Kara sat staring at the TV. A repeat of one of the old black and white *Avengers* episodes was on channel 12, but she wasn't paying attention. It had been a long day. She was emotionally drained and exhausted. Her body cried out for sleep but the prospect terrified her.

No sleep.

Sleep was a luxury she couldn't afford. Sleep was when you lost control. So the answer was to stay awake all night. She had coffee, she had the television. Jill was peacefully asleep upstairs. Kara would stay down here, and stay awake.

Janine. The name had plagued her all through the hellishly long day. Writing had been impossible because she couldn't stop thinking about Janine. If indeed there truly was a Janine inside her, where had she got the name? Since her unconscious had presumably created Janine during Kara's childhood, where had it dug up a name Kara had never heard as a child? Or at least did not remember hearing. Maybe the source of the name was locked away with the personality that bore it.

But another question haunted her: Did Janine really exist? Or was what had happened here these past two days a part of her own reaction to Kelly's death? She clung to that explanation. She had to.

She could probably clear it up with a simple phone call to her mother. Or could she? What could she say? *Mom? Did Dad rape Kelly and me on a regular basis when we were kids?*

No way.

Shuddering with revulsion, she got up and poured herself another cup of coffee, then settled herself on the straight-back wooden chair and tried to lose herself in the irrelevance of a three-decades old British television show.

It beat thinking.

FEBRUARY 16
5:45 A.M.

KARA REALIZED SHE HAD BEEN ASLEEP.

She jumped up from the chair and stared frantically around the living room. Good God, it was morning already! *Body by Jake* was on the TV. How long had she been out? Was anything different? Had she done anything while she was out? She checked her feet—clean. But that hadn't meant anything yesterday. She scanned the kitchen. Everything seemed the same there except for—

—the carving knife on the counter.

Feeling weak and sick, Kara stumbled toward the kitchen.

Please, God, no blood. Don't let there be blood on that blade.

There wasn't. The blade was clean. It was Dad's ancient carving knife. It had been new when it was a wedding gift thirty-five years ago. He'd honed it so many times over the years, standing before Thanksgiving turkeys, Christmas hams, and summer steaks, that the blade was now half its original width. Kara had never thrown it away. It had always been special. Now she didn't want to touch it. But she did.

As she lifted it gingerly and carried it to the sink, she saw that the point was broken. She didn't remember ever noticing that before. What could—?

"Mom?"

It was Jill's voice from upstairs. She sounded a little frightened. Probably looking for her. Kara hurried to the foot of the stairs.

"I'm down here, hon. Everything okay?"

She held her breath. *Please say yes.*

"Sure," Jill said, smiling from the top of the stairs.

Kara exhaled.

Jill said, "But who's Janine?"

Biting back a scream, Kara fought off the blackness that crowded the edges of her vision and forced herself up the stairs.

"Wh-where did you heard that name?"

"You okay, Mom?"

"Just tell me!"

"I read it. Mom, what's wrong?"

"Where? In the bathroom?"

"No. In my bedroom."

Kara brushed past her alarmed daughter and hurried to the bedroom at the far end of the hall. She burst through the door and didn't notice anything at first. Then she saw the thin letters sliced into the wall above Jill's bed.

Janine loves little girls
Just like Daddy

Kara couldn't hold it in any longer. She stood in the doorway and screamed.

▼

6:50 A.M.

They made it to the New Jersey Turnpike in record time.

After Kara had calmed herself and soothed a very frightened and mystified Jill, she called Dr. Gates. He wasn't available yet, according to the answering service. Kara couldn't wait. She had to get away from the farm, away from those words carved in the wall above Jill's bed. She threw some clothes in a couple of suitcases, loaded the car, and fled for New York.

As she drove, she could not escape the vague, ominous feeling that she was heading toward even worse trouble. She laid that off to her long-time aversion to New York, and the cruel irony of having to run for help to the city she loathed.

Along the way, Kara pulled into every rest stop she saw and called Dr. Gates' number. It wasn't until the Adm. Wm. Halsey Plaza near Newark Airport that she reached him.

"Strange things are happening," she told him. "Frightening things."

Dr. Gates' voice conveyed all the concern of a man inquiring about a train schedule.

"What, for instance?"

She didn't want to talk about them now, and she didn't want him to put off seeing her.

"I'm only half an hour from the city. I'll tell you when I get there. When can you see me?"

"Well . . . my schedule is already filled, perhaps I can—"

"It's got to be today. If you can't squeeze me in, perhaps you can recommend someone."

Kara didn't want to see anyone else, but she sensed Dr. Gates would never send her to a rival.

"Well, since you seem to think this is an emergency, perhaps I can add you on at the end of the schedule. Please be at my office at five."

"I'll be there."

She hung up, feeling a little better. The foreboding still clung to her like a shroud, but at least she was doing something about whatever was happening to her. She had taken the first step toward beating this. And she *would* beat it. Kara had structured her life so as to maximize her autonomy. No one controlled her. No one ever would.

Especially not something or someone who called herself "Janine."

▼

10:29 A.M.

Rob recognized her voice immediately. It gave an instant lift to an otherwise dreary Monday.

"Kara! What's up? How's the farm?"

"It's fine," she said. She sounded subdued. "Rob, there's something I've got to ask you."

Rob glanced around the squad room. His desk was situated near its center, surrounded by everybody else's. He wished he had more privacy, but the enclosed office went to the lieutenant. It didn't matter much at the moment. Karpinsky and Reddington were in the corner, arguing animatedly with Rob's partner, Augustino Manetti; Madsen and Carter were at their own desks, banging out reports on their typewriters. There was enough racket to cover his end of the conversation.

"Sure. Go ahead."

"You were with me on Thursday in Dr. Gates office when he hypnotized me, right?"

"Right."

"Were you with me all the time? I mean, did you ever leave the room?"

"Not for a second. Gates did. He left to get some files. But I never budged from my chair."

"So he didn't plant any post-hypnotic suggestions in me then, right?"

Rob was becoming concerned now. And he could tell Kara was upset.

"Kara, what's this all about?"

"A couple of weird things happened over the weekend."

A wavelet of nausea rolled through Rob's stomach.

"What sort of things?"

"I don't want to talk about it now. But you're sure nothing happened while I was hypnotized? No one named 'Janine' spoke from me?"

"Gates kept calling for 'Janine' to speak, but she never did. Only when he called you 'Kara' did you answer him. You just looked like you were asleep the whole time, except when . . ."

"When what?"

The sight of Kara turning her head and looking at him with that awful grin flashed before his eyes.

"When you looked at me and smiled."

"I didn't say anything?"

"No. It was when Gates was out of the room. You just . . . smiled."

Calling that grimace a smile was like calling a rabid wolf a puppy, but he didn't want to upset her more than she already was, not if it wasn't going to change anything.

"Why didn't you tell me?"

"I didn't think anything of it." *I didn't* want *to think anything of it*. "How bad is this, Kara?"

There was a long pause, then a tremulous sigh, then:

"I may have the same thing as Kelly."

Rob gripped the phone with muscle-cramping intensity.

"Where are you? I'm coming to get you."

"I'm okay, Rob. I'm handling it. I've got an appointment with Dr. Gates at five. I'm going to start treatment with him right away."

"I'll meet you there and sit in like before."

"No. Thanks, but that won't be necessary this time."

"I don't trust him, Kara."

"*I've* got to start trusting him now. I don't have any choice."

"There are plenty of shrinks in the city."

"But he's already familiar with this case. I'll have to start from scratch with anybody else."

She made sense, but Rob still didn't like it.

"Okay. Call me when you're through. Let me know what he says."

"Rob—"

"I care, Kara. Dammit, I still care. I don't want anything bad happening to you."

"Thanks, Rob," she said in a smaller voice. "That helps. I'll call."

After hanging up, Rob checked his watch. He wondered if he could get to talk to Doc Winters today. He wanted to clear up a couple of questions about Lazlo Gati.

▼

5:06 P.M.

"You can go in now," the receptionist said.

It was a replay of last Thursday, only this time Kara was alone. She had left Jill at Aunt Ellen's for the afternoon. The poor kid wasn't sure what was happening, she just knew it wasn't good. Kara would have loved to have been able to explain everything to her, but how? She had told her that she wasn't feeling well and had come to New York to see a doctor who could help her. Jill wanted details but Kara had managed to avoid them. For now.

Kara had called Marge, her supervisor at the hospital, to explain her absence. She still had some time off coming to her and was going to have to use up what was left. Marge didn't sound too happy. She told Kara that if she couldn't do the job, they'd have to find somebody else. Kara had hung up with the feeling that the world was closing in on her. She didn't need this extra pressure, not with her mind playing tricks on her and her book falling farther and farther behind schedule.

Dr. Gates was behind his desk as usual. His blue oxford shirt picked up the blue of his eyes. His light brown tie was almost the same sandy shade of his wavy hair and mustache. His expression was as neutral as ever.

He motioned her toward a chair.

"Have a seat, Miss Wade, and tell me all about the 'strange things' that have been happening to you."

Kara gave him a brief description of the weekend's unsettling incidents, from her soiled feet on Saturday morning to the message carved over Jill's bed. Dr. Gates listened in silence, twirling that key ring on his finger. When she finished, he rose from the desk and walked to the window. His expression was troubled when he turned back to her.

"I was afraid of this."

"Of what? Tell me what's happening. That's why I'm here."

"Isn't it obvious? Janine—your second personality. She's no longer dormant."

"That's just it: It's too obvious, and too bizarre. I can't buy that. I can't buy Janine's existence."

Dr. Gates returned to his high-backed swivel chair behind the desk. His face was once again impassive.

"Denial is your first hurdle on the road to recovery. You must get over that before we can start meaningful therapy."

"But isn't there another explanation? Couldn't I be doing this to myself in some way? I mean, it's such a coincidence that you should tell me about Kelly's second personality and the possibility of my having one called Janine, and then *wham,* Janine starts writing on walls. It's all a little too facile."

"You're overlooking the hypnosis session," Dr. Gates said gravely. "I was against it from the beginning but you insisted. I warned you it was dangerous. I warned you it might awaken something best left dormant. It appears I was right."

Dr. Gates' smugness would have infuriated Kara under different circumstances, but the sick dread seeping through her now left little room for anything else.

"But two sisters with multiple personalities . . . it sounds so far fetched."

"On the surface, yes. But not quite so far fetched when you consider the specifics of your case: two genetically identical children subjected simultaneously to identical trauma. Given those circumstances, is it so outlandish to suppose that the psychological defense mechanisms would also be identical?" He ticked points off on his fingers "Same genes, same trauma, same response. It is logical."

Kara was numb.

"When do we start therapy?" she said.

"Today, if you wish."

"I wish. What kind of therapy?"

"Just let me worry about that," he said with a small, condescending smile.

The sudden surge of anger within her energized Kara. Anything was better than feeling afraid.

"I am not an idiot, Dr. Gates. If this is going to work I have to know what's going on. I am not a child and will not be led through the dark by the hand."

He stared at her a while before answering.

"Very well. I plan to use free association at the start. I'll have you lay back in the recliner and begin talking off the top of your head about your childhood. I'll be searching for what we refer to as 'blocked' areas. When I have identified a pattern of blocks, I will put you under hypnosis and try to unblock those areas. If I'm successful, you will then begin the most difficult part of the therapy: you will have to face the painful memories you have repressed since childhood."

"And that will do it?"

"Theoretically, yes. Once the repressed memories are free, once you have dealt with them emotionally and intellectually as Kara, there will be no more need for Janine. She will either go dormant permanently or cease to exist."

It sounded sensible to Kara. She felt the first stirrings of hope.

"Let's get to it."

"There's something else you should know," he said, holding up a hand. "It will not be as easy as it sounds. It will take a *long* time, perhaps years, during which you will come to hate me, call me an incompetent, a charlatan, and want to quit. But you must have faith. You must stay with the therapy."

A cold lump of fear formed again in Kara's throat.

"Years? You mean I've got to spend *years* wondering whether I'm going to turn into this other person who writes on walls and God knows what else?"

He shook his head and pulled a pad from the top drawer of his desk.

"We can do something about that. Your second personality appears to be adopting a pattern of activity similar to your sister's: Janine takes over only when you are in periods of lighter sleep."

That was a relief.

"Then I'm safe during the day."

"For now.

"What does that mean?"

" 'Kara' is your primary personality, the dominant one, the personality through which you deal with the workaday world. This is a strongly entrenched, well-integrated, adult personality that has no need for 'Janine.' So 'Kara' remains in the driver seat while 'Janine,' the relatively minor personality, remains in the passenger seat. She has been dormant for a quarter century or so and hasn't the power to push 'Kara' aside and take over—except when 'Kara' is asleep. But the more time she logs in control, the stronger she will become. And some day she may well be able to assert dominance any time she wishes."

Kara fought the horror crawling through her. Not to be in control . . . to be dominated by a stranger, even if it was of her own creation . . .

"What can I do?"

"It's what *we* can do: suppress her. Don't give her time in the driver seat. That's why I'm prescribing something that will keep both you *and* 'Janine' asleep all night."

He handed her the slip. It was for thirty Halcion tablets.

"You prescribed these for Kelly. They obviously didn't help her too much."

Dr. Gates' smile was small and bitter.

"Your sister wouldn't take them if she had to work the next day. She said they made her groggy in the morning. Which they might."

Groggy in the morning ... a small price to pay for controlling Janine. Kara held up the prescription.

"Guaranteed to work?"

"Nothing is guaranteed in psychiatry. But they will give you an edge. Take one every night, Miss Wade."

Kara folded the slip and dropped it in her purse. She nodded toward the recliner.

"Shall we get started?"

▼

6:26 P.M.

"Hey lady!" Rob called from his car window as he saw Kara come out of the medical arts building. "Need a ride?"

She glanced at him with a get-lost look, then her face relaxed into a smile. A worn, tired smile, but a smile nonetheless. She came over to the car.

"How long have you been waiting here?"

It had been an hour. He hadn't been able to see Doc Winters today, so he'd set it up for tomorrow. He'd got here around five thirty and had begun to fear he'd missed her.

"Too long. Get in. I'll drive you where you're going."

She got in the other side, leaned back against the head rest, and closed her eyes. She looked beat. Rob reached over and squeezed her hand. She didn't pull away.

"Tough day?" he said.

She nodded. "You wouldn't believe."

"Want to tell me about it over a drink?"

She opened her eyes and looked at him.

"A drink would be nice."

He didn't want to take her to Leo's so he found a restaurant on Eighth and parked by the fire hydrant. The place had upscale decor with lots of neon in the window, the kind of place that could charge twenty-five bucks for portions that wouldn't feed a toddler. But it was nearly empty so they got a table near the rear. No menus, just drinks. Rob ordered a scotch, Kara had a chablis.

She was reticent, but slowly he drew the events of the weekend out of her. It was chilling. Those words carved over Jill's bed gave him the creeps.

He said, "I think you did the right thing, getting out of there. I only wish you had someone else as a doctor."

"You keep saying that. Do you know something about Dr. Gates that I don't?"

"Nothing bad. Everyone I talk to says he's tops. I just don't like him."

"Neither do I. He's got all the warmth of an earthworm. Not the sort you look forward to spending an hour a day, three days a week with."

"That often?"

"Monday-Wednesday-Friday. He's going to jump me into heavy therapy at first to see if we can get a quick response. As I said, he's not Dr. Warmth, but if he knows his stuff and can get me through this, then he's the one I should be with."

"I guess so. I just—"

"It's all my fault!" she blurted. Tears glistened in her eyes. "If only I'd listened to him and not tried that hypnotism, none of this would be happening."

"Don't blame yourself, Kara. You had to know if—"

"And now I do! Rob, I'm frightened! To think that I was standing over Jill's bed with my father's old carving knife, cutting words into the wall! It makes me sick!"

"You'll be all right. They don't come any tougher than you, Kara. If anyone's going to lick this thing, it's you."

Rob desperately wanted to raise her spirits and would have said anything to buck her up, but he believed what he'd said. Kara was strong. He had real faith in her mental toughness.

"I hope so," she said, sniffing and wiping her eyes with a napkin. She finished her wine. "Can we get out of here?"

"Sure."

▼

"Staying at your aunt's?" he said as he drove toward the East Side on Twenty-fourth. With all the little businesses closed and no trucks double parked to load and unload, it was an easy trip.

"For now. I don't know what I'm going to do long term. This could be a lengthy siege. I may have to move here."

Rob was ashamed of the tiny surge of delight those words elicited. He knew how she hated the city.

She said, "During the day I'll be at Ellen's with Jill.

She'll sleep there, too. But for the time being I'm going to sleep over at Kelly's."

"Alone? Why on earth would you want to do that?"

"I don't. But Dr. Gates suggested it. He said I should spend my nights there until we see how things go. Otherwise I run the risk of Jill seeing me as Janine. I don't want that. What if she had awakened when I was carving those words over her bed? What if she'd tried to talk to me then, someone who looked like her mother but *wasn't?* I can't risk frightening her like that. Or worse, run the risk of hurting her when I'm Janine."

"How long can that go on?"

"I don't know. Until we're sure the sleeping pills Dr. Gates gave me will keep Janine asleep, too. Then I'll feel safe being in the same house with Jill."

Rob shook his head. This sounded almost like one of those corny old *Psycho*-type movies. All that was needed now was a walk-on by Betty Davis or Joan Crawford.

But this was no movie.

"I'll stay with you," he said.

Rob surprised himself. *Where did that come from?* He could feel the small hairs at the back of his neck rise at the thought of meeting the Janine side of Kara.

Kara looked at him, a slight, skeptical smile playing on her lips.

"Thanks, Rob. That's kind of you, but it won't be necessary."

"You can't always do everything on your own, Kara," he said, hiding his hurt at being rejected, and annoyed at his big mouth for setting himself up for it. "Sometimes you have to admit that you need help."

"I know that." Her smiled broadened. "And when I do, you'll be the first one I call."

They said little during the rest of the drive back to

her Aunt Ellen's. Rob hoped all along the way that Kara would ask him in for dinner.

She didn't.

▼

9:30 P.M.

After dinner, after tucking Jill in and repeating for what seemed like the hundredth time the not-quite-true explanation of why her mother had to sleep at Aunt Kelly's for a few nights, Kara returned to the apartment house on East Sixty-third. Her stomach twisted slowly into a knot as she climbed the front steps. What would tonight bring?

In the vestibule, a business card protruding from the slot in the 2-C mailbox—Kelly's—caught her eye. It was from Ed Bannion.

Kara Wade—
Call me re: Kelly's estate.
E.B.

He'd written his home number on the front.

Kelly's estate? Kelly didn't have an estate. Kara decided to call him tomorrow.

In the apartment, she tried to shed the dread and apprehension that clung to her as she wandered through the empty rooms.

This was where Kelly had tried to fight the same problem. And Kelly had lost.

But Kelly hadn't been taking her sleeping pills—at least that was what Dr. Gates had said. Kara would. She'd take one every night if it proved helpful.

But that wasn't all she'd do.

She marched into Kelly's bedroom and pulled all the sleazy underwear, blouses, sweaters, skirts, and other paraphernalia from under the night tables and dresser and stuffed them into two of the Dagostino bags Kelly had stored between the fridge and the wall. When everything was packed, she took the bags out to the corner of Sixty-third and First and left them under the street light. She was reasonably sure they'd be gone by the time she made it back to the front door of the apartment house. Absolutely sure they'd be gone within the hour.

When she got back to the apartment, she locked the dead bolt and hunted around for a place to hide the key. Dr. Gates had told her that in cases of multiple personalities the quiescent personality was unaware of the other personality's activities during its active phase. Kara didn't know of any other key in Kelly's apartment, so she figured that if Janine should take control during the night, she would not be able to leave the apartment if Kara hid this one well enough.

She finally decided on the right rear corner of the top rack in the oven. Who in their right mind would look there for a key?

Don't ask.

After that she showered. As she lathered up, Rob's words from the afternoon came back to her:

You can't always do everything on your own, Kara.

How many times in her life had she heard that? From her mother and father, from Kelly, from friends. Nobody seemed to understand her. She didn't want to do everything on her own. She wasn't looking to cut herself off. She just wanted to be able to stand free and clear. She'd take help when she couldn't provide it herself—like seeing Dr. Gates for therapy—but what she *could* do on her own, she *would* do on her own.

Maybe she'd picked it up from her Amish neighbors, who were "beholding to no one," as they put it. But Kara sensed it went deeper than that. The need for autonomy, to control her own life, seemed to be engraved on her soul. Which made the possibility of another personality taking over at any time—even if it was just for a few seconds—especially loathsome.

She got ready for bed. She wished she could do a little writing but she was exhausted. She didn't think she'd need a sleeping pill, but she was going to follow doctor's orders strictly. At least for now. She took one of Kelly's leftover Halcions, settled in Kelly's bed with one of Kelly's back issues of *Rolling Stone*, and tried not to think about Kelly. Or Janine. Or how alone and afraid she was. And how comforting it would be to have someone to talk to right now. And how stupid she'd been for refusing Rob's offer to stay the night.

Somewhere between comforting and stupid, Kara fell asleep.

LETTERS FROM

Purgatory

Poor little fool. She came back.

He's absolutely elated. How he gloats and struts! So taken with how clever he is. The Napoleon of Plotters, the Machiavelli of Manipulators.

Makes me ill!

How I'd love to teach the swine a lesson. Thinks I'm helpless, harmless, not the slightest possible threat to his great intellect. I hate that most of all . . . even if he's right. He knows I'm totally without resources.

No. Perhaps not totally. Have my own intellect. Don't see why I can't manage to be as deceitful and crafty as he. Not beyond my capability to get a message of warning to this new one.

Wouldn't that be wonderful! What a coup! With no resources other than what I can steal and hide, to warn her away from him. Wouldn't that take the wind out of his sails! Oh, he'll punish me, I know, punish me severely, but it would be worth it. Just to show him, to let him know he hasn't beaten me into complete submission. I'm still here. I can still act.

He'll not take me for granted any more after I do this.

If I can indeed do it. Have to try.

First thing I'll need is her address.

FEBRUARY 17
8:06 A.M.

KARA AWOKE FEELING GROGGY AND NOT PARTICULARLY well rested. She shook herself to full alertness and slipped from the bed. She saw that she was still in the same flannel nightshirt she had put on last night. The bedroom looked the same. No words carved in the walls. She ran her hands over her body. No new bruises or cuts of scrapes. She ran to the bathroom. No writing on the mirror. She checked the living room and the kitchen. No knives on the counter, and the key was still in the oven, exactly where she'd left it.

She slumped against the counter, weak with relief.

"Okay," she said to no one in particular. She thumped her fist on the countertop. *"Okay!"*

▼

10:00 A.M.

"Thanks for seeing me on such short notice, Doc," Rob said as he dropped into the chair opposite the desk.

Doc Winters peered at him over his reading glasses.

He tapped his desk top with a ballpoint; *Navane* was inscribed on the barrel.

"You said it was urgent."

"It is, kind of. It's about Dr. Lawrence Gates—"

"What is it with you and Gates? You got something personal against him, Harris?"

Rob was startled by Doc Winters' vehemence.

"Not at all. I've only met him twice. I don't particularly like the man, but it's not personal."

"A lot of people don't like Larry Gates, but that's not a cause for police harassment."

"I'm not harassing anybody! Did he tell you that?"

"No. I haven't had cause to speak to him for a couple of years now, but let me tell you something about Larry Gates. I know he presents this cold surface to the world—"

" 'Cold' is an understatement."

"I won't argue that. I don't know why he does it. I'd think it would be counterproductive to a successful psychiatric practice. But then, financial considerations aren't much of a motivating force in the life of a man of his wealth. And besides, from what I understand, it hasn't adversely effected his patient flow."

Rob said, "I doubt the patient I know would be going to him if it weren't for his special qualifications in the area of her problem."

"That multiple personality you mentioned? Well, as I said, she couldn't be in better hands. But you know, I did see Larry's cold facade crack once: when his brother Gabor contracted pneumonia."

With the mention of Gabor, Rob's interest surged.

"When was that?"

"During Larry's residency—third year, I believe. Gabor caught the flu but didn't kick it. Being an invalid, he quickly developed pneumonia. Larry had one of the pulmonary guys admit him to Downstate so he could keep an eye on his brother while going about his regular duties as a psychiatry resident." Doc Winters leaned forward and pointed his ballpoint at Rob. "He never left the hospital once during Gabor's illness, Harris. He *lived* there. That's the real Larry Gates."

Rob was surprised. Maybe he had Gates pegged wrong.

"Gabor survived, I gather."

"Yes."

"But died later."

"Years later, somewhere in his forties. His longevity was a testament to the care he received from Larry."

"Why do you say that?"

"Gabor Gati was a nightmare. Grotesquely deformed by multiple congenital defects . . . nearly blind, aphonic—"

"Pardon?"

"Mute. Couldn't speak. I doubt very much that his intelligence was above the idiot level. His body was bulbous and scoliotic, with atrophic limbs. He was totally dependent. Couldn't feed or clothe or change himself. Quite repulsive, actually. But Larry was intensely devoted to him. He had hidden Gabor from the Nazis and had helped him escape the Commies—he wasn't going to let some lousy bacterium claim his brother." Winters shook his head. "Quite a guy."

"Sure sounds it," Rob said but decided to withhold the Nobel Prize just a little longer.

"Now what was it you wanted to see me about?"

"Gates signed Gabor's death certificate. That struck me as irregular."

Winters' brow furrowed. "In most cases it would be. Highly irregular for a first degree relative to sign. But not illegal. Larry is a licensed M.D. and qualified to sign. And he acted as Gabor's attending physician most of the time, so he would have been most familiar with the particulars of Gabor's medical history. It's a unique case. I don't see anything to get excited about."

Rob sighed and rose from the chair.

"Neither do I. Just checking. Thanks, Doc."

"It's okay. And relax about Larry Gates. He's dedicated. Hardly ever takes a vacation, from what I hear. A workaholic, perhaps, but a good man."

"If you say so, Doc, that's good enough for me."

But that doesn't mean I have to like him.

▼

1:37 P.M.

The voice of Ed Bannion's secretary came through the intercom.

"There's a Kara Wade on seven-six. Says it's personal."

Ed felt a quick surge of excitement.

"Got it, Nancy." He jabbed the blinking button. "Hello! You're a hard woman to find."

"I went back to Pennsylvania for a while. I got back yesterday. I got your note."

"Yeah." He laughed. "After calling a few dozen times, I figured that was the best way to get hold of you."

"What's this about Kelly's estate?"

"She didn't have a will."

"How do you know?"

"I checked. A will was never filed for her."

"Why would you check?"

Ed detected a note of hostility creeping into Kara's voice. Maybe she thought he'd been prying.

Well, she was right. He had been rooting around for a way to maintain contact with her and had come up with an ingenious solution. He figured that if Kelly Wade was like most single people in her age bracket, she didn't have a will. They hardly ever do. Only if they're married and have kids do they start thinking about who's going to get what they leave behind if they kick the bucket unexpectedly.

He was right. Kelly had died *in testate*.

"I'm just trying to help, Kara. Trying to repay a debt. Kelly helped my family through her profession, now it's my turn to help Kelly's through *my* profession."

He'd made up that story about his mother being in the hospital, but what he was about to tell Kara was all true and legally sound. He just had to make sure he didn't come on too strong as he tried to sell her on it.

"If you want to avoid probate, if you want access to her bank account or accounts—I have no idea what she had—you'll have to be named administrator."

"I don't want her money."

"It's not as vulturish as it sounds. She's got bills due, I'm sure—utilities, charge cards, etcetera. They'll need to be paid, otherwise her creditors can take her estate to court."

There was silence on the other end of the line. Ed let it run its course.

"I never thought of that," Kara said finally.

"Of course, you didn't," Ed said, trying to sound jovial. "That's what us legal eagles are for. Besides, if you don't take over her accounts, the Government will. I'm sure you can put them to better use."

"I guess so. What do I do?"

"I'll do most of it. I'll act as your counsel and go before the surrogate and file to have you appointed administrator of Kelly's estate. That should be no problem. Since she had no husband or children, her twin sister is the obvious choice—unless your mother or father protest."

"No one will protest."

"Fine. Then you can pay off her bills from her account, clean out her apartment, take whatever you want to keep as memories, and be fully in the clear legally."

"What will this cost?"

"It's on the house. *Quid pro quo.* Should I get the paperwork started?"

Say yes! Please say yes!

"All right," she said slowly. "This is very considerate of you."

"Think nothing of it. Now, we'll have to get together and have you sign a few papers. Is tomorrow good for you?"

"Only the afternoon. I have an appointment in the morning."

Ed had to babysit some money men from the West Coast all afternoon and evening tomorrow.

"How about Thursday?"

"Thursday would be better. I have the whole day free."

"Good. I'll meet you at Kelly's and we'll go someplace for lunch."

Another hesitation. *Say yes, Kara.*

Finally: "Okay. That sounds nice. See you then."

Ed hung up, jumped up, and was doing a little victory dance around his desk when his secretary walked in.

"Are you all right, Mr. Bannion?"

Ed stopped abruptly and straightened a few papers on his desk top.

"My foot fell asleep. But now I'm fine, Nancy. Just fine."

And I'm going to be even better!

▼

11:02 P.M.

Kara dragged herself back to Kelly's apartment with the promise that if the next few nights went as well as last night, she'd pronounce herself safe to sleep at Ellen's. It was the only way she could cajole herself into returning. The thought of another night alone in that apartment was daunting.

That was why a warm glow suffused her when Rob popped out of his car and intercepted her at the door to the apartment house. It would be good to have company for a while.

"I can't stay," he said. "I just wanted to see how you were doing. I called a few times but there was no answer."

"I'm fine," she said. "Come on in. I'll fix you a drink. Or coffee. Whichever you prefer."

He looked surprised. "You sure?"

"Absolutely."

▼

One drink turned into two as they sat on the couch and talked while VH-1's music videos danced across the TV screen. And the more they talked, the more Kara realized that all her old feelings for Rob were very much alive. She felt so comfortable with him, so safe. And warm. Then her eyes caught sight of his pistol in its clip holster, resting on the end table.

"God, I wish you weren't a cop."

"I think maybe it's genetic, passed down from my dad. I can't help it."

"Okay. Then I wish you weren't a cop in New York City."

"Where, then?"

"Someplace that wasn't full of junkies, pimps, pushers, rapists, and killers. I'm afraid for you."

"That's just it, Kara. I don't see this city as full of junkies, pimps, pushers, rapists, and killers. They're not the city. They've just gravitated here because of its size. Manhattan is like a big pond. They're the scum that floats on top. They get all the attention. They're what too many outsiders see and remember most when they come here. The pond scum may make the pond look uninviting, but they're not the pond. I work for the rest of the pond—the people you don't notice, the ones who live here and work here and make it go. Like your Aunt Ellen. Like . . . Kelly. I'm here for them. I'm no Sir Galahad in a suit of armor and I'm not Dirty Harry, but in a lot of ways I'm what stands between them and God knows what. I bitch about the rules and regs and the politicians as much as the next guy, but I do take what I do seriously, and I do mean to do it well."

Kara stared at him. She realized that she had never truly appreciated Rob. She had loved him, yes, and probably still did, but she had never really appreciated his depth. She sensed something rare in him, something to be nurtured and cherished.

Impulsively, she leaned over and kissed him on the lips.

"They're lucky to have you."

A retread video of "Do That To Me One More Time" began to run on VH-1.

"We used to dance to that," Rob said, "Wanna?"

Kara smiled. "Yeah. I wanna."

They rose and slipped into each others arms and began to sway to the music. Rob wasn't much of a dancer but Kara couldn't have cared less. She gave in to the pleasurable warmth of his arms around her, the faint residue of his Old Spice after shave.

"It's been a long time, Rob."

"It's been forever."

They kissed. A long kiss. Kara felt the warmth gathering in her. Reflexively she began to pull away, then she fought the reflex. She felt his tongue probing. She opened to it. Soon they were pulling at each other's clothing.

"Ten years!" Rob whispered. "I've been waiting ten years for you to come back!"

Kara said nothing. She knew she really hadn't come back in any true sense. But here, tonight, now, she was back. And she wanted to be with Rob.

He ran a finger up her left arm to the deltoid.

"Look at the definition. You've been working out?"

"Nautilus and aerobics."

She shivered as his finger continued over her shoulder and down to her breast where it circled the nipple. They kissed again.

"I've missed you like crazy," he whispered into her ear.

"I've missed you, too, Rob. Especially like this."

He pulled his head back and smiled at her.

"I didn't know feminist writers went in for this sort of stuff."

"We like it as much as the next person. Maybe even more."

"I suppose you want to be on top."

"You've got it."

Laughing, they made their way to the bedroom where they took turns being on top.

Eventually they ended up side by side. Kara lay with her head on his shoulder.

Rob said, "We got to try this more often. Ten years is just a tad long for a dry spell. Think we can get together again before the end of the century?"

"I think I'd like that. This was wonderful, Rob."

And she meant it. She couldn't remember the last time it had been this good. She felt relaxed, content, emotionally complete. She knew the feeling wouldn't last long, but she relished the sensation while she could. She realized how much had been missing from her life. She knew it wasn't just the orgasm, it was the intimacy. She had been avoiding intimacy since she'd left New York. It had become a pattern of behavior: Don't get to know a man well enough to allow an emotional bond to develop. Keep him at arms' length at all times. A couple of the members in one of the women's groups she belonged to had misinterpreted that and Kara had found it necessary to put them straight: She wasn't interested in a relationship with *anybody*. The pattern had developed into a reflex, one she'd had to suppress tonight.

She was glad she had. This was good, this was right, this was rare and precious. Snuggled against Rob, with his arm around her shoulder, she felt warm and secure, and best of all, *alive*.

She drifted off to sleep.

LETTERS FROM

Purgatory

I've done it! I've sent out the warning! What a stroke of genius! What a brilliant move, even if I do say so myself!

And the swine hasn't the slightest idea what I've done. Obviously. If he did he would be raging at me. And punishing me severely.

I cannot escape punishment.

So what? That was a given when I began this little project. If he intercepts the warning, he'll make me suffer. If she receives the warning, she will show it to him, or someone else will tell him of it, and the result will be the same, although probably worse in the latter scenario.

So, whether I succeed or fail, I shall suffer dearly. The anticipation of it is worse than a sword poised over my neck, waiting to fall. Decapitation—ha! That would be a pleasure compared to what I face.

But whatever I suffer shall be worth it. Not for her sake alone. At first I thought my scheme to warn her was pure selflessness, but that's not the case. No. I'm doing this more for myself than for her. This is my Spartacan uprising, my storming of the Bastille, my Boston Tea Party. With this act I put him on notice that he has not broken me.

I only hope my warning reaches her. For if it does, and

if she heeds it, I will have wounded him, and he has never been wounded before. Knowing that is worth any punishment.

It should reach her by Thursday.

And then all Hell may break loose.

FEBRUARY 18
2:32 A.M.

ROB AWOKE IN THE DARK TO A DELICIOUS FEELING. HE HAD A huge erection. And it was in Kara's mouth. He groaned and arched his back as she worked her lips and tongue up and down the shaft. There'd been oral sex during their affair ten years ago, but never like this. This was fabulous. Rob closed his eyes and drifted on the pleasure.

He felt Kara's weight shift as she straightened up and straddled him. And then he was inside her and she was bucking her hips up and down, sliding him in and out of her at an ever-increasing rate. He looked up as she leaned over him, her breasts bobbing, her eyes closed, her upper lip caught between her teeth. When he reached up and ran his palms over her hard nipples she moaned and increased the tempo of her hips. Rob matched her thrust for thrust until they reached a furious pace. Finally, when he knew he could hold back no longer, Kara suddenly stopped her undulations. As he exploded within her, she straightened and stiffened and shuddered as a soft, high-pitched scream escaped through her clenched teeth. Then she collapsed beside him and they both lay there panting.

When he caught his breath, when he could speak again, Rob turned to her.

"Kara, that was fantastic. What—"

Without a word, Kara turned her back to him.

"Kara?" He propped himself up on one arm and shook her shoulder gently. "Kara?"

She was sound asleep.

Rob stared at her bare back in the darkness as a mix of feelings washed over him. He was annoyed and he was confused, but there was something else. He didn't recognize it at first. An alien feeling, a new experience: he felt . . . used.

Which was ridiculous. Kara didn't use people. Kara wasn't—

A thought struck him with an icy shock that sent cold tendrils writhing along his body.

Who had he just made love to? Kara . . . or Janine?

Rob didn't sleep the rest of the night.

▼

7:52 A.M.

Kara noticed that Rob was unusually subdued at breakfast. He'd always been a morning person. Even last week, after sleeping in a chair all night, he'd been unbearably cheery. Not today. He looked tired and seemed troubled as he leaned against the kitchen counter and sipped his coffee. Preoccupied.

Not Kara. She was *up*.

Two—count 'em—*two* nights in a row with no craziness. No writing on walls, no stunts with knives, nothing! And no sleeping pill last night.

Maybe good sex was a better medication than Halcion.

Either way, everything was beginning to fall into place. If she continued on this kind of even keel she might consider finding a therapist in Philadelphia to work this through. Between the Jefferson Medical Center and Hahnemann she was sure she could find a psychiatrist of Dr. Gates' caliber to continue her treatment. She'd mention it to him during their session today.

And it would be so good to be back in Pennsylvania. She could ship Kelly's things home and sift through them at her leisure, keeping the personal items—the yearbooks, the photos, her records, things like that— and giving the rest to a charity.

But returning to the farm meant leaving Rob. A part of her—a big part of her—didn't want to leave him. Last night had been wonderful, and waking up with him beside her had made the morning brighter. There had to be a way they could work something out.

She watched him and felt the desire rise up in her again. She wondered at that. Making love to Rob last night must have started some sort of chain reaction within her, causing her body to want to make up for all the years without him. It had been too long. She was actually sore down there. She even had a vague memory of a sex dream last night during which she'd practically raped Rob. And strangely enough, Dr. Gates seemed to have been there. A weird dream. But dreams weren't the real thing. She'd been disappointed when he got up and took a shower first thing this morning. She'd been hoping for a reprise.

"Something bothering you, Rob?"

At the sound of her voice he started and sloshed a little coffee onto the back of his hand.

"No. Everything's fine. Why?"

"You've hardly said a word all morning."

He smiled and Kara thought it looked a little forced. "Sorry. A lot of things on my mind, I guess. All sorts of stuff piling up at the precinct. There don't seem to be enough hours in the day." He glanced quickly away from her, then back. "Are you seeing Dr. Gates today?"

"Eleven a.m. sharp. Every Monday, Wednesday, and Friday. But I don't know for how long."

Concern leapt into his eyes.

"What do you mean?"

"Well, things seem to be pretty much under control at the moment. Nothing's happened here like it did at the farm."

"Maybe, but you can't quit therapy."

"I've no intention of—" Something was going on here. "Rob, what's wrong?"

A tortured expression flickered across his face, and then he put down his coffee and slipped his arms around her. He squeezed her so tightly for a moment that she couldn't breathe, then he relaxed.

"I just want you to be all right, that's all."

Kara looked into his eyes and saw that he meant it. She kissed him.

"I *will* be all right, Rob. I'm going to see to that." She glanced at her watch. "But I've got to get going. I want to be back at Ellen's when Jill wakes up. I want to have breakfast with her."

"I'll give you a lift."

"That's okay. I'll walk. I feel good this morning."

She could tell by his bleak expression that Rob felt anything but.

They parted at the front entrance. Kara waved and headed uphill toward Second Avenue. She kept up a brisk pace. She wanted to squeeze in some school work with Jill between breakfast and her appointment with Dr. Gates. Kara didn't like her missing all these class days, but she didn't know what else she could do at present. Until she knew for sure how long she'd be staying here, they'd both have to play it by ear.

The sun was warm on her back. It was a bright, crisp, beautiful winter day, with hardly a breeze stirring the air. She had to admit it: New York City could be nice sometimes.

▼

The steel band that had been constricting Rob's chest all morning loosened a bit as he watched Kara walk away. All night he had lain awake trying to think of a way to ask her if the woman astride him in the middle of the night had been Kara. He had searched the still darkness for just the right words, the perfect framing of the question so that she wouldn't be hurt and insulted if the answer was yes, and she wouldn't be frightened out of her mind if it was no.

He'd come up with nothing. From the moment she'd awakened beside him he had tried to ask her, but at the last moment would lose his nerve.

This wasn't like him. He could interrogate with the best of them, asking the most personal, the most outrageous, the most leading, self-incriminating questions without batting an eye. But Kara wasn't a suspect. He couldn't bear to hurt her.

For all her outward toughness, Rob still sensed something fragile within Kara. He had to be very careful. He had lost her once. He didn't want to lose her again.

He watched her turn downtown onto Second Avenue and disappear. He hoped Dr. Gates was as good as Doc Winters said he was. Rob had a feeling Kara needed more help than she realized.

▼

12:48 P.M.

Kara cradled Jill on her lap in Ellen's dining room.

"So, bug. Are you bored here?"

"Oh, no!" Jill said. "Lucia lets me help her in the kitchen, and when she doesn't need help mixing stuff, I watch the VCR. It's got great stuff, Mom. I'll show you."

"That's okay, Jill. I've—"

But Jill was off and running. Kara followed. The TV was running by the time she reached the den.

"You see, you put the thing in here and the movie comes on the TV. I was watching *Neverending Story* before lunch. See? It's still on. It's really good."

Kara watched a boy sitting atop a seemingly endless snake with a dog's head as it wound through outer space.

"And I saw *Flight of the Navigator* and *Pinocchio*— that was scary—*Old Yeller*—that made me cry. And Aunt Ellen's going to get me a new Disney movie every day! It's so great! Can we get one, Mom?"

"We'll think about it."

Kara vowed that when she finished her book she'd blow part of the final advance payment on a VCR. God, she had to get to work on it. But she couldn't think, couldn't organize her thoughts. Lately everything in her head seemed jumbled. She needed to get back to Pennsylvania, and soon.

But for now, the VCR was a blessing. With no school and no friends, Jill would have been bored stiff without it.

"When the movie's finished, we'll take a walk to a museum. How does that sound?"

"The one with the funny name?"

"Not the Guggenheim. Today it will be the Museum of Modern Art. But you can call it what you used to call me: MOMA."

Jill smiled and together they watched the end of her movie.

▼

9:30 P.M.

Kara headed back to Kelly's apartment early. She was tired. On the way she went over the morning's session with Dr. Gates. He had been his usual remote self, sitting behind his desk, twirling his key chain and contributing little more than a few noncommittal grunts while she free associated about her childhood. The whole thing seemed like an exercise in futility. But no doubt everyone thought that at first.

Patience, Kara, she told herself. *Patience.*

But she knew patience had never been her strong suit. She tended to want results yesterday, if not sooner.

She thought she had seen a slight reaction in Dr. Gates when she told him of her tentative plans to move the therapy to Philadelphia if things continued as smoothly as they had since Monday. It hadn't been much of a reaction. The slightest lifting of the eyebrows, the slightest down-turning of the mouth. Nothing more. Perhaps it had been her imagination. Perhaps she had simply wanted to see him react.

Two more nights, she told herself as she slipped the key into the vestibule's inner door.

She had promised herself that if the next two nights proved uneventful, she would abandon Kelly's apartment and begin sleeping at Ellen's. That would be easier for herself, and especially better for Jill.

As she turned the key, she glanced at the row of mailboxes to her right. She noticed the envelopes through the window of the 2C/K. *Wade* box.

Probably bills.

Which reminded her of Ed Bannion's offer to help her become administrator of Kelly's estate. It was sounding better all the time. Good to know that a seed of kindness you had planted while alive could reap benefits after you were dead. Even in New York.

Kara wondered where the mailbox key was. Probably on Kelly's key ring which was still in the personal effects—evidence bag at the Midtown North precinct house.

As she entered the apartment she realized that she no longer felt like some sort of graverobber whenever she walked through the door. She was getting used to it. She was almost comfortable here.

She hid the apartment key in the same place as the other night—in the rear of the oven—and then made a quick search for the mailbox key. No luck. She'd ask the super for a duplicate in the morning.

As she toweled herself off after her shower, she realized that she hadn't heard from Rob all day, which was a bit strange. But he had said he was loaded down with work.

She sat on the edge of the bed and debated taking the Halcion tonight. What if she didn't really need it.

Don't be a jerk. Take it as directed. Kelly didn't and look what happened to her.

Kara swallowed one and turned out the light.

▼

11:44 P.M.

Ed Bannion stood in the lobby of the Waldorf shaking hands with the very tanned Murray Weiss and Jay Delano, accepting their thanks for a wonderful dinner and wishing them in turn a safe flight back to the coast in the morning. Weiss and Delano were producing a feature that was to be shot entirely on location in Manhattan and this had been one of many trips to firm up budgets and leases and contracts and permits and the myriad legal documents necessary for a location shoot.

They were turning in early tonight—they had an early flight out of JFK tomorrow.

The three of them had started off first thing this morning and crunched numbers all day long. After that it was drinks and a long leisurely dinner at Le Cirque with three wines and after-dinner cordials. Ed was feeling loggy. They seemed fine.

Different metabolism. Or because they were still on L.A. time. That had to be it.

As Weiss and Delano headed for the elevators, Ed glanced past them and caught sight of a familiar blond haircut just entering an elevator; it belonged to a slim, shapely woman in a leather mini. She was on the arm of a swarthy man wearing a business suit and a turban. Ed froze for a moment. She looked just like Kelly Wade—no, *Kara* Wade!

And then the elevator doors closed.

Ed shook his head to clear it. He felt dizzy, frightened. It was like seeing a ghost. Too many after-dinner snifters of Irish Mist. That was it. The liquor was affecting his vision.

He turned and hurried outside for a cab.

Thursday

FEBRUARY 19
11:40 A.M.

KARA MADE IT BACK TO KELLY'S APARTMENT BEFORE ED showed up.

Another good morning, right from the start: bright sunshine, the apartment key just where she had left it, and no writing on walls or mirrors. She'd had breakfast with Jill, tutored her in math and reading, and had a nice long talk with Ellen.

She had vague memories of another sex dream. Only tiny, tantalizing fragments remained ... a Hindu ... all sorts of weird positions ...

She wondered if it was the Halcion.

And once again she was left with the vague impression that Dr. Gates had been there. Not visible, not a participant in the dream, but *there*.

She guessed that wasn't so unusual. Dreams were supposed to be subconscious rehashing of the day's events. She'd had a session with Dr. Gates yesterday, and he was playing an important role in her life right now, so it wasn't surprising he'd be a presence in her dreams.

But where had the Hindu come in?

As she passed the mailboxes in the vestibule, she noticed that Kelly's seemed even fuller than last night. She'd asked the super about a key earlier this morning and he said he'd get her a replacement—for five dollars. Fine. She'd paid him.

Back in the apartment now, she found that a small envelope had been slipped under the door. It was the new mailbox key.

At that moment the buzzer from the vestibule rang. It was Ed. Instead of buzzing him in, she went down to meet him. She had to get the mail anyway.

Ed was looking dapper in a Burberry coat and a cashmere scarf. His brown hair was slightly windblown but otherwise he looked perfectly put together. He carried a slim briefcase that appeared to be polished cordovan leather.

"You're looking great!" he said with a smile as she opened the vestibule door.

"A bit of an exaggeration," she said, "but thanks anyway."

She felt shabby in her jeans and sweater, but she hadn't taken much time to pack on Monday morning. Her mind hadn't been on her wardrobe.

Ed held the door for her while she opened Kelly's mailbox and pulled out a stack of envelopes.

"Bills?" Ed said as they headed for the stairs.

Kara took a quick look at the return addresses.

"That's the way it looks."

"Then I'm just in time. Legalman to the rescue."

Kara gave him a smile. He was trying very hard to be nice.

In the apartment he set his briefcase on the floor and said, "Want to have lunch first and then get to the paperwork?"

"Why don't we—"

Kara stopped when she spotted Dr. Gates' return address on one of the envelopes. She pulled it out and stared at it.

"What's the matter?" Ed said.

"This envelope . . ."

Dr. Gates' name was on the return address sticker in the upper left corner, a West 21st Street address. Probably his home. But the rest was strange. It was a Consolidated Edison payment return envelope, but the Con Ed address had been heavily scratched out with pencil and the address of Kelly's apartment written below it. But even stranger was the new addressee.

" . . . it's addressed to me."

It wasn't sealed. The flap had been torn open and then tucked back inside. Within was an electric bill, folded around a check. Kara was baffled.

"What on earth—?"

"There's writing on the back," Ed said, pointing to the reverse of the bill.

Kara turned it over and stared at the hasty scrawl. She felt her throat constricting as she read.

> *Kara Wade—*
> *Get away from Dr. Gates, as far away*
> *as you can. He takes over your body*
> *while you sleep and uses it for his own*
> *pleasures. You cannot fight him. Run*
> *far away or you will end up like your*
> *sister. RUN!!!!*

Kara felt as if the temperature in the apartment had plummeted forty degrees. Gooseflesh broke out along her arms. She shook her head in wonder.

"This is the craziest thing I've ever seen."

And it was precisely because it was so very crazy that it bothered her so. Some nut knew her name and address, and knew she was one of Dr. Gates' patients. Great. This was just what she needed.

But worse than that—the words struck a responsive chord within her—as if she had half suspected the same thing. She shivered.

Ed reached for it. "May I?"

His brow furrowed as he read it. He looked up at her, questioningly.

"What's this all about?"

"Dr. Gates was Kelly's psychiatrist. I've had a few sessions with him myself, lately. I haven't the faintest idea who this is from, but I'd assume it's one of his patients."

"Yeah. But why write on the back of an electric bill?"

"I don't know, but I'm going to find out."

"The police?"

"Right. This mentions Kelly."

With a trembling finger, she dialed Rob's number at Midtown North. While the phone was ringing, she looked at Ed and noticed that he seemed strangely tense all of a sudden.

▼

Ed thrust his suddenly sweaty palms into his coat pockets.

The police! Couldn't he ever come here without the police getting involved?

He went to the table and picked up the electric bill again.

And this! Were these twins a magnet for madness? *He takes over your body and uses it for his own pleasures.* What kind of craziness was that?

Kara spoke a few words into the phone and then hung up.

"Rob's not in, but I left a message for him to call when he gets back."

Thank God for small favors.

He wanted to change the subject.

"Speaking of craziness," he said, "I was in the Waldorf late last night and I saw someone who looked exactly like you. Was it you?"

"Afraid not. I went to bed early."

"Yeah. I didn't think it was you. Didn't dress like you. Had this red leather miniskirt on, black stockings."

She stared at him. "What was I . . . I mean *she*, doing?"

"She was getting into an elevator with some towelhead."

"Towel-head?"

"Yeah. You know, a guy with a turban. Some sort of Indian or Hindu character."

He smiled at her but she didn't smile back. Instead, the color slowly drained from her face.

"What's wrong, Kara?"

She didn't answer. Instead she ran into the bedroom. Ed followed at a discreet distance and stood in the doorway. He watched in amazement as Kara darted about the room like a madwoman, turning over the two night stands one after the other and searching the spaces beneath. Next she went to the big dresser and pulled out the bottom drawer. Her anguished cry drew him into the room.

"Are you okay?"

She was down on her knees before the dresser. She had something red clutched against her chest. She looked up at him with a look that Ed instantly recognized—the same helpless, tortured look that he'd seen on her sister's face before she went through the window at the Plaza.

"Sweet Jesus!" he said. "What's wrong?"

With tears glistening in her eyes, she held up something red, something leather. He didn't know what it was. Just then the phone rang. She dropped the red leather thing and ran into the front room. He could hear her on the phone, talking to "Rob," asking him to get over here as soon as he could.

It took him a moment but he finally recognized the red leather thing lying at his feet. It was a miniskirt.

▼

Rob stared at the note scrawled on the back of the Con Ed bill. It was rank insanity. His skin crawled at the thought of what kind of mind had dreamed this up—and then addressed it to Kara.

"This is scary stuff."

"You're telling me!"

Kara looked spooked. Her eyes had a haunted, hunted look as she sat at the table and twisted her hands together. Ed the Lawyer had scooted off as soon as Rob had showed, all but falling over himself in his hurry to get out the door, leaving behind some papers for Kara to sign, saying he'd pick them up some other time.

Something about that guy . . .

"But that's not the worst of it!" Kara said. She held up a leather miniskirt, a pair of black panty house, and a black ruffled blouse. "Look at this!"

After Ed had left, she had told Rob about her dream, and what Ed had said about spotting her last night with somebody wearing a turban.

"Maybe you missed it when you cleaned things out the other night," Rob said, not believing it himself. Oh no, not after his Tuesday night with Kara. How could he?

"I didn't miss it, Rob. I threw out every sleazy thing

I found. This was *not* under the dresser when I turned in Monday night!"

He could see she was getting more upset.

"Okay, okay. Take it easy. I was just trying to offer an alternative explanation."

Her expression was bleak. "Rob, what's happening to me?"

"I don't know. And I don't know how to help you. But I'll do anything I can. You know that." He tapped his finger on the Con Ed bill. "I do know I can do something about this, though."

"What?"

"Show it to the guy whose return address is on the envelope."

With Kara along, Rob drove back to the precinct house. Handling them by the edges, he xeroxed the check, the front of the envelope, and both sides of the bill. Then he sealed each of the three in clear plastic evidence envelopes.

"I'll get them dusted for prints as soon as possible. That'll be a futile exercise with the envelope, what with all the people who've handled it legitimately since it was mailed, but the bill may yield something useful."

Kara only nodded. Her mind seemed elsewhere.

"I want your prints, too."

"Why?"

"To eliminate them. You handled the letter. Even if we don't get a single print off it, that note will still be useful in keeping your sister's case open."

"Really?" Some interest began to show in her eyes. Good.

"Sure. The part about how you'll 'end up like your sister' can be construed as a threat to you, plus it implies foul play in Kelly's death."

"Do you think it's a threat?"

"No. I think it's meant as a warning. There's a

screwed up mind out there that knows something about Kelly's death—or things it knows something—and has sent you a warning. I don't think he means you any harm."

" 'He'? How do you know it's a he?"

Rob handed her the xerox of the note.

"Doesn't that look like a man's handwriting?"

She nodded. "I guess so."

He snapped his fingers. "I ought to submit this for handwriting analysis. That could be real interesting. But for the moment, we're going to see how the esteemed Dr. Gates reacts to this."

Kara was watching him closely.

"You're really looking forward to that, aren't you?"

Rob grinned, unable to suppress the gleeful anticipation rising through him.

"Are you kidding?" he said. "I can hardly wait."

▼

1:57 P.M.

"Ask the doctor to squeeze us in between appointments," Rob told the receptionist.

Her tone was dubious. "I'll see what I can do."

Rob gave her his best and strongest tough cop stare.

"Do. It's a police matter. Very important."

They sat in the waiting room with one other person, an attractive woman of about twenty-five. Rob watched her read a magazine and nibble steadily at her already well-chewed fingernails. When the current appointment exited the consultation room, Rob nudged Kara and rose to his feet. He headed for the inner room door without waiting for the receptionist's okay.

"Just a minute, sir—" she began.

Rob ignored her. He didn't want to give Gates time to set himself up. He wanted to catch him off guard and keep him that way. Maybe the doctor would let something slip.

"Dr. Gates," he said, marching up to the desk and looking down at him, "we have a new development in the Kelly Wade case. I need to question you about it."

"I resent this intrusion, Detective Harris," he said, appearing properly indignant. "Certainly this could have waited until after hours."

"No, sir, it couldn't." He pulled the xeroxes from his pocket and unfolded them. He glanced at Kara standing uncertainly behind him. "Ms. Wade received this today. I need your input on it immediately."

Rob handed the sheets to Gates and then seated himself in the chair closest to the desk where he could get a better angle on the doctor's face. He wanted to watch his expression as he read.

Rob had arranged the sheets in a specific order. First the envelope face, then the check, then the front of the electric bill, then the reverse side.

Gates' brow furrowed as he looked at the first page. It remained furrowed until he reached the fourth. Then his eyebrows shot up and he started as if someone had goosed him.

"This is incredible!" he said glancing quickly at Rob and then back down.

He glanced once at the first sheet, then went back to the fourth, shaking his head. Rob saw anger and outrage in Gates' expression, which he had expected, but he saw something else that surprised him: a sort of grudging admiration. There was even an instant when Rob could have sworn that a rueful smile had flitted across the doctor's face.

Finally he put the papers down and leaned back in his chair.

"Well!" he said. "This is quite interesting!"

"Interesting?" Kara said. "Is that what you call it?"

Rob had been concentrating so on Gates that he had forgotten about Kara. She was still standing behind him.

"Yes. Although I suppose it was quite frightening for you."

"You might say that."

Kara settled into the other chair before the desk.

"Have any idea who it is?" Rob said.

"I know exactly who she is."

"She?"

"Yes. A paranoid schizophrenic. Delusions of being controlled by another are quite common among individuals with that diagnosis."

"But this patient doesn't say anything about herself being controlled by you. She wrote to Kara, and she mentions Kelly."

"Yes. But she believes I control her, as well. It's not uncommon for the paranoid schiz to see their therapist as a powerful individual with mystical powers to control people, especially themselves. After all, the purpose of my interaction with them is to help them change their behavior through therapy and medication. It's not a big step to interpret that as robbing them of control of their lives. That way they can blame me for their bizarre behavior. It's quite common, really."

It sounded plausible to Rob, but it wasn't getting him where he wanted to go.

"What's her name?" Rob asked.

"You have *chutzpah*, Detective Harris," Gates said with a condescending smile. "I will give you that."

"Does that mean you refuse to identify her?"

"It does. You knew I would before you asked."

"I can get the courts involved in this."

"And I can suffer a memory lapse."

An impasse.

"I will find her, Dr. Gates. I know she must have regular access to you."

"Why do you say that?"

"She knows about Kelly, she has Kara's address, and she used your personal mail to send her message."

He smiled that irritating smile again.

"In that case, detective, I suggest you put my receptionist at the top of your list."

"She already is."

They stared at each other until Kara broke in.

"May I change the subject for just a moment?"

▼

Kara knew they didn't have much time and there was something she simply had to ask Dr. Gates.

"Someone said they saw me in the Waldorf late last night."

Dr. Gates offered her a bland expression.

"And?"

"I didn't go there—at least as far as I remember."

"Did this person say it was you, or someone who merely looked like you?"

"Looked just like me and wearing a red leather miniskirt. This afternoon I found a red leather miniskirt hidden where Kelly—or Ingrid—used to hide her sleazy outfits."

"You told me you have been hiding the apartment key every night. This morning—was it still in the place where you had hidden it last night?"

"Exactly."

Dr. Gates leaned back and began twirling his key ring.

"Let us consider this logically, Miss Wade. If there is only one key to the apartment and it hadn't been used, then you could not have been in the Waldorf last night. It was someone who *looked* like you."

"What about the miniskirt?"

"Was it the same style as the ones you say Ingrid had hidden?"

"Exactly. Same brand and everything."

"Doesn't it seem rather unlikely that your other personality, Janine, would have exactly the same taste in what you term 'sleazy' clothing?" he leaned forward and stared at her. "Do you see where this is leading?"

Obviously he wanted her to draw her own conclusion, and when she looked at it in this light, there was only one.

"Well, it's possible the skirt got jammed up under the drawer when I cleaned out the space beneath it Monday night, but it doesn't seem likely."

"Does any other explanation fit the facts as we know them?"

"No."

"Then we are left with an unfortunate coincidence and nothing more. Please do not allow yourself to be upset by something like this."

Easy for you to say, she thought, yet she did feel some of the tension ease out of her. Not much, though.

"What if Janine knows where I hide the key?"

"Multiple personalities have no interaction. When one is in command, the others are experiencing a 'black-out,' just as you experienced over the weekend when Janine took control. I assure you, she does *not* know where you hide the key."

Kara wasn't completely convinced, but she had to admit she felt better. Maybe she hadn't been at the Waldorf last night after all.

Dr. Gates rose to his feet.

"And now if the two of you will please take your leave, I can continue with my scheduled appointments.

And as for this—" He held up the xeroxed sheets. "She will not bother you again."

"How can you be so sure of that?" Rob asked.

Dr. Gates' smile was almost sharklike.

"Because I am going to have a long talk with her."

▼

"He's lying," Rob said as soon as they got on the elevator.

Kara felt a sudden stab of fear.

"About what? About me at the Waldorf?"

"No-no," he said quickly. "Not that. About the note you got. That's not a woman's handwriting."

"I didn't know you were an expert."

"I'm not. But I know someone who is."

When they got to the lobby of the medical arts building, Rob thumbed through a small address book and then made a call. As she watched him talk on the phone, she realized that there were two sides to Rob Harris. There was the young man she had known ten years ago—the gentle lover, the awful amateur chef, who still existed. Then there was the other side—the cop. She had seen that side today at the precinct house, a man who knew his job, who had confidence in his abilities, who had the respect of his colleagues. She'd met his partner, Augie, she'd watched him banter with the others and talk shop with them. He was more than comfortable in the detective squad room—he *belonged* there.

She knew with a pang that there was no hope of his ever leaving there willingly.

"Okay," he said, turning away from the phone. "Professor Jensen will see us now. He's a handwriting expert the Department uses from time to time. A Philosophy prof at

NYU. Pretty weird duck, but handwriting's his hobby, and he's damned good at it."

New York University's Washington Square campus wasn't far from Dr. Gates' office. Rob drove her past the huge stone arch that marked the square. The lower seven or eight feet of its two supports were darkened with overlapping scrawls of graffiti. It made her think of a giant with dirty feet. Parking was no problem with Rob's Vehicle Identification card. He led her into a modern looking glass and brick building filled with students hanging around between classes. Black seemed to be the 'in' color—clothing, eye make-up, fingernail polish, even hair when it wasn't green or orange. Most of the kids seemed to have invested a lot of time and effort into distorting whatever natural attractiveness they might have possessed.

Professor Jensen's office was on the fifth floor. Younger than Kara had expected, he was maybe forty, very thin, balding in front with long dark hair trailing over the collar of his shirt.

"Ah, yes," he said when Rob walked through the door. "Detective Harris. I remember you now. What have you got for me?"

Kara noticed how he was rubbing his hands together in anticipation. He was really into this handwriting thing.

"Nothing too detailed. Just want to know if the author of this is male or female."

"Ah! A debatable determination. Some authorities say you can't tell."

"No?"

"But I can. Not a hundred percent, of course, but I've got an excellent record. Let's have a look, shall we?"

Rob handed him the xeroxes. Professor Jensen took them to his cluttered desk.

"You don't have the originals?"

"Back at the precinct house. If you need them, I'll get them."

"These should suffice for the moment."

He pulled a magnifying glass from the top drawer, then bent over the sheets.

"The writer is male, I'd say. Little doubt about it."

Rob nudged Kara with his elbow and gave her a self-satisfied I-told-you-so look.

Professor Jensen was staring at the xerox of the envelope.

"Deucedly strange way of sending a letter, wouldn't you say?"

Kara was trying to remember when she had last heard someone say 'deucedly' when Rob reached over and picked out the xerox of the check.

"Any chance they were written by the same guy?"

Jensen brought the magnifying glass into play again. Bewildered, Kara turned to Rob. He held a finger to his lips. *Trust me.*

"Hard to say," Jensen said. "If I had a longer sample of the second hand . . ."

Suddenly Kara remembered something and fumbled in her shoulder bag, praying she hadn't lost it. Here it was.

"Will this do? It's a prescription."

Jensen took it and laid it out on the desk in line with the check, the note, and the envelope face. He leaned back, then hovered close, finally he crossed his arms in front of his chest and simply stared.

"Odd," he said, and stared some more. "My immediate impulse is to say that these are two different people. The downstrokes and loops are similar but not completely. And yet . . . there's a common factor here, a unifying influence. I can't tell you in concrete terms, but after you've analyzed enough handwriting, you get a subliminal feel for the *gestalt* of a sample. These two *feel* similar to me, and yet they're not."

Rob said, "Could the man who wrote the check and the prescription have been trying to disguise his handwriting when he wrote the note and addressed the envelope?"

"Possibly. But I get a feeling that it might have been the other way around."

"What do you mean?"

"Perhaps the author of the note was trying to imitate the handwriting of the man who wrote the check."

▼

Kara slumped in the passenger seat of Rob's car as it idled at the curb. Professor's Jenkins' analysis had shaken her to the core.

"Do you think Dr. Gates could have sent me that message? Why would he do such a thing?"

"I don't know. Mind if I smoke?"

"Yes. And if he didn't, why would he lie about whoever did? Why would he say it was a female when it was a male."

"That might have been just to protect his patient. We both know what a fanatic he is about confidentiality."

"Do you think Dr. Gates is as tightly wrapped as he should be?"

Rob looked at her and shrugged.

"I don't like the guy, but that's a gut thing. The people I talk to who should know give him high marks, especially when it comes to multiple personalities."

"What if he's a multiple personality himself? What if his other self wrote me that note to warn me away from him?"

Rob's eyes widened and his voice became hushed.

"What if it was his Evil Twin?"

"Not funny, Rob. I'm serious."

"Sorry. It seems jut a little too far out."

But an idea that was even farther out kept nagging at Kara's mind. It was so ridiculous and outrageous that she didn't want to mention it, but it was there and it was going to keep on nibbling away at her until she brought it out.

"Try this for far out: What if Dr. Gates *can* take over your body while you sleep?"

"And use it for his 'personal pleasures'?" Rob said with a slow smile. "Kara . . ."

"I know how it must sound to you, but it's different on my end. You're not living under the threat of someone named Janine taking over your body and doing what she wants with it. When you've lost the absolute control you always assumed you had, crazy things start to sound plausible."

"I need a cigarette," Rob said.

He got out of the car and walked around the front to Kara's side where he squatted against the pole of the No Parking sign. As he lit up, he motioned Kara to roll her window down.

"Those things will kill you," she said.

"You make me nervous when you talk like that."

"Just consider it. What if that note I got isn't completely out of left field? What if Dr. Gates entered my mind when he hypnotized me and he's been taking over whenever he wished? What if he was doing the same thing to Kelly? What if that warning is from one of his past victims?" She forced a laugh that came out sounding strangled. "What if I'm completely bonkers for even mentioning this?"

Rob was staring at her.

"Please don't laugh like that again," he said. "It's scary."

"My *life* has become scary, Rob. Does all that I said

sound as crazy and impossible to you as it should to me? Tell me it's absolutely impossible."

"It's absolutely impossible."

"Good. Then I'll sleep easier tonight." She coughed. "Can I roll the window up now? You're getting smoke in the car."

Rob took a final drag and flipped the cigarette away.

"Where do you want to go?" he said as he got behind the wheel.

"Ellen's, if you don't mind."

"What about tonight? You staying alone at Kelly's again?"

"Definitely."

Kara loathed the idea of spending another night alone in that apartment, but until she was sure . . .

"I'd offer to keep you company," Rob said, "but tonight's my turn to do a shift on a stakeout we're running on a murder suspect's apartment. But I'll come over first thing in the morning and see how you are."

Kara watched his eyes as he spoke. Something wrong there. Was he avoiding her for some reason? Or was she getting as paranoid as the person who'd written her that note?

Suddenly she felt very alone.

▼

10:32 P.M.

Ed had been calling Kara's apartment—actually, it was Kelly's apartment—every fifteen minutes since 6:30. It wasn't all that much trouble. He had no plans for the night and his phone had a last number auto redial function, so all he had to do was press one of the extra buttons and the phone did the rest.

Ostensibly, his purpose would be to go over some of the legal documents he'd left with her this afternoon, but really all he wanted was to hear the sound of her voice, to make sure she was all right.

Why is this so important to me?

Ed wasn't sure he could answer that. All he knew was that since she'd opened that weird note in front of him today, and since he'd seen that lost, lonely, helpless, frightened look on her face when she found that miniskirt under the dresser, he'd been feeling more protective toward her with every passing hour.

Somehow she had become his responsibility. Madness, he knew, but that was the way he felt. She needed someone to watch over her or she might, as that note had said, end up like her sister.

On the sixteenth try, she picked up.

He talked her a little small talk and could sense the tension in her. Poor kid. She was really spooked.

"Is your detective friend coming over?"

"No. He's on a stakeout."

Damn! Ed had stayed away for fear of running into that cop again, and the guy was somewhere else for the night. Too bad. It was a little too late now to be popping over there.

He talked her through the forms and had her sign and initial where she was supposed to. When it was all finished, he thought he'd give getting a late date with her the old college try.

"There. That wasn't so hard. I'll have a messenger come by for them in the morning. Or better yet, why don't we get together for a drink tonight and you can give them to me then."

"Thanks, Ed, but I'm bushed," she said, and really sounded it. "This has not been a good day and I'd like to see it over and done with."

"That note, huh?"

"Right. That note—and the handwriting analysis of it."

"Really?" This was starting to get exciting. "What did it show?"

"Nothing conclusive, but it raised some frightening possibilities."

"Like what?"

She told him about how her psychiatrist had said he knew who had sent it and that it was a woman, but that a handwriting expert had said otherwise, and had not been able to entirely rule out the possibility that Dr. Gates might have written it himself.

Ed was almost dizzy when he wished her a good night and hung up. He sat in his living room, staring out at the glittering skyline.

A lot of strange shit going on in poor Kara Wade's life. And it kept on getting stranger and stranger.

And who was helping her? That cop Harris, who was supposed to be her friend, just seemed to be adding to her worries. He should have been shielding her from the disturbing news about the handwriting. She had enough to worry about.

And her psychiatrist, this Dr. Gates. Some help he was. If he was lying to her about whoever wrote that note, what else was he lying about? She was probably paying him an arm and a leg for help and he was doing nothing for her. That would be bad enough, but was he doing something *to* her?

The thought brought Ed to his feet. Where had *that* idea come from? He began pacing the living room.

Kelly and Kara. Both patients of this Dr. Gates. Both with that same heart-rending look—Kelly a couple of weeks ago, Kara today. Something going on here. Something definitely not kosher.

Hell, he thought with a grin, *neither am I.*

He grabbed the phone book and found only one psychiatrist named Gates. His office was on Seventh Avenue. Without giving himself time to reconsider, Ed memorized the address, grabbed a coat, and headed for the street.

Outside, he flagged a cab. Traffic was light. Less than ten minutes later he was standing in front of a smallish office building near the Chelsea-Greewich Village border. There were lights over the front entry, lights on in the lobby, but no guard. Without thinking, he tried the doors. All locked.

What the hell am I doing here?

He backed off about twenty feet and paced back and forth as he stared at the front doors. He'd tried speed a few times in college, and he felt now like he had then—hyper, fidgety, wired, can't-sit-down, can't-stand-still, ready to do or try anything no matter how crazy as long as it involved movement.

What he wanted to do now was crazy. He wanted to get into this Dr. Gates' office and go through his records and see what they had to say about the Wade twins and what kind of plans he had for Kara. Maybe there'd be a clue there that would incriminate Gates. Maybe he was the guy responsible for the haunted look on Kelly's face before she died, and on Kara's face today. Kara had mentioned both Kelly and she being hypnotized by Gates. Maybe he had planted some bizarre posthypnotic suggestions in both their minds.

He heard footsteps and saw some dapper gent with sandy hair and a mustache wearing a blue cashmere overcoat walk up to one of the front doors. He used a key from the ring he was twirling on his finger to unlock it, and then walked inside.

A key. That's all it took. No guard inside. Just a key and you were in.

An even crazier idea was forming in Ed's mind. He pushed it away. It was insane. But the more he fought it, the more powerful and insistent it became. The excitement of it grew, tingling through his limbs, until it consumed him.

I'm going to break into Dr. Gates' office!

Yes! He'd do it! Jesus, yes, he'd do it tomorrow night! If he gave himself longer to think, he'd talk himself out of it.

The idiocy of it made him giddy. He laughed out loud as he went off in search of a cab back home.

▼

Rob hadn't really lied to Kara this afternoon. He was on a stakeout, but it wasn't a murderer's house he'd been watching. It was Dr. Lawrence Gates' Chelsea townhouse.

He'd followed Gates from his office to his home around dinner time—a walk of about seven blocks—and had watched the three stories of lighted windows until about midnight. That was when Gates had stepped out of his front door and begun walking west. Rob nurtured a twinge of excitement as he followed him in his car, expecting him to flag a cab on Seventh. Maybe this wouldn't be a waste of time after all. Maybe he'd learn something about the secret life of Lazlo Gati/Lawrence Gates, M.D.

But Gates simply walked downtown and returned to his office.

At midnight?

What doctor returned to an empty office at this hour?

Rob parked near the corner and watched, thinking maybe a patient would show up for an emergency consultation. He saw a figure standing in the shadows on the downtown side of the Kramer building. Whoever he was, he gave out a high pitched laugh and walked away.

A nut. Maybe one of Dr. Gates' nuts.

Rob kept watching, but no one showed up.

He settled back in the seat. He had a feeling this could turn out to be a long night.

▼

Kara sat on the edge of the bed, trembling. She was exhausted, and she had taken the Halcion a few minutes ago, but she didn't see how she was ever going to get to sleep tonight. Not after all that had happened today.

She had thrown the leather mini away. And she had combed the undersides of the night stands and pulled the dresser apart. There were *no* other items of sleazy clothing left. If she found something tomorrow, she feared she'd have a breakdown.

But strangely enough, the discovery of the skirt today wasn't what was bothering her the most now. It was that note. That crazy, bizarre, frightening note.

He takes over your body while you sleep and uses it for his own pleasures.

She found it especially disquieting in light of the vague memory of Dr. Gates' presence in the erotic dreams she had experienced the past two nights.

What am I thinking?

She had to stop worrying about impossibilities and deal with the real and plausible. Kelly's multiple personality had been real and plausible in light of what Dr. Gates said and what Kara had found hidden around the apartment. A multiple personality disorder would easily explain the happenings at the farm over the weekend. Multiple personalities were an established psychiatric fact; books had been written about them.

Despite all that documentation, Kara still could not accept the existence of a second personality within her. So if she couldn't accept Janine, why was she even considering a psychotic's fantasy about Dr. Gates controlling her body while she slept?

She turned out the light and pulled up the covers. She had to learn to trust. Trust Dr. Gates and his ability to help her straighten this out. You had to trust your therapist.

She smiled in the darkness. Taking over someone else's body while they slept. Now *that* was crazy.

FEBRUARY 20
12:30 A.M.

ON YOUR FOURTH BRUSH PAST KARA WADE'S MIND, YOU find her deep enough in NREM sleep to permit undetected entry.

At last.

You've been waiting over an hour now, and you are impatient. You slip in quickly and immediately suppress her consciousness. When you're satisfied that she is locked down in stage 3 sleep, you relax and let yourself flow through her nervous system, taking control of her motor cortex, tapping the inputs of her sensory system.

You become aware: of the soft flannel touch of her nightgown against her skin; of the pillow against the back of her head; of the slight burning in her stomach, hyperacidic from the stresses of the day; of the dry, slightly sour taste in her mouth; of the susurrant flow of air through her lips and nose as it fills her lungs; of the sounds of the still active city as they filter into the darkened bedroom.

And now, once again, she is yours.

You've *become* Kara Wade.

Her skin, her muscles, her bones, her breasts and

genitalia, her five senses, all yours to do with as you wish.

And you wish to get out of this bed.

You throw back the covers and turn on the light. Then you pull the flannel nightgown over your head and step before the full length mirror on the closet door to look again.

What a wonderful body.

You never tire of looking at Kara Wade's body, of *wearing* Kara Wade's body. You run your hands over her breasts—*your* breasts now—and feel a delicious tingle as the nipples rise under your gentle caress. Kelly's breasts were slightly higher, slightly firmer, the nipples pinker, but Kelly was a nullip. Kara has borne a child and that causes certain inevitable changes.

You loved Kelly's body and were shattered when you lost it. You had such good times with it—something about her attracted men like flies. Hardly a one refused your advances when you were wearing Kelly. That was why you were determined to have Kara from the moment you saw her standing in the doorway to your consultation room. You knew it would be just like having your dear sweet Kelly back. And it is. Only better. Much better.

You take a deep breath, thrusting the breasts outward and drawing in the abdomen. A beautiful shape. Enough body fat to give her that feminine roundness, but not an inch of flab. And that natural blonde thatch between her legs—superb.

You flex the muscles in the arms and legs and buttocks, feeling their high tone, their excellent conditioning. Kara takes superb care of her body, much better than Kelly ever did. This is a body that can go the distance, that will never tire. You wish you could stay with it permanently.

And to think she was almost warned away. You very

nearly cried out when you saw the note. The audacity of it. Meddling in your affairs. Punishment was swift and severe—and continues even now. Yesterday's note was the first—and last.

But you mustn't distract yourself with these matters now. Your time in Kara's body is limited—after all, you have to allow her *some* rest—and you wish to make the most of it. You pull on jeans and a sweater, not bothering with underwear, then open the closet. Inside, you drop to your knees and pull out a loose section of molding along the floor. From inside you pluck a pair of keys and a wad of bills, mostly hundreds. You peel off the smaller bills and five hundreds, and return the rest to the cubby hole.

So convenient to be able to use the same old hiding place for the keys and money, but Kara ruined your hiding places here for the kinds of clothes you prefer to wear on your evening jaunts. You'll have to find a new place. There's always the house in Chelsea. You could keep the clothes there, but that would run the risk of being seen going in and out night after night. You don't want any link between Kara and her therapist outside the office.

A locker. That's it. You'll find a locker somewhere to store the clothes, somewhere between the apartment and the hotel district. And you can change in the hotel room you'll be renting for the night. That will work.

Or why not simply throw the clothing away each night after you use her? You certainly don't have to worry about economizing.

You'll decide later. Right now you have to get down to that all night boutique in SoHo that carries the things you like, and then you'll have to find a hotel.

You unlock the apartment door with your key. The other is for the Chelsea House because every so often you have to visit home with the borrowed body, usually to pick up a fresh supply of cash. You peek down the hall. Empty. Good. You don't want to be seen by any of the neighbors.

You smile with Kara's lips. You don't have to worry about that meddlesome detective lover of Kara's spotting you as you leave, either. You caught him following you in his car tonight during the walk from your house to the office. Let him sit outside the office all night if he wishes. He'll learn nothing.

That detective—he's the only fly in this otherwise perfect ointment. He could ruin everything if Kara becomes too involved with him. Should that come to pass, you'll have to think of a way to scare him off. That might be fun. You could have terrorized the fellow on Tuesday night, but instead you settled for a quick fuck—and not a bad one, actually—and then left Kara to sleep away the rest of the night. The detective wasn't bad in bed, but night after night the same lover would bore you. No variety there.

And, cliche though it might be, variety is indeed the spice of life.

Twirling the key ring on your finger, you hurry down the hall to the stairs and try to decide on which of the big hotels to use tonight. You've always been fond of the Waldorf with its international clientele. That Hindu fellow last night had practically memorized the *Kama Sutra*. Between his agile tongue and rock hard penis, he bought you and Kara's body to orgasm five times! He was worth three ordinary fellows. Too bad he left for India this morning. A repeat performance would be something to look forward to.

But no. Even if the Hindu was available tonight you would find someone else. That is your new rule. Never twice with the same man. Never a New Yorker or a New Jersey or Connecticut native. The further away the home, the better. One night stands, only.

Of course, that increases the risk of VD or even AIDS, but that is a risk you'll have to take. Not that you're at risk for contracting the disease yourself, but something like AIDS will wreck a beautiful body like Kara's, and then you'll be forced to go out and find a new one.

Kara isn't the only body you have available to you, but it's certainly the best. You'll still use the others now and then to maintain contact and to give Kara a rest. But Kara is going to be your new Number One, slipping perfectly into the slot vacated by her sister. Too bad Kelly is dead. It would have been nice to alternate between them. Too bad you can only control one body at a time. Putting Kelly and Kara in bed together is a magnificent fantasy.

The thought of the late great Kelly brings to mind something you've been meaning to do. You'll have to get over to Wheatley's office and change your will again.

Out on the street you have no trouble finding a cab. Three of them practically have a fight trying to pick you up when Kara stands on the corner and raises her hand.

You love being beautiful.

You give the lucky driver of the first cab an address on Greene Street and settle back in the seat, savoring the sensations bubbling through you. Even after all these years, it's still a thrill to switch bodies, especially to a newer one. Still a thrill to sway it through a hotel lobby or bar and draw hungry stares from all the men— all the straight ones—and even a few women. You won't balk at matching Kara up with another woman if the opportunity presents itself, but it's more difficult to arrange. Men are so much easier to acquire, even in pairs.

You prefer to wear a woman. Their bodies are so

much more versatile, and they are capable of so much more pleasure than a male. In your vast experience playing either sex you've concluded that there is really no comparison. A woman's body is a vastly superior sexual instrument. The problem is, as always, finding a sufficiently accomplished musician.

You've been borrowing bodies for, what?, nearly forty-five years now. Ever since you were about six years old. Not with your present degree of expertise and subtlety, of course. You had to learn by trial and error. There were no teachers in this art.

You remember how it started. It was just about the time the family was preparing to flee the old country. Everything was in turmoil, emotions running high, conflicting, confused. That was when you began experiencing flashes of those emotions. Not from within, but from without. *Others'* emotions. You would follow those emotions and find yourself looking through the eyes of your sister, Marta, or one of your brothers, seeing what they saw, feeling what they felt, actually *inside* them.

But you couldn't maintain the contact. Not in those days. And the other minds would rebel, push you away. They wouldn't know it was you, that it was *anybody*. They just knew that something was wrong and subconsciously reacted against you. But you kept on trying, probing. You had to. And by trial and error you discovered that you achieved your best results during the night when they were asleep. You could enter them then without resistance. And as long as they stayed asleep, you could make their arms and legs move. Eventually you learned to keep them asleep and unaware. That done, you could get them up and walk around in their bodies.

But instinctively you knew right from the start that yours was an ability that had to be kept secret. You could do something that other people could not—although you suspected your sister Marta had some undiscovered capability like yours. So maybe it was genetic. You'd caught hints in the family history that there may have been others with a power like yours, but nothing definite. And those records are long gone now.

But what does it matter, really? It is a fool's game to root about for causes. The why and how is irrelevant. You power exists, you know how to use it, you *love* using it. Where it comes from *simply doesn't matter*.

Whatever the cause—accident or heredity—you knew your ability would cause fear in other people, so you kept it a secret for much of your childhood.

With adolescence, you became bolder and perfected your technique.

On Green Street, you pay the cabby and go into the Nite Owl Boutique to pick out some sexy clothes. The owner's eyes light up at the sight of Kara's familiar face—she thinks she's still dealing with Kelly. Dollar signs flash in her eyes and she comes over immediately to help.

As you browse through the racks of low-cut tops and high-cut skirts, and undergarments with unconventional but strategic openings, you think about how far you've come. From listening in on emotions to taking absolute control over—all but *owing*—this fabulous body.

Life is good.

And going into psychiatry proved to be a stroke of genius, even if you do say so yourself. It gives you access to people with emotional problems, a majority of whom are women, since women as a rule are far more apt to admit to emotional problems and seek help for them. A certain percentage of those women, purely as a result of the law of averages, are young and attractive. You've skewed the curve in your favor by letting it get around that you treat nurses on a courtesy basis. When you find a young attractive woman who fits your criteria of suggestibility, you edge her down a circuitous path that will convince her that she might have a multiple personality disorder. When she allows you to hypnotize her, you establish contact, entering her mind and making a little nest for yourself there. It's akin to leaving a marker. After that, you can find her whenever she's in range—like reaching out in the dark and finding a familiar object—and take her over whenever she's sleeping. You make her body do a few rude things during the night, thus confirming the multiple personality diagnosis beyond all doubt. After that she's yours whenever you want her, as soon as she goes to sleep.

The sleep part is important. Once you've worn a body a few times in sleep, you're capable of taking over whenever you wish. But if you do so while the individual is alert and conscious, the victim knows she's been taken over. She might even recognize you. That would never do. So you only take over patients who have been convinced they have a multiple personality disorder, and only when they are asleep.

It's a delicate juggling act, really. You must keep them frightened and off-balance enough so they stay in therapy, but not so frightened and distraught that they become discouraged or disillusioned with you and go somewhere else. With the right amount of hope and a sufficient number of set-backs, you can keep them dangling indefinitely.

And when you tire of them ... you *cure* them.

Some of them cure themselves by moving away. Your range is limited. You can reach as far as Hartford and the Catskills and a ways west of Philadelphia. And even when they are that far, there is no sensation of transit—one instant you're in your own body, the next instant you're in another's. But at the extremes of your range the bond is so tenuous, the strain of maintaining contact so enormous, that there is nothing to be gained by the effort. Except in Kara's case. During the weekend after she returned to her farm it exhausted you to make her body do a few simple things, such as writing on the mirror and the like, but it was worth the effort. It brought her back to New York.

You've never failed. Your arrangement has worked perfectly for years and there is no reason it cannot go on for as long as you live. No matter how old your brain and your own body become, you can always have a young body to occupy.

You carry your packages from the Nite Owl and find a cab to take you to the Helmsley Palace on Madison and 50th. You rent a room there—registering as Janine Wade—paying in advance in cash. Then you stop at the pharmacy to pick up some make-up and essentials. Half an hour later you walk Kara's provocatively dressed body down to the bar. In no time you have a Stetson-hatted Texan in tow. He's big, he's horny, and this is his last night in town. He's perfect.

▼

2:45 A.M.

You lay alone on the bed in Kara's body, vaguely frustrated. The Texan was all right, but after the Hindu last night he was something of a letdown. You can see that you're going to have to go back to picking up doubles again. You've shied away from that sort of thing since the fiasco at the Plaza two weeks ago, but you don't see that you have much choice if you're going to make these little jaunts worthwhile.

You get up, wash off the make-up, use the Massengill vinegar douche you picked up earlier, and put the new clothing back in the Nite Owl bags. You've decided to store them in a locker at Grand Central. That way they'll be convenient to midtown and you won't have to waste so much valuable time going down to SoHo.

Dressed again in the jeans and sweater and coat, you head for the lobby. The exhilaration of a few hours ago has worn off, and because the evening has not turned out as well as you hoped, you're feeling somewhat low. It's at times like these that questions of morality arise and circle you like whispering shades from unkempt graves.

What right have I to do this?

The question doesn't arise nearly so often as it did during the early days. But tonight it creeps back. You face it squarely.

No right at all.

Then why? Why do you do it?

You know the litany. You do not flinch from the response.

Because I can! Because I must! Because I love it! Because I cannot stop! But most of all because without it I might as well be dead!

Besides. You are one of a kind, a law unto yourself. That is your justification. Isn't that enough?

▼

3:30 A.M.

Movement at the front of the Kramer building caught Rob's attention through his half closed eyes. He straightened up and squinted through the foggy windshield.

Gates. Leaving his office.

Christ! What had he been doing in there all this time?

Gates began to walk uptown. Since Seventh Avenue ran downtown only, Rob couldn't follow. He took a gamble. He started the car and took the next even numbered street east up to Sixth Avenue, raced uptown to Twenty-first and came down the street with his lights out. He pulled in by a fire hydrant at mid-block and waited.

Gates showed a few minutes later. He went up the steps to his front door and disappeared inside. Five minutes later all the lights went out.

Rob debated extending the watch, then decided against it. He had a feeling Gates wouldn't be going anywhere until his office opened in five and a half hours.

A wasted night. Or maybe not. At least he knew Gates hadn't been out snooping around Kelly's apartment playing mind games on Kara. But he was puzzled as to what it was in Gates' office that would keep him occupied until this hour.

Sooner or later he'd find out. Rob had no doubt about that. Patience and vigilance—sooner or later they paid off.

He turned on the headlights and headed home.

▼

9:32 A.M.

Ed had tried to age the coveralls quickly by bunching them up on the floor and stomping all over them. It had added wrinkles, but still they looked too clean. The same was true of the tool box he carried, even though he had taken a hammer to it.

Nothing I can do about it now, he thought as he entered the Kramer Medical Arts Building.

But he'd skipped shaving and showering this morning and was pleased with the slightly grubby effect.

He walked up to the directory, found Dr. Gates listed on the third floor, and took the elevator up. That was when he began to sweat.

This is crazy! I could get disbarred for this!

The best thing to do was turn around now, go back to the apartment, and go to work late. He had called in sick this morning but he could always tell them the virus had passed as suddenly as it came and he felt fine now.

No! You're going to do this. You're going to go through with it. No backing down.

When the elevator door opened, he marched out and found Dr. Gates' office. The door was flush steel. He took a deep breath, readied his best grin and Bronx accent, and pushed it open.

"Mornin'!" he said to the receptionist behind the desk. "How's it goin' t'day, sweetheart?"

"Can I help you?" she said, fixing him with a frosty stare.

"Yeah. Y'havin' any trouble witcher locks?"

She shook her head. "No. Why do you ask?"

"Complaints. Loadsa complaints. Mostly on da fourth floor, but de owners want me t'check ev'ybody out as long as dey got me here."

"I can't allow you to disturb Dr. Gates' patients—"

"Nah, don' werry. Jus de outta door here. Lemme see yer key set."

She reached for her bag and then stopped.

"I don't know . . ."

Ed had been afraid of something like this, but he had a plan of action prepared: *Bull your way through.*

"I should look atcher rest room keys, too."

Still she hesitated.

"C'mon, lady. Watcha tink I'm gonna do, steal 'em? I ain't got all day. And if sumpin goes wrong wit da cylinder or da tumbluhs later, yer boss'll hafta pay outta his own pocket. Know what I'm saying'?"

She handed him a ring with two keys on it— probably the lobby key and the office door key—plus the two restroom keys that she kept in her drawer.

Ed smiled at her. "Tanks, sweets. Dis'll only take me a minute."

He checked out the lock on the door. It was a simple dead bolt with a knob inside and a keyhole outside. He found the right key on the second try and turned it back and forth. It worked perfectly.

"Hear dat?" he said, putting his ear down to the face plate as the bolt slid in and out. "Yer cylinders is dry. I'll fix dat in a jiffy."

He took out the can of graphite spray he had bought this morning and squirted some into the keyhole. He tried the key again.

"*Much* better! Okay, I'm gonna check out yer rest rooms and da front. Be right back."

Without giving her a chance to protest, Ed closed the door and hurried down the hall. He took the stairs two at a time down to the lobby, walked quickly through the front doors, then sprinted down to the locksmith on Fourteenth Street. He threw the office and main entrance keys on the counter.

"One copy of each! Quick!" he said, puffing.

Jesus, I'm out of shape!

The man behind the counter gave him a sidelong look, but made up the copies and charged him four bucks plus tax. Ed had a five ready. He slapped it down, told him to keep the change, then sprinted back to the Kramer building.

He took the elevator up to allow him to catch his

breath, then strolled back into Dr. Gates' office. The receptionist looked relieved to see him.

"Here y'are, sweetheart. Ev'ryting works fine. No problemo."

"Thank you," she said, her cool and distant manner returning.

Now came the fun part of his plan: the psych-out. If he left too fast she might start wondering about him. So Ed had decided to make her *want* him to leave.

"Say, y'doin' anyting tonight?"

"Yes."

"How about t'morra?"

"Sorry, but I'm involved."

"Yeah, well, hey, I'm involved, too, but dat don' mean we can't go out an have a lil fun, if know what I mean."

"I'm *very* involved, now if you'll—"

He held up his hands.

"Hey, sor*ree!*"

Just then the door marked "Consultation" opened and a middle-aged man stepped out.

"Hiya, doc," Ed said.

"That is *not* Dr. Gates," the receptionist said. "Now, will you please leave?"

"Cert'nly. But how 'bout I drop by 'roun' five and we'll get a drink somewheres? Howzat soun'?"

She ignored him.

Shrugging dramatically, and with a great show of reluctance, Ed picked up his toolbox and left. He strolled to the elevator. The car that came for him was empty. When the doors closed and he was alone, he began to laugh. He leaned back and held his fists up to heaven.

"You did it, you clever bastard, you! You fucking-ay *did* it!"

His heart was pounding, he was bathed in sweat, but he'd never felt so alive in his life. And the best part about it all was that it had been *fun*! Jesus! He'd almost be willing to do this sort of thing for a living!

The car stopped on the second floor and he straightened up. An old lady with a walker came in, assisted by a younger woman. Ed tried to look serious, but he felt too good. He rode the rest of the way down grinning like an idiot and jingling the two brand new keys in his pocket.

But the grinning and jingling came to an abrupt, panicky halt when the elevator doors opened on the lobby and he saw Kara waiting outside. For an instant Ed couldn't breathe, couldn't move, then he noticed that she wasn't looking his way. Her eyes were down, her face pale, her expression blank. Her mind looked to be a million miles away.

Ed wasn't going to wait for her to look up. He hoisted the tool box onto his shoulder, blocking his face from Kara, then he pushed past the old lady, almost knocking her over, and hurried for the street, never looking back until he was a block away.

And all along the way, he thought of Kara. She looked like she had the weight of the world on her shoulders. He had to find a way to help her, and he was convinced a clue to doing that lay in Dr. Gates' office.

Well, he'd find out for sure tonight.

He was actually looking forward to that.

▼

10:07 A.M.

"I have spoken to the patient who sent you the note," Dr. Gates was saying, "and I can assure you, he will never bother you again."

Kara tried to ignore the lie about the "him" behind

the letter, telling herself it was just Dr. Gates' way of protecting patient confidentiality.

She nodded without really listening. She had other things on her mind. Another erotic dream, for instance. She didn't remember much besides a cowboy hat . . . and Dr. Gates' presence.

She yawned behind her hand.

That was another thing. She was so *tired* lately. Maybe it was because of the dreams, maybe it was because she hadn't been able to workout all week. Or maybe the Halcion was staying in her system.

Still, she didn't dare stop it because it seemed to be doing the job. The apartment key had been right where she had hidden it. She'd even tied a strand of her hair around it last night, and the strand was still in place this morning. So, if nothing else, she could be sure she hadn't left the apartment last night.

Rob had stopped by first thing this morning. He looked exhausted. He said he had another stake out tonight so he wouldn't be able to stay over.

Just as well. Kara intended to hit the sack early tonight. *Very* early.

▼

2:33 P.M.

Lieutenant Mooney had the Kelly Wade folder on his lap as he slumped in the swivel chair behind his desk. He was whining again.

"Why are you doing this, Harris?"

"I'm not *doing* anything, lieu. I'm just telling you that there's new evidence in the Kelly Wade case and it's got to stay open."

"That's a kook letter! It doesn't count!"

"It's addressed to Kara Wade and says, in effect, get out of town or wind up dead like your sister. Where I come from, that's a threat. And it may mean that Kelly Wade herself was threatened before she died."

Rob watched Mooney mull that, watched him try to find a way to make an end run around it, watched him give up.

"Damn it, Harris. Okay. So what are we doing with this 'threatening' note?"

"It's down in fingerprints now. We got a set from the victim's sister yesterday, and we found a set of Dr. Gates' from when he registered for a handgun in 1980. Both of those are all over the bill and the check. But they've picked up a third set. That's the one we're running down now."

"And when that comes up as blank as the set from the hotel room, what're you going to do?"

"I'm going to start shaking Dr. Gates' tree and see if any rotten apples fall out."

"Okay," Mooney sighed. "But make sure you do it all legal like. Make sure all your paperwork is done. I don't want no harrassment calls from this shrink."

"Right, lieu. But I know you'll be behind me a hundred percent if he does call, right?"

Mooney tossed the file across the desk.

"Oh, yeah."

Rob glanced at his watch. If he hurried his afternoon paper shuffle he could be down by Gates' office in time to start following him again. The guy had to go someplace besides his office and his home.

▼

11:35 P.M.

"Time to move," Ed thought, but he didn't move.

He had the jitters now. It was one thing to pull a fast one on a receptionist. It was something else entirely to enter a locked building with a stolen key and rifle through the confidential files of a state licensed physician. We weren't talking fun and games, here. We were talking breaking and entering.

Ed had already put himself through the man-or-mouse shit and had run the line about A-man's-got-to-do-what-a-man's-got-to-do through his head at least a thousand times by now. It didn't help. But he was going to goddamn do it or never be able to look at himself in the mirror again.

Taking his coffee with him, he got up from his window seat at the all night Burger King on Twenty-third Street and headed for the door.

B and E time.

He walked down Seventh Avenue. He was still dressed in his overalls, but beneath them he wore khaki slacks and a flannel shirt—in case he had to run and needed a quick change of appearance. He'd left his tool box at home. All the tools he needed were the keys in his right pocket and the flashlight in his left.

He slowed as he passed Barney's, checking the window displays—he preferred Brooks Brothers—and stopped short of the Kramer building. What if someone spotted him going in, or questioned him? What would he do then?

First off, he wouldn't worry about it. And if he was stopped, he'd just say he was Dr. Gates and hope whoever it was didn't know the doctor by sight.

Ed glanced around. No one in sight. He hurried up to

the lobby door with the key ready, hoping it was the right one, and thrust it into the lock. It fit. It turned. He pulled it open and scooted inside. He didn't bother with the elevator—that would mean standing where he was visible from the street—but went directly to the stairs. His mouth was dry as sand by the time he reached Dr. Gates' office door. He didn't allow himself to pause and think. He used the second key and opened the door. If anyone was inside he'd say he was part of the cleaning crew and would come back later.

Dark inside except for the glow from the fishtank and the blip on the computer screen. And quiet. He closed the office door behind him, turned the bolt.

Made it!

He felt weak. He had to take a pee. He wanted to turn around and get out of here. But that would have been stupid after coming this far and taking all these risks. No turning back now. He pulled out his flashlight and began his search.

The reception area he knew from this morning. He went into the consultation room. He dearly would have loved to turn on the lights but he was afraid lighted windows might draw attention from someone on the street. Maybe he was being overly cautious, but he was taking every precaution he could think of.

Nothing in the consultation room, at least nothing he was looking for. He wanted the files. There was a flush oak door behind the desk. He opened it and was faced with three more doors. The middle turned out to be a small private bathroom.

Thank God! he thought as he stepped in to relieve his aching bladder. *Never should have had that third coffee.*

The room behind the left hand door was lined with file cabinets. And it was windowless. He flipped on the light and pulled on the handle of the nearest drawer. It wouldn't budge. Same with all the others. Every cabinet was locked.

Ed spent a few moments cursing Dr. Gates with every four-, ten-, and twelve-letter word he knew. He'd never imagined he might run into locked files inside a locked office.

As he turned to make his way back to the consultation room, he noticed that the third door was standing ajar. He pushed it open and shone his flashbeam inside.

Another windowless room, only empty. But the walls ... they were covered with fabric. Thick fabric. The floors and ceilings too. He stepped inside and checked the inner surface of the door. That was covered too. He touched it. Soft. Then he realized where he was.

In a padded cell.

Saturday

FEBRUARY 21
12:05 A.M.

KARA HUNG UP THE PHONE. SHE WAS GRATEFUL THAT ROB cared enough to call and check on her, but was uncomfortable with the implication that she needed someone to watch over her. Or was she being too analytical?

She lay back in bed and waited for the Halcion to work.

No dreams tonight. Please, no dreams.

She wasn't up to any sex tonight, real or imagined. Peace, that was all she wanted. And a reasonably normal life, one in which she would feel safe sleeping in the same house as her daughter.

Actually, she was spending more time than usual with Jill these past five days. And Jill, with the adaptability of a nine year old, had been quite content to go to parks and places like the Museum of Natural History when her mother was around, and watch the VCR when she wasn't. Today Kara had tried to watch a Disney movie with Jill. But it was *Freaky Friday*, the one in which Jodie Foster switches bodies with her mother. It struck Kara as too much like that damn crazy note. She'd had to leave the room.

And her book . . . her book was going nowhere while

the deadline kept creeping up. She didn't want to blow this. She was counting on that second payment on the advance. But more than that, she believed in her book, knew it would be an important contribution to the women's movement. If only she could get back to work on it.

Tomorrow ... she'd force herself to work on it tomorrow ...

Right now she felt sleep creeping over her. She blanked her mind and welcomed it.

▼

Rob sat in his car, smoking and sipping Dunkin' Donuts coffee as he watched Gates' townhouse. He was waiting for the lights to go out so he could call it a night.

Rob had been asking around about Gates. Nobody knew too much about him. Seemed to be a real homebody. Took vacations from his practice but never left town. No social life that anyone knew of. His world seemed to consist of his home and his office, and occasionally a trip to the hospital. Gates could walk to all three: a few blocks downtown on Seventh Avenue and he was at his office. A few blocks further down and he was at St. Vincent's on Eleventh Street in the village. That was his world. Family dead, no friends, no close ties to the medical community. The guy lived in a vacuum.

Actually, he lived in a Victorian townhouse. Rob knew the type well: four floors and a basement. Once upon a time, before the recent regentrification of Chelsea, he had lived in one of these townhouses, two blocks down on Nineteenth. He had been a rookie then and had been rooming with Tony Morano, a friend from the Academy. But they had shared one of seven apartments in a subdivided building just like Gates'. Two apartments per floor and one in the basement.

Gates had a whole townhouse to himself. That took bucks. Big bucks.

Rob flipped the cigarette butt out the window.

Come on, Lazlo Gati. Lock up your castle and go to bed.

Just then the front door opened and Gates came down the steps. He started toward Seventh Avenue, just as he had last night. He was heading back to his office.

Muttering under his breath, Rob started his car and prepared to follow.

▼

Ed flipped the light switch in the padded cell. A fluorescent tube flickered to life behind a metal grille in the ceiling. There was no furniture, just the door, four walls, floor and ceiling, all padded.

It was the damnedest thing. Whoever heard of a padded cell in a psychiatrist's office? What for? In case someone went berserk during a session? Ed smiled. Maybe it was for after they got the doc's bill.

Seriously, though, what kind of people did this Dr. Gates treat that he needed a padded cell?

And who cared, anyway? This wasn't helping him help Kara.

As Ed turned to go, he noticed a row of buttons on the inside of the door. He recognized it immediately as an electronic combination lock. Six push-button numbers, and a "Lock" button.

It struck him as odd that there would be a "Lock" button on the inside. He could see providing a way to let yourself out should you get locked in accidentally, but why would you want to lock yourself *in* here? Weirder and weirder.

But again, this wasn't what he had come here for. He turned off the light and returned to the consultation room, making sure to leave the door closed behind him, just as he had found it.

It was time to get out of here.

He entered the waiting area and closed the consultation room door behind him. As he started toward the outer door, the glowing blip on the computer screen caught his eye.

I wonder . . .

He slipped behind the desk and looked at the screen. One word glowed in the upper left next to the blinking cursor.

READY?

Ed typed in YES and hit the Return key.

The screen beeped and replied with: CODE?

Oh, sure. Didn't that figure. Everything else was locked up tight, so why shouldn't Gates have access codes for his computer files.

For the hell of it, Ed typed in GATES and hit Return. He was rewarded with:

INELIGIBLE COMMAND
CODE?

Ed tried again with LAWRENCE, LARRY, MD, NUTS and made a final stab with SHIT. Each was answered with the same message as the first. He was about to give up when he remembered that reference book in the library, the one used by all shrinks to code their diagnoses. The DSM-III-R. He racked his brain trying to remember the code for Multiple Personality Disorder. He'd read it so many times he could almost picture it in his mind. In fact, he *could* picture it. And the code number was 300.14. He punched that in.

The screen beeped and a list of names popped up.

Now we're cookin!

He hit the Scroll button and searched for "Wade" as the list of names slid up the screen.

▼

Rob pulled into the curb half a block down from the Kramer building and waited for Gates to catch up. The only way this sort of move could backfire was if Rob had guessed wrong and Gates was not going to his office.

Nope. There he came. Striding along like he was out for his morning constitutional.

Crap. Another long night.

▼

Ed was flabbergasted. He hadn't actually counted, but a big part of Gates' practice was diagnosed as Multiple Personality Disorder. All were women, and most were in their twenties and thirties. The books Ed had reviewed had said the disorder was rare. If that was true, Dr. Gates had tapped into a rich vein of multiple personalities.

But that wasn't all that had disturbed Ed. He had scrolled through Kara's file and then Kelly's. They'd been very similar. That was to be expected, he guessed, what with their being twins with the same disorder, but a number of paragraphs appeared word for word in both files. That bothered him. He picked a few other names at random from the list.

They all had the same psychiatric history. Classic Multiple Personality Disorder. Their histories were described each time in almost the exact same wording. It was almost as if Dr. Gates were using a computer boilerplate method for his medical charts, the way Ed's legal department used computers to piece together the paragraphs of various contracts.

The more Ed read, the more he became convinced that the psychiatrist was doing just that.

And then he heard the key slipping into the lock on the outer door and turning.

Oh, Jesus!

Ed slid from the chair and ducked behind the desk, so terrified that he was sure he was going to wet his pants. What was he going to—?

The flashlight!

He popped his head up, saw it, grabbed it, and dropped back down just as the lights went on. He crouched there, holding his breath and praying, promising God that he'd start going back to church every Sunday instead of just Christmas, Palm Sunday and Easter as he did now. He was in the middle of promising to receive communion every Sunday for the rest of his life, and trying to think of something else to promise, when whoever it was who had come in walked straight through the waiting area and into the consultation room, closing the door behind him.

Ed gave him thirty seconds. He watched his Movado count them off one by one, then he rose to his feet and tiptoed to the door. He unlocked it, slipped out into the hall, and eased it closed behind him. He debated half a second about relocking it, then decided to hell with it. He headed for the stairs at a brisk walk. It was all he could do to keep from sprinting.

▼

Rob was slipping into a doze when his beeper went off.

"What the hell—?"

He got out of the car and went to the booth on the

corner. He called the precinct house and learned that Tommy Doyle was looking for him.

"Been trying to reach you all night, Harris. You on a plant or somethin'?"

"What is it, Tommy?" Rob said, yawning.

"The print report you were waiting for on that electric bill came in. They made a match on the third set of prints."

Rob was suddenly wide awake.

"Anyone we know?"

"No name, but it matched the partials they found in the hotel room on that Kelly Wade case you've been hauling around."

Rob's insides tightened. He thought he had been blowing the threat in the letter out of proportion to keep Kelly's case open. But now there was a direct link to Kelly on the night she died. So maybe this wasn't from a harmless kook. Maybe there was real danger to Kara.

"Thanks for finding me, Tom. I—damn!"

Someone in coveralls had just come out of the Kramer building and had taken off down the street at a run. It hadn't been Gates—too short, hair too dark.

Rob hung up and started after him, but he was already out of sight, up one of the side streets. He was tempted to follow, but that would leave Gates unattended. And Gates was the one he was really interested in.

Rob returned to his car and settled back with his eyes fixed on the entrance to the Kramer building.

▼

Ed ducked into the first alley he found and shucked his coverall. The February night air cut through his flannel shirt but he didn't care. He wanted to be rid of that thing.

He hurried up to Sixth Avenue and looked for a bar. A place called Edwin's beckoned from across the street. He hurried over. It was dark and smoky and almost full. Perfect. He ordered a double Absolut on the rocks. They didn't carry Citron, so he told the bartender to squeeze a lime in it.

Sweet Jesus, what a night!

Who'd have thought that Gates—he assumed that had been Gates who'd come in—would return to his office after midnight?

I could have been caught!

But he *hadn't* been caught. In and out with no one the wiser. He'd *done* it. His own *Mission Impossible*.

He sipped the drink and wondered what to do with what he had learned. But *what* had he learned?

Why would a psychiatrist be manufacturing medical histories for his patients? It didn't make sense, and he didn't know what he could or should do about it. But one thing was for sure: He had to tell Kara. And soon.

Why not now? She might be asleep, but he had to unburden himself. He had to share what he had done and learned with somebody else. He went to the pay phone and called her.

Her voice when she answered was cautious but alert.

"It's me. Ed."

"Ed?" She almost sounded as if she didn't know who he was.

"Yes. Look, I know it's late, but I've just come across some really important things that I've got to tell you about."

"Tonight? Now?"

"Yes. Can I come over?"

"I'm very tired, Ed. I don't think—"

"It's about Dr. Gates."

There was a long pause on the other end, then:

"What about Dr. Gates?"

"I've just learned something about him. I think there's something funny going on."

"I'd very much like to hear about this, Ed. Where are you?"

"In a dive on Sixth, but you don't want to come here."

"Can I meet you someplace convenient for both of us?"

Ed faced through a mental list of places that would be comfortable for Kara and wouldn't turn him away in his present state of dress.

"How about the bar at the Warwick? It's on Fifty-fourth and Sixth, about halfway between us."

"I'll meet you there in half an hour."

"Great."

Ed hung up and wondered why his previous elation seemed to have faded. If anything, it should have been boosted by the prospect of meeting Kara tonight. She'd certainly agreed readily enough after he said it had to do with Dr. Gates, but she'd sounded strange. Distant.

Well, she'd said she was tired. It had to be that.

He finished his drink and went out to the street to see if he could find a late cruising cab, otherwise it was going to be a long cold walk up to the Warwick.

▼

Rob watched the entrance to the Kramer building and pondered the identity of the owner of the third set of prints on the electric bill. Whoever had left them had been in the Plaza with Kelly on the night she died. He was getting closer. A key to the mess was dancing somewhere beyond the edges of his consciousness, just past his reach.

He also wondered who had come out of the building a while ago. That, too, gnawed at him. If only he'd been in his car at the time, he would have had a better look. All Rob could say now was that he'd carried a vague resemblance to that guy Ed who'd been hanging around Kara.

Ed . . . there was a strange bird. Didn't seem to be a threat. Actually seemed to be helping with the legal details. Nice of him to bring over those estate papers for Kara on Thursday. Or maybe he had the hots for her.

Rob jolted upright.

Thursday! Ed had been with Kara when she got that letter! He could have touched it. He *must* have touched it! He'd read it!

"Shit!"

And Ed had known Kelly! So he could have been with her the night she died! He was the guy who could fill in all the blanks.

Rob jumped out of the car and ran back to the phone. He called Kara's number. If she knew where Ed lived, or even had his home phone number, Rob could haul him in for questioning. *Now!*

As Kara's phone began to ring, Rob glanced up at the Kramer building. Gates be damned! Let him doodle around up there till sunrise. He could wait. This was the first real lead on this case and he wasn't going to waste any time getting to it.

Kara's phone kept on ringing. And ringing.

Tiny pulses of apprehension scattered through him. He knew she was taking sleeping pills, but the phone was right next to the bed. And he knew she was there—he'd spoken to her around midnight.

Something was wrong.

He made a quick call to Doyle, told him to pull the personal effects bag on Kelly Wade and have it ready, then he ran for his car.

▼

The Warwick bar was almost empty by the time Ed finished telling Kara of his evening's exploits. He searched her face for some sign of approval. It was slow coming, but finally a warm smile lit her features.

"You did all that for me?"

"Well, yes. I felt I owed it to you . . . and Kelly."

"But what if you'd been caught?"

"That's a risk I was willing to take. You've got to be ready to take a few risks or else life isn't worth much."

Ed drained his third double vodka. He was feeling pretty good. Damn good—about the night, about himself, about being here in this almost deserted bar with Kara.

"What do you think I should do, Ed? I'm so confused."

He looked at her. She was beautiful. In the dim light, despite the jeans and loose sweater she was wearing, she reminded him more of her sister than ever. But she was obviously tense. She sat across the tiny circular table, nervously twirling a key ring on her index finger. And she was asking him for advice. He tried to organize his vodka-muddled thoughts.

"As I see it, you've got two choices. You can get out of the city and put as much distance as you can between this guy and yourself." For selfish reasons, Ed didn't like that idea. It meant he wouldn't get to see her anymore. "*Or* . . . you could take the bull by the horns and go to the State Board of Medical Examiners and demand a complete investigation of this man's record keeping and practice methods."

She was staring at him with those big blue eyes. They were hypnotizing.

"What do *you* think I should do?"

"I think you've got the courage and integrity to take this to the State and protect others as well as yourself. That's what I think you should do."

She put her hand on his and squeezed as the last call came from the bar.

"Thanks for your confidence, but I'm still not sure. Is there someplace we can talk about this some more?"

"There's my place." The words just popped out, but Ed was glad they did. "We can talk there as long as you want."

"That sounds perfect. Let's go."

With that she was up and heading toward the door. With an excited, anticipatory tingle in his groin, Ed dropped some money on the table and hurried after her.

▼

Rob had stopped off at Midtown North, grabbed the effects bag from Doyle, and run out. As he raced east to First Avenue and then uptown, he shook Kelly's apartment keys free of the tangle within and had them ready when he slammed to a halt in front of her building.

Out of instinctive courtesy, he rapped on the door and waited a couple of seconds before unlocking it and rushing inside. Main room, kitchen, bedroom, bathroom—all empty. No sign of struggle, just empty.

Where the hell could Kara be?

A chilling thought struck him: What if it wasn't Kara out there roaming the city? What if it was Janine?

Or worse yet: What if this Ed Bannion character was some sort of head case who had lured her someplace tonight with the intent of seeing that she ended up like her sister?

Rob had to find Bannion. But how? He had his office number but no one would answer at this hour. And the morning might be too late.

Rob grabbed Kelly's Manhattan white pages thumbed them open to the *B*'s. He found *Bannion*. There was a truckload of them. Limiting himself to the *E* or *Edward*

Bannions narrowed it down some, but there were still plenty.

He sat down by the phone and began calling.

▼

As you inspect Ed Bannion's Upper West Side apartment through Kara's eyes, you think of how the night has been little more than a series of shocks, one after the other.

The first shock was the early morning phone call at Kara's apartment from someone called Ed who said he had startling information about Dr. Gates. That simple statement forced you to cancel all your plans for returning to the Helmsley tonight. You've been playing the rest by ear.

The second shock came when you recognized Ed Bannion as one of the brothers from the Plaza the night Kelly went through the window. Ed was the one on his knees behind you at the end, doing you from the rear. The one who bit you.

You masked your surprise then, but you nearly gave yourself away when Ed Bannion dropped the bombshell: that your office had been invaded, your computer security breached, and that you had walked right past the culprit less than an hour ago without suspecting a thing.

You wander the bleached hardwood floors of Bannion's apartment while the owner uses the bathroom. You inspect the glass and chrome tables, the Italian leather sectional. The man has no taste. There's no theme, no harmony, no personality to the decor. These are just *things* he's bought. They have no meaning to him beyond the fact that they are considered the right things to have. It's as if he furnished the place with random snippets from the "Home" section of the Thursday

Times. An empty man living an empty life in an apartment filled with *things*, whose only passion has been the job which obviously bores him to tears now. Else why would he have tried the hair-brained stunt of breaking and entering tonight?

Taking over Kara Wade has engendered a Gordian knot of complications, but you aren't ready to surrender this wonderful body yet. You eye a set of carving knives jutting from a block of teak on the kitchen counter. Alexander the Great's abrupt and efficient method for unsnarling stubborn knots comes to mind.

You examine the knives, and choose the one with the longest, thinnest blade, then hurry into the bedroom and shove it under the bed. You're standing by the picture window when Bannion returns. He sways slightly as he crosses to the bar and begins to make himself another drink.

"Do you really think you should have another, Ed?" you say, kicking off Kara's shoes and moving languidly across the room.

You're thinking that if Bannion doesn't get too drunk, you might yet salvage something out of this night.

"I'm celebrating."

Gently, you take the bottle from Bannion's hands and put Kara's arms around him.

"You don't need to get drunk to celebrate. As a matter of fact, that could interfere with the kind of celebration I have planned."

You watch a flush creep up Bannion's cheeks.

"Wh—what kind of celebration is that?"

"The kind of celebration that happens when a very grateful girl is alone with a brave man she admires very much and finds very attractive."

"This isn't necessary."

"Yes it is."

You back up a step and pull off the sweater to reveal Kara's breasts.

"Do you like them? Touch them."

Bannion's mouth is hanging open as he stares at you. He seems paralyzed. So you lift his hands and place them on her breasts.

"That feels good, Ed. Rub them."

Bannion is getting into it now. Kara's jeans are the next to go. They're loose and fall to the floor when they're unbuttoned. You step back again and spread your arms.

"What do you think of this body, Ed? Isn't it glorious?"

"It's fabulous!"

"Yes, it is. And now I want to see your body, Ed. But only a little bit at a time." You kneel before him and unzip his fly. "We'll start with this area here."

▼

Ed was dimly aware that a small part of his brain was very upset, was shouting at him, in fact. But he couldn't make out the words through the fog. A warm fog, a haze of vodka lit by bright red glowing waves of pleasure rippling over him.

Kara was so much like her sister Kelly, so *much* like Kelly, she even gave head like Kelly, and now she was on her hands and knees on the bed, facing away from him, and he was standing behind her, sliding in and out of her doggy style. Almost a replay on that night in the Plaza a couple of weeks ago, except there was no black garter belt to hold on to, and Phil wasn't here and Ed had her all to himself.

Maybe it was because this was so much like the night at the Plaza that the worry-wart corner of his brain was so upset. But after all, Kara and Kelly were identical twins. Why shouldn't they be exactly alike?

Well, they weren't *exactly* alike. Kara's body was firmer, the flesh more taut, better toned. He thought that in a pinch, if given the choice, he might prefer Kelly's slightly thicker layer of padding, but either way it was a no-lose proposition.

Kara turned her head and looked at him over her shoulder.

"Do it faster! And harder! I want to *come*, damn it!"

A chill ran over his bare skin as she bucked her buttocks hard against him. Something about that sounded so familiar.

She turned her head again. She smiled.

"And this time, don't bite me."

The words struck him like the shock wave of an atomic bomb detonating on the bed. He felt himself shrivel. As he fell limp from within her, he backed away until his buttocks came up against the cold surface of the bureau. His mouth worked, trying to speak. How could she know? No one could know that but Kelly. Not even Phil knew that he'd bitten her. Ed had been ashamed to tell him.

She sat on the edge and looked at him. Her stare made him want to cover himself. He had been naked for a while, but now he felt like a specimen in a jar.

"Well, Ed Bannion," she said in a low voice that was almost a whisper. "What are we going to do with you?"

"Who are you?" Ed said, whispering as well.

"I've got many names, Ed. You've met me before, but I told you then that my name was Ingrid."

"No! That's not possible! You're lying!"

"Am I? You were with your brother. His name was Phil or Bill or something like that. You said you were in the textile business. You lied to me. That wasn't nice. And you bit me. That caused all sorts of complications."

Ed was frozen against the bureau like a child's tongue to a wrought iron rail in the dead of winter. The thing before him looked like Kara, and it used Kara's voice—though not the way Kara used it—yet it was not Kara. It knew things Kara couldn't possibly know, things only her dead sister could know.

"How—?" It was all he could manage.

She got up and began pacing before him, moving slowly, completely unconscious of her nudity. That such a beautify body could be parading before him naked and fill him with only fear and loathing amazed Ed.

"How? That should be obvious, shouldn't it? I'm not Kara. I'm Dr. Gates, using Kara's body, just as that note said. And it's a wonderful body, don't you think?" She smiled at him, a deadly cold, bone-chilling smile. "Let me explain. Don't worry. I'll be brief."

▼

But it's so hard to be brief. You must keep reining in your narrative, forcing yourself to hold back a wealth of details as you tell Ed Bannion your story. Perhaps it's because you've never before had the opportunity to tell anyone your story. It has been bottled up inside for your whole life, fermenting like champagne, building up pressure, crying to be released. And now that Ed Bannion has allowed you to pop the cork, the story is gushing and foaming from you in an effervescent torrent.

"So you see," you say, forcing yourself to bring your truncated, expurgated autobiography to a close, "I have developed the perfect cover for my talent. Quite ingenious, don't you think?"

Bannion, still nude, still cowering against the bedroom bureau, says nothing. He has not been a terribly receptive or appreciative audience.

"Oh, and those files you discovered in my office computer? You were right. They were indeed boiler-plated. I dictate the original reports, Miss Carney types them into the computer, then hard copies are filed in the locked cabinets. But with my special patients, I change the computer files, giving them the typical characteristics of a Multiple Personality Disorder. That's in case anything untoward happens to them—as it did to Kelly Wade. If there's an investigation of her death and my records are subpoenaed, I'll simply print out an altered medical record that nicely explains the erratic behavior that caused her death. I've been at this a long time, Ed. I have all the angles covered. I've covered contingencies most people would never think of."

Poor Bannion. He looks so pathetic standing there, trembling. But he believes. It's there in his eyes. He's completely convinced.

Which means it's time.

You reach under the bed and search for the kitchen knife.

▼

"What are you doing?" Ed said, finding his voice at last.

Kara had reached under the bed, and now she was sitting there with the sheet pulled over her lap. What could she have under the sheet. One of his slippers?

Who the hell cared? He wanted her–him–*it* out of here!

And *it* was the only term that seemed to fit. What sort of a creature was Gates that he could take over bodies like this? And Ed was now completely convinced that Gates could do it. How else to explain what it knew? Gates had to have been inside Kelly Wade that night to know what had been said! So bizarre—a demonic nightmare. But Ed knew he was awake.

And he had to get this . . . *thing* out of here!

But how? He wished he had a gun. All the times he'd planned to pick one up but put it off. He decided to try the direct approach. And if she wouldn't go, he'd throw her out. He outweighed her by fifty pounds. It might be an unpleasant scene, but he had to get her *out*!

"You'll have to leave. I don't want you here."

She said nothing. Only stared at him, her hands under the sheet on her lap.

His heart thudding, he stepped toward her.

"Out!"

▼

You debate the situation. Is there a way you can leave Bannion here alive? Certainly he'll talk. He'll go to the State Board and lodge a complaint. He might even go to the papers. He'll be branded a madman, but the damage will be done. The reputation of Dr. Lawrence Gates will be permanently smeared.

That would ruin everything.

Regrettably, there is no other viable option.

There can be no hesitation. Kara is strong and in excellent condition, but she is still a woman and no match for Bannion's extra weight.

"Didn't you hear me?" Bannion says, a tremor of fear in his voice. He takes another step closer. "I said *out!*"

You grip the knife handle. With a single motion you rise and lunge at Bannion. The man's eyes goggle when he sees the blade. He tries to block it with his hands but the blade slips under them. It drives forward with all of Kara's strength behind it, the sharp point piercing the skin at the lower edge of the sternum, slicing up through the diaphragm and into the heart. You wrench the blade left and right to make sure you pierce the myocardium, then you yank it free.

Bannion's eyes bulge wide, his face blanches with agony and the horror of death as he clutches at his chest and epigastrum. Blood bubbles between his fingers. He makes a gurgling sound in his throat as he drops to his knees, then topples face first with a loud thunk onto the hardwood floor.

You watch Bannion a moment. You've never killed before. It's not pleasant to watch someone die. Why do some personality types find this rewarding? Most unpleasant. But most necessary in this case, unfortunately.

You hurry to the bathroom. There's blood splattered on your hands and your breasts. You wash it away—there are definite advantages, it seems, to committing murder in the nude. You scrub the knife as well and return it to its teak block.

You take one last look at Bannion. Miraculously, he's still alive, but just barely. Blood pools under him, crimson foam bubbles at his lips.

Such a waste. But at least your secrets are safe.

You return to the living room where you slip back into Kara's sweater and slacks and hurry from the apartment. As you close the door behind you, the phone begins to ring.

Sorry. No one lives here anymore.

It's too late to do anything else tonight. You'll have to go straight back to Kara's apartment. The Friday night revelers will still be out in droves. A cab should be easy to find. Especially in Kara's body.

▼

Rob sat in Kelly's apartment and slammed the phone back onto its cradle. He was having no luck so far with the list of Bannions. He'd called every single one. Yet with the number of no-answers he'd had, he couldn't be sure if he'd already hit the right one.

He tried being analytical.

Wouldn't Ed have given Kara his home phone number?

Rob searched the apartment and found the papers that Ed had left with Kara on Thursday. His card was there, with his home phone number and address written on it. West 70th. It figured.

He called the number and let it ring for a long time. He was about to hang up when the ringing was broken by a clatter, as if the receiver had fallen on the floor.

Then a voice like death came over the wire.

▼

The ringing of the phone drew Ed from the wonderful lethargy that enveloped him. He was cold, colder than he had ever been in his life, but it didn't seem to matter. He was in that floating, dreamy state before sleep when consciousness is still hanging on but everything is fluid, everything is peaceful, everything and anything is possible.

He felt wet. His chest and abdomen were soaked. Probably with blood. Somewhere in his brain a voice— probably the same unheeded voice as before—screamed that he was dying. But that wasn't true. Couldn't be. He'd been stabbed, yes, but there was no pain now. Only cold. And you couldn't die of cold. Not in a heated Coronado apartment. Not with what he laid out a month in mortgage payments.

His outflung arm was only inches from the phone wire where it jacked into the wall. He stretched and reached it. He tugged on the wire and the phone dropped to the floor with a bang that sent shockwaves vibrating through his skull.

The trimline receiver tumbled to a rest near his head. Ed tried to reach the receiver, to bring it closer to his lips, but his arms wouldn't respond. He tried to shout but the words gurgled in his throat, emerging as a barely intelligible croak.

A tinny voice rattled out of·it.

"Hello? Hello? Is this Ed Bannion? From Paramount? Hello? This is the police calling."

Ed didn't recognize the voice. He tried again to make his voice work.

"Help ... dying ..."

Why had he said that? He wasn't dying. Just tired. And very cold.

"What? What did you say? Did you say you're dying? Hello?"

It sounded a little like Kara's detective friend, Harris. Ed tried to speak again, to reassure Detective Harris that he was all right, but no words came. He was so tired. Too tired to talk. Maybe later.

Who is this? Hello, damn it!"

Finally the voice clicked off, replaced by silence. Blessed silence. Now he could get some sleep. So tired. And so cold. If only he could get warm, everything would be perfect ...

... perfect ...

He roused himself. What if that panicky voice in his head was right? What if he went to sleep and didn't wake up? He had to warn them about Dr. Gates, about what he was doing to Kara, and to others. But how? Even if he could manage to dial the phone, he couldn't talk. He could just barely move his finger.

Move his finger ...

▼

Rob didn't know who the hell that had been on the phone, but it was somebody in extremis. He called Doyle and told him to get a radio car over to the address, then headed for his own car.

He hadn't been able to tell if the voice was male or female, but its owner was surely dying. He prayed it wasn't Kara.

If Bannion had harmed her in any way . . .

He screeched to a halt before Bannion's apartment building. A blue and white radio car was already there, its red lights flashing. He ran inside. The vestibule door was open, *Bannion* was listed on the fifth floor. He found two uniforms waiting outside 5-A.

"You Harris?" said the older-looking one with the thick black mustache. "I'm Grosso. You the one who called this in?"

Rob nodded. "No answer?"

"Nothing."

"Let's break it in."

"Ay, I don't know—"

"The guy on the phone said he was dying. That's reason enough. Come on."

The two uniforms glanced at each other, then shrugged. The three of them hit the door at once. That was enough.

Rob leaped into the apartment with his service revolver drawn, his eyes darting about the neat, spacious, well-lit living room.

"Kara! Kara, you here?"

Silence. He checked out the dining room and kitchen, then moved to the bathroom. He heard Grosso's voice call from the bedroom.

"Yo! Harris! Here he is!"

Rob rushed to the bedroom. Grosso was squatting next to a naked prone male body, his index and middle finger on the throat. There was a huge amount of blood on the floor, pooling out from under the corpse.

Rob looked closer. It was Ed Bannion, the man he had been trying to find all night.

"Ain't even cold yet," Grosso said.

Rob had only met Bannion twice, but seeing him murdered like this got to him. He'd seen hundreds of murder victims but this was the first one he had ever known. He felt queasy. And angry. Now he might never know what went on in Kelly's room at the Plaza that night.

He was about to turn away when he noticed the way the blood was smeared near Bannion's right hand, almost like—

"Is that writing over there by his hand?" Rob asked and moved to the far side of the corpse.

Grosso bent for a closer look. "Shit, yeah, I think it is!"

Rob knelt on the throw rug next to Bannion's body. There were letters traced in blood on the polished wood:

The rest was smeared.

" 'Gates?' " said Grosso. "He talking about the Pearly Gates?"

The sudden burst of excitement in Rob was almost unbearable.

"I don't think so," he said. "I think he named his killer."

He rose to his feet and motioned Grosso away.

"Don't touch a thing! Don't touch a goddamn thing until Forensics gets here and photos and prints everything."

He stepped back and stared at the body. The uneasiness rose up in him again. Bannion was here dead, but where was Kara? Where the *hell* was Kara?

▼

Kara awoke with a start. There were sounds in the outer room, footsteps, rustlings.

Someone's here!

She leaped from the bed. She was weaponless, defenseless. And terrified. As she lifted the phone and prepared to dial 911, she peaked through the open door. The breath clogged in her throat. A man there. In a bomber jacket. He looked like—

"Rob?"

He whirled, his features tight with shock at first, then they relaxed with relief.

"Kara! You're here!"

"Of course I'm here. I've been sleeping here all week as you well know! But what are *you* doing here? And how on earth did you get in?"

He rushed forward and grabbed her shoulders—gently, but there was no escaping his grasp.

"Where have you been all night?"

"Right here. Where else?"

"No. You weren't here. *I* was here, but *you* weren't!"

Something in his eyes was starting to frighten her.

"Rob, what are you talking about?"

"I called here a couple of hours ago but got no answer."

"I talked to you—"

"No. After that. I got worried so I got Kelly's key from the effects bag and let myself in. The place was empty. I used your phone for I don't know how long." He let go of her shoulders and pointed past her. "Look. The phone book's right where I left it."

Kara looked and felt terror begin to crawl through her. She hadn't had the phone book out all week. She pushed past Rob and ran for the oven. The key was still there, and the strand of her hair was still wrapped around it. She looked at Rob.

"Rob, I couldn't have left here. The key's right where I put it."

She watched him shake his head slowly and knew with sinking certainty that he was telling the truth. He had been here and she had not.

How? She wanted to scream it. *HOW?*

He came over and led her to the couch. He eased her down and then sat next to her. Close.

"There's something else you should know, Kara." His eyes were locked on hers. "Ed Bannion is dead. He was murdered an hour or so ago."

"Ed? Oh, God! Ed?"

For a moment the room spun about her, but she willed it to stop. But she couldn't stop the tears.

"Poor Ed! What a horrible way to die!"

She felt Rob stiffen beside her.

"What way, Kara?"

"Stabbed to death. How awful!"

"How did you know he was stabbed?"

Know? God, how *did* she know?

"I . . . I don't know! Didn't you tell me? Please say you told me!"

Rob's headshake was slow and deliberate.

"My God, what's happening to my life, Rob? Everything's going crazy around me and I can't seem to do anything about it! What's happening?"

He held her gently and said, "I don't know, Kara." He said, "I don't know," over and over.

FEBRUARY 23
8:22 A.M.

"I HOPE YOU ENJOYED YOUR RDO, ROB," AUGIE MANETTI said as he dropped a stack of papers on Rob's desk.

Sunday was Rob's regular day off, and he had spent most of it with Kara and Jill. He had been itching to stay on the Bannion killing but he felt Kara needed him around until she got used to the idea that someone she knew had been murdered. So he had stayed away from the precinct house all day. Besides, Manetti was his partner and was familiar with the Kelly Wade file. Rob had filled him in on all the details of the Bannion case. Officially, it was out of Midtown North's area, but because Rob had said it tied in with the Wade death the case had been assigned to Midtown North. Rob expected to be called into Mooney's office any minute.

Yesterday had not been the best of days. Kara had swung between depression and anxious agitation. But he had enjoyed being with Jill. The kid was a joy. Plus having her along had forced Kara to keep it light most of the time.

Rob dragged them around on a tour of his personal favorite sights in Manhattan, from the New York Yacht Club on 44th Street with its second-story windows that looked like the sterns of Spanish galleons, then to the Dakota, then for a ride on the Roosevelt Island cable tramway, and finally to the top of the Chrysler Building. Kara seemed to perk up a little, but whenever Jill was out of earshot, Kara had rambled on about strange dreams, and Gates being there. Rob was beginning to worry about her mental stability.

Maybe today would be better.

"What's the beef?" Rob said to Manetti.

"This Bannion case—it's turning into a pretzel."

Manetti dropped into the chair next to Rob's desk. He was a compact, well muscled man with jet black hair, fashionably short on top and sides, and long in the back. He and Rob had come up about the same time and often worked together.

Rob said, "The unknown prints from the Plaza and the electric bill match Bannion's, right?"

"Right. That was a damn good guess."

"A deduction, my dear Augie. A deduction."

"No shit, Sherlock. But I went you one better. I had the M.E. take a bite impression from Bannion. And guess where it found a perfect match?"

"Kelly Wade's shoulder!"

"Riiiiight!"

Mannetti held out a hand, palm up. Rob slapped it.

"That's better than prints!" Rob said.

"You know it. The prints don't say when he was there. But the bite match says he was with Kelly Wade at the very end. And I expect the DNA match on the semen to show he was *in* her as well!"

Rob wondered how Kara would take that. Not well, he figured.

"Nice work."

"Found the murder weapon, too. One of the kitchen knives. Traces of Bannion's blood in the groove between the handle and the blade. No prints on it, though."

"Still, it sounds like you had yourself a pretty good Sunday, Augie."

"Up to a point. Then things get screwy. I mean, Bannion writes the name of Kelly's psychiatrist in his own blood on the floor. But nowhere in the place is there a single print that belongs to this Dr. Gates."

"Damn. Probably wore gloves."

"Maybe. Maybe not. Because you know whose prints the place is lousy with?"

"I can hardly wait to hear."

"The other Wade girl. Kelly's twin. What's her name—Kara?"

Rob froze. He stared at Manetti. He wasn't kidding. Why would he? He didn't know of Rob's past history with Kara—or of his continuing interest.

"Christ!" Rob said.

"My sentiments exactly! See what I mean about screwy? We got a dead guy named Bannion we can link to the death of Kelly Wade, maybe not as her killer, if indeed she was killed, but right there on top of the scene of her death—and right there on top of her, as well, if you know what I mean and I think you do. And we can put Kelly Wade's twin sister at the scene of this Bannion guy's death. But whose name does Bannion write on the floor in his own blood? The psychiatrist who was treating Kelly Wade!"

"You want another twist in your pretzel?" Rob said, still numb from the news that Kara had been in Bannion's apartment.

"Sure. Why not? Hit me."

"Dr. Gates is Kara Wade's psychiatrist, too."

"No shit!" Manetti clapped his hands and laughed. "I'm gonna have to write a book about this one!"

A book, Rob thought. Kara was writing a book. He hoped she wouldn't have to finish it in jail.

"So!" Manetti said. "What do we do now? Pick up the twin?"

Rob stopped himself from shouting *No!* But it wasn't easy. He forced himself to lean back in the chair and look as if he were seriously considering the suggestion. He had to buy Kara some time. She hadn't killed Bannion. He was sure of that.

At least he thought he was sure.

"Not yet. If her prints were on the knife or if Bannion had written *her* name on the floor, we'd have her all but sentenced. But they're not and he didn't. He wrote 'Gates.' So I'm going to look into Gates. In the meantime, why don't you run a background check on Kara Wade."

That ought to buy us a couple of days.

"Will do."

Manetti headed for his desk while Rob sat and brooded at his own. He was faced with unanswerable questions.

But what would he do when the time ran out? And how could he tell Kara she was at Bannion's place without sending her off the deep end?

The only way he knew how: Come right out and say it.

▼

1:30 P.M.

"Maybe I *was* there, Rob," Kara said.

She was surprised at how calm she felt. But after all, she had been anticipating this moment all day. Memories of the other night's dream had prepared her for it.

"You were there, Kara," Rob said. "Fingerprints don't lie."

She nodded, echoing him. "Fingerprints don't lie."

"But another thing they don't do is tell us *when* you were there."

"It was probably Saturday morning. But just my *body* was there. *I* wasn't."

"You mean . . . Janine."

She didn't answer him. They were sitting twelve stories up in the front window of Ellen's co-op, overlooking East 46th Street. They were alone in the living room for the moment. Ellen was out at a luncheon. Jill was in the kitchen helping the cook with a batch of tollhouse cookies. Kara looked down at the snarled traffic below as she debated whether or not to tell Rob what she had come to believe. It was so incredible, so outre, that she scarcely believed it herself. But it explained everything.

And it was the reason she had skipped her session with Dr. Gates today.

"I don't know," Rob said slowly. "I don't know if this multiple personality thing is going to carry much weight with a jury if the evidence puts you in Bannion's apartment Friday night or Saturday morning."

Kara took a deep breath. *Might as well go for it.*

"Maybe it's not a multiple personality disorder. Maybe it's Dr. Gates."

Rob stared at her. "I don't get it."

"That letter I got—on the back of the electric bill? Maybe it's true. I think it's possible Dr. Gates can take over bodies and use them."

She explained what she remembered of her dream from Saturday morning—disjointed snatches of monologue as her own voice told Ed Bannion Dr. Gate's story of how he used women's bodies for "fun," of a knife, of blood, and Ed falling to the floor.

Rob's expression was stricken. "Kara . . . Kara . . ."

"I know how crazy it sounds, but doesn't it explain everything? It explains the note—it's from one of his former 'toys'—and it explains this so-called Ingrid personality in Kelly and this Janine in me. And most of all, it explains why Ed wrote Dr. Gates' name on the floor instead of mine!"

"Kara, there isn't a jury in the world that will buy that."

Kara fought the sinking, trapped feeling that threatened to overwhelm her. The apartment walls seemed to be closing in.

"I'm in big trouble, right?"

Rob nodded. "Your prints are all over the apartment, you can't account for your whereabouts at the time of the murder, and you've got what might be construed as a motive."

"Motive? I didn't know he'd . . . he'd been with Kelly until you told me yesterday!"

"You know that and I know that, but—"

"But what will a jury say? Is that it?"

Rob shrugged and remained silent.

"Do you think Ed might have thrown Kelly out that window?"

"He was there."

Yes. Ed Bannion had been there, and he'd *bitten* Kelly! He'd also been alone with Kara in Kelly's apartment. She felt cold all over.

"Then what was he doing hanging around me? Do you think he wanted to kill me?"

"Maybe. I doubt we'll ever know."

"And what about the other man they say was with Ed at the Plaza? Is he out there lurking about?"

Rob reached over and squeezed her hand.

"I'll be keeping an eye on this place—and it's *here* I want you to stay. Not that apartment."

Kara felt her back begin to stiffen at being told where to stay, but she made herself relax. Rob was right.

"But what if I'm . . . dangerous after I go to sleep?"

"Can't you talk to Ellen? Find some way to lock you in a bedroom when you call it a night?"

Kara thought about that. She could tell Ellen and Jill she'd been sleepwalking.

"That might work. What are you going to be doing?"

"I'm going to be all over Gates. He's in this up to his neck. Not like you say—sorry, but there's no way I can buy that. But he's involved. After all, it was *his* name Bannion wrote on the floor. So that means the good doctor's got some questions to answer. And I'm the guy who's going to be asking."

The grim determination in Rob's eyes offered her a glimmer of hope.

Jill came running into the room, a plate in one hand and her ever-present chopsticks in the other.

"Rob! Rob!" she cried, then caught Kara's sharp look. "Mr. Harris! Look at this!"

Kara watched his face brighten at the sight of her. He put an arm around her waist and drew her close. With the contact, all the tension seemed to run out of his body.

"What are they?"

"Guess!"

"Spotted rocks."

She giggled. "No! They're uncooked cookies."

"Don't look like cookies to me. Cookies are flat. Those are round."

"They flatten when they cook. But watch this!" She picked up one of the balls of raw cookie dough with her chopsticks and popped it into her mouth. "See? I can do it now!"

"Well, I'll be!" Rob said, hugging her closer. "You did that just like a real Chinese! Can I have one?"

Jill picked up another with her chopsticks and got it to Rob's mouth.

"Hmmmm," he said. "Tell the cook it needs more vanilla."

"Not me!" Jill said. "*You* tell her!"

Jill ate another dough ball.

"You know," Rob told her, "you're so good with those, I think we can take you to a sushi bar."

"What's that?"

"That's where they eat raw fish on rice balls."

Jill made a sour face. "Eeeeuuuuu!"

Kara watched Rob rock his head back and laugh. She had to tell him about his daughter. And soon. Before he figured it out on his own.

▼

2:55 P.M.

Rob sat in Gates' waiting room and surveyed some choice photos of the murder scene. The best was a close-up of the writing on the floor. Rob had made sure the photographer had set the lamp so that the light reflected off the still-wet letters. He was anxious to show this to Gates and watch how he reacted to seeing his own name written in blood.

Kara was innocent and Gates was guilty. He firmly believed that. He had no right to. He hadn't a shred of evidence to back that up. It was a gut feeling.

Or was he fooling himself? This was why cops were supposed to stay away from cases in which they were emotionally involved. Emotions clouded judgment. Were his feelings for Kara clouding his?

Rob began to turn the photo over on his lap, then snapped it back to face up. From this angle, the smears to the right of "Gates" had looked like an "equals" sign, followed by a "K."

The hairs at the back of his neck began to rise. *Gates is Kara?* Rob stared at it from all angles. Was that what Bannion was trying to say? That Gates was in Kara? Like the note on the electric bill had said? Like Kara had said less than an hour ago?

The number of people who believed in that crazy idea seemed to be growing. Was it possible that—?

Rob shook off the thought. No. Couldn't be. Something like that simply wasn't possible. The smeared end of Bannion's scrawl—the "=K" part—had to be a trick of the light. People did a lot of awful things to each other in New York, but they didn't take over each other's bodies.

When Gates' patient came out, Rob scooted into the consultation room as he had done before, without waiting for the receptionist to warn the doctor.

"Detective Harris," Gates said in a bored tone. "What brings you back?"

"Your friend Edward Bannion is dead," Rob said without preamble.

It had the desired effect. Gates stiffened and blurted:

"My friend?"

Any uncertainties Rob had harbored about Gates being involved in Bannion's death evaporated with those two words. He took grim satisfaction from the fact that Gates' first response was not to ask who was Edward Bannion or what the hell Rob was talking about, but to challenge the idea that he was a friend.

He shoved a particularly gory crime scene photo under the psychiatrist's nose.

"Sure. Don't you recognize him?"

Gates took the photo and studied it. The blood and the corpse did not seem to faze him.

"I've never seen this man before in my life."

"Really?" Rob handed over the close up of the scrawl. "The last act of his life was to write your name."

Gates was clearly jolted by the sight of his name written in blood. But Rob had to hand it to him: he recovered quickly.

"This could mean anything. It doesn't say 'Dr. Gates' and it doesn't say 'Lawrence Gates,' it just says 'Gates.' That could mean anything."

"Yeah," Rob said softly, staring at him, "but you know and I know that he means you."

"Are you accusing me of murder?" Gates said.

"You said it, not me."

Gates leaned back and smiled. He picked up the key ring from his desk top and began twirling it on his finger.

"All right, Detective Harris. Let's assume you are accusing me of the murder of a man I have never even heard of until this very moment. Let's play this game through. I have no motive, and no opportunity."

"Can you account for your whereabouts at the time of the murder?"

"Which was?"

"Approximately two-thirty a.m. Sunday morning."

"I was here, in my office, working on patient charts. And I have the best witness in the world."

"Really. Who's that?"

"A member of the city's police department. You."

Rob felt the surprise break through onto his face.

Gates's smile broadened.

"Come now, Detective Harris. Did you really think your pathetic attempts to shadow me went unnoticed? I know you've been watching me. It's been quite amusing, really."

But I wasn't outside your place all night! Rob thought. He had been at Kara's before the murder and at Bannion's after. Plenty of time for Gates to sneak out and kill Bannion.

But he wasn't going to tell Gates that. Not yet.

"If you think you were shadowed before, pal, you wait."

The smile faded from Gates' face, replaced by a look of cold contempt.

"Don't look for trouble, detective."

"I won't be looking for trouble—just looking for you. No matter where you go, you're going to look up and see me. I'll connect you to Bannion, and then you'll be mine. You can file harrassment charges, but that won't stop me."

"Harrassment charges? Do you think I'd have to stoop to that? Against *you?* Do you really think I couldn't lose you any time I wished? Do you actually believe that someone like you would be any sort of match for a man with my intelligence and knowledge of the human mind? Don't make me laugh!"

"That's the last thing I want to make you do, pal," Rob said.

He gathered up his photos. The guy was guilty. Rob could smell it. A grim, cold determination crowded out the anger that had built up during their exchange. He was going to nail Gates, or lose his badge trying. He headed for the door.

"Be seeing you."

LETTERS FROM **Purgatory**

At last! The punishment is over!

This was by far the worst ever. So weak I can barely write. Not physically weak, but weak in the spirit, in the mind. This time he brought me to the precipice of madness. I know my grip on sanity has been tenuous at best, but this time nearly undid me. A few hours more of his torture and I fear I'd have been irretrievably mad.

And I failed! That's the worst part. Got my warning to her but she didn't heed it! Maybe the little fool deserves what's happening to her! Maybe—

No. That's unfair. It's too much to ask anyone to believe something so far beyond her own capabilities, something without precedent in her own experience or knowledge, something that should be impossible.

But perhaps I haven't failed completely. He's disturbed about something. Something's gone wrong. Don't know what it is, but he's upset. Detect ripples on the customarily serene surface of his sublime indifference to the world. His supreme confidence in his ability to deal easily with whatever the lesser mortals around him might do appears to have been challenged.

Am I responsible for that? I pray so.

Also sense that tonight he will answer that challenge. I hope his opponent is mentally agile. A survivor.

I'll be cheering for him. I hope the opponent kills the

swine! Or maybe I'll get the chance. If I can, I'll do it. I know I can do it now!

I won't be punished again!

FEBRUARY 24
12:10 A.M.

GATES WAS PLAYING IT COOL. HE CAME OUT OF HIS TOWN-
house and didn't even glance around. Walked up to
Seventh and down to his office, just like every other
night since Rob had been watching him.

Which made Rob a little uneasy. Gates was going to
pull a stunt tonight. He could smell it in the air. When
and how were both up to Gates, which put Rob at a dis-
advantage. He had to be ready for anything.

Rob parked on Seventh and settled in for his watch.
He locked his car doors and checked to make sure the
safety strap on his holster was undone.

▼

12:25 A.M.

You enter her mind so easily now, like sliding down a
smooth, lubricated chute into a warm spring. You settle
into a familiar groove within that warmth. It fits you
perfectly. But of course, it should. It's custom made to

your personal specifications. You lock her consciousness into sleep and take over.

There's an instant of shock when you open her eyes.
You're not in Kelly's apartment. You turn on the light. It's
a small room, tastefully and expensively furnished. Is
Kara staying over at the Aunt's she talked about? That
would seem to be the case.

Well, that should present just a minor difficulty. If
everyone in the apartment is asleep, you can slip out
and be on your way.

You're going to miss this body. It's the best you've
ever had. Not that you're going to harm it in any way.
That would be a sin. But what you've got planned for
it tonight will take it out of circulation indefinitely.

For you've decided how to take care of the impudent
Detective Harris. A suitably ignominious end. Not only
will he be stabbed in exactly the same manner as the
man whose murder he is investigating, but it will be by
the very same hand—the hand of the woman he seems
to care so much about.

The irony of it appeals to you. And as he's dying you
will tell him in the voice of his lover who you really
are, and what you can do, and why it is impossible to
follow you when you do not wish to be followed.

And then you will laugh in his face.

After that, Kara Wade will undoubtedly be tried for
murder. She may get off on an insanity plea, and you
will gladly testify on her behalf about her multiple personality disorder, but even so, she will be institutional-
ized. She will not be free to come and go as you wish.
However, you might look in on her from time to time
to see if there are any interesting sexual experiences to
be had in a maximum security institution.

You throw on some clothes and glide to the door. If
the apartment is dark and quiet you'll slip to the kitchen

for a knife then out into the city. You turn the handle and pull.

The door won't budge. You rattle it—not too loudly—and pull again. It's locked. You look and see that it's one of those old fashioned doors with a keyhole and a lock bolt. And the key's not there.

It's got to be somewhere. You turn the room upside down but you can't find it.

Has Kara had herself locked in her room for the night? You wouldn't put it past her. It's an ancient, simple, and effective solution. And it has you stumped.

You're tempted to punish her body, damage it, even disfigure it as you abandon her, just to show her who's boss. But that will interfere with your plans. You need her in good condition. If you stay away for a few days, she'll let down her guard. And then you'll make your move.

But now it's time to return to Chelsea where Detective Harris is watching. You don't need your special ability to outwit a cretin like Harris. There are other ways short of killing him to demonstrate that he is no match for a mind of your caliber. This might be an even better way to prepare him for his end. Humiliate him first. Confound him. Lose him when he tries to follow you. Night after night, demonstrate his impotence against you.

And when he's completely demoralized, *then* you drive the knife home with Kara's hand.

This will be fun. You can start tonight.

You neaten up the room, turn off the lights. You hurry back to bed and leave Kara Wade's body in sleep.

▼

1:08 A.M.

Rob raced down Twenty-first Street. He sighed with relief when he saw Gates walking up the steps to his front
door. The doctor had left his office unusually early tonight and Rob had been afraid he had something sneaky
planned. If he did, he would have pulled it during Rob's
end run with the car. But there he was. Home sweet
home.

Was this it for the night? Rob didn't trust Gates
enough to think so. He'd give him another couple of
hours before quitting.

He got the car settled into its customary spot by the
fire hydrant and zipped up the battered, fleece-lined
leather bomber jacket to ward off the cold. He was just
lighting a cigarette when he saw Gates bounce down
his front steps and head back toward Seventh again.

Maybe he'd left something at the office. Rob started
up the car. He wasn't going to let Gates out of his sight
this time. He didn't wait for him to get to the end of the
block but pulled out and crept the car along behind
him. No need for subtlety anymore. Each knew where
the other stood.

At the corner, Gates suddenly turned right instead of
left. He began hurrying *up* Seventh Avenue. And the
traffic ran downtown only.

Here we go!

Rob found another hydrant on the corner and pulled
in next to it. He jumped out and sprinted after Gates.

The doctor had a half-block lead. At the corner of
Seventh and Twenty-second he got into the rear of a
waiting cab. It lurched away, heading east on Twenty-
second.

Rob grinned. That sly bastard! Must have called from

his home and had a radio cab waiting for him! Rob paused long enough to get the cab's number off the roof light, then he searched Seventh Avenue for a cab of his own. None in sight. He kept running, past Twenty-second on to Twenty-third which was a two-way. Better chance to find a cab there.

He did. He flagged it down and flashed his shield as he leaped inside.

"Police. Put on your 'Not in Service' sign and move it up to Sixth! Fast!"

The driver was dark, his voice thickly accented.

"Begging your—"

"You'll get paid. *Move it!*"

The driver moved it. The card on the visor said his name was Achmed Moustaffah. Rob didn't care if he was Colonel Qadaffi as long as he could handle his rig and knew the streets.

The light was green ahead at Sixth. Rob directed Achmed to the curb at the corner. Now the hard part. Was Gates continuing east or turning uptown? When the red came, he watched. He'd give the other cab twenty seconds to—

Suddenly a radio cab went by on Sixth, heading uptown.

"See that cab?" Rob said. "Forget the light and follow it."

Achmed turned to him and grinned.

"Really? This is true what you say? 'Follow that cab?' Four years I have driven and so many movies have seen and have prayed that someone would say this to me! You are making me so happy!"

"If you don't shut up and start driving, we'll lose him!"

With a screech of balding tires, Achmed wheeled through the red light onto Sixth.

"Have no fear! We shall not be losing him!"

Rob slid over on the back seat until he was behind Achmed. He crouched down and watched Gates' cab ahead through the space between the driver and the window post.

The smart way to do this, of course, would have been to have a back-up ready. But Gates was not officially a suspect, so there was no back-up to be had. And even if there were, Rob wouldn't have used it. This was between him and Gates. Anybody else would get in the way.

Okay, Doc. You've made your move. Let's see where it takes us.

▼

You look through the rear window of the cab and see no one following. A delivery truck, an off-duty cab. Easy to spot a tail at this hour of the morning.

You face front and settle back in the lumpy seat. You're disappointed. That was too easy. You almost wish for a decent challenge. This is like beating a street urchin at chess.

Well, no sense in following through with the rest of the route you had planned. No need for it now. You've achieved checkmate on the first move.

You tell the driver to let you off at the Plaza. He drops you on the Central Park Side. You walk in the bar entrance, past the stairway down to Trader Vic's, and into the Oak Bar with its dark paneling, the ornate white ceiling, the tiny lamps in sconces on the walls and pillars. You notice the sign. "Occupancy by more than 240 persons is dangerous and unlawful." You can't imagine sharing this room with 239 people.

You take a table by the window where you can see the park, and order a snifter of Remy Martin. You swirl it in the glass and inhale the vapors as the liquid warms, savoring the irony of sitting completely unnoticed in a place where only weeks ago, in a different body, you were notorious.

You are about to drain your snifter when the waiter sets another on your table.

"I didn't order this," you say.

The waiter smiles and nods his head toward the other end of the room.

"Compliments of the gentlemen at the bar, sir."

Startled, you scan the bar. Your eyes freeze on a man in a brown leather jacket standing with his foot resting casually on the brass rail. He smiles and hoists a glass of beer in your direction.

Harris!

The insolent pup! How did he find you? You were certain you left him gawking on that street corner back in Chelsea.

Well, never mind that now. He was lucky this time. And you did want a challenge tonight, didn't you?

Time for the second phase of your plan to elude him.

You leave enough money for the drink and a tip, then you exit the bar and rush through the small lobby toward the main entrance, the one by the fountain, facing Fifth Avenue. You turn left toward Central Park South. As soon as there's a break in the traffic, you hurry across the street toward the Park.

▼

Rob watched Gates enter Central Park's southeast corner. He couldn't believe Gates wanted to spend any real time in there. Too risky. He could run into a bunch of wilding kids and be left as hamburger along the side of the path. He guessed from Gates' soft look that he wasn't in great shape, which placed another mark against a long trot through the Park.

A diversion, I'll bet.

Rob moved to his left along Central Park South until he was half way between Fifth and Sixth. He pressed himself back into the darkened, canopied doorway of Mickey Mantle's and waited.

Sure enough, ten minutes later Gates emerged from the park at the head of Sixth Avenue and crossed back to the downtown side of Central Park South. He disappeared as he hurried down Sixth.

Rob cut through the alley near Mickey Mantle's, emerging on 58th Street, then he ran full tilt up to Sixth and turned downtown. He spotted Gates immediately on the far side of the avenue. Rob hugged the store fronts, keeping to the shadows. His big worry now was Gates grabbing a cab and leaving Rob in the dust.

Rob watched Gates cross 57th, saw him pause, look around, then duck down the steps of the subway entrance on the far corner.

Rob stayed in the shadows by his own subway entrance, catercornered from Gates'.

Good for you, Doc. Never would have thought of you taking the subway.

Rob allowed himself to relax a little. He had practically grown up on the subway. He knew it inside and out.

Gates had just entered Rob's realm.

▼

You buy a token and wait near the foot of the steps, watching for Detective Harris to appear. Suddenly there are footsteps descending but it is a tall lanky black man wearing what looks like a soft leather fez. His eyes challenge you as he passes. You look away. When you hear the rumble of an approaching train on the level below, you dash down the stairs to the platforms. You don't care where the train is going because you're only going to take it one stop. The wind gushes from the downtown side. Excellent! You run for it. The doors open at your approach, as if they've been expecting you. You find a car near the middle and step inside. But you don't sit down. Instead, you peer up and down the platform. You're taking no chances this time. There is no sign of Detective Harris. You watch until the doors close, sealing you in.

You smile as the train lurches forward. You've done the unexpected. Normally a man of your stature would not stoop to riding the subway. But you thrive on doing the unexpected.

The first stop is almost immediate. Forty-ninth Street. That's too close to where you got on. You decide to take the train one more stop.

See? Sometimes you even surprise yourself—you've changed your own plans in mid-play.

Let Harris try to catch you now.

▼

Rob crouched near the top of the stairway furthest uptown on the platform. He'd come underground via the other entrance. Apparently the doctor was unaware of the multiple stairways to and from street level at each stop.

Rob watched as Gates scanned the platform. He waited until the doors were closed and the train was in motion, then he made his move. He ran down the steps, darted across the platform, and grabbed one of the safety chains that swung across the space between the last and next-to-last cars. He slipped between the chains and stepped onto the platform between the cars.

He paused there a moment to catch his breath and get

himself together. That move had been a lot easier when he was fifteen.

He slid the door open and entered the next-to-last car. Leaning forward against the train's momentum, he made his way toward Gates' car, somewhere near the middle. He found the doctor hanging on a strap and staring out the windows at the darkness of the tunnel.

He walked by and gave him a sharp elbow in the ribs.

"Sorry."

Gates turned, a glare in his eyes. But the anger abruptly turned to shock.

Rob gave him a polite smile, as if he were just another passenger.

"Wish they'd learn to drive these things a little smoother," he said, then continued forward to the next car.

He hid his grin from Gates. That expression on the psychiatrist's face was worth the risk of jumping on a moving subway. Any day.

In the second car from the front, Rob found a heavy black woman in a nurse's uniform standing by the door, obviously waiting for the next stop. That would be Forty-second Street. She had a face like James Earl Jones with a Roseanne Barr style body. Perfect.

When the train stopped at Forty-second, Rob exited the car in a half crouch on the nurse's downtown side, then slipped behind the nearest pillar and waited. He was sure Gates would not want to stay on the subway any longer. Well, pretty sure. This was pure gamble now. Rob stayed behind the pillar, not moving a muscle as the train slid its doors closed and began to roll toward Thirty-fourth Street. He peered into the passing cars. If he saw Gates, the chase was over. The psychiatrist would have won tonight. Rob would have to start again tomorrow night.

But he didn't see Gates. He must have got off.

But still Rob didn't move. When the train was gone, he heard what he had expected: a single pair of footsteps hurrying up the stairs.

▼

You watch every passenger who gets off the train, then you wait until the doors are all closed. And still you wait until the train has been swallowed by the subway tunnel. You are alone on the platform. The detective did not get off the train.

You turn and hurry up toward the street, planning what to do next. This has been a very unsettling experience. Detective Harris was exceedingly lucky tonight and very cocksure about it. He knocked you in the ribs on the subway car, then pretended you were a stranger. An insult. An assault. Even though the chase isn't over yet, he has succeeded in humiliating you. He'll be bragging about this to his policemen cronies tomorrow, calling you a fool.

Oh, it will be good to have Kara Wade's hand sink that blade into his gut and twist it!

But that will have to wait. What to do now? If you return to Chelsea he might well be sitting in his car outside your front door, waiting for you. Laughing at you.

You come up to the cold, crisp air. The neon sleaze of Times Square assaults you. You ignore it. Your mind is on more important matters. What to do next?

An idea strikes you. Why return home at all? Spend the night at a hotel. A wonderful idea.

You look around. But you certainly won't stay here in the Times Square area. The Grand Hyatt is just a few blocks east. And the Helmsley Palace is further uptown. You were at the Helmsley as Kara a few nights ago.

Now you'll have to be there as yourself. Oh, well, it's a comfortable place.

No sooner do you raise your hand to flag a taxi than one pulls into the curb. You reach for the door but it opens by itself. A familiar, grinning face appears out of the rear interior.

"Need a ride, Doc? I'm heading your way."

The shock is like a stab in the throat. This is not to be borne! How can this buffoon know your every move? It's not possible! Not natural!

You lurch away, into the street to find another cab, one for yourself, to take you away from this city hireling who trails after you like a tin can tied to your tail. Rage is a living thing inside you. You'll kill him with your bare hands if you ever get the chance!

Suddenly there's the blare of a horn, unbearably loud, screeching tires. You spin. Lights, so bright, so close—

▼

"Oh, shit, man! Oh, *shit!*" Rob's cabbie was saying as he leaped from his taxi.

Rob was ahead of him, running around the back of the cab to where Gates lay sprawled face down on the pavement.

The driver of the van that struck Gates was running around in circles, grabbing anyone who might have been a witness, pleading with anyone who would listen.

"You saw him run out in front of me didn't you? I had no chance to stop! The light was green! He jumped right in front of me! It's not my fault!"

Rob wanted to shut him up.

"It's all right. I'm a police officer. It wasn't your fault. Now back off while—"

Gates groaned and got to his knees. He looked

around in a daze. Finally his eyes focused on Rob. There was a wild look in them.

Rob took a cautious step forward.

"Just stay where you are, Gates. We'll get an ambulance."

Gates lurched to his feet and reached for Rob, staggering toward him. He was bleeding from a cut on his forehead.

"El ment!"

"Easy, Gates. You're hurt. Why don't you sit on the curb here.

As Rob put out a hand to steady the injured man, Gates leaped at him.

"Nen tibet! Kedeshen, nen tibet!"

He grappled with Rob, slinging one arm around him and pulling at his jacket with the other. There was a crazed look in his eyes. Rob tried to push him away without knocking him down again.

"Hey, be cool, Doc. You're going to—"

And then Rob felt Gates' probing hand latch onto his holster.

He's going for my gun!

Rob shoved Gates violently away but felt the revolver pull free, saw Gates click off the safety. Rob grappled for it. Gates was in his face. He looked demented. He was breathing like a set of leaky air brakes. Flecks of saliva salted his lips as he wheezed in a faint, frantic, high-pitched voice, saying the same thing over and over.

"Nen tibet! Nen tibet!"

Gates had wormed one of his fingers through the trigger guard but Rob had jammed his thumb behind the trigger. Gates twisted the pistol viciously, pointing the barrel straight up, but Rob held on. He knew he was a dead man if the gun got away from him.

Suddenly Gates stiffened and shuddered. His eyes

widened and he suddenly tried to pull his hands free of the revolver. The move took Rob by surprise. His thumb slipped from behind the trigger, leaving it free to move.

The retort was deafening. Rob winced away from the muzzle flash, felt the burn and sting of the ignited powder. Out of the corner of his eye he saw Gates jerk upward, saw the top of his head explode in a fountain of red. And then the revolver was all his again and Gates was staggering backward with outflung arms. He managed two steps, during which his eyes were wide, shocked, losing their light. For an instant, his mouth twitched. He said something that sounded like *"Kissinum,"* then he toppled flat onto his back like a fallen tree.

Rob stared at him, feeling numb, feeling sick. All around him voices were saying how crazy the guy was, first running out in front of a car and then attacking a cop and trying to steal his gun. Rob barely heard them. He was staring at Gates' supine form. From this angle he could see the small round hole under Gates' chin where the bullet had entered. It wasn't even bleeding. He stared at that hole until the first blue and white unit arrived.

FEBRUARY 25
11:30 A.M.

"HOW YOU HOLDING UP, ROB?"

It was a measure of Lieutenant Mooney's sincere concern that he called him by his first name. Rob was surprised that he knew it. Mooney perched on the edge of his green desk in his gray office; Rob sat in the chair before it.

"I'm doing all right."

"You did a full shift yesterday. You could have taken today off."

"I don't need an extra day off."

Why was everybody treating him like he was going to fall apart?

"I remember the first time I shot somebody—"

"That's just it, lieu. I didn't pull the trigger. It was *his* finger in there. Not mine. And if he didn't take the bullet, it might just as easily have been me. Or someone on the curb."

Rob realized he had raised his voice and was getting steamed. He leaned back in the chair and shut up.

"Hey," Mooney said. "Easy. Just asking."

"Sorry, lieu. It's just that the whole thing never should have happened."

That was the part that bothered Rob the most. He was furious with himself for letting someone like Gates get his hands on his revolver. It was the kind of thing that should only happen to a rookie. Not to a guy with his experience. If Rob had been more on the ball he wouldn't have to see blood and bone and brains erupting from the top of Gates' head like a mini Mount St. Helens every time he closed his eyes.

"But it did happen. He fooled you. You thought he was hurt, you let down your guard, and he pulled a fast one on you. Don't let it get you down."

"It's not. But it means I'll probably never know the connection between Gates and Bannion and the Wade women. Three of them are dead and the fourth only came to town a couple of weeks ago, so she knows nothing."

"I'm glad you brought that up. I've been going over these files and here's my scenario: Gates either hypnotized Kelly Wade or got her hooked on schnozz, then pimped her out to do tricks with some wealthy contacts or friends. Bannion got too rough with her and threw her out the window. Gates got pissed at losing such a valuable asset and killed Bannion. Gates tries to elude police surveillance, attacks an officer in front of witnesses, and is fatally shot during the struggle. Three cases closed—bim, bam, boom." He handed the folders to Rob with a satisfied grin. "I like the way you work, Harris."

"Hey, lieu, that doesn't fit the facts at all. Gates was loaded. He didn't need to rent out his patients."

"He did it for kicks, then. He was kinky. The motive doesn't matter now that there's not going to be a trial. He did it. And he won't be doing it no more. Case closed. All *three* cases closed. Understand?" Mooney's face was getting red and his neck was beginning to bulge out over his collar. "We've got other deaths that need investigating. Get to them. Have a nice day, Harris."

Rob sighed. He knew from years of experience that when Mooney got like this there was no talking to him. He got up and headed for the squad room.

"You, too, lieu."

Rob tossed the files on his desk. These cases weren't closed by a long shot. But they weren't solvable, either. And if they were left open he'd have to file semiannual DD5 Supplementary Complaint Reports on each one. And Mooney would have to review each one.

Why not close them up? Officially, at least. That would get Kara off the hook—she couldn't be a suspect in a closed case.

But in his head Rob planned to keep them open. And if something new popped up, he could always reopen them officially.

And that day would come. He didn't know when, but he had a gut feeling this wasn't the last he'd seen of these three cases. In fact, he had an urge to combine the three into a single file: the Wade/Bannion/Gates case.

Especially after touring the back rooms of Gates' office yesterday.

He had shown up at the office at nine and told the receptionist as gently as he could that her employer was dead. The woman had shown no emotion other than disappointment at being out of a job. While she was emptying her desk, he had strolled through into the back rooms for a peek.

The file room had been tempting. He would have loved to get into those locked cabinets, but he had no warrant for a search and no probable cause to obtain one.

The other room had been the real shocker. A padded cell. With electronic combination locks inside and out, no less. He'd asked the receptionist how often Dr.

Gates had had occasion to use it and she told him she hadn't even known it was there.

No. There was too much here that was unexplained. Rob knew he hadn't heard the last of Lazlo Gati/ Lawrence Gates, M.D.

Manetti stopped by Rob's desk.

"That background on Kara Wade is ready. The Pennsy folks don't have much on her, but they're sending it down the wire. Should hit the printer any second. Still want it?"

Rob shrugged. "I'll stick it in the Bannion file. The case is closed. They're *all* closed."

Manetti laughed. "Move-'em-Out Mooney strikes again."

Rob went to the corner room where the printer and FAX machine sat. The printer was an old high-speed dot matrix that printed each line with a scream like Sam Kinison with hemorrhoids. He ripped off the fact sheet and speed-read through it. He grabbed Manetti as he passed.

"Hey, Augie. Who did this?"

"Lancaster County Sheriff's office, Why?"

"It's garbage. They don't have the date of her wedding, and they've got her kid's birthdate screwed up."

Manetti gave him an elaborate Brooklyn shrug.

"So call 'em, Rob."

Rob went back to the sheet. Kara's date of birth, her school records, her college degree and major, her job at the hospital, and even her performance record were all there. So was the kind of car she drove (a five-year old Buick), her credit record (excellent), her voter registration (Independent), and so on. But Jill's birthdate was off by a year. They had her as nine and a half and she was really only eight and a half. And there was no record of a marriage. No mention of Kara's late husband's employment and credit record. No mention of her being a widow. Nothing at all about her late husband. It was an extremely consistent deficiency, almost as if the guy had never—

"Jesus H. Christ!" he said aloud.

But if she'd never married, then who was Jill's—?

Suddenly Rob felt weak all over. Jill ... the first time he had met her ... in Gates' waiting room ... she'd said she was nine and a half ...

Nine and a half! That jibed with the background sheet. Jill had been born six months after Kara left New York!

Six months!

That meant—!

Rob's hand shook as he reached for the phone.

▼

12:30 P.M.

Kara waited for Rob's knock on the door. He'd called a short while ago asking if they could get together and talk—alone. He had insisted on alone. The doorman had buzzed up to say that he was here.

Alone. Kara wondered at that. And his voice had sounded funny. Thick, and hesitant. As if he'd had too much to drink. She hoped he wasn't drinking so early in the day. But if he was, she guessed it was understandable. After all, he'd killed somebody yesterday.

What a shock that seven a.m. call Tuesday morning. Rob on the phone, very subdued, telling her that Dr. Gates was dead. Killed by a bullet from his gun. He'd given her most of the details, and she'd culled more from the eyewitness accounts in the morning paper.

Her shock hadn't lasted long. It quickly turned to joy, to overwhelming relief. She knew that shouldn't be.

She shouldn't want to dance and sing because her psychiatrist was dead, but the news triggered something deep within her that wanted to pop champagne and shout for joy. She felt like a lifer in Sing Sing who'd just been let free.

The feeling had lasted all day. She'd wanted to see Rob last night but he had been up for thirty-six grueling hours by then, with most of the last twelve spent answering questions and filling out reports. He had wanted only to sleep. Sleep was something that Kara found elusive for most of the night. She'd felt too up, too buoyant. The feeling was still with her. It was unsettling to feel so *good* about a man's death.

She opened the door as soon as Rob knocked. He'd chosen a good day for a private tete-a-tete. The cook was off and Ellen had taken Jill out to lunch at Rumplemeyer's.

She went to hug him, figuring he'd need a hug after what he'd been through yesterday, but Rob brushed past her without saying a word. A couple of sheets of paper were rolled up in his hand.

"It's good to see you, too, Rob," she said, wondering why he was acting this way.

"We alone?" he said, wandering in a circle around the living room.

"Yes. I told you—"

"Good. Read this."

He handed her the sheets of typed paper. It was all about her.

"What's this?"

"It's about someone who was never married. Who's daughter was born a year earlier than she told me."

Kara felt her mouth dry up. She stared at him.

"Then you know."

His stood flatfooted with his shoulders slumped, his face a stricken mask, his brown eyes wide.

"She's mine?"

"Ours."

Kara took a step toward him and stopped. She'd had this planned for years, how she'd explain all the reasons, good ones, that had compelled her to leave him in the job he loved while she raised their child far from the city she could not bear to live in. How she was going to tell him immediately after the child was born. And how "immediately" had dragged on and on as she put off telling him that he was a father indefinitely. Eventually the delay stretched to an unconscionable length and she became too ashamed to tell him.

And even now, as he stood before her, already aware that Jill was his child, the words threatened to fail her again.

"You've got to understand, Rob. I—"

He began to sob. His chest heaved, tears filled his eyes and ran down his cheeks. Kara was shocked speechless. She had never seen Rob cry, had never thought he could. She stepped to his side and touched his arm. She never thought in a million years he would react this way.

"Rob, I'm so sorry I never told you, but—"

"She's mine?" he said. "She's really mine?"

"Yes."

He smiled then. With tears streaming down his cheeks he smiled and began laughing between the sobs. It was an awful sound, and made him look insane.

"All the way over I was praying it was true. Ever since that night when you two had dinner at my apartment she's been popping into my mind. I keep thinking if I ever had a kid I'd want her to be like Jill, I'd want her to *be* Jill! And when I'd think about the two of us getting back together I'd think of maybe even adopting her. But I don't have to adopt her! I'm already her father!"

Kara too felt like laughing and crying.

"But what about all that bullshit about your husband being killed on the Penn Turnpike? It was so convincing."

"Years of practice. And I wanted to see how you'd react." She paused. "Then you don't hate me?"

"No! I'm madder'n hell, but I don't hate you. You did such a great job with her! I think this is the happiest day of my life!"

He hugged her and Kara began to cry with him.

"I'm so glad you found out. I've been looking for a way to tell you but the time was never right. But I knew I had to tell you before we went back to Pennsylvania."

She felt him stiffen. He pushed her back to arm's length.

"Pennsylvania? You're not taking her back to Pennsylvania! Not now! Not when I've just learned about her!"

"Rob, that's where her home is, that's where she goes to school—"

"No way! You've kept me out of her life for nine and a half years. No more. That little girl needs a father and I'm going to be it. I don't know how we're going to tell her, and maybe we won't be able to tell her till she's older, but god damn it, even if she doesn't call me 'Daddy,' I'm going to *function* as her daddy! Am I making myself clear?"

"But Rob—!"

The phone cut her off. She went to answer it.

"Tilsdale residence."

"Is Miss Kara Wade there?" said a woman's voice.

"Speaking."

"One moment please for Mr. Wheatley."

Mr. Wheatley? Who one earth was—?

"Hello? Miss Kara Wade? This is Gordon Wheatley,

attorney for the estate of Dr. Lawrence Gates. Can you come over to my office immediately?"

Kara could feel sudden tension coiling within her.

"What for?"

"This has to do with Dr. Gates' estate. It's quite important."

"I want nothing to do with you or his estate."

"I assure you, it's quite to your advantage to—"

"I'm too busy!"

There was a pause, then Mr. Wheatley sighed.

"Then may I come over? It is extremely important."

Kara was taken aback by the request. She didn't know lawyers made house calls.

"How . . . how long will it take you?"

"Only a few minutes. I'm just a few blocks away on Park Avenue. And I'll only take a moment of your time."

"Okay. I guess so. But don't be long."

▼

It wasn't long. Kara knew that Rob was about to lay a guilt trip on her—one she richly deserved—but she managed to forestall that by telling him about the mystifying call from Dr. Gates' attorney. It seemed only minutes later that Gordon Wheatley showed up with his secretary.

"This is most irregular," he said as he trooped into the living room. He was a thin, waspish man in his late fifties with wire rimmed glasses and an unruly shock of white hair. "But Dr. Gates' wishes for his estate have been most irregular since the day he made out his first will with us twenty years ago."

"How so?" Kara said.

"I'm not at liberty to discuss that, as I'm sure you'll understand. But let me say that I would not have been

unhappy if Dr. Gates had taken his legal matters elsewhere long ago."

Rob stepped forward.

"What's this all about, Mr. Wheatley?"

"This." Mr. Wheatley stuck his hand out, palm up,
toward his secretary. "Miss Capwell?"

She placed a small manila envelope on his palm. Mr.
Wheatley in turn handed the envelope to Kara. The envelope was heavy and it jingled. She didn't like the
idea of receiving anything from Gates, especially after
he was dead.

"What's this?"

"A list of the assets in his estate and the keys to his
home on Twenty-first Street."

"But why?"

"You own it now."

Kara was aghast. She had to sit down.

"I *own* it?"

"Yes. You are his sole heir. He left everything he
owned to you. Counting the mines in West Virginia,
that increases your net worth by approximately thirty-
two million dollars."

Rob nearly fell into the seat beside her. Kara could
barely speak.

"But I don't want it! I don't want anything of his!"

"You may refuse it, of course, but I would think
about that. There will be a formal probate of the will,
but he left specific instructions that immediately after
he was pronounced dead, these keys were to be deliv-
ered to the heir he had named." He cleared his throat.
"We had some difficulty reaching you, otherwise you
would have had them sooner."

"When did he name Kara his heir?" Rob asked.

"Last week. I will be in touch with you again soon,
Miss Wade, under more formal circumstances, I hope.

However, it was imperative that this particular term of his will be carried out as written. Good day."

Kara didn't show him or Miss Capwell out. She sat with Rob on Ellen's couch and stared at the envelope in her hand. Finally, Rob spoke.

"I don't care if you keep it or not, Kara, but I've got to see the inside of that house. I've *got* to."

Kara looked at him, unsure of what to do. Then she realized that she wanted to see it, too.

"Let's go."

▼

1:24 P.M.

"The lights are on," Kara said as they stood before Gates' house.

It was a tall, narrow Victorian row house of dark brown stone, looming behind a wrought iron fence. Each floor had its own large bay window. A tiny patch of winter-browned lawn sat on either side of the short slate walk that led to the front steps.

"They've been on since Monday night," said Rob close by her side. "Let's go. I've got to be back at the precinct soon."

He opened the low iron gate and walked ahead of her. Kara held back. Something within her—the same something that had rejoiced with the news of Dr. Gates' death—was afraid and was trying to hold her back. She overcame it and followed Rob up the steps to the front door.

There were two front doors. The outer one was unlocked. As she stood in the vestibule with Rob, Kara tried to peek through the designs in the frosted glass of the inner door but couldn't see much.

"Why don't I go first," Rob said as she turned the key in the lock.

"I can take care of myself," she said.

"I'm sure you can, but since we're dealing with a guy who qualifies as the Daffy Duck of the New York State Medical Society, maybe I should just check the place out to make sure he doesn't have any crazies living with him."

"You're thinking of that padded cell in his office?"

"That, and some other things."

"All right," Kara said, suddenly glad Rob was along. "Be my guest."

She stepped into the front hall behind him. On her right was the common wall Dr. Gates shared with the house next door. A long narrow staircase ran up along that wall. An ornate chandelier, festooned with heavy red glass grapes, hung overhead. Far to the rear, daylight filtered in through the tall windows overlooking the rear courtyard.

Just inside the front door on the left wall of the foyer was an alarm panel. A red light glowed at the top of the panel. The numbers *1-7-4-2-3* were written on a tag tied to the key ring. Kara punched them in and the light turned to green.

"We're in."

"Let me check the basement first," Rob said.

He stepped down the hall to a door that opened into the space under the stairs and went below.

As Kara watch him go, she remembered that incident in Philadelphia a few years ago where they found three women chained in the basement of someone's house. She shuddered with revulsion.

She spun and stared the length of the foyer. For a moment she had thought someone was there. The foyer was empty. But she couldn't escape the feeling that she wasn't alone.

Be careful, Rob.
To distract herself, she began to look around.

▼

Rob entered the basement cautiously, wishing at first for a flashlight. But when he flipped the switch he found he didn't need one. There were plenty of incandescent bulbs hanging among the pipes in the exposed ceiling.

The basement was not quite what he had expected. There were the usual crates of odds and ends, and a furnace and a water heater at the rear. But it was smaller than he had anticipated. And it was clean, warm, and dry—heated and dehumidified. There was green industrial grade carpet on the floor and relatively new oak planking on the walls. Part of the area appeared to have been walled off but there was no access to the space.

He sniffed the air. There was a sour smell. Maybe Gates was having some trouble with his sewer line. Maybe it was time to call Roto-rooter.

One thing was sure at least: Nobody was hiding down here.

▼

Kara explored the first floor. All the ceilings seemed at least fifteen feet high. She peeked into the front room. It was a small study with curtains drawn across the bay window. A computer terminal sat on a desk. The next room was a bathroom with ornate tiles and an old fashioned paw-footed tub. Next came the kitchen and pantries. She opened a few of the cabinets. One of them was stocked with jars of baby food.

She was standing there and staring at the rows of Gerber Junior Meals, trying to imagine what use Dr.

Gates could possibly have for them, when she felt suddenly weak. *Hungry . . . so hungry*. Her knees wobbled as the room whirled about her once, then stopped. Then she was fine.

What had caused that? And then she remembered that in the turmoil of Rob's visit and Mr. Wheatley's bombshell about inheriting this house, she hadn't got around to eating lunch.

Promising to grab a bite soon, she moved on to the rear of the house which was taken up entirely by a large dining room with a huge marble fireplace.

She heard Rob on the stairs and hurried back to the foyer.

"All clear," he said. "On the small side, but it's *clean*. Looks like whoever does the rest of the house vacuums and dusts the basement as well. Never seen a clean basement before."

"That kind of goes with the rest of the place. It's immaculate. But he looked like the fastidious sort, didn't he."

Rob was rubbing his jaw, looking at the gleaming oak paneling running around the foyer.

"Yeah. Real fastidious. But something's up. Got to be. Why would he leave you his house?"

Kara only shrugged. She couldn't answer that question. At least not yet.

Rob said, "Let's give the rest of the place the once-over and then get out of here."

The second floor had a bedroom in the bay-windowed front section, but the rest of the level was one huge library. Bookshelves ran from floor to ceiling around the entire open space. Two ladders on rollers stood ready to give access to the top shelves.

"I've never seen this many books outside of a public library," Rob said.

"They look old and rare. I don't know much about

book collecting, but I'll bet he's got some choice first editions here."

She pulled out a copy of *Huckleberry Finn*. The book was dated 1884. Suddenly it slipped from her fingers. For an instant her hand felt numb, tingling, as if recovering from a novacaine injection, and then it was fine again.

"Oops!" she said and replaced the book on its shelf. She wondered if her blood sugar was low.

"So much for the second floor," Rob said, heading for the stairs. "Now for three. The Magical Mystery Tour continues."

The third floor had been opened up into one huge room. The windows at each end were hung with heavy draperies and the walls were covered with an assortment of rugs and hangings. Plush carpet hid the floor. A grand piano dominated the rear end of the room; the front section was taken up by an eight-foot high projection screen set up before the draped bay window. It was flanked by racks of electronic equipment arrayed in two arcs. Along the side wall were shelves holding thousands of record albums, tapes, and CDs. A television projection unit was suspended from the ceiling, aimed at the screen. And in the center of it all was a single reclining chair.

Kara noticed Rob being drawn to the front section as if by a magnet.

"Look at this stereo rig!" he said.

"That's all it is? Just a stereo?"

Rob laughed. "Right. 'Just a stereo.' Kara, this is to the average stereo what the space shuttle is to paper airplanes. He's got a turntable that plays both sides of a record, reel-to-reel, cassette, and even eight track tape players, a ten-disk CD player, plus for video he's got VHS, Beta, and videodisk." Rob was like a little boy in a toy store at Christmas. He approached one of the coffin-sized, fabric-covered boxes situated around the room. "Look at these surround-sound speakers! Christ! There's enough wattage here to blow the roof off!"

"I'm surprised his neighbors haven't had the police on him."

"That's what I think all these drapes and wall hangings are for. They're like baffles. They keep the sound from bouncing off the walls as well as vibrating through. He's fixed himself a miniature concert hall here."

Kara looked through the titles of some of the albums.

"He must have every opera by every diva whoever warbled a note."

"You like opera?" Rob said, coming over to her side.

"Can't stand it." But as she stood there with her hand on the record rack, she thought she heard an operatic voice wailing faintly in the back of her mind. She shook her head and it was gone. She moved to his classical section.

"He's got composers I've never even heard of," she said.

"No ZZ Top?"

"Not a one."

"Guess there's no accounting for taste." He put a hand on her arm. "Let's go. I've got to get back."

"I want to look around some more," Kara said. "It's safe, don't you think?"

"Nobody here but us. You really want to stay?"

"I want to check out his study, see if he's got any papers that will give me a clue as to what he was all about—and why he left it all to me."

"You sure you want to know?"

"I think so."

Kara didn't say so, but she was still half-convinced that Gates had somehow used her body. She wanted to find a way to contact the person who had sent her that warning note. She wouldn't rest easy until she knew for sure.

Rob had her follow him down to the front door.

"Make sure you keep it locked while you're here, and turn on the alarm when you leave."

"Yes sir!"

"Now—when can we get together tonight? We've got a lot of talking to do, and some decisions to make."

She'd known this was coming.

"How about after dinner? Meet me at Ellen's and we can go someplace."

"Ellen knows?"

Kara nodded. "Ellen, my mother, and Bert. They're the only ones. And Kelly, of course."

Rob's eyes were intense as they bored into hers.

"Of course. Everyone but me. And Jill. We've got to figure out when to tell her."

"Yes. I know."

Kara wasn't looking forward to tonight's discussion.

Rob hovered outside until she had locked the door behind him, then waved good-bye and hurried off.

As she turned away from the door, Kara felt her arms and legs give way, as if someone had severed all their nervous connections. As she went down, a voice spoke in her mind.

"At last! I thought he'd *never* leave!"

FEBRUARY 26
12:17 A.M.

ROB WAS CRUISING MANHATTAN.

I'm a father! Jill's my daughter!

The two thoughts kept echoing in tandem off the inner walls of his skull. They'd kept him awake, kept him wired. Which was why he was up and out and doing something he never did: driving around the city.

He cruised the avenues, using Harlem or the Park as his uptown boundaries, and Canal Street downtown. Traffic was light. He drove at a leisurely pace, staying in the center lanes to let the cabs and everyone else in a hurry slip by on either side. The street lights glimmered on his windshield and off the passing cars, the neon from the various store fronts refracted through the steam rising from the street vents. The city had its own brand of beauty. He felt enough at peace with himself tonight to enjoy it. He smiled. Stopping to smell the roses, Manhattan style.

He wished he could have got together with Kara tonight but she had called around 4:30 or so to tell him that she wasn't feeling well. She seemed to have picked up an intestinal virus or something and was going to spend the rest of the afternoon and evening in bed.

Probably the best idea. She hadn't sounded well at all. Rob had been tempted to drop by Ellen's and hang around with Jill anyway but had canceled the idea. He was afraid he might start crying again.

Christ, hadn't that been a scene this afternoon! He didn't know where it had come from but all of a sudden he'd been bawling like a wimp. And in front of Kara, too. Embarrassing as all hell, although it hadn't seemed to bother her in the least.

Anyway, his throat tended to get tight every time he thought of Jill, so maybe it was better if he hung loose on his own tonight.

He was tooling up Sixth into Chelsea when impulse pulled him left onto Twenty-first. He was glad he no longer had to camp out here every night. He came to a complete stop in front of Gates' house.

The lights were on.

That wasn't so strange, really. If Kara hadn't been feeling well, she probably hurried back to Ellen's without bothering to turn them off.

He wondered if she'd locked the door.

Rob double-parked and ran up the steps. He tried the door. Rattled it. Good. She'd locked it behind her. But through the glass he spotted the green light glowing on the alarm panel. She'd forgotten that. He rattled the door again, then walked back to his car. He'd have to remind her about the alarm. It would be a sin to let vandals get hold of that library, or that fabulous stereo rig.

He put the car in gear and started rolling again, thinking about instant fatherhood.

▼

Kara wanted to scream but had no voice, wanted to run, crawl, claw a path away from here but had no limbs, none at least that would obey her. And what good would blind flight do? The horror was within her, all around her, it permeated her flesh, it encapsulated her like a steel bubble.

Horror, gut-wrenching panic, rage—they'd been her world since this afternoon. And they were with her even now, but they were under control. She could almost say she was calmer now—as calm as a madwoman in a straitjacket. She had to hold on. That was all she could do. She could feel her sanity jittering on its already frayed tether, blindly straining to pull free and flee into the waiting darkness.

After the horrors of the past ten hours it was a wonder that she retained any control at all.

She knew a few things. She knew it was night, and knew she was in the dining room. She could smell and hear, she could taste her dry mouth but could not move her tongue or lips, could see but was incapable of moving her eyes. She'd been a prisoner within her own body since this afternoon.

This afternoon . . .

Now that her body was in one of its quiet periods, the insane events of the afternoon and evening rushed back in a flood . . .

At first she had simply lain there on the floor inside the door. The voice didn't speak again. Eventually she became convinced that she had suffered a massive stroke; some sort of brain aneurysm had ruptured.

But then she started to move.

First the fingers of the right hand, then the left, moving independently of her volition, without her permission, rippling up and down like a pianist playing rapid scales. Then the arms bent, the knees straightened. She sat up. Kara had a sense of the muscles moving but she was exerting no effort, she felt no strain.

The terror was building inside her. Her body was like a runaway machine. A moment ago she had been plead-

ing with her limbs to move, now she was trying to stop
them. Her body turned over onto its hands and knees
and began crawling down the hall. *Where am I going?*

Her body crawled into the big dining room. It headed
straight for the couch and pulled itself up onto the cushions. She was panting but had no feeling of breathless-
ness.

And then the voice spoke again.

"There! That's better! A cushion is much preferable
to a hard floor any day, don't you think, Kara?"

She tried to scream but still she had no voice.

"Don't be afraid, Kara. You're in no danger."

Panic swirled around her again. She felt as if she
were sealed inside a tight cubicle of foot-thick glass,
banging frantically, desperately on the walls with no
one to hear her but this disembodied voice.

Where was it coming from? It sounded like . . .

Then her eyes closed.

Kara panicked. She was in total darkness. It was like
being blind. She fought to raise her lids but they might
as well have been someone else's for all the response
she elicited.

The last thing she remembered seeing was the gold
mantle clock over the fireplace. It had read 3:20.
Through the darkness she heard faint noises from the
street outside—horns, trucks shifting gears. She had always hated the incessant street sounds of New York for
keeping her awake, for intruding on her concentration.
Now she loved them. They proved that she was still
alive. And she heard the clock's chime—once on the
half hour, once for each hour of the day on the hour.

When her eyes reopened, the afternoon light was fad-
ing and the clock said 4:32.

"I feel better now. Stronger."

Her body sat up, then stood and walked a few wobbling steps around the dining room before stumbling back to the couch.

"Though not strong enough to negotiate the steps, I fear. But that is not important now. What is important is a little phone call we must make."

Kara watched her hand reach out and lift the phone receiver, saw it dial 4-1-1. She heard the operator come on the line.

And then she heard her own voice speaking.

"Manhattan, please. The Midtown North police precinct."

Her own voice, speaking someone else's words. Mentally she jumped at the sound of it, but her body remained still. She heard the recorded answer, then watched her hand punch in the number.

She listened as she asked for Detective Harris, heard herself explain how she wasn't feeling well and wanted to go to bed early tonight. She heard the concern and disappointment in Rob's voice and tried to scream out, *Rob! No! It's not me! Not me!* But instead her voice went on lying, promising that they'd get together tomorrow.

After hanging up with Rob, her eyes closed and she spent another couple of hours in terrified darkness, listening to the clock and the street.

When her eyes opened again she saw that it was almost seven.

"We'll have to call Aunt Ellen."

She thought she had become inured to shock by then, but she was jolted by watching herself dial Ellen's number and listening as her voice glibly informed her aunt that she would be staying at Kelly's again and would explain later.

"There! That should give us a respite."

Sudden fury blazed up in Kara. She wanted to attack

this thing, this voice . . . but it was only a voice. How did you attack a voice?

And *who* was the voice?

She thought she knew. Words formed in her mind. A question. Mentally, she spoke the thought.

You're not Janine, are you?

"No."

Something about the voice . . . something familiar. The rhythm, the choice of words. She was sure now who it was.

Are you Doctor Gates?

"Doctor Gates is dead."

Then who—?

"Quiet! I need to rest."

There came another period behind closed eyelids, a long one during which Kara thought she might have slept—not because she felt safe enough, but to escape the horror temporarily, and maybe to awaken and learn that it was all a terrible nightmare.

She was roused by abrupt movements of her body, and by noises from the front door. Someone was rattling it.

The dining room was dark but light poured down the hall from the chandelier. Her body rose from the couch and walked unsteadily but stealthily to the kitchen where it pulled a long-bladed knife from a drawer.

She waited. The door rattled once more, briefly, then all was silent.

"That, I would say, was your friend, Detective Harris. Even after midnight, when he believes you home and asleep, he is still nosing round. He is going to be trouble."

Kara had no doubts now.

You are *Doctor Gates!*

"I told you: Doctor Gates is dead."

Then who are you? And why are you doing this to me?

"You'll know in a moment. I believe I'm strong enough now." Her body moved to one of the cabinets and she pulled out two jars of junior foods, the kind Kara used to feed Jill when she was a baby. Then she was heading across the hall toward the door to the cellar.

"I'm not being coy. It's simply that it's easier to show you who I am than to explain. And now you will see."

Steadying itself on the banister, her body started down the cellar stairs.

▼

Rob turned downtown on Seventh after leaving the townhouse. As he passed the Kramer Medical Arts building, he checked his coat pocket. He still had them: the keys he had taken from Gates' secretary this morning. He pulled into the curb.

Up in the office he searched Gates' desk for keys to the filing cabinets but found nothing. Frustrated, edgy, he sat in Gates' high-backed chair. He realized that it wasn't the files that had drawn him back to the office. It was the other back room—the padded cell. He needed one more look at it.

He propped the cell door open with copies of the *PDR* and *Dorland's Illustrated Medical Dictionary*—he didn't want to be accidentally locked in here. He'd probably die of starvation before anybody found him. He turned on the overhead light and stood in the center of the cell.

What on earth had Gates used this for? Who had he kept here?

The questions plagued him. Questions existed to be

answered. They never went away until they were answered.

He paced the narrow dimensions of the room, tapping on the padding with the heel of his hand and the side of his shoe. It was thick. If you were the sort who was inclined toward such things, you might be able to knock yourself out by banging your head against these walls, but you wouldn't be able to crack your skull. You might even—

Something crunched.

Rob's shoe had tapped against a slight bulge in the lower padding. Something else was under the fabric. He reached down and found a split seam along the floorline. Dropping to his knees, he wriggled his fingers up under the fabric. There was paper crammed in there. He vised a couple of sheets between his fingers and yanked them out. Then he pulled more out. The space was stuffed with scraps from notepads, prescription blanks, used envelopes, all covered with tiny script. And a pencil, short, looking as if someone had sharpened it with his teeth.

Rob studied the script. He was no handwriting expert, but these looked like they were written by the same hand that had sent Kara the warning note. And they were dated.

Rob began setting them in order. He had some reading to do.

He had a feeling one of his questions was about to be answered.

▼

The basement was small, as Rob had mentioned earlier. Had it been less than twelve hours since they'd arrived here together? It seemed ages. After all the high ceilings upstairs, these low-slung pipes overhead gave her a hemmed-in feeling, seemed to press down on her.

Her body took her to a paneled partition. Her hand reached up among the pipes and pulled a lever. Something clicked inside the wall. She pushed on a panel which dropped back then slid to the left, revealing a small room.

A foul odor wafted out—urine, feces. Had she been in control of her body she might have gagged.

"Unpleasant, isn't it? But if I've got to smell it, so should you. I've been living in that for almost two days."

A Tiffany-type floor lamp threw a cone of light on the room's single piece of furniture. A crib. In the crib was the source of the odor.

"Let me introduce myself properly. My name is Gabor. This is my body."

Had she a voice, Kara would have screamed. In the crib was a wrinkled, shrunken thing with thick, mottled skin and whispy white hair trailing off its scalp. The head was too big for its body—adult-sized on a body no bigger than the average five-year old's. It's face was a caricature of humanity with its flattened nose, its drooling, toothless mouth, its white-coated eyes stared blindly upward. In contrast to its short, warped, wizened limbs, its body was a bloated, corpulent, barrel-chested mass, the pelvis sheathed in a stained, fouled diaper.

"Loathsome, aren't I?"

Kara was numb. Had she been able, she wasn't sure she would have dared to frame a reply.

"You needn't worry about injuring my feelings. Even I find myself repulsive."

She detected something behind the words, a cosmic rage, a tragic self-loathing.

But this is Doctor Gates' house!

"The man you know as Doctor Gates was my brother, Lazlo. The body, at least, was Lazlo's. The intellect you dealt with, pouring your heart out to in your therapy sessions, was I. Gabor. So, in a real sense, Doctor Gates isn't dead. *I* am Doctor Gates. *I* went through pre-med and medical school, *I* sat through those tedious lectures, *I* studied those dry texts till my eyes burned like heated coals in my head, *I* passed those tests and board exams, spent those years in residency. The medical degree and license may have Lazlo's name on them, but they are the result of *my* work. They are *mine*."

Where . . . where was Lazlo all this time?

"With me. A passenger in his own body. Like you."

Oh, God!

"It wasn't so bad for him. I left him alone at times. And after all, we were brothers. Twins, would you believe? *Twins!* Like you and Kelly. Yet something went wrong with me in utero, early on, when we were both little more than collections of cells. My body became distorted while his grew perfectly. Twins should share, don't you think?"

Poor Lazlo!

"Never mind him. He's gone. And my body needs tending. First a quick change of diaper—I prefer the Huggies to Pampers—and then we'll feed me. It's been two days since I've eaten and I'm starving. That's what the junior foods are for. I use them when I haven't got time to puree something more appetizing. After dinner, a sponge bath. As you'll soon learn, I take good care of my body. I bathe it every day."

Kara wanted to cry at her helplessness, but she had no tears.

Let me go! Please let me go!

"Lazlo used to plead for release in the early days, but he stopped after a while when he came to realize that it would do him no good. You might as well do the same. We're going to be together for a long, long time, Kara."

▼

With Kara's hand you spoon the food into your mouth—your other mouth, the mouth you were born with. You're glad you were finally able to escape from that body this afternoon. The hunger was becoming unbearable.

But that's over now. You're in control again, just as you planned. Everything has gone according to your contingency plans. You've foreseen everything. You always knew there was a possibility that Lazlo would meet with an untimely end, so you prepared for that. You knew that, by law, his immediate heir would be his brother, yourself, Gabor. But since your body is itself incapable of meaningful communication, you knew Gabor would be declared incompetent and all your inherited assets placed in trust under some sort of guardianship—out of your control.

That would never do. So you arranged for Gabor to 'die.' Then, as Lazlo, you made a will and left all of your assets to the woman in whose body you were most comfortable at the time. There has been a string of heirs. For the past year it was Kelly Wade. Just a week ago you changed the chief beneficiary to Kara. Fortuitous timing. And brilliant anticipation. You should be proud.

Why then do you feel so empty?

It's not the hunger. It's not the trauma of two nights ago. It's Lazlo. He's gone. He's dead. He gladly killed himself to escape you. That has hurt you deeper than you ever thought possible.

You miss Lazlo. Miss the familiar workings of his

body, miss his companionship. And after all, he was your twin brother.

Now he's dead. You can trace his death back to Kelly Wade. It began with her. If she hadn't managed to jump out that window at the Plaza, you would still be occupying Lazlo's body and going about your usual business. But Kelly's death brought Kara to town, and Kara was a temptation you couldn't resist. But Kara's boyfriend is a cop, a tenacious one. And if he hadn't harassed you so, you would not be in your present position—the sole surviving member of the Gati family.

It's Harris' fault. If he hadn't hounded you, you would not have fled onto 42nd Street and been hit by the car. The impact temporarily severed your contact with Lazlo, giving him a chance to try to steal Harris' pistol. When you returned to Lazlo, you discovered yourself in mid-grapple with Harris. You tried to let go of the pistol but your finger was stuck. When you tried to yank it free, the gun went off.

And that is all you remember. The impact of a bullet tearing through the brain you were occupying traumatized your consciousness. You lay in a coma for almost a full day. You're still weak. You could barely occupy Kara when she arrived here.

But you're getting stronger. And when you are this close to your real body, it is easy to stimulate and control the almost reflexive actions of chewing and swallowing while maintaining control over Kara. You spoon the junior meal into your toothless mouth. Although you can't taste it (thank goodness) you know the nutrients flowing into your body from this lumpy gruel will make you stronger.

But although everything has gone according to plan, all is far from perfect. Difficult days lie ahead. Kara has a daughter, plus she's been having an affair with Detective Harris. The detective will be easy to be rid of. All you need do is find another lover and let Harris know that he has been replaced in your heart. It may prove messy for a while, but eventually that should serve to sever all ties with him. Although you would love to see him as dead as Lazlo, you will have to be satisfied with merely breaking his heart instead of shoving a knife blade through it.

The child, though, presents a major problem. You will not be able to fool her for long. She will never guess exactly what is wrong with her mother, but she will know she is not the same. She will sniff you out and raise a cry.

Something must be done about the child.

An accident. That is the best way. A terrible accident. A fall, perhaps. Like her Aunt Kelly. These Wades— such an accident-prone family.

Suddenly Kara's mind is shouting, startling you.

You can't do this! It's unconscionable! Your own brother, and now me! How can you live with yourself?

You've wondered that yourself at times. And whenever you do, you look down at your misshapen body and consider the alternative. And you know you do not want to live there.

You do not answer her. You are concerned with the strength she is showing. You could feel her fighting for control of her hands as they changed your diaper. One or two times she almost drew them away. This concerns you. Not that she'd ever be able to wrest control back from you, but it takes more effort to control her than it did Lazlo. She's much stronger willed than he ever was. Luckily, she doesn't know her own strength. And to assure that she doesn't get an opportunity to find out, she will have to be housebroken quickly.

You have an idea. When the feeding is finished and your bath is done, you'll start her first lesson.

▼

Rob sat on the floor of the padded cell, numb and drained by what he had read in the scraps of paper scattered across his legs.

Madness. Pure madness.

But strangely coherent madness.

Maybe that was because the author was so convinced that he was Lazlo Gati, whose body had been usurped by his twin brother Gabor during their teenage years and never returned to him except for brief periods during which he managed to write this diary of sorts. According to this diary, Lazlo was locked in this padded cell during those periods of freedom while Gabor frolicked in other bodies, mostly female.

Utterly crazy. But who *was* this crazy man? Where was he now? That was the scary part. His last entry was three nights ago ... when Lazlo was still alive. That was the disturbing part: there had been no entries since Lazlo's death.

Rob stood and tried to shake off the crazy story. He smiled. Here he was, sitting in a padded cell, trying to make sense of the ravings of a certifiable nut case. There was a major flaw in the story: Gabor Gati had been dead for years. His death certificate was on file downtown ...

... signed by Lazlo.

He shook himself. It all seemed weirdly logical—*if* you could accept the premise that Gabor was still alive and could actually control another person's body.

But if he was alive, where would he be?

In the Chelsea house, of course.

Rob felt spicules of ice forming in his blood.

Lazlo Gati—or Dr. Gates, or whoever the hell he was—had left everything to Kara. And one of the terms of the will had been that she be given the keys to the Chelsea house immediately.

Christ!

And Rob had left her there alone. He wondered if her sudden illness had anything to do with Gabor? Or if—?

What am I saying? Get a grip, Harris!

He stood in the center of the padded cell and took a few deep breaths. It was late, he was tired, and his imagination was having a field day. Kara was at Ellen's. He'd go home himself, get some sleep, and see Kara first thing in the morning to make sure she was all right.

To make sure she was still Kara.

▼

1:35 A.M.

She was in a cab going east on 42nd Street. Kara huddled sick and miserable, limbless and voiceless within her own body, searching for a way out.

"Lazlo died right over there," Gabor told her, pointing out the window with her finger.

Is that why you brought me here?

"Of course not."

Then why am I naked under this coat? It's too cold for this sort of thing.

"I've already told you twice: Your taste in clothes is terrible. I'm going to have to buy us a whole new wardrobe. Something with style."

Kara prayed that was the truth, but she feared he had something else in mind. Something awful.

You won't find anything open at this hour.

"We're not looking for clothes now."

Then what—?

"Patience, my dear."

He told the cabbie to pull to the curb and wait, then stepped out onto the sidewalk. She felt the wind run icy fingers up the insides of her thighs.

Where are we going?

"Straight ahead."

They were walking toward a brightly lit store. Yellow and white incandescent bulbs strobed deliriously in its smudged and smeared show window, their light racing madly around its border. A neon sign blinked "ADULT BOOKS" in turquoise while another blared "PEEP SHOW" in red.

You're taking me there?

"Yes. Have you ever been in one?"

Never!

"Then this will be a new experience for you."

Inside the door was a square room, its walls lined floor to ceiling with porno magazines—men with women, women with women, men with men. To the rear was a curtained arch, keystoned with a sign that said, "PEEPS." A narrow platform ran across the front of the store, supporting a glass display case and a cash register. Behind the case stood a portly, short, balding, middle-aged man wearing a greasy Guns n' Roses T-shirt and a two-day stubble. There were two male customers in the store who quickly headed for the back when they saw her.

The man on the platform leaned over the display case and looked down at her.

"Can I help yiz, lady?" he said in a voice like a chainsaw.

"I'm looking for a tool," Kara's voice said as she stared into the dusty display case.

Lined up on the shelves behind the glass were a good two dozen different models of vibrators and dildos.

You're not serious!

"Hush. I'm choosing."

"Why fool with a tool when you can have the real thing?" the counterman said, leering through his stubble.

"How about yours? Is your tool available?"

His smile broadened. "Anytime!"

"Interesting. However, I believe I'll take that one there."

Kara watched in horror as her finger pointed to a twelve inch pink vibrator formed in the shape of an erect penis. Gabor could only be buying it for one reason. It made her sick to think about it.

No!

The counterman took it out, wrapped it up after it was paid for, and handed her the package with a lascivious smile.

"Batteries not included."

"Quite all right. I have plenty at home."

"Okay. But if dis don't work, come back an' I'll show you da real ting."

"I just might take you up on that."

You wouldn't! Kara said as they exited the store.

"I might. Just to teach you a lesson if you prove bad company for me."

But he's dirty and ugly and probably crawling with diseases!

"Probably. But I can always replace you should you become debilitated by disease."

The sick helplessness of her position began to weigh more heavily than ever on Kara. But she refused to be cowed.

What kind of monster are you? she said as her body settled again in the back seat of the cab. *And what kind of a man wants to be in a woman's body?*

" 'Man?' What makes you think I'm a man? You saw my body. Genetically it may possess a 'Y' chromosome, but that's it. During my formative years my perceptions were drastically limited and I was never treated as a male—or a female, for that matter. I was treated as a sexless, mindless sibling. A doll. A pet. My own body had no experiences to influence my sexual orientation. But when I began getting out of my body and into others, I found the female sexual response more intense, more fulfilling. And speaking of sexual response . . ."

Kara watched her hands slip the vibrator from the brown paper bag. Her body leaned back in the seat and spread her legs. The hands slipped the vibrator under her coat.

Was this why he'd left her clothes at home? He wasn't—! Not here in the cab!

No. Don't!

"A shame we don't have any batteries."

God, please don't!

She felt the cold plastic begin to work its way inside her. Even without a voice, she managed to scream.

▼

6:05 A.M.

Kara watched her hand carve a thick slice off the loaf of seedless rye.

"You know the plan now? And when we get to your Aunt Ellen's you will coach me so I don't make any mistakes."

Kara still burned from the humiliation in the cab a few hours before. She refused to answer.

"Don't be rude, Kara. We are going to be living together in this body for quite some time to come. You have to accept that. We can be bickering enemies or civil companions. But I warn you, if you give me trouble, there will be more incidents like the one in the cab. And they will escalate until you behave like the good little girl I know you can be. The choice is yours."

I choose to be set free, damn you!

"That is not an option."

Kara fought the black depression thickening around her. She was utterly helpless, completely at Gabor's mercy—and he didn't have any.

Even without any mistakes, Ellen's going to think my moving in here is pretty strange.

"What she thinks doesn't matter. She merely has to hold the door as you and your daughter move out."

Mention of Jill drew her up from the depths.

Why Jill? You didn't say anything about her before!

"You can't very well abandon her. Not a devoted mother like you."

Were Kara's skin responsive to her emotions, it would have crawled at the thought of this thing in her body pretending to be Jill's mother.

No! Let her stay with Ellen!"

"Not a chance."

Kara's rage exploded. She wished she could take that knife and—

Suddenly her right hand pulled the knife from the bread and slashed toward her left. The blade never reached her flesh. But it came close, stopping within an inch or two of her arm.

"Well, well! Spirited, aren't we? You caught me by surprise there. But it won't happen again."

I hate you! I'd rather die than live like this!

"You think being a passenger in your own body or a little autoeroticism in the back of a cab is the worst that could happen to you? You're wrong, my dear. I've been kind to you. I've allowed you to keep in touch with the world through your senses. But I don't have to do that. I can cut them off."

Go ahead. I don't care.

"Really? We'll see. Say good-bye to smell and taste."

The odor of the bread was gone but other than that, Kara didn't notice much difference.

"Now . . . sound."

Silence such as Kara had never imagined possible—even the subliminal rush of blood through her arteries was gone. Only the voice remained.

"Now sight."

Darkness engulfed her. Darkness so profound its impact was almost a physical blow. More than an absence of light. A darkness that had never *known* light.

"Frightening, isn't it? But tolerable because you still have your senses of touch and proprioception. You can still feel the air against your skin, your feet on the floor; you still know up from down. But not for long."

I'm not afraid.

"You should be. You are about to experience true, complete sensory deprivation. I used it to punish Lazlo when he was naughty, and he dreaded it. I will use it to punish you, as well. And if you do no prove to be a pleasant companion, I shall leave you in the deprivation state permanently."

Huddled in the vast empty darkness, Kara was terrified but refused to let him know.

Do your worst.

"Very well. Your first punishment will be brief, but it will seem eternal. Good bye."

Suddenly the floor went out from under her. She was tumbling, racing into a silent black infinity. All points of references were gone. There was no up or down or near or far. She was exploding and contracting in cycles. If only she could stop this endless falling, but there was nothing to hold onto. Everything was gone.

She hadn't realized it would be like this. Never in her darkest imaginings had she encountered terror like this. There was nothing here! *Nothing!* He had to let her out, let her back into the world!

She screamed but there was no sound. Only the endless fall into the eternal silent darkness.

▼

As you cut another slice from the rye loaf, you notice that your hand is trembling. That was close. Too close. She has an extremely powerful will, this one. Much stronger than Lazlo's. She broke through your motor restraints. You will have to keep her tightly reined. No telling what she might do if she gets loose.

Thus the punishment. And let her think that you can keep her in sensory deprivation permanently should you so choose. Don't let her know that it is an effort for you, that you can only keep her deprived so long, and then you must let her up. Let her think you release her out of beneficence instead of necessity. That should help keep her in line.

Oh, Lazlo. If only he were alive. It was so much easier with him. He could be dominated, trained to behave. You knew just what to expect from Lazlo.

Although on rare occasions he did manage to surprise you. That note to Kara on the back of the electric bill. It had infuriated you that he had dared to interfere, yet you had to grant him a grudging accolade for his craftiness.

And you punished him severely, of course. Just as you are punishing Kara now.

As you eat, you remember that you must check and make sure that Wheatley has followed the terms of the will as to the burial of Lazlo's body. You don't want your brother lying in the morgue any longer than necessary.

You finish your toast and coffee and wipe the crumbs from the dining room table. It is time to welcome Kara back to the world of the senses.

"Hello, Kara."

There is a long pause. Finally, her voice comes to you. It is small and weak.

Please don't ever do that to me again!

"The choice is up to you, my dear. You merely have to be civil company and we shall both live in peace. Right now, however, it is time to go."

It's too early to go to Ellen's.

"Correct. We are first stopping at the office of the late, lamented Lawrence Gates, M.D."

▼

The office is empty of life except for the fish in the tank. You feed them. Eventually you'll move them to your house. You don't want them to die.

You notice that your desk drawer is open. Someone has been searching your office. Detective Harris, no doubt. You check the file room and see that the cabinets remain closed and locked. You glance into the padded cell.

What's that.

Her voice is stronger now. You flip on the light to show her.

"That, my dear, is a place where you will be penned from time to time. During those periods, your body will be totally yours again."

Where will you be?

"Sometimes in my own body—find it remains in better health if I return to it once in a while—but most times I will be using someone else's body. Variety, you see, is the spice of life."

Is this where you left Lazlo when you took me over at night?

"Exactly. Lazlo, you see, developed a nasty habit of injuring himself when I left him locked in a normally furnished room. He did it to embarrass me, so that I would have a black eye or a swollen lip when I returned to take control of him again."

Good for Lazlo!

"I thought you'd appreciate that. As a result of his persistence in these pranks, and the fear that he might one day do permanent damage to himself, I had this padded cell installed here. I would have loved to have had a similar cell installed in the house, but after seeing all the talk and consternation caused by this one, even though it was in a psychiatrist's office, I decided against it. I have striven always to maintain a low profile. Here. Let me show you how it works."

You close the door and push the "LOCK" button.

"There. We're locked in. To get us out, all I have to do is tap in the combination."

You blank out Kara's vision to do this.

No! Please!

"Don't worry, my dear. Only your sight and only for a few seconds. Letting you see the combination would defeat the purpose of having a lock, now, wouldn't it?"

You allow her to see again as the door swings open.

"And don't try to memorize the movements of my hands. I change the combination periodically."

If Lazlo was locked in here, who sent me that note?

"Lazlo, of course. A most ingenious prank, I must say. Although perhaps I was a bit lax with him. When I locked him in here one night while visiting you, I forgot I had three or four bills in stamped, addressed envelopes in the pocket of my sport coat. He had a pencil hidden somewhere, so he opened the electric bill and wrote to you on its back; then he readdressed the envelope and stuck it back with the others. I dropped the lot of them into the mailbox the next day, never realizing what he had done. He was quite a character. I'm going to miss him."

Did you . . . punish him?

"Of course. Severely! You had only a taste of the punishment. I cut Lazlo off for an entire day. So don't try anything like it."

Kara says nothing. You wonder about her. You hope she will become compliant. You're not paired with her permanently, but it will be some time before you can arrange to transfer all your assets to someone else. You are stuck with her for now. You must convince her to be a good little girl.

"And now we go to your aunt's."

▼

The arrival at Ellen's went far more smoothly than Kara had anticipated. Which only deepened her depression.

Lucia, the cook, let her in on the first knock.

"Miss Kara. I didn't know you were out. Can I fix you some breakfast?"

"No, thank you," Gabor said in her voice, "but could you fix something for Jill? We'll be leaving soon?"

"Of course. What would she like?"

"Quick! What's her favorite?"

Waffles.

"If waffles wouldn't be too much trouble—?"

"No trouble at all!" She bustled back toward the kitchen.

Gabor took her body on a quick tour of the apartment.

"Your aunt has good taste. Money doesn't seem to be an object."

Kara didn't answer. She didn't care what Gabor thought of Ellen's decor. She was frightened. It was bad enough that she was enslaved to Gabor, but the thought of Jill within his reach was almost more than she could bear. If only there was a way to keep Jill away from him. Even if only for a little while. Just long enough to find a way to fight her way free of Gabor.

For somewhere within her consciousness was a conviction that this would not be a permanent thing, that sooner or later she would escape Gabor. She held onto that conviction with an iron grip. It and her fear for Jill were the only things keeping her sane right now.

"Where's your daughter's room?"

Leave her out of this!

"Come, come, Kara. I thought we had settled this. We must take Jill with us. Too many questions, too much unwelcome scrutiny if we leave her here. Plus, that would break her heart. I may be many things, Kara, but I am not without feelings."

Kara saw no use in withholding Jill's location. He could find her easily enough without her help.

The bedroom at the end of the hall.

"Thank you."

Kara had to admit that Gabor was very good with Jill. He woke her gently and explained that they'd be staying in the city for a while but in a different place, a big new house with a giant TV screen and the loudest stereo in the world. Jill was excited, all trusting smiles. Kara wanted to cry out to her, wanted to gather Jill in her arms and hug her tight against her. But she could do nothing. Jill hopped out of bed and into her robe and ran down the hall for her waffles.

"You never told me what a darling little thing she is!"

Kara didn't want him to touch her or even talk about her, but she felt that telling him so would only give him more power over her. And he had more than enough already.

Yes. I raised her myself.

"So you told me. You've done a splendid job."

Kara wanted to tell him where he could shove his compliment, then realized that the orifice would be hers.

Thank you.

The next hour went quickly, with Gabor doing a credible imitation of her, making up plausible explanations to Ellen as to why she and Jill were moving out. Soon they were ready to go. Jill had eaten her waffles, the cook was tearfully kissing her good bye, and their few belongings were packed up.

Then Rob showed up.

"What's *he* doing here?"

She could sense the agitation behind the words.

I don't know. We were supposed to get together last night, but you called me in sick, remember? Maybe he just wants to see how I'm doing.

Rob drew her aside into the living room.

"Kara, what's going on?"

"I'm moving. Is that any concern of yours?"

"Hell, yes it is! I don't want my daughter living in that man's house!"

"His *daughter?* What is he talking about?"

Rob is Jill's father.

"You told me her father was dead!"

I lied.

"Bitch!"

But I lied to Rob, too. He only found out yesterday. What's the matter Gabor? Do lies bother you? You lied to me about my father. He was a good and decent man and you made me suspect him of the worst foulness!

"Never mind that! What do I tell him!"

You figure it out.

"Don't do this! You'll pay!"

The 'punishment?' I'll risk it.

She dreaded the thought of another instant of total sensory deprivation, but it would be worth it to see Gabor squirm.

"I'll hurt her!"

What?

"Your daughter. I'll hurt her. A child can have nasty accidents, trip and fall against sharp things. I'll do it if you don't cooperate."

Fear for Jill was a knife with nowhere to strike.

You beast! You subhuman—!

"She'll suffer!"

Kara capitulated. Again. That was all she seemed to be doing lately. Was that going to be the story of her life from now on?

All right! Tell him he didn't want me to take her back to Pennsylvania and so I'm acquiescing.

She listened as her voice told him that. But Rob didn't seem satisfied. He kept staring at her as if looking for a flaw.

"Kara," he said. "You remember the night we met at CBGB's?"

"What's that mean?"

It's a trick question. We met at McSorley's.

"He's suspicious then?"

Obviously.

"Why?"

I don't know!

"No," she heard her voice say. "We met in McSorley's. How could you forget?"

"Oh, right," Rob said with a grin that looked somewhat relieved. "McSorley's. Same neighborhood. I get mixed up sometimes. Say, do you remember . . .?"

▼

You listen to Kara and you parrot the proper replies to this detective, and in the back of your mind you realize that there is real trouble here.

You had planned to be rid of the detective by giving him the cold shoulder, refusing to see him, never returning his calls. Sooner or later he would give up. Or so you thought.

Now you know that will never happen. There is more than mere romance involved here. This is a living bond of flesh and blood named Jill. You know that no matter how you spurn him the detective will keep returning—not to see Kara but to see his daughter.

The detective must be disposed of.

But how?

You must think on this. Carefully.

And most certainly, you cannot let Kara know until the last moment.

▼

10:22 A.M.

Rob picked up his phone on the third ring.

"Harris."

"Ah, Detective," said a familiar voice. "Professor Jensen here. Those handwriting samples you left me this morning?"

The scribbled notes he'd found in the padded cell.

"Yes? Did you—?"

"Definitely the same as the writing on the back of the Con Ed bill."

"You're sure?"

"No question about it."

"Great! Thanks a lot."

Yeah. Thanks a *whole* lot. That meant whoever had been locked in that room had sent Kara the warning. But *who*?

This was getting crazier and crazier. He needed something to point *away* from the craziness, not *to* it.

Rob sat at his puke green desk and brooded, shutting out the sounds of the detective squad room. He glanced up and saw Manetti typing away at his desk.

"Augie! We got anybody Hungarian here?"

"Sure," Manetti said without looking up. "Varadi."

"Varadi? I thought he was Italian."

Now Manetti looked up. His expression registered his disdain.

"Italian? What, you kiddin'? Mike's got red fucking hair! And freckles! How many *paisans* you seen with red fucking hair and freckles?"

"Sorry."

He went to find Varadi.

Kara had given all the right answers this morning, except as to why she was moving into Gates' Chelsea house. She hadn't even wanted to visit it yesterday, and now she was moving in with Jill.

Something was very wrong.

Rob found Varadi by the water cooler.

"Mike. You speak Hungarian?"

Varadi's expression was guarded. It didn't go with his boyish face and freckles.

"Yeah. A little."

Rob kept thinking of the phrase Gates had used over and over just before the gun went off.

"What's *el ment* mean?"

"*El ment?* Means 'He's gone.' Why?"

"How about *kissinim* or *kissinum*?"

It had been Gates' last word as he fell dead.

"That's 'thank you.' What's up? Going to a Hungarian restaurant? I can recommend—"

"Thanks, Mike."

Rob hurried back to his desk. *He's gone!* and *Thank you!* Jesus H. Christ! Why would Gates say stuff like that? If Rob were a mental case, he'd probably say that could mean only one thing: Lazlo Gati had killed himself to escape the control of his brother Gabor.

But Rob wasn't a mental case. He was a New York City cop. And if he wanted to stay a New York City cop, he would keep these thoughts to himself.

Only one thing to do at this juncture: Stick like glue to Kara and Jill. He'd move in with them if he had to. Anything to stay close. Something was going on. He didn't know what—or if he did, he couldn't bring himself to say it out loud—but he was going to find out for sure.

The phone rang again. It was Kara.

"Rob, do you have any free time tomorrow?"

"I'm off. One of my floating days off."

"Would you mind stopping by the Chelsea house and helping me with a few things? I want to make some changes."

"Sure! Be glad to! See you around nine?"

He hung up. How about that? She wanted 'to make some changes.' Wasn't that just like a woman in a new house? Maybe all his fears were groundless.

Whatever. He'd be on West Twenty-first Street bright and early tomorrow morning.

▼

9:35 P.M.

Kara couldn't stand the noise any longer.

God, that's awful. Can you say you actually enjoy that caterwauling?

After Jill had gone off to bed, Gabor had seated Kara's body in the recliner on the heavily draped third floor. With a remote electronic control he had started up the CD player. Seconds later, operatic voices began blasting through the room. He tilted the chair back, closed her eyes, and Kara found herself enclosed in darkness, listening to a woman screeching in Italian. She had to admit, though, that the sound system was impressive. She could almost believe that she was in an opera house listening to a live performance. But that did not make her enjoy what she was being forced to hear.

"That is not caterwauling. That is Mirlella Freni singing Verdi's *Ernani* at La Scala. It's beautiful."

It's awful. But not as awful as how you have perverted your ability.

Her eyes opened.

"Perverted?" And to what use, pray tell, do you think I should have put my talent? The good of humanity? Don't make me laugh."

Kara had pulled herself from her depression. Having Jill around helped. She had set her mind to work on getting free of Gabor. It wouldn't be easy—he was so much more experienced at this—and it might even be impossible. But she had to try. And to have any hope of success, she had to know more about what made him tick.

Why not? Think what you might be able to do for coma patients. Maybe you could wake them up. Or schizophrenics. Maybe you could put their minds back on track.

"Perhaps. Perhaps not."

But you've never even tried. You have this power and you could have contributed something, but instead you're nothing but a—a voluptuary!

"Voluptuary. I like that word. You have an excellent vocabulary, Kara. But you have not thought your scenario all the way through. Here I am, the hero of the medical world, snatching lives back from the depths of coma and psychosis, the wonderful Gabor Gati! But what happens when they all go home for the night? Where is Gabor? Gabor is in a crib in a diaper being fed gruel by a nurse. He can't watch films on TV, he can't choose the music he'd like to hear, he can't even speak to carry on a conversation. And where are the friends and company and conversation Gabor might want? They're somewhere else, and glad to be there, glad they don't have to look at that blind, shrunken, deformed, ugly little geek they use during the day!"

That's the way you see yourself. Aren't you engaging in what you psychiatrists call 'projection?'

"Very good! It is exactly that. But don't try to psychoanalyze me, my dear. I'm way ahead of you. Do you think I have no perspective on myself? I do. I know I am egocentric, and even narcissistic in my own way. And I might even be considered a sociopath. But I exist outside the terminology created for the common *Homo sapiens*. The developmental defects that so grossly altered my body altered my brain as well. I'm different from you. I'm different from everybody. Your rules don't apply to me. I am a species apart."

Hitler probably thought the same way.

"Perhaps I am rationalizing. But I'm not a megalomaniac. I've no plans to sneak about, impregnating

women with my sperm in order to start a super race of
my kind."

It probably wouldn't work anyway.

"I agree. But if I were the B-movie power-crazed
monster you're implying I am, I'd certainly give it a
try. But I'm not interested in ruling the world. I don't
care about the world. I care about Gabor. I came into
this world trapped in a blind, mute, deformed body incapable of experiencing anything beyond the most rudi-
mentary sensations. But I found a compensatory power
within me that allows me to experience all manner of
sensation via the bodies of others. So I use that power.
It would be a sin, after all, to waste it."

*Did your power come with a gift for moral contor-
tions as well, or did you develop that on your own?*

"I don't explain myself, Kara. Even to myself."

Maybe you—

Kara felt her body start as something tapped her
shoulder.

It was Jill, tired, rubbing her eyes.

"I can't sleep with all that noise," she said above the
blare of the opera.

The sound ebbed as Kara's thumb pressed the vol-
ume control.

"And you didn't kiss me good night."

Had Kara's muscles been responsive to her moods,
they would have bunched into cramped knots. The
thought of Gabor kissing Jill . . .

"Sorry, my dear. Let's get you back to bed."

"And how come you keep calling me 'my dear?' "

"Because you *are* my dear."

"What do you usually call her?"

"Honey." Or "Bug."

"How quaint."

He led her down to the bedroom and did a decent job
of tucking her back in.

"Don't forget my kiss!"

Kara's body bent and her lips kissed Jill on the cheek.

"And a hug!"

Kara felt Jill's arms go around her neck and squeeze.

"I love you, Mom!"

Had she eyes and tears, Kara would have wept. That hug and those words were meant for *her* and Gabor was stealing them. She raged blindly.

I'll get us out of this, Jill! Someway, somehow, I'll get free of him!

A calm, monstrously self-assured voice replied.

"No you won't."

FEBRUARY 27
8:22 A.M.

"WHERE YOU GOING WITH THAT FOOD, MOM?"

You freeze for a moment. You were doing what you always do: preparing breakfast for your body in the basement. You reached into the pantry for some junior foods to take downstairs, but you forgot the child.

Up to this point, the morning has gone quite well. Jill is a charming child, bright, intelligent, good-natured. She stirs some lost, long-dormant part of you. A child. Progeny. The future. You realize with a pang of loss that you will never have a child of your own, that an entire wing of the Gati family has reached its terminus in you. That perspective has escaped you until now. The tragedy of it makes you grieve.

But now the child has seen the baby food and wants to know about it.

You tell her, "I'm going to take some of it downstairs. To make more room up here."

"How come it's here?"

"Someone with a baby probably lived here before we moved in."

"Why'd they leave it?"

"I don't know," you say, unable to keep a snap out of your voice. "Stop asking so many questions."

The child starts as if she'd been slapped.

Don't talk to her like that!

"I'll speak to her the way I choose. Doesn't she ever stop asking questions?"

Never. How else is a child to learn? How do you think you learned?

"By stealing. I never had a childhood of my own. I had to siphon it off from others."

Asking's better than stealing.

"I had no choice."

Awww. I'll get some violin music for you.

You don't know how long you can tolerate sharing a body with this woman. Her contempt for you is a cold damp wind on the back of your neck. Her rage at having control of her body torn from her is a palpable thing, a growing weight on your shoulders. Her sense of self is too strong, too deeply seated to allow you a comfortable coexistence.

If only you had known. So many people live their lives with no sense of direction, no firm sense of self, easily influenced by the latest fashion, allowing themselves to be blown hither and thither. Life would be so much easier now if Kara had been one of those.

But what alternative do you have? You are stuck with her until other arrangements can be made.

"Want me to help you bring some of those downstairs?" Jill asks, her wide brown eyes looking up at you, unsure of what she's done wrong, anxious to make amends.

But the last thing you need is this child trailing behind you down to the basement. You cannot let her learn that you live down there.

"No, thank you, dear," you say as gently as you can. "I can handle this myself."

"Okay," she says.

You pull a spoon from the drawer.

"What's that for?"

Another question. You bite down on your tongue.

"Nothing, dear."

You start toward the basement but she's right behind you.

"You stay up here, dear. I'll only be a few minutes."

"I don't want to."

"Go up to the top floor and turn on the television. You can watch cartoons on the giant screen."

"I don't want to. I don't like being up there alone. I want to come with you."

"Well, you can't."

Her lower lip starts to tremble. Tears begin to rim her dark eyes.

"Mommy, I'm scared up here!"

You try, but you can't keep the edge off your voice.

"That's too bad. You'd better get used to it because you're going to have to stay here alone lots of times, starting now."

You step into the stairwell and close the door behind you. There's a latch inside the door. You snap it home.

As you hurry down the stairs, you hear her terrified cries as she bangs on the door.

You beast! You bastard! How could you—

"Enough! My patience is frayed. I can see that your child is going to be a terrible problem. Something will have to be done about her."

Kara's voice is suddenly conciliatory.

She'll be all right. She's just got to get used to this place. And when she gets into a school around here she'll be out most of the day. She's no trouble, really.

"I'm sure everything will work out," you say.

But privately you know that the present situation is intolerable. Despite whatever precautions you may take, it seems inevitable that the child will discover the reason for your multiple daily trips into the basement. And what about those times when you want to leave Kara's body and re-enter your own for brief periods, or return to some of the other bodies that you've used in the past? What will you do then? You will have to leave Kara in the padded cell in the office. What are you going to do with the child—hire a babysitter?

No, this will never do. You need complete privacy in your house. Three's a crowd, as the old adage goes. You must be rid of Jill. Perhaps a private school in another state, a sleepaway academy during the school year and summer camp the rest of the time. Plenty of parents do it. That might work. And then again it might not. You need a solution you can be assured of, a permanent solution.

And suddenly you know.

Your fondness for the idea grows as you spoon the cereal into your mouth. Because it might solve the problem with Kara as well.

And it can happen toady. You've already planned an 'accident'—a fatal one—for Detective Harris. Why not involve the child in that same accident? A tragic pair of deaths. And as a possible lagniappe—the breaking of Kara Wade. Witnessing the deaths of her child and her lover, watching her own hands cause those deaths and being utterly impotent to do anything to save them will break her will, crush her spirit. It has to.

And after the accident, life within Kara Wade will be much more pleasant, and far more secure. Not only will there be no police detective sniffing around her, but the child will be gone. You will have your house all to yourself again. And Kara Wade will have learned to be a compliant, submissive hostess.

Life will be good again.

You glance at your watch. Detective Harris will be here soon. You'd better get upstairs and set the stage.

▼

Jill opened the front door for him. Rob's throat tightened at the sight of her. His voice became husky.

"Good-morning, Miss Wade. How are you today?"

"All right, I guess," she said and turned away.

Rob caught her arm and gently pulled her around to face him.

"That was the most unconvincing 'all right' I've ever heard. What's up, Jill?"

She sniffed. "I don't like it here."

He went down on one knee beside her and put his arm around her waist. Touching her gave him a warm feeling like he'd never known. Her dark hair and complexion—they were his. He could see that now. Part him was part of her. The realization awed him.

"Nobody likes a new place if they still like the old place, but there's lots of neat stuff here."

Rob didn't care if she didn't like this house in particular, but he wanted her to like New York. Because he wanted her to live here and be near him.

"Too many steps," she said.

"For an energetic girl like you? Think of what good exercise it'll be for your legs. Why, in no time you'll be running—"

"And Mom's changed."

The rest of Rob's words twisted and tumbled and caught in his throat as a wave of arctic cold seeped into his spine.

"What do you mean, 'changed?' "

"She's not the same. Like she's a different person."

The cold began spreading to the rest of his body.

"When did she change?"

"Yesterday. Just like in the movie. Except yesterday was Thursday."

"What movie?"

"*Freaky Friday.* I saw it at Aunt Ellen's. It's about a girl who switches places with her mother."

"What kind of switch?"

"She winds up in her mother's body and her mother winds up in her's. Only that didn't happen with Mom. I'm not in her body. Someone else is."

Rob felt himself begin to tremble as his daughter spoke his worst fears. He could barely form the words.

"Why . . . why would you say something like that?"

"Because she talks different. And she yells at me."

Rob forced himself to relax. Maybe Jill was feeling the disruption of being moved from place to place the past few weeks. From the farm to Ellen's, and now to the townhouse. And Kara had been under tremendous stress, so she might be a little short these days. Stir those kind of changes into someone at an impressionable age like Jill, add a movie like *Freaky Friday* or whatever it was called, and the result was a child who thinks her mother is someone else.

A good explanation, Rob thought. *Why doesn't it make me feel any better?*

"I'll straighten her out," he said, giving Jill an extra squeeze before releasing her. "Where's this freaky mom of yours, anyway?"

"Upstairs. Listening to music."

"Let's go see her."

He took his daughter's hand and together they climbed toward the top floor. He heard the music long before he reached her. He stopped on the second floor and listened to the booming basso males and shrieking falsetto females, all drawing their notes from deep within the abdomen, maybe as far down as the pelvis.

Opera.

The wave of cold hit him again.

"Your hand's getting all sweaty, Rob."

"Sorry."

He wiped his palms on his pants legs.

Your mother hates opera.

Despite the bright sunlight outside, the third floor was dark. He found Kara lying back in the recliner, the opera blaring from the six-foot speakers around the room. Her face was relaxed, peaceful. She could have been asleep. He leaned over and spoke into her ear.

"Since when are you an opera fan?"

She opened her eyes and smiled, reached up with her arms and pulled his head closer. She kissed him on the lips, long and passionately. Rob began to respond, but he wasn't comfortable kissing her like this in front of Jill.

"I'm glad to see you," she said when he pulled away.

"It's mutual. But opera?"

"There's so much of it here I thought I'd give it a try. The music's not bad. I just wish I knew what they were saying."

"I can live without knowing. You said you needed my help up here?"

Rob noticed how she used the remote control to turn off the stereo from her chair. She seemed right at home. *Too* at home.

"Yes," she said, rising from the chair. "I want to take down those drapes from the rear windows and let in some light. It's like a mausoleum in here."

She was right about the gloom. And it was a very Kara thing to do. She was always one for open windows and letting the air through. He walked over and pulled the drapes aside to take a look. The window was huge—three five-foot panes stacked floor to ceiling. The drapes were suspended from a heavy rod bolted to the ceiling.

"This'll let in some light, all right. But how do I get up there?"

"I thought we might try one of the ladders from the library."

"Good idea. I'll get one."

"I'll help."

"That's okay. I can manage."

Rob removed his jacket and laid it atop one of the record cabinets. He pulled his clip holster and revolver from the small of his back and folded them in his jacket. Then he headed for the stairs.

▼

What are you up to? Kara asks as you watch Detective Harris descend to the second floor. Her words writhe with suspicion.

"Nothing, Kara. Nothing at all."

You love this room just the way it is—like a tomb. Why are you pretending to want to change it? Tell me!

"It's very simple, really. Your detective friend is suspicious of you. That's why he keeps asking questions about your past together. I'm doing this to allay those suspicions. Seeing me making changes in the house will put him more at ease, make him more willing to overlook any gaffes I make as I pretend to be you."

There is a lengthy pause. Then:

I don't trust you.

"I realize that. But it doesn't matter."

You don't tell her what you're really planning. Better to let her learn as it happens. The shock will drive it all more deeply home.

And it will happen soon. Very soon.

▼

With growing unease, Kara watched Rob set up the ladder next to the window. Maybe Gabor truly was trying to allay Rob's suspicions, but somehow that didn't ring true. She had a feeling he was up to something.

She had to admit, though, he was certainly acting like a devoted parent where Jill was concerned, whether for Rob's sake or to make up for locking her out of the cellar earlier, Kara couldn't say. But when Jill wanted to go downstairs, Gabor convinced her to stay, and even turned on the projection TV so she could watch *Pee Wee's Playhouse*.

"She's not going to see much on that screen once I let the light in," Rob said.

"We'll adjust," Kara's voice said. "I think opening this floor up to that southern exposure is worth the loss of a little daytime TV, don't you?"

"I guess so."

Rob locked down the spreader on the stepladder, checked its stability, then began to climb.

"Want me to steady it?"

"Nah. I'll be okay."

But to reach the center curtains, Rob had to climb to the very top and perch on the head step. The ladder wobbled under him.

"Maybe you'd better steady it after all," he said.

Her hands braced the side rails as Rob reached under the valance and unhooked the left curtain. When he let it drop, blinding sunlight poured in on an angle through the five-foot sheets of glass. He looked down at her.

"How's that?"

"Great. Now the other one."

As Rob worked on the right curtain, Kara noticed that her right hand had moved from the ladder's side rail to the front pocket of her jeans. It pulled out a key ring and began twirling the ring on its index finger.

What are you doing that for?

"I want to see if he notices."

He will *notice!*

"I hope so. Because I want him to know before he dies."

Sick terror engulfed Kara.

No! What are you going to do?

"Watch."

Rob dropped the second curtain. More sun poured in.

"There we go. Now, you said you wanted the drapes—"

His eyes widened as he looked down at her. Kara could see his eyes fixed on her hand and the twirling key ring.

"It's you!" he said in an awed whisper. "God damn it, it's *you!*"

Kara heard her voice shout *"Yes!"* and then her hands were pushing hard against the stepladder. Before Kara could even attempt to hold them back, the damage was done. With all Rob's weight at the top, the ladder toppled easily, vaulting him toward the huge panes of glass. With a terrified cry, he grabbed a pleat of one of the side drapes but it pulled free and he crashed into the top pane. It shattered with a bell-like clang, and then all the glass was coming apart, in shards large and small, in squares, triangles and daggers, catching and throwing flashes of sunlight as they spun and tumbled in all directions.

Kara heard Jill shriek in terror behind her. Rob's body twisted and contorted within the flying glass, one hand still clutching the side drape, the other grasping at empty air. He fell out of sight, pulling the drape after him. A silent scream ripped from Kara as she saw the fabric catch for a second on the edge of the window frame. She thought it might hold, then it too slipped from sight.

NO!!!

▼

You watch the detective fall to his death. It's a three-story drop. And if the fall in itself isn't enough, there's a patio below ringed with a wrought iron fence. The fence is directly below the window. It's not spiked, but it will break Detective Harris in two when he strikes it.

But now for the second part of the plan: the child.

You turn and see her horrified face as she runs up to where you stand. All you have to do is grab her arm and propel her the rest of the way through the shattered window, to follow her father down in death. She's at your side now. You reach for her arm—

There's movement at the window. It catches the corner of your eye. You look. It's a hand—bloody, but rising over the corner of the floor-level sill, grasping the side of the frame.

The detective didn't fall all the way!

He's alive! Kara cries. *Thank God!*

You rush forward and see that he somehow managed to grab hold of the cornice that runs along the back of the house at the level of each floor. And now he's climbing back in! He's got to be stopped! He's barely holding on by his fingertips.

"I'll remedy that!"

A quick slash or two at his hands with one of these glass daggers littering the floor should send him down to where he should already be.

Don't! Leave him alone!

You pick up a slim, sharp shard of glass. This should do it. As you shift it in your hand it slips. You grab for it with the other hand and feel a piercing pain in your palm—

—and suddenly the world is dark and your body is

bloated and thick and small and your limbs are scrawny things that you can barely move.

"NO!"

▼

Kara's knees suddenly went out from under her and she fell forward, nearly tumbling out the window herself. The pain in her palm was blinding. She turned her hand to look at the bloody glass dagger protruding from both sides. All the way through! Pain blazed anew, higher than before as she pulled it free.

And then Kara realized that *she* had turned her hand, *she* had removed the glass—not someone else.

"I'm free!" she screamed aloud. "Oh, God, I'm *free*!"

But how? Why? Her mind raced. Kelly had got free of him—and Kelly had a deep bite mark on her shoulder. Lazlo had got free of him—right after being knocked down by a car.

Rob had raised his head and shoulders above the sill. He glared at her with a mixture of fear and fury.

"Pain, Rob! *Pain!* That's the key! Pain cuts the contact, breaks his control!"

As he levered himself over the sill and onto the floor, Rob looked at her with confused eyes, full of mistrust.

"It's me, Rob! Really me! I'm free of him!"

God, it was wonderful to speak her own words, have control of her own limbs. But for how long?

She picked up a piece of glass in her good right hand and stared at the left's bleeding palm. There might be a way to hold Gabor off. She clenched her teeth and drove the point of the glass into her injured hand. She screamed with the burst of renewed pain.

"Kara!" Rob shouted. He was inside the window

now, staring at her with horrified eyes. "What the hell—?"

"It'll keep him away!" she said, gasping through her teeth. "God, it's got to!"

"Then it's true? Gabor is behind this whole thing?"

His eyes were wild, as if he still didn't believe any of this was really happening. But he'd mentioned Gabor. That meant he knew!

"Yes! Gabor—the monster!"

"Where is he?" he said.

Kara could hear Jill behind her, sobbing, scared half to death, calling her name.

"In the basement," Kara said. "Behind the paneling. Get down there, Rob. Kill him!" Those words sounded so alien, but she knew it was the only way. "Kill him before he comes back. Don't ever let him do this to me again! *Please!*"

She plunged the glass into her hand again.

▼

Rob's gut churned as Kara screamed again with pain.

"Christ, Kara! You won't have a hand left!"

He glanced around the room. There had to be something he could do. And then he saw it. The velvet tie-back from the side drape he had hung onto when he was falling lay on the floor amid the shattered glass. He grabbed it and held it up.

"What are you going to do with that?"

"Tie you up."

She frowned, then smiled with relief.

"Yes! Oh, thank you!" She looked down at the bloody glass dagger in her hand. "I don't know how many more times I can do this!"

Rob wasn't sure he could stab himself even once. He was sure, however, that he was in the presence of the bravest woman—the bravest *person*—he had ever known.

He helped her over to a ladderback chair that was set against the wall by the record shelves. Kara dropped into it and pushed her hands around the back of the chair.

"Good knots, Rob. I don't want to get free."

As he looped the cord around her wrists and arms and through the rungs of the back, Jill began screaming.

"What are you doing to my mother? Stop it!"

"It's okay, Jill," Kara said in a soothing voice. "I asked him to do this."

"But you're *hurt!*"

"I know. But I did that to myself. Rob's not hurting me. He's doing this so I don't hurt myself any more."

"But *why?*"

"There's a bad man in the basement who's making me hurt myself. Rob's only going to tie me up for a few minutes while he makes the man stop, then he's going to let me go. Right, Rob?"

Rob kissed her on the forehead. He'd never loved her more than he did at this moment.

"Right." He looked Jill right in the eye, hoping she'd see no threat in him. "And then I'm coming back upstairs and letting her loose. And then we're all getting out of here. For good! But whatever happens, don't let your mother get loose till I get back!"

He could tell Jill wasn't buying the whole package, but at least her panic seemed to be under control.

"He's right, Jill. Don't let me get loose. Okay?"

Hesitantly, she nodded.

Rob pulled the cord as tightly as he dared around Kara's wrists. He didn't want to cut off circulation, but he didn't want her getting out, either. Not after what she'd done to him a moment ago.

Rob shuddered at the memory of that fall. If the

drape in his right hand hadn't caught for that second, allowing his left hand to grab hold of the cornice—

He stepped over to the record cabinet and pulled his revolver and holster from his leather jacket. He looked at Kara and nodded once, then ran for the stairs.

"There's a lever up among the pipes by the wall. Pull it down!"

"Got it!"

He took the steps down three at a time.

▼

You keep thrusting but you can't get back into Kara. Twice you've tried and each time you were rebuffed by blasts of pain. But the third time is lucky. You are back in. There's sunlight, cold air from the broken window, pain in the left hand but not enough to break the bond. As you snatch the reins of control, you hear Kara cry out.

No! Not again!

"Yes! Again! And this time—"

You can't move her arms. A chair—you're in a chair. *Tied* in a chair! You pull frantically on the cord that binds you. And the detective is nowhere in sight!

"Where is he?"

In the basement, Gabor. Getting ready to riddle your filthy little body with holes!

Her rage, her hatred of you is an angry surf, it pummels you, swirls around you and tries to drag you under. Too strong, this one. Too angered at having her life taken over. But you hang on to control and continue to struggle with the cord that binds your wrists. They loosen slightly, but not enough to make a difference. You can get free of them eventually, but eventually will be too late.

No! This can't be! You fight the panic. You can't let them beat you! Not these two inferiors. You must think!

And then you notice Jill standing before you, tears in her eyes, looking frightened and confused.

"Jill, honey," you say, remembering her mother's pet terms for her. "Untie me, bug."

You feel Kara's rage and desperation beating against you anew.

No! Leave her out of this!

"You said not to," Jill says. "Not until Rob comes back from stopping the bad man in the basement."

Those deadly words are all the more chilling from the mouth of a child. You search for a plausible reason for Kara to have changed her mind.

"I know, bug, but I forgot to tell Detec—Rob something very important. There's a dangerous trap in the cellar. The bad man set it. And if we don't tell Rob right away, he'll get hurt! You don't want him to be hurt, do you?"

"No," she says, her eyes and voice filled with uncertainty.

"Then untie me. Quickly! Please, bug! There's no time to waste if we're going to save him!"

Jill's face is tortured for a moment, then she runs around to the back of the chair.

It's too late, Gabor! Kara says. *He's found you by now! Any minute now and I'll be free of you forever!*

You realize that she's probably right but you must try.

The child whimpers as she struggles with the knots. You feel something pull free. There's a little extra room around your wrists. You yank them free of the cord, leap up, and grab Jill by the arm. Terror propels you down the stairs, dragging the frightened child after you.

What are you doing, you monster? Leave her out of this!

You could drop Kara into limbo to shut her up but that would distract you for a moment, and you need every second, every ounce of concentration at your disposal if you're going to have a chance of surviving.

On the first floor, you stop in the kitchen and pull one of the carving knives from a drawer, then head for the basement.

It's too late, Gabor! Too late!

But you know that as long as you're still alive and still in Kara's body, it's not too late.

You begin shouting as you enter the stairwell.

▼

Rob had been pounding on the paneling, reaching up among the pipes, but had found nothing. There was an empty space behind the panels, he could hear that, but his questing hands hadn't come in contact with anything that felt like a lever—

Until now.

His hand closed around a short length of L-bar. He pulled down on it and heard a click inside the paneling. A section sank inward. He was pushing on it, trying to find a way in, when he heard someone shouting on the stairs.

Kara's voice! How did she—?

"Don't do it Harris! I've got your daughter and if I die, so does she!"

Rob heard Jill's terrified sobs before he saw her. And when she came into view, Kara was holding a knife at her throat.

Not Jill!

A current of panic buzzed through Rob for an instant. Then he drew his pistol.

"Give me the gun, Harris," said Kara's voice.

The menace in her eyes, her expression—so alien.

And to see her pressing the point of a knife against Jill's throat sickened him.

"No way, Gabor."

"I'll cut her. I will."

Rob noticed that the faint trace of accent he used to hear in Gates' voice had wormed its way into Kara's. He looked into Jill's eyes, saw the hurt mixed with the fear.

"That's not your mom, Jill. That's someone pretending to be your mom. Just stand quiet and I'll get us out of this."

"I sincerely doubt that. The *gun*, Harris!"

"Forget that. I give you the gun, you'll shoot us both."

Rob ransacked his brain for a way to bargain out of this. The first step in any hostage situation was to keep everyone talking so you could think.

"I don't want that," Kara's voice said. "This is merely self defense. I'll let you go. I just want to protect myself."

This from someone who just moments ago had pushed him out a third story window.

"Right. You'll let Jill and me waltz out of here."

Kara's face hardened. Her hand moved the point of the knife up to Jill's right eye. Jill whimpered with terror.

"I'm going to start cutting her, Harris. Starting with this eye. And I'm going to keep cutting her until you put that gun on the floor and slide it over to me."

Rob felt beads of sweat burst from every pore on his body. He pointed his revolver at the section of paneling that had moved and spoke through his teeth. His voice was low, almost a whisper.

"One drop of her blood, Gabor . . . I see one drop of blood and I empty this pistol into that wall. And then I go through that wall and I get hold of whatever's left of you in there and I tear it apart with my bare hands."

"Jill won't be much to look at by then."

"But you'll be dead."

"Will I? I'm living in Kara now. Maybe Kara will die with me. And maybe my body will die but I'll go on living within Kara. The situation is unprecedented. Anything could happen."

And either way, I lose, Rob thought.

"The pistol, Harris. Slide it over."

But as long as he held the pistol, Rob knew he had a chance. There was a way to save Jill: kill Kara. Rob raised the pistol in the two handed grip and sighted at the middle of Kara's forehead.

She smiled at him.

"You'd have made a good general, Harris. Sacrifice one platoon to avoid losing both. Go ahead. Shoot. Can you do it? To Kara? She's in here with me, looking down that barrel just as I am. Pull the trigger . . . *Rob.*"

He lowered the pistol. He couldn't do it. Maybe if he just wounded her, the pain would free her from Gabor, but it was too risky. Most of her body was hidden behind Jill. He couldn't risk hitting Jill.

Rob could feel the balance of the stand-off shifting toward Gabor. Inevitable. Gabor controlled the two people Rob cared about most in this world. He felt as if he were being torn apart, slowly, one small piece at a time.

"*Now*, Harris!"

▼

You've wasted enough time. The longer you let this drag on, the greater the chance something will go wrong for you.

I wish he'd pulled the trigger! Kara says.

"I doubt that."

At least Jill would be safe.

You sense her sincerity, and you wonder at the depth of a mother's feeling for her child. You can't imagine sacrificing your own life for anyone.

But enough talk with Detective Harris. He cannot be threatened into dropping his weapon, so it is time for action. You're not anxious to cut the child—it will be most unpleasant—but this is a desperate situation. You are fighting for your own existence. All it takes is one short jab. You need only move your hand an inch or less and the point will pierce the child's eye. That will bring Harris to his knees. And then you'll be in control.

This will teach Kara a lesson, too.

"Watch carefully, Kara. I'm going to demonstrate who is the master here."

Panic spews from her in a fountain.

No! You're not—!

"Watch!"

Kara's voice becomes an inarticulate scream in your mind as you draw the knife back a bit, preparing for the jab, then—

You can't move it!

The knife is frozen in the air. Now it's moving away! *Away!* It's Kara! She's reasserting control! But this is impossible! You knew she had a powerful self, but you never dreamed—

You try to force her back but her rage is a living thing, clawing at you. Kara's protective instincts have been uncaged, released from some primitive part of her hindbrain, and they are now roaring through her like prehistoric beasts. Racial memories, encoded in every cell of her body, are bursting free. Every woman who has ever persevered through a life of domination . . . every mother since the dawn of time who has ever fought to save her child . . . it's as if they've all suddenly risen up and joined her against you.

You've misjudged this woman. You hope it was not a fatal error. You fight back with all your power, your greater experience. You must win! You *must!*

▼

Kara shouted with triumph as she forced the knife blade away from Jill's face. She could only control one arm at a time, it seemed—Gabor kept her left arm wrapped tightly around Jill—but Kara controlled the important one. The ferocity of her anger astonished her, and even frightened her. But it was the fuel she used against Gabor, and it was working. She could do it! She could beat Gabor!

"The panel!" she said to Rob in a voice so strained she barely recognized it as her own. "Slide it—*uhn!*"

The effort of speaking cost her some control over her hand and the knife blade darted toward Jill's eye again. She stopped it in time, but she didn't dare speak again.

▼

Something was happening. Rob watched Kara's body tremble violently. Her right arm spasmed. She'd said something about the panel. *Slide it?*

He backed away to the panel and pushed against it. It didn't move back but it slid a bit to the left. He kept it moving, and then he was looking into a small room with a crib. Two steps and he was standing over it. Rob's gorge rose as he stared down at the mottled, bloated diapered thing looking up at him with opaque eyes.

Here he was. This was Gabor. Rob ratcheted back the hammer on his revolver and leveled it at Gabor's oversized head. He squeezed the trigger but couldn't pull it. Gabor's words came back to him. What if killing Gabor's body left him alive in Kara's, and permanently in control?

Kara lurched into the room, still clutching Jill, still brandishing the knife. There seemed to be a tug of war going on. The knife would slash toward Jill, then pull back. Over and over.

As Kara struggled toward the crib, straining and jerking like someone moving the wrong way in the rush hour commuter tide, trying to go up the steps while the horde was flowing down, Rob stepped aside. He sensed a titanic struggle roaring beneath the surface, one he was barred from entering. He had no choice but to wait and see what would happen, and stand ready to grab Jill and pull her free at the first opportunity.

▼

Close, closer. Kara pushed her body toward the crib. It was like moving under water. And the closer she got, the stiffer Gabor's resistance as she sensed him drawing strength from his own panic.

Within a yard of the crib, she stalled. Gabor seemed to have dug in his heels in a last desperate effort to hold her back. Even her unquenched fury wasn't strong enough to push her beyond that point.

Why didn't Rob shoot him? What was he waiting for? She didn't dare risk speech—it might allow Gabor the upper hand.

Hand . . . the knife was still in her hand, forgotten as they fought toward and away from the crib. She called up all her reserves. A garbled chorus, an unintelligible blend of an unimaginable number of voices echoed down the millennia and roared in her ears as she tightened her grip on the handle . . .

And plunged downward.

Kara screamed with the pain of the blade sinking deep into the muscles of her thigh. Jill screamed, too. But suddenly Kara's body was her own again. She pushed Jill child toward Rob.

"Get her out!"

And then she lunged at the crib.

Ahead of her, she saw Gabor's body rear up and look at her with its blind eyes. His slack mouth hung open, his tongue moved, as of trying to form words.

Kara didn't hesitate. She shoved the blade forward between the bars and rammed it into Gabor's barrel chest. He made a hoarse cry like the squeal of a pig and then Kara was leaning over the crib, slashing and stabbing. There were no more cries after the first, and the thrashing stopped soon after. The only noise was the hiss of the knife slicing in and out of him and the small whimpering noises coming from deep in her own chest. But she kept driving the knife into his body, over and over. She slashed him for Jill, and she slashed him for her father whose memory he had defiled, but mostly she slashed him for herself. She closed her eyes so she wouldn't have to see the carnage she was causing, but she couldn't stop ... couldn't stop ... couldn't stop. She had to keep it up until there was nothing left of him, until there was no chance that he would ever defile her or threaten Jill ever again. And even now when she knew he had to be dead, and her wounded leg was threatening to give out under her, her arm kept stabbing, as if it had a life of its own.

Suddenly Rob was there, holding her arm, pulling the knife from her hand.

"It's over, Kara," he said. "Christ, it's over. You can't kill him any more."

Her leg gave way and she fell against him. Rob lifted her and carried her from Gabor's room up to the first floor where he stretched her out on the settee in the foyer. She saw Jill staring at her from the kitchen doorway, her fingers jammed into her mouth.

"It's all right now, honey," Kara said, reaching out her good hand to her. "I'm okay, now. The man in the cellar won't make me do bad things any more. He's gone for good."

Rob went over to Jill and she clung to him, using him as a shield between herself and her mother. That hurt Kara, but what else could she expect? It was going to take a long time to heal the trauma of this morning.

"It's okay, Jill," Rob said, drawing her toward Kara. "Your mother's okay now. It was like you said, like *Freaky Friday*, but the bad man who was in your mother is gone, and he can't come back. Give her a hug. She's a very brave lady, and she needs you now."

With a small cry, Jill rushed forward into her mother's arms. Kara crushed her against herself and began to sob. They stayed locked together while Rob got a hand towel from the bathroom and tied it around her thigh. Then he headed toward the basement stairs.

"Where're you going?"

"Some unfinished business."

He closed the door to the basement behind him. A few moments later she heard a series of muffled retorts from below. Like gun shots. Rob reappeared a short while later.

"What . . .?"

"Five to the head," he said grimly. "Insurance."

Kara closed her eyes. "Thank you."

FEBRUARY 28
6:48 P.M.

"WHAT DID YOU DO WITH HIS BODY?"

Kara had been afraid to ask, but she had to know.

Rob looked at her from the other end of the couch in the front room of his apartment.

"Food for the fishes. Even if he's found—and he won't be—he can't be identified. Gabor Gati is officially dead. The crib and its mattress were left in a vacant lot in the South Bronx. And the bloody sheet went up in flames in the fireplace. It's done. Over. *Finis*. We can now go about getting our lives back on track."

"Amen," Kara said.

She leaned back on the cushions. The sutures in her left palm and right thigh were starting to pull. The wounds had been easily explained as glass cuts, and luckily she hadn't severed any tendons in her hand. The wounds to her body would be healed in a week or so. But the rest of her . . . she didn't know if she'd ever get over the past three weeks.

And Jill. She was worried most about poor Jill. But the child appeared to be bouncing back better than either Kara or Rob. She was having a ball playing nurse to her mother. She came out of the kitchenette now holding a glass of cola.

"Here you go, Mom."

"Thank you, Nurse Jill."

Kara would have preferred something stronger, but with the Percodan running through her system for the pain, she decided to stick to soft drinks.

"I'll think I'll make myself a refill," Rob said, jiggling the ice in his scotch glass.

"And I'll pick up this mess," Jill said. She straightened the newspapers, the magazine, picked up Rob's key ring—

—and twirled it on her index finger. Twirl-twirl-stop. Twirl-twirl-stop.

Kara's stomach plummeted. She leaped up from the couch and grabbed her arm.

"Jill! Jill, look at me!"

The big blue eyes turned toward her, wide and innocent. Kara could barely hear her over the pounding of her heart in her throat.

"Mommy, you're hurting my arm!"

Kara loosened her grip but did not let go.

"Why did you do that?"

"Do what, Mom?"

"Twirl those keys on your finger? Tell me!"

"I . . . I saw you do it! Mom, why are you mad at me?"

Kara released her arm and hugged her.

"I'm not mad, bug. I'm just frightened."

Oh, God, was she ever going to be free of this?

Yes! she thought. Yes, she would get free of Gabor's lingering taint on her life. She would put this all behind her and start out anew with Jill. And with Rob. And eventually, she would be able to look at the world without seeing Gabor's shadow everywhere. Eventually, this would all become a dim memory, a barely remembered nightmare.

But for now, for a while—she hated herself for even thinking it, but she had no choice—she was going to have to keep a close watch on Jill.

SPINE-TINGLING
HORROR FROM TOR